BETTY

THE ULTIMATE

Betty Neels's novels are loved
by millions of readers around the world,
and this very special ***12-volume collection***
offers a unique chance to recapture the pleasure
of some of her most popular stories.

Each month we're bringing you a new volume
containing two timeless classics—irresistible love
stories that belong together, whether they share the
same colourful setting, romantic theme, or follow the
same characters in their continuing lives...

As a special treat, each volume also includes an
introductory letter by a different author. Some of the
most popular names in romance fiction are delighted
to pay tribute to Betty Neels; we hope you enjoy
reading their personal thoughts and memories.

We're proud and privileged to bring you
this very special collection, and hope you enjoy
reading—and keeping—these twelve wonderful
volumes over the coming months!

Volume Ten

***—with an introduction from popular
Modern Romance™ author***

Sara Craven

**Two stories featuring unexpected
springtime proposals by Betty Neels:**

LAST APRIL FAIR
THE COURSE OF TRUE LOVE

We'd like to take this opportunity to pay tribute to **Betty Neels**, *who sadly passed away last year. Betty was one of our best-loved authors. As well as being a wonderfully warm and thoroughly charming individual, Betty led a fascinating life even before becoming a writer, and her publishing record was impressive.*

Betty spent her childhood and youth in Devonshire before training as a nurse and midwife. She was an army nursing sister during the war, married a Dutchman and subsequently lived in Holland for fourteen years. On retirement from nursing Betty started to write, inspired by a lady in a library bemoaning the lack of romantic novels.

Over her thirty-year writing career Betty wrote more than 134 novels and was published in more than one hundred international markets. She continued to write into her ninetieth year, remaining as passionate about her characters and stories then as she was with her very first book.

Betty will be greatly missed, both by her friends at Harlequin Mills & Boon® *and by her legions of loyal readers around the world. Betty was a prolific writer and has left a lasting legacy through her heartwarming novels. She will always be remembered as a truly delightful person who brought great happiness to many.*

THE ULTIMATE COLLECTION

Volume Ten

LAST APRIL FAIR

&

THE COURSE OF TRUE LOVE

Two full-length novels

Harlequin Mills & Boon Limited,
Eton House, 18-24 Paradise Road, Richmond, Surrey TW9 1SR

ISBN 0 263 83652 5

Set in Times Roman 11¼ on 12½ pt.
141-0503-103254

Printed and bound in Spain
by Litografia Rosés, S.A., Barcelona

Dear Reader

I discovered the novels of Betty Neels well before my own career for Harlequin Mills and Boon® began, and was immediately captured by their charm. It's an enchantment that has lasted for over twenty-five years, and will continue even though dear Betty is no longer with us.

I have an almost complete collection of her books, and read them over and over again, drifting off to a world of Dutch interiors, mouth-watering food, and happy endings that can make you laugh and cry all at once. They're an instant lift—the fictional equivalent of hot buttered toast, or a box of favourite chocolates. Betty wrote the ultimate timeless fairy story.

Betty, herself a nurse, and married to a Dutch husband, knew the Netherlands well, and made it come alive for her readers. Her heroines were not always beautiful, and usually curvier than fashion dictates. She wasn't scared of words like 'plump' or 'Junoesque', and all of us for whom the diet starts tomorrow will always be glad of that. None of us doubted that the ultimate marriages would be happy ones, and that for her heroines and their chosen men everything really would be for the best in this best of all possible worlds. Because she made us believe in real love. What an achievement. And how sorely I shall miss scurrying home with a new 'Neels' for a few hours of pure escapism.

Betty Neels was a true star, who will continue to shine for future generations of romance readers.

Sara Craven

LAST APRIL FAIR

by

Betty Neels

Last April Fair, when I got bold with beer
I loved her long before, but had a fear to speak.

John Clare, *Shepard's Calendar*

CHAPTER ONE

MRS GREGSON'S elderly voice, raised in its never-ending vendetta against the nurses making her bed, penetrated throughout the entire ward; it even penetrated Sister's office, so that its occupant rose from her work at her desk with a sigh, opened the swing doors and made her way down the long ward to where her troublesome patient lay. She was a very pretty girl, tall and slim and nicely curved in her navy uniform. She had corn-coloured hair, cut short and swinging around her neck, with a fringe over her blue eyes and a nose which tilted very slightly above a softly curved mouth so that despite her twenty-six years she reminded anyone meeting her for the first time of a small eager girl wanting to be friendly with everyone.

She reached the bed just as its occupant, sitting in a heap in the middle of it clutching a blanket round her frail person, drew breath to begin on a fresh round of abuse. 'Yer ter leave them blankets,' she shrilled, 'me bed's fine—it don't need making.'

'And what is our Doctor Thorpe going to say when he comes presently and finds you in that untidy heap?' Phyllida Cresswell's voice was quiet and quite unworried by Mrs Gregson's tantrums.

''E won't say nothin', 'e'll be too busy looking at yer pretty face.'

Phyllida wasn't in the least put out. 'There you go again, making up stories. You just wait until I tell his wife!'

Mrs Gregson cackled happily. 'Just me little joke, Sister dear, though you mark my words, some feller'll come along one day and run orf with yer.'

'It sounds exciting,' agreed Phyllida. 'And now how about this bed?'

'Well, if yer say so…'

Phyllida smiled at the old lady, smiled too at the two student nurses and started off down the ward again. It was a good thing that Philip Mount was the Surgical Registrar and rarely came on to her ward; Mrs Gregson's sharp eyes would have spotted that they were rather more than colleagues within minutes. Phyllida frowned slightly. Philip was getting a little too possessive just lately. It wasn't as though they were engaged. Her frown deepened; perhaps it would have been better for them both if they had been, although she couldn't remember that he had ever suggested it, merely taken it for granted that one day they would marry. And he was a good man; there weren't many like him, she knew that; not particularly good-looking, but well built and pleasant-faced and rarely bad-tempered, ready to make allowances for everyone—she wasn't good enough for him and she had told him so on several occasions. But he had only laughed at her, refusing to take her seriously.

She went back into her office and sat down at her desk again and picked up the telephone. There was the laundry to warn about the extra sheets she would need, the dispensary to argue with over the non-arrival of a drug she had ordered, the office to plead with for the loan of a nurse because one of her student nurses had gone off sick—she sighed and lifted the receiver.

The day went badly, with no nurse to replace the one who had gone off sick, two emergencies, Doctor Thorpe's round and him in a nasty temper and not nearly enough clean linen returned from the laundry. Phyllida, a sunny-tempered girl, was decidedly prickly by the time she went to her midday dinner, a state of mind not improved by her friends wanting to know why she was so ratty, and made even worse by one of her friends demanding to know if she had had words with Philip.

'No, I have not,' she declared crossly, and thought suddenly that a good row with him would be better than his even-tempered tolerance when she was feeling ill-humoured. She added rather lamely: 'I've had a foul morning and Doctor Thorpe was in one of his tetchy moods; the round took for ever.'

The talk became general after that and presently, back on the ward, she regained her usual good nature so that Mrs Gregson stopped her as she was going down the ward to say: 'That's better, Sister dear. Black as a thundercloud yer've been all morning.' She grinned, displaying impossibly even false teeth. 'We ain't such a bad lot, are we?'

Phyllida had stopped to lean over the end of her patient's bed. 'You're the nicest lot of ladies I've ever met,' she assured her.

Mrs Gregson nodded, satisfied. 'Going out this evening?' she wanted to know.

Phyllida said that yes, she was and she still had a lot of work to do as she went on her way. She and Philip were going to have dinner with his elder brother and his wife. They lived in Hampstead in a pleasant house; privately she found them a dull couple with two dull children, but they seemed content enough and she had, upon occasion, detected a gleam of envy in Philip's eye at the sight of their comfortable home with its neatly kept garden, well-behaved dog, gleaming furniture and shining windows. She frowned a little as she bent to take her newest patient's blood pressure. It wasn't that she didn't like cleanliness and order and furniture polish, but somehow there was too much of it. She thought with sudden longing of her own home, an old rambling house in a village near Shaftesbury, standing on high ground so that it creaked and groaned in the winter gales and captured all the summer sun there was on its grey stone walls. Her father was the village doctor with a practice scattered miles in every direction and her mother ran the house with the help of old Mrs Drew who was really past it, as well as coping with the large untidy garden, two dogs, a variety of cats, an old pony and some chickens and over and above these such of her four children who might happen to be at home, and they usually brought friends with them.

It was late March, thought Phyllida, neatly charting her findings; the daffodils would be out and the catkins, and in the wilder corners of the garden there would be violets and primroses for the picking. She had a week's holiday due to her, only a few days away now. The thought cheered her enormously and she felt guilty at the relief of getting away from Philip for a little while—perhaps while she was at home she would be able to make up her mind about him. And really, she chided herself as she went from bed to bed, with a nod and a word for the occupants, there should be no need of that. He was a splendid man, generous and honest and thoughtful—he would make a perfect husband. He would be dull too. She wiped the thought from her mind as unworthy and concentrated on his good points so that by the evening when she went off duty she was almost eager to see him.

She took extra pains with her face and hair as she changed out of her uniform and then poked around in her wardrobe. She had clothes enough, for unlike many of her friends she had no need to help out at home, but now she dragged out one dress after the other, dissatisfied with them all, until, pressed for time, she got into a grey wool dress with its matching long coat, tied a bright scarf round her neck, caught up gloves and handbag and skipped down the austere staircase of the Nurses' Home. Philip was waiting in the hospital yard. That was another nice thing about him; he never kept her waiting and he never grumbled if she were late. She smiled widely at him as she got into the elderly Rover he cherished with such care.

'I've had a foul day, Doctor Thorpe was as sour as vinegar and they sent up two chest cases. What about you?' she asked.

'Oh, quite a good list, one or two tacked on, of course, but Sir Hereward was in a good mood.' He turned to smile at her. 'Shall we go to Poon's?'

Phyllida didn't really like Chinese food, but she agreed at once. Poon's was well away from the hospital and not expensive, and although Philip wasn't mean, he hadn't anything other than his salary. They drove through the City, cut into Long Acre and into Cranbourne Street and turned into the Charing Cross Road. There was a good deal of traffic as they turned into Lisle Street and found a parking meter, and the restaurant was crowded too. Phyllida sat down at the corner table found for them and let out a long contented sigh.

'This is nice. I love my work, but it's good to get away from it. I've got a week's holiday in a few days, too.'

'Going home?' Philip was studying the menu.

She chose sweet and sour pork before she replied. 'Yes.' She gave him a questioning look.

'I've a couple of days owing to me...' His nice face beamed at her across the table.

'Then come down for them. I'm going on Sunday evening—when can you manage to get free?'

'Wednesday—until Friday midnight. Your mother won't mind?'

Phyllida laughed. 'You know Mother, she loves a house full—besides, she knows you well enough to hand you a spade and tell you to dig the garden—a nice change from whipping out appendices!'

They spent a pleasant evening together, although thinking about it afterwards, Phyllida had a feeling that they had both been trying too hard; trying in a self-conscious way to turn their rather vague relationship into something more tangible. She couldn't think why, not for herself at any rate. She was fond of Philip but she was almost sure that she didn't want to marry him, and yet her sensible brain told her that he was so right for a husband.

She lay awake for a long time thinking about it and then overslept so that her breakfast was a scrappy affair of tea and toast, and for all the good her sleepless night had done her, she might just as well not have given Philip a thought, and indeed she had no time to think about him at all during the morning. She still had no student nurse to replace the one who had gone off sick and one of the three remaining nurses had gone on holiday. She took the report with outward calm, had a few succinct words with Linda Jenkins, her staff nurse, picked up the pile of post for her patients and started off on her morning round, casting a practised eye over the ward as she went. They might be short-staffed, but the girls were managing very nicely; the beds were being made with all speed and those ladies well enough to get up were being settled into the armchairs arranged at intervals down the long ward, a scheme intended to encourage the convalescent ladies to get together and enjoy a nice chat among themselves. Phyllida had discovered long ago that they became so interested in swapping their illnesses that they forgot to grumble at their own aches and pains, the awful food, the tepid tea, the unfeeling nurses… None of which was true, but she quite understood that they had to have something to gossip about. She paused now by a group and listened to Miss Thompson, a pernicious anaemia who ruled the new patients with a rod of iron since she had been in and out of the ward for years now, describing the operation her sister-in-law had just had. Miss Thompson had the bloodcurdling and quite inaccurate details of it so pat that Phyllida's lovely eyes almost popped out of her head. When Miss Thompson paused for breath she asked drily: 'Did she recover, Miss Thompson?'

She knew that she shouldn't have asked the question; now she would have to listen to a long-drawn-out blow-by-blow account of the unfortunate lady's return to health and strength. She passed around her letters and began a mental assay of the off duty for next week while she stood patiently. When Miss Thompson had at last finished, Phyllida, mindful of hurt feelings, merely remarked that some people had remarkable experiences, admonished the ladies to drink their mid-morning coffee when it arrived and went on her way. She recounted it all to Linda over their own coffee later and chuckled her way into a good humour again, so that when she thought of Philip during a rare few minutes of leisure later that day it was with mild pleasure at the idea of him spending a couple of days at her home.

She only saw him once before she started her leave, and for so short a time that they could only exchange a brief remark as to when he would arrive. She still felt pleased about him coming, but her pleasure was a little dimmed by his matter-of-fact manner, and his 'See you, then' was uttered with the briskness of a brother. True, they had encountered one another in the middle of one of the busiest corridors in the hospital, with nurses, porters and housemen milling up and down, but, thought Phyllida, suddenly annoyed, 'if he loved her as much as he said he did, he could surely have looked at her with rather more feeling?' She left the hospital the following evening, glad that she hadn't seen him again.

She drove down to her home in the neat little Vauxhall Astra, a present from her parents on her twenty-first birthday, five years ago, and although she could have afforded to exchange it she had never felt the need; it went well and she understood it as well as she would ever understand any car. She fastened her seat belt, gave a last glance at the rather grim hospital behind her and drove out into the busy street to meet the London traffic.

It took her quite some time to get out of London and on to the M3, but she was a good driver and not impatient. Once on the motorway she sent the small car racing along and at its end, took the A30 to Salisbury. It was almost empty of traffic by now and she made good time to the town, working round it to the north and picking up the A30 again on its further side. She was on home ground now and although it was getting on for ten o'clock, she didn't feel tired. Just short of Shaftesbury she turned off on to the Tisbury road and then turned again, going through pleasantly wooded country and climbing a little on the winding road. Over the brow of the hill she slowed for a minute. The lights of Gifford Ferris twinkled at her almost at its foot, not many lights, for the village was small and off the main road. But it was by no means isolated; there were other villages within a mile or two on all sides; any number of outlying farms and main roads to the north and south. Phyllida put her foot down and sent the car scuttling down the hill and then more slowly into the village's main street. It had a small market square with a stone cross in its centre, a handful of shops around it besides a comfortable hotel, and at the top of the hill on the other side one or two old stone houses. She stopped before one of these and jumped out, but before she could reach the door it had been flung open.

'Your mother's in the kitchen, getting your supper,' observed her father placidly. 'Nice to see you, my dear—did you have a good trip?'

She kissed him soundly. 'Super—almost no traffic once I'd

left London. Something smells good—I'm famished! I'll get my case…'

'Run along and find your mother, I'll bring it in. The car will be all right there until the morning.'

Phyllida walked down the long narrow hall and opened the kitchen door at its end, contentedly sniffing the air; furniture polish, the scent from a bowl of hyacinths on a table, and fragrant cooking. They spelled home.

Her mother was at the scrubbed table in the middle of the room, cutting bread. She looked up as Phyllida went in, dropped the knife and came to meet her. 'Darling—how lovely to see you, and how nice you look in that suit. There's watercress soup and mushroom omelette and buttered toast and tea, though Father says you're to have a glass of sherry first. He'll bring it presently.' She returned Phyllida's hug and added: 'Willy's here just for a few days—half term, you know.'

The younger of her two brothers appeared as her mother spoke, a boy of fourteen, absurdly like his father, with tousled hair and an air of never having enough to eat. He bore this out with a brotherly: 'Hi, Sis, heard you come, guessed there'd be food.'

She obligingly sat down at the table and shared her supper while their mother cut bread and wondered aloud how many more meals he would want before he settled to sleep.

'I'm growing,' he pointed out cheerfully, 'and look at Phylly—she finished growing years ago and she's stuffing herself.'

'Rude boy,' observed his sister placidly. 'How's school?'

Her father came in then and they sat around, all talking at once until Willy was sent off to bed and Phyllida and her mother tidied the kitchen, washed up and went to the sitting room with a tray of coffee.

It was a pleasant room; long and low-ceilinged and furnished with some nice pieces which had been in the family for generations. There was comfort too; easy chairs drawn up to the open fire, a vast sofa with a padded back and plenty of small reading lamps. Phyllida curled up on the sofa, the firelight warm on her face and dutifully answered the questions with which her mother bombarded her. They were mostly about Philip and cunningly put, and she answered them patiently, wishing illogically that her mother didn't seem so keen on him all of a sudden. She had been vaguely put out after Philip's first visit to her home by her mother's reaction to him. 'Such a nice young man,' her parent had declared, 'and so serious. I'm sure if you marry him he'll make a model husband.' It hadn't been the words so much as the tone in which they had been uttered, and ever since Phyllida had been worried by a faint niggling doubt at the back of her pretty head; a model husband sounded so dull. But this evening she could detect no doubt in her mother's voice—indeed, her parent chattered on at some length about Phyllida's future, talking about the wedding as though it were already a certainty.

Phyllida finished her coffee, observed rather tartly that no one had asked her to get married yet and when her mother remarked that she had understood that Philip was coming to stay for a couple of days, pointed out very quickly that it was only a friendly visit—it made a nice restful change after his work at the hospital. Mrs Cresswell agreed placidly, her still pretty head bent over some embroidery, and presently Phyllida went to bed.

Being home was delightful—pottering in the garden, helping her mother round the house, going for long bike rides with Willy, helping in her father's surgery. Phyllida relaxed, colour came back into her London-pale cheeks, her hair seemed more golden, her eyes bluer. Her mother, looking at her as she made pastry at the kitchen table, felt certain that Philip would ask her to marry him when he came.

She was right; he did, but not at once. He wasn't a man to rush his fences, and it wasn't until the morning of his second day there that he suggested that they might go into Shaftesbury for her mother and do some shopping, and Phyllida, called in from fetching the eggs from the hen-house at the end of the garden, readily agreed. She had been glad to see Philip when he had arrived, but not, she confessed to herself, thrilled, but they had quickly slipped into their pleasant, easygoing camaraderie and he was an undemanding companion. She put a jacket on over her slacks, combed her fringe, added a little more lipstick and pronounced herself ready.

Shaftesbury was full of people and cars; it always was, probably because it was a small town and built originally on top of a hill and its shops were concentrated in two main streets. They had done their shopping, chosen a variety of cakes from the fragrant bakery hidden away in an alley where the two streets met, and sat themselves down in the buttery of one of the few hotels for a cup of coffee before Philip made any but the most impersonal remarks.

'Wouldn't you like to leave hospital and have a home of your own?' he wanted to know.

Phyllida chose a bun, not paying as much attention as she should have done. 'Oh, yes,' she said casually, 'I'd love it. Have a bun?'

'Then why don't you?'

She looked up then, suddenly realizing what he was going to say. 'Don't, Philip—please...'

He took a bun too. 'Why not? You must know that I want to marry you?'

'Yes—well, yes, I suppose I did, but not—not urgently.'

He was a very honest young man. 'If you mean I'm beside myself with impatience to get married, you're right. But I've given the matter a great deal of thought lately and I'm sure you're the wife for me; we know each other very well by now and I'm more than half in love with you.' He smiled at her across the table. 'How about it, Phylly?'

She knew that she was going to say no. Perhaps, she thought desperately, she had never intended to say anything else, but it was going to be hard to say it. For one thing, she was strongly tempted to accept Philip's matter-of-fact proposal. They would live together happily enough, she would take an interest in his work and he would be a kind and considerate husband, of that she was sure. She would have a pleasant enough life with enough to live on, a nice home, friends of her own sort and children. She would like several children; only she had the lowering feeling that Philip would want a neat little family of a boy and a girl. He would be a splendid father too and the children would be good, obedient and reasonably clever. In fact, life wouldn't be what she had dreamed—a vague dream of a man who would sweep her off her feet, treasure her and love her and never on any account allow her to wear the trousers, and more than that, would fill his house with a brood of healthy, naughty children.

She sighed and said gently: 'It wouldn't work, Philip.'

He showed no rancour. 'Why not? You must have reasons.'

She frowned. 'I like you very, very much—I think for a while I was a little in love with you, but I'm sure that it's not enough.' She looked at him with unhappy blue eyes. 'I'm sorry, Philip—and I don't think I shall change my mind.'

He said calmly: 'You're in love with someone else?'

'No. Oh, no, no one at all, that's why it's difficult...you see, you're so right for me. I respect you and admire your work and the way you live, and I like being with you, only I don't want to marry you.' She added miserably: 'It would be such a mistake, and the awful thing is I don't know what I want.'

Philip finished his coffee with the air of a man who wasn't in the least defeated. 'I'm not taking no for an answer,' he told her quietly. 'I won't bother you, but I'll wait.'

'But it won't be any good.' She looked like an unhappy little girl, her short upper lip caught between her teeth, her eyes enormous under the fringe. She felt suddenly peevish. If she could get away, right away, he would forget her because he didn't love her, not with the sort of love which just didn't want to go on living without her—he might even fall in love with someone else quite quickly. It struck her then that he was the kind of man who didn't need to love like that; he was a calm, even-tempered man and too much love would choke him. When he only smiled and offered her more coffee she didn't say any more, for what was the use?

Philip didn't allow her refusal to make any difference between them. He spent the rest of the day with her, treating her with the same good-natured affection that he had always shown her. He went back to London that day after tea, saying all the right things to her mother and father and reminding Phyllida cheerfully that they would be going to the Annual Dance at the hospital together two days after her return: 'Though I'll see you before then,' he had assured her.

She watched him go with mixed feelings; real regret that she didn't love him and a faint touch of temper because he seemed so unmoved about her refusal—or was he so sure that she would give in? The thought made her even more peevish.

The moment he was out of sight her mother remarked: 'Well, dear, are you going to marry him? I'm sure he must have asked you.'

Phyllida hadn't meant to say anything about it—not just yet anyway, but she perceived now that her mother would go on gently asking questions until she got an answer.

'Yes, he did, and I said no.'

'Oh, good.' Mrs Cresswell took no notice of her daughter's surprised look. 'He's a very nice man, darling, but not your sort.'

'What is my sort, Mother?' Phyllida didn't feel peevish any more.

Her mother washed a tea-cup with care; it was old and treasured like most of the china she insisted on using every day. 'Well, he doesn't have to be handsome, but eye-catching, if you know what I mean, the sort of man who would take command in a sticky situation and know just what to do—and not let you have your own way unless he thought it was good for you.'

'A bigheaded tyrant,' suggested Phyllida.

'No, dear, just a man who would never take you for granted; take great care of you without you ever knowing it, and know exactly what he intended doing with his life—and yours, of course.'

'A paragon. Mother, I never knew you were romantic—does Father know?'

'He married me,' observed her parent placidly. 'What will

you do about Philip? I mean, you can't help but see him often, can you?'

Phyllida had piled the tea things on to a tray, on her way to putting them away in the carved corner cupboard in the sitting room. 'I hadn't thought of that,' she said slowly. 'It would be sense to leave, I suppose.'

'Well, think about it, darling.' Her mother spoke briskly. 'It could be done easily enough.'

Phyllida gave her a faintly mocking look. 'Mother, you have no idea...'

'No, dear, but things can always be done, however awkward, if only one applies oneself to them.'

Nothing more was said after that. Phyllida went back to London two days later, reluctant to give up a job she liked and go through all the fuss and bother of finding another one—and outside London, she supposed gloomily.

She didn't see Philip until the evening of the dance; indeed, she had taken care to keep out of his way, going to great lengths to avoid their usual meeting places, keeping one eye on the ward door in case he should come to see a patient referred for surgery.

But she had to see him again eventually. They met in the entrance hall, shortly after the dance had started, he very correct in his black tie, she prettier than ever in a pearly grey chiffon dress and silver slippers.

Her hullo was a trifle awkward, but Philip didn't seem to notice. He took her arm, asked her where she'd been during the last two days and suggested that they went into the big lecture hall, decorated for the occasion, and danced. It wasn't until they had circled the place at least twice that he asked: 'Had second thoughts, Phylly?'

'About what?' And then, despising herself for the remark: 'No, I haven't, Philip, and I'm not going to—truly I'm not.'

He laughed down at her. 'No? Shall we wait and see? We meet most days, don't we, so it won't be a case of "Out of sight, out of mind"—you're very used to me being there, aren't you?'

She met his eyes. 'Yes. You mean you'll wear me away like water on a stone.'

'Nicely put, although I wouldn't describe you as stony. You'll change your mind.'

Perhaps it was because he looked so smug and sure of himself that she resolved then and there to look for another job. She didn't say anything though, but danced the night away, mostly with Philip but with all the other men she knew as well. She enjoyed herself too; tomorrow was time enough to think things out.

She hadn't got much further by the following evening when she came off duty. It had been a busy day with several of her patients not doing as well as she had hoped, so that she felt too depressed to do more than take off her cap and put her feet up on the sofa in the Sisters' sitting room. She closed her eyes the better to think and then opened them again as the door opened and Meg Dawson, Surgical Ward Sister and one of her closest friends, came in. 'There's a phone call for you, Phylly—your mum.'

Phyllida had taken her shoes off as well. She padded down the passage to the phone box at its end and picked up the receiver. Her mother's voice, very youthful still, sounded very clear. 'Phylly? Father wants to talk to you.'

Phyllida was surprised; she and her father got on splendidly, but he was a busy man, not given to telephone conversations unless they concerned a patient. She said cautiously: 'Yes?'

Doctor Cresswell didn't waste time. 'You mentioned leaving, Phylly—if you do, there's a job going in about three weeks' time.'

A sign from heaven, thought Phyllida childishly. 'I could leave then—I've still another week's leave due, so I'd have to work three weeks notice…' She knew that her father was nodding his head even though he didn't speak. 'What sort of job?'

'A patient of mine until I referred her to Sir Keith Maltby—I attend her parents too. A girl of eighteen with erythroblastic leukaemia—I wasn't called in until she had been ill for some time, sent her straight to Sir Keith who got her into hospital;

she was there two months, had several courses of cytotoxic drugs and has improved considerably, gained weight, taken an interest in life. Her mother came to see me today, says Gaby has set her heart on going to somewhere sunny—they want to take her on a short cruise—Madeira and the Canaries, but they want a skilled nurse to keep an eye on her and recognise the signs and symptoms if she should have a relapse. All expenses paid, and fare of course, and a decent salary—about three weeks, they think. Of course you realise that Gaby hasn't very long to live. Sir Keith agrees with me that she should be allowed to do what she wants within reason—her parents are wealthy, fortunately. It would get you away, my dear, if that's what you want.' And when Phyllida didn't answer: 'I could arrange for you to see these people—the name's de Wolff—they've booked for a cruise leaving on April the sixth, that's not quite four weeks away.'

Phyllida heard herself say that yes, she would like to meet the de Wolffs and that provided they liked her, she would be prepared to take the job. 'I've a couple of days off, but not till the end of the week, that would be too late to give in my notice—look, Father, I'm off at five o'clock tomorrow and on at one o'clock the next day. I'll drive down in the evening, see them in the morning and drive straight back—I can just do it provided they'll make an appointment early in the morning.'

'Splendid, my dear. I'll see to it and ring you back.'

So she found herself the next day rushing off duty, racing into her outdoor things and driving as fast as traffic permitted out of London. The appointment was for half past nine on the following morning and to save time she was to go to the de Wolffs' house, as it was on the London side of Shaftesbury and she could drive straight on back to work after the interview. She hadn't told anyone about it and she hadn't seen Philip. She had toyed with the idea of going to the office and giving in her notice that morning, but there was always the chance that the job wouldn't turn out to be what she expected. She got clear of London at last and belted for home.

CHAPTER TWO

MRS CRESSWELL was waiting with supper, and her father came from his study to talk to Phyllida while she ate it. 'Gaby's a nice enough girl, poor child—difficult at times, I gather from her mother, but it has to be remembered that she's very ill. She has no idea how ill, of course, although her parents have been told. Not that they've accepted it well; they simply cannot believe that a girl of eighteen can die. They're both energetic, social types and can't understand why Gaby isn't the same.'

Phyllida carved another slice of her mother's home-baked bread. 'You don't like them,' she stated flatly.

'I wouldn't go as far as to say that, shall I say that I regret their attitude towards illness and death—two inconvenient states they simply refuse to recognise, but I'm glad they're so eager to take Gaby on this trip. Sir Keith tells me it's only a question of three months or so.'

'Oh, Father, how awful—isn't there anything at all to be done?'

He shook his head. 'You know that yourself, my dear. Thank heaven it's extremely rare—other forms of leukaemia have a much more favourable prognosis these days.'

Phyllida left home after breakfast the next morning, to drive the few miles to the de Wolffs' home. She joined the main Salisbury road presently and then turned away on to a country road leading to Berwick St John, and after another mile came upon the house she was looking for. It was Edwardian, much gabled and ornamented with beams and plasterwork in an attempt to make it look Tudor. It was large too, spick and span as to paintwork and altogether too perfect for her taste. She thought with sudden nostalgia of her own home only a few miles away and so very different, its ancient oak door almost always open, its mullioned windows wide, with curtains blowing a welcome. There were no curtains to be seen here and no open windows.

She got out, crossed the gravel, so smooth that she felt guilty treading on it, and rang the bell. The man-servant who opened the door matched the house exactly; correct; unwelcoming and without any warmth. He begged her to enter, ushered her into a small panelled room furnished with expensive, tasteless furniture, and went away.

Both Mr and Mrs de Wolff entered the room a moment later, bringing with them an air of brisk efficiency and charm. They bade Phyllida seat herself, and without any preliminaries, proceeded to put her—as Mr de Wolff observed—in the picture. 'You shall see Gaby presently,' promised Mrs de Wolff, and smiled charmingly at Phyllida. She was a handsome woman, in her forties but not looking it by reason of exquisite make-up and beautifully cut hair, and a casual tweed suit which must have cost a great deal of money. She smiled a lot, thought Phyllida, and she quite understood what her father had meant when he had told her that neither she nor her husband wanted to accept the fact that Gaby's illness was a terminal one.

'The specialist takes a grave view, of course,' said Mr de Wolff, teetering on his toes before the fireplace, like the chairman of a board meeting, 'but we're both so healthy ourselves we take a more optimistic view. This little holiday should do her the world of good, and she's so keen to go.'

'You will notify the ship's doctor of her illness?' asked Phyllida, 'and I should want her medical notes with me so that they can be referred to if necessary.'

Mrs de Wolff frowned, and just for a minute all the charm had gone, but it was back almost at once. 'Of course we'll see to all that, Miss Cresswell, you can safely leave us to arrange everything just as it should be. We shall consult Sir Keith, of course—such a pity that he's in Scotland, otherwise you could have gone to see him, but I'm sure your father has told you all there is to know about Gaby.' She got to her feet. 'Would you like to see her now before you go? We do so hope you'll come with us, but it's for you to decide of course.'

She crossed the room and rang the bell and when the unsmiling manservant came, asked him to let Miss Gaby know that she was wanted in the morning room.

The first thing Phyllida thought when she saw Gaby was how very pretty she was, small and slim to the point of thinness and far too pale, with a cloud of dark hair to match her dark eyes. This thought was followed at once by a second one, that the girl looked far more ill than her parents had made out. She seemed a docile little creature too, replying meekly to her mother's remarks about how much she wanted to go on holiday with them, and what she intended to do. But she offered no remarks of her own, although she smiled at Phyllida and went on smiling when her father said that she was a spoilt girl and had everything she could possibly want. He sounded very pleased with himself as he said it, and Phyllida wondered if he had stopped to think that having everything one wanted wasn't much use if one wasn't going to be alive to enjoy it.

She stayed for another half an hour, asking questions as discreetly as possible as to her duties. It would be mostly companionship, she gathered, and the giving of Gaby's medicines and pills, as well as a number of small routine tasks—temperature and pulse and blood pressure and making sure that her patient slept well. She rose to go presently, reiterating that she would want the case notes with her, and reminding the de Wolffs that the ship's doctor would have to be informed. Gaby had gone with some small excuse so that Phyllida could speak openly now. A little uneasy because of the de Wolffs' casual attitude towards their daughter's illness, she said gently: 'You do know that Gaby is very ill? I know it's hard to believe—and you're quite happy about her making this trip?'

Mrs de Wolff's charming smile slipped again. 'Quite happy, Miss Cresswell,' she said with finality. So Phyllida left it at that, only staying to arrange to meet them all on the morning of the sixth.

'We shall be driving up,' explained Mr de Wolff. 'We'll pick you up at the hospital, that will be the easiest way, I think.'

They wished her goodbye, and the manservant ushered her

out into the chilly March morning. She had driven for ten minutes or so when she said out loud: 'Well, they could at least have offered me a cup of coffee!'

She reached Salisbury by continuing along the same country road from the de Wolffs' house, stopping on the way to have the cup of coffee no one had offered her, and once through Salisbury she made for London without waste of time.

At the hospital she had the leisure to change into uniform, write out her resignation and present herself at the office. The Senior Nursing Officer was considerably astonished, but in the course of her long and successful career she had learned when not to ask questions. Beyond expressing a sincere regret at Phyllida's decision to leave, she said nothing other than to wish her a successful future and advise her to give the office due warning as to the exact date of her departure.

'You have a week's holiday still, Sister Cresswell, and I expect you can arrange to add your days off to that. I shall have to appoint someone in your place, but in the meantime I think that Staff Nurse Jenkins is quite capable of carrying on. Do you agree?'

'She's very good, Miss Cutts, and the patients like her. The nurses work well for her too.'

'In that case I see no reason why she shouldn't apply for the post.' Miss Cutts nodded kindly in gracious dismissal.

Phyllida, speeding to the ward, felt intense surprise at what she had done. Probably if she had stopped to think about it, she would have decided against leaving, but now it was done she felt relief as well. She still had to see Philip and explain, but she would bide her time and choose the right moment for that.

But the matter was taken out of her hands. He came on to the ward to take a look at a suspected duodenal ulcer which would probably need operation, and instead of leaving at once he followed Phyllida to her office, shut the door behind him and asked her quietly: 'What's this I hear about you leaving?'

'Oh, dear—so soon?' She turned to face him across the small room. 'I only saw Miss Cutts half an hour ago and I haven't told a soul—I was going to talk to you about it, Philip.' She pushed her cap away from her forehead. 'Not now, though—I've heaps to do.'

'You're off at five o'clock? I'll meet you at Tony's at half past six.' He went away without another word, leaving her to wonder for the rest of the day if she had made the mistake of her lifetime. Even now, if he overwhelmed her...she wondered at the back of her mind if he felt strongly enough about her to do that. With a tremendous effort she dismissed the whole thing and attacked her work; there was enough of that to keep her mind off other things; the duodenal ulcer not responding to medical treatment; Mrs Gregson springing a mild coronary upon them; the young girl in the corner bed with undulant fever, so depressed that no one knew what to do next to get her cheerful again, and the sixteen-year-old anorexia nervosa next to her, taking precious time and patience with every unwanted meal...

Tony's was a small unassuming restaurant within five minutes' walk of the hospital and much patronised by the doctors and nurses. Phyllida arrived punctually and found a table for two by one of the windows. There was no view, only the drab street outside, and she sat staring at it until Philip slid into the seat opposite her.

His 'Hullo—shall we have the usual?' was uttered in his normal calm way and when she nodded: 'And now what's all this nonsense about leaving?'

'It's not nonsense, Philip. I've given Miss Cutts my notice and I leave in three weeks' time—just under, as a matter of fact. And I've got a job.'

Just for a moment his calm was shaken. 'A job? So you'd arranged it all some time ago?'

'No.' She explained carefully and added: 'I'm sorry, Philip, I like you very much, I told you that, but the best thing to do is for us to stop seeing each other.'

He said with faint smugness, 'You're afraid I'll wear you down.'

She stared at him, her blue eyes clear and honest. 'I don't know,' she told him earnestly, 'but if you did, it wouldn't be right.'

The waitress brought them the soup of the day and Phyllida studied it as though it was something of vital importance. Presently she said: 'It's difficult to explain, but when I marry I want to be so in love with the man that nothing else matters; there'd be no doubts and no wondering about the future and where we'd live or how.' She looked up from her soup and gazed at him from under her fringe.

'And you don't feel like that about me? Phylly, grow up! You're living in a fairy tale—there's no such thing as that kind of love, only in romantic novels. I'm surprised at you, I thought you were such a sensible, matter-of-fact girl, with no nonsense about you.'

Phyllida picked up her spoon and gave the Heinz tomato a stir. That was the trouble, she thought silently, he'd got her all wrong. She was romantic and full of nonsense; he had confused the practical, sensible young woman who ran the medical ward so efficiently with her real self, and looking at him now, she could see that he still thought it.

He was half way through his soup by now. 'Well, trot off if you must,' he told her cheerfully, 'and come back when you're ready. I daresay I'll still be here.'

She sat silently while the soup was replaced by pork chops, frozen peas and a pile of chips which might have daunted any girl but her, who ate like a horse and never put on an inch. When the waitress had gone again, she said patiently: 'I'm not coming back; this job is only for three weeks—I don't know what I'll do after that.'

It annoyed her that he still looked complacent, but to say more wasn't going to help. Deeds, not words, she told herself silently.

'What is this job?' he wanted to know.

She told him, and being an opportunist, picked his brains. 'I don't know a great deal about it—I've never seen a case, though I've nursed one or two lymphoblastic leukaemias and they did rather well.'

'This one isn't likely to—it's rare, so rare that there aren't enough statistics, but it's a terminal illness, I'm afraid. Have you got the notes yet?'

'No. Sir Keith Maltby has been looking after her, but he's in Scotland. Father will get the notes from him, though, he's already telephoned him about it. He doesn't object to Gaby going on this cruise—he says she can do what she likes provided her parents understand that the moment she shows signs of deterioration they must get her to hospital or fly her back without delay. The ship's doctor will have all the facts; Mr de Wolff has undertaken to see about that. There's plenty of money, I believe, so there's no reason why anything should go wrong from that side of it.'

As she spoke, she wondered uneasily why she didn't quite believe what she was saying. Perhaps because she had taken a faint dislike to Mr and Mrs de Wolff—quite an unfounded one, based entirely on his brisk attitude towards his daughter's illness, and his wife's calculated charm. Phyllida gave herself a mental shake, agreed with Philip that it would be interesting to see Madeira and the Canaries even if her chance to do so might be limited, and then applied herself to responding suitably to his unshakable friendliness.

It remained unshakable too for the next few weeks, and she felt guilty because she was unable to feel regret at her decision, largely because Philip made no secret of the fact that he expected her to come running once she had brought Gaby back home again.

'Any ideas about the next job?' he asked her airily. 'A bit difficult while you're away, isn't it? It'll mean an enforced holiday while you find something to suit you and then go after it. You might not get it either.' He sounded so satisfied that she could cheerfully have thrown something at him.

Leaving the ward was harder than leaving Philip, she discovered; she had grown fond of it during the last few years; it was old and awkward to work in and there were never enough staff, but she had loved the ever-changing succession of patients, and some of those, like old Mrs Gregson, were so upset at her going that she had promised that she would come and visit them the moment she got back from the cruise. Unthinkingly she had mentioned that to Philip and been furious with herself for doing so when she saw the knowing little smile on his face, smugly sure that she was making an excuse to return to the hospital and see him. She managed not to see too much of him, though, going home for her days off so that she might collect Gaby's notes and listen to her father's sound advice, as well as root around in her bedroom to see what clothes she should take with her. It would be warm for most of the time and last year's summer dresses looked depressingly dull. She decided to travel in a jersey suit and the silk blouse she had bought in a fit of extravagance, pack some slacks and tops and buy one or two things in London.

There was a nice selection of cruise clothes; her modest list lengthened as she went along the rails. In the end she left the shop with a new bikini, three cotton dresses, sleeveless and light as air, and because they were so pretty, two evening dresses, one in pink crêpe with not much top and a wide floating skirt, and the other of white organza. She wasn't sure if she would have the chance to wear them, but there was no harm in taking them along. She already had a flowery-patterned long skirt and several pretty tops to go with it and a couple of short silky dresses from last year.

She packed her bags, arranged to have the rest of her luggage sent home, bade goodbye to her friends at a rather noisy party after the day's work, and retired to bed, but not to sleep at once. There was too much to think about—Gaby and her treatment and the still vague disquiet because she didn't know too much about it, although the notes were comprehensive enough and her father had primed her well. Presumably the ship's doctor would keep a close eye on her patient, and after all, her parents would be there. Slightly reassured, Phyllida allowed her thoughts to turn to Philip. She had contrived to bid him goodbye at the party, with people milling around them so that there was very little chance to say much. She had tried to sound final, but he hadn't believed her. It was annoying and she worried about it, getting sleepier and sleepier until she nodded off at last.

She left the hospital in some state, for the de Wolffs arrived for her in a chauffeur-driven Cadillac; it took up a lot of room in the forecourt and Phyllida, turning to wave to such of her friends who had managed to spare the time to look out of their ward windows, saw their appreciative grins. She got in beside the chauffeur after a final wave and caught Mrs de Wolff's eye. It didn't look in the least friendly and she wondered why, but she smiled at Mr de Wolff, and spoke to Gaby, who answered her eagerly and with encouraging warmth. Phyllida, a charitable girl who seldom thought ill of anyone, supposed Mrs de Woolff had had a trying time getting ready for their holiday. She settled herself in her seat, resolving to do her best to see that Gaby wasn't only well looked after, but kept amused too, so that her parents could enjoy themselves too.

They arrived at the dock with only a very short time to spare before embarking—done deliberately, Mr de Wolff explained, so that there would be no delays for Gaby in getting on board. Phyllida took her patient's arm as they walked slowly up the gangway, for Gaby looked exhausted, then followed the steward up to the Sun Deck. They were to share a de luxe cabin and she looked around her with deep satisfaction; she was used to the normal comforts of life, but this was luxury. She sat Gaby down in a comfortable chair, noted with satisfaction that their luggage was already waiting for them, and took a quick look round.

The cabin was large, even for the two of them, with beds widely spaced, a comfortable sofa, a table and two easy chairs. The window was large and the lighting well arranged and the adjoining bathroom all she could have wished for. It only needed a pleasant stewardess to offer to unpack for them to complete her satisfaction, but she declined this service and asked instead if they could have a tray of tea, for Gaby looked as though she could do with something of the sort. It was barely midday and Mr de Wolff had told her they would be going to the second sitting for their meals, still an hour and a half away;

ample time to unpack, check unobtrusively that Gaby was fit to go to the restaurant, and try to get to know her better.

They drank their tea without interruption. The de Wolffs hadn't appeared; probably they realised that Gaby was tired and needed to rest. Phyllida unpacked for both of them, not bothering her patient to talk. After lunch she would search out the doctor, show him the notes and ask for any instructions he might care to give her. Gaby could rest on her bed in the meantime. The girl looked fagged out and Phyllida frowned a little; the job was full of uncertainties and Gaby was a very sick girl. She wondered again if it had been wise of her parents to allow her to come on the cruise and then conceded that if the girl had set her heart on it and had so little time to live, they were only doing what any loving parents would want to do. It was a pity that Sir Keith hadn't seen Gaby for some weeks, but the de Wolffs had said that he had agreed to the trip, so it must be reasonably safe for Gaby to go. Phyllida dismissed her gloomy thoughts and started to chat quietly, hanging away her patient's lovely clothes as she did so.

They shared a table with Mr and Mrs de Wolff at lunch, both of whom dominated the conversation, talking animatedly about the places they were to visit, the various entertainments on board and how splendid it all was for Gaby, who ate almost no lunch, replied docilely when she was spoken to, and attracted a good many admiring glances from the surrounding tables.

Phyllida did too, although she wasn't aware of it; she was too concerned about her patient.

The meal was a leisurely one, passengers serving themselves from a long buffet of cold meats and salads, arranged in mouth-watering abundance. Gaby's parents didn't seem to notice that she was drooping with fatigue, so that Phyllida took affairs into her own hands and when the steward brought the coffee, excused both herself and Gaby, whisked her to their cabin, tucked her up on her bed, and went in search of the doctor's surgery.

It was three decks down, adjacent to a small hospital. The doctor was at his desk, a young man with a pleasant open face, talking to the ship's nurse. Phyllida took a dislike to her on sight and felt that the feeling was reciprocated; she didn't like heavy make-up and brightly tinted nails on a nurse, nor did she fancy the hard blue eyes and tight mouth in what should have been a pretty face. However, her errand wasn't with the nurse. She introduced herself briskly, stated her business and waited for the doctor to speak.

He looked bewildered. 'But I haven't heard...' he began. 'I've had no information about this Miss de Wolff. Perhaps you'll tell me about her, Miss—er—Cresswell.'

It took a little time, although she gave the information concisely and without personal comment. When she had finished he said thoughtfully: 'Of course I'll look after her and do everything in my power to help. You say she's entered a period remission? Then it's quite possible that she'll be able to enjoy this cruise, to a limited extent, of course—and return home at least none the worse. May I keep these notes and study them? I'll see that you get them back. Perhaps if I were to call and see Miss de Wolff...this evening, or later this afternoon after tea?'

Phyllida agreed. 'I thought we'd have tea in the cabin and then dress without hurrying.'

'Very wise. I think you should suit your activities to her mood. You say she insisted on coming on this holiday?'

'Well, yes, so her parents told me—perhaps it was just a flash in the pan; she's not shown anything but a—a kind of docile acceptance.'

The doctor rose to his feet. 'Would you like me to talk to her parents?'

Phyllida considered. 'If when you've seen her you think it necessary, yes, please.' She hesitated. 'They seem to think that this cruise will put her on her feet again. They can't accept...'

'I know—it's hard for people to realise. Miss de Wolff has no inkling?'

'None that I know of, but I don't know her very well yet. I'll tell you if I think she has.'

They parted in friendly fashion and Phyllida started off down the long corridor taking her to the other end of the ship, to be overtaken almost at once by the nurse.

'I thought I'd let you know that you'd better not expect too much help from me,' she began. 'I have quite a busy time, you know, and I have to be on call round the clock.'

Phyllida stopped to look at her. 'That's OK, I'm sure you must be pretty busy. I don't expect I'll need any help, thanks all the same.'

The other girl gave the suggestion of a sniff. 'If you need any advice...' she began.

Phyllida's large blue eyes flashed. 'I expect I'll be able to cope,' she said gently. 'I've been Medical Ward Sister at St Michael's for four years.' She smiled widely, added 'goodbye' and went on her way, her blonde hair flying round cheeks which were a little pinker than usual, by reason of her vexation.

The doctor was very good with Gaby, matter-of-fact and friendly, taking care not to alarm her by questions which might give her reason to think. And afterwards, on the pretext of fetching some pills in case Gaby felt seasick, Phyllida went back to the surgery.

He said heavily: 'Well, Miss Cresswell, if she'd been my daughter I'd never for one moment entertained the idea of her coming on a trip like this, however much she'd set her heart on it. And she's not wildly enthusiastic about it, is she? Is she spoilt? She didn't strike me as being so.'

Phyllida shook her head. 'I don't think so. She's very quiet and agrees with everything her parents suggest.' She didn't add the unspoken thought that Gaby appeared to be in considerable awe of her parents and anxious, almost painfully so, to please them.

'Well, I'll have a word with them and take a look at her each day. You'll come to me at once if you think it necessary, won't you?'

Phyllida felt better after that, and after due thought went along to the de Wolffs' cabin. It surprised her to discover that they were put out over her visit to the doctor. 'There was really no need,' declared Mrs de Wolff sharply. 'Gaby is a little tired, but otherwise she's recovering very well. We don't want ideas put into her head.'

'I don't think anyone will do that, Mrs de Wolff—after all, she's been under a doctor for so long now, she can't find it strange if the ship's doctor pays her a visit.' She turned to Mr de Wolff. 'I thought you were going to tell him about Gaby—he knew nothing at all about her.'

'I considered it unnecessary.' Mr de Wolff spoke pompously and looked annoyed. 'After all, if Sir Keith gave his consent to this cruise, I hardly suppose that we lesser mortals need to interfere.'

Phyllida went pink. 'I have no intention of interfering, Mr de Wolff, but Gaby has a severe illness and you asked me to look after her and I intend to do so. How long ago is it since Sir Keith Maltby actually saw her?'

Her employer went a rich plum colour. 'That's beside the point, Miss Cresswell. All we ask is that you carry out your duties.'

Phyllida drew a calming breath. She was wasting time; he had no intention of telling her. 'Where would you like us to meet you before dinner?'

She heard his sigh of relief. 'Oh, in the Neptune Bar—about eight o'clock.'

Gaby seemed better when Phyllida got back to their cabin, and became quite animated over the choice of the dress she should wear. She decided on a plain, long-sleeved blue silk sheath, for no one would dress on the first night at sea, and Phyllida put on one of last year's dresses, a very plain one; she considered it made her look just as a nurse out of uniform should look.

The evening went off very well after all. The doctor had introduced himself to the de Wolffs in the bar, offered his services should they be required and went away before the two girls arrived, and if Gaby didn't eat a good dinner, at least she seemed to be enjoying herself. All the same, she went quite willingly to bed when Phyllida suggested it, and Phyllida, quite tired out, went too.

The days formed a pleasant pattern; they breakfasted in their cabin and then spent a leisurely morning sitting on deck, and if Phyllida regretted not being able to join in the deck games and wander off to chat to some of the other passengers, she didn't admit it, even to herself. It worried her that they saw so little of Gaby's parents, who seemed to think that meeting their daughter at lunch and dinner was sufficient, nor did they express anxiety over her condition or ask Phyllida how she was progressing. Luckily the weather was calm and getting warmer, so that by Sunday morning they were able to wear cotton dresses and lie in the sun for a time. It was while they were doing this that the doctor joined them for their mid-morning beef tea and Phyllida, in a casual voice masking her worry, mentioned Gaby's headache. 'Quite a troublesome one,' she added lightly, 'it just doesn't go away.'

'Ah, yes—one of those sick headaches, I expect,' observed the doctor, taking his cue smartly.

Gaby nodded listlessly. 'Yes, I was sick in the night—Phylly had to get up—that's why I feel so dozy now.'

The doctor didn't stay long, and presently, while Gaby slept, Phyllida went in search of him. 'Do you think it's infiltration of the meninges?' she asked anxiously. 'My father told me about that. Should I tell her parents? She seemed so much better—we haven't done much, but she was beginning to eat a little and take an interest in things.'

'Where are her parents?'

'They play bridge a good deal of the time and they've made a good many friends.'

'They don't see much of Gaby? Not enough to notice if she's better or worse?'

'No.'

'I'll have a word with them if you like, and I'll have another look at her later on. I don't like the headache and sickness, it may possibly be what you suggest.'

By the evening Gaby was worse, the headache was persistent now and so was the sickness, and she had become irritable, so that nothing Phyllida could say or do was right. And when the doctor came to see her just before dinner he looked grave. 'I'm going to advise you to disembark at Madeira,' he said. 'There's a good hospital there, and while I don't think she needs to go there at the moment, if you were to stay in an hotel she could be moved quickly. Better still, her parents could fly her back home straight away. I don't think she should stay on board, we haven't the facilities.'

Phyllida nodded. 'You'll see Mr and Mrs de Wolff? Shall I say nothing to Gaby until it's all arranged?' She paused. 'I shall have to pack.'

'Yes, of course, I'll go and see them now.'

She went back to the cabin and sat down with a book. Gaby wasn't sleeping, but she didn't want to talk either. It was half an hour before Mrs de Wolff opened the door and came in.

'Well, here's a fine state of affairs!' she exclaimed angrily. 'All our plans changed just because Gaby feels a little under the weather! Still, the doctor knows best, I suppose. My husband's radioed for rooms for you both at Reid's Hotel and we'll see you safely there tomorrow before we get back to the ship.'

Phyllida stared at her. 'But aren't we all going ashore?'

'Good heavens, no. We've planned it all nicely—we shall go on to the Canaries and pick you up on our way back next Saturday. Gaby will be better by then. We've talked to the doctor, so you have no need to worry, Miss Cresswell. We feel confident that you can look after Gaby very well until we return—it's only five days and we simply can't miss any of this cruise and there's no need for us to do so. Besides, we've been looking forward to it for some time.'

She went and peered down at Gaby. 'You do look a little pale, darling. You'll feel better on dry land, I expect, and you girls can have a few days' fun on your own.' She patted Gaby's head and Phyllida saw the girl wince. 'We'll leave you plenty of spending money.'

When she had gone Gaby said wearily: 'Mummy always thinks that if she gives me enough money everything will be all right.'

'I expect you'll enjoy it just as much as being on board ship,' said Phyllida soothingly. 'Now, I'm going to pack our things, and suppose we have dinner here this evening? You choose what you'd like to eat and get a long night's sleep. Now I'm going to take these books back to the library.'

She went to see the doctor too, and he wasn't in the best of tempers. 'I've made it plain to Gaby's parents that she's extremely ill and possibly heading for a relapse, and I suggested that you should all fly back from Madeira tomorrow, but they won't hear of it—told me that if the specialist considered her fit enough to take a holiday that was good enough for them, that we're probably over-anxious. They agreed readily enough to Gaby going ashore with you—said they'd pick you up at the end of the week. Are you at all worried?'

'I'm in a flat spin,' confided Phyllida. 'Anything could happen, couldn't it? And here we are, thousands of miles away from home and her parents refusing to face up to her being ill. Do you think she'll be all right? I'll take the greatest care of her.'

'If she keeps quiet and with you to look after her she might get over this bad patch, but she really needs to be flown home and taken to hospital, but her parents utterly refuse. They say that this has happened before and she's always got over it.' He sighed. 'At least Mr de Wolff has all the particulars of her case and I've written a covering letter; he's promised to deliver it himself at the hospital and arrange for a doctor to call and see Gaby—probably tomorrow in the evening or the following morning. We shall be back here on Saturday and if Gaby is no better, I'll do my best to persuade her parents to fly her back.'

Phyllida agreed. The doctor had done all he could, she would have the hospital close at hand and a doctor, so perhaps she need not worry too much. Gaby's father had said that these little relapses, as he called them, had occurred before and Gaby had always pulled through with a little extra care. But there were a number of drugs she should be having—perhaps they would have them at the hospital in Funchal. Phyllida didn't quite trust Mr de Wolff's casual view of his daughter's condition, but she had to take his word for it. She packed for them both, saw Gaby into bed for a good night's sleep and went to bed herself.

There was no hitch in the next day's plans. Gaby was cheerful, and after a good night's sleep seemed better. They went ashore just before lunch, went straight to the hotel and lunched there with Gaby's parents before they rejoined the ship. Their goodbyes were brief; they didn't look back as they left the hotel.

Phyllida and Gaby had adjoining rooms overlooking the gardens going down to the sea, with the swimming pools and tennis courts at their edge. They were spacious and airy and Phyllida made her patient comfortable in a long chair on the balcony before unpacking once more and then going to see about meals. When she got back Gaby was sitting up, looking quite animated, watching the guests in the pools. 'I'm going to like it here,' she declared, and looked happy for the first time, 'just with you. We don't need to do anything, do we? I mean, go on excursions or shopping? Daddy gave me some money to hire a car, he said we could tour the island, but I'm not keen, are you?'

'Not a bit,' lied Phyllida. 'I'm all for being lazy. And by the way, Doctor Watts from the ship wrote a note to one of the doctors at the hospital here asking him to pop round and see you this evening or tomorrow, just in case there's anything you need.'

Gaby hunched a shoulder. 'I wish people didn't fuss so. I'm quite all right if only I didn't have this headache.'

'Well, that's why he's coming, I expect; if it's no better he'll be able to prescribe some different tablets. Would you like to stay up here for tea? Or we can have it on the terrace—it looked super and there's a lovely view.'

Gaby settled for the terrace and presently they went downstairs and found seats in a shady corner, and Gaby, Phyllida was pleased to see, enjoyed her tea, talking quite animatedly about her clothes and the boutique they had stopped to look at in the hotel's foyer.

The rest of the day passed pleasantly. They dined at a small table by themselves, but several people around them stopped to speak and Gaby, once more in a happy mood, preened herself in their admiring glances. Phyllida went to bed happier than she had been since the cruise started. Gaby might not be better physically, but she was a whole lot happier. The thought that it was because her parents weren't there crossed her mind, but she dismissed that as unlikely. They gave Gaby everything; she had more clothes than she ever could wear, lovely jewellery, and every luxury that money could buy. She was almost asleep when the notion that Gaby had everything but real love and interest from her parents came into her head. She could have wept at the sadness of it.

Gaby felt so well the next morning that she put on one of her prettiest sun dresses and lounged by one of the swimming pools while Phyllida swam around, but as the day became warmer they moved back to the terrace, ate their lunch there and only went back to their rooms so that Gaby might rest. But they went outside again for tea and stayed there until dinner time, when Gaby changed her dress for a rather too elaborate silk one, but she looked so happy that Phyllida told her that she looked a dream and would turn all heads. Which she did. As they said goodnight later, Gaby said sleepily: 'It's been a lovely day—I'd like to stay here, just with you, Phylly, for ever and ever.'

Phyllida dropped a kiss on the pale cheek and made some laughing reply before she went to her own room.

Gaby was awake and sitting up in bed when Phyllida went in the next morning and she left her to have her breakfast and went downstairs to have her own, wondering if it would be a good idea to suggest that they might take a taxi to the Country Club and sit there for an hour or two before lunch. She didn't hurry over her meal. Gaby didn't like to be disturbed until she had finished her breakfast; it was almost ten o'clock as she got up from the table. She went back upstairs, pausing to speak to some English guests on their way out. When she knocked on Gaby's door there was no answer; probably she was reading and hadn't heard. Phyllida opened the door.

Gaby wasn't reading. She was lying back in bed, unconscious.

Phyllida drew a startled breath, pulled herself together in seconds and went quickly to the bed. The first thing she did was to press the bell, the second to feel for Gaby's pulse, so faint and threadlike that she had difficulty in finding it. Her breathing was so light and shallow that she had to bend down in order to check it. No one had answered the bell, so she rang again, took the tray off the bed, pulled the pillow into a better position and when there was still no answer to her summons, ran to the door. Something must be done, and fast, if it were to be of any use.

CHAPTER THREE

PHYLLIDA WASN'T a girl to panic, but now she had to get a tight hold on herself, making her mind work sensibly when all she wanted to do was scream for help and leave everything to someone else. This wasn't hospital, it wasn't even England; she knew no one, she wasn't even sure where the hospital was. Gaby was desperately ill—worse than that, Gaby was going to die. Somehow or other she would have to get a message to her parents, find a doctor, get her to hospital. Phyllida took another look at Gaby, lying so still in her bed, and went downstairs as fast as she could, running across the foyer to the reception desk.

There was no one there. She banged the bell and was angry with herself because her hand shook, and when no one came she couldn't stop herself crying in a shaky voice: 'Oh, please won't someone come?'

'Will I do?' asked a voice behind her.

It belonged to a very tall, powerfuly built man with what she immediately decided was a face she could trust, though at that moment she would have trusted a snake.

'Yes,' she didn't hesitate. 'I'm looking after a girl—she's desperately ill and her parents are cruising round the Canaries—I don't know exactly where they are. I need a doctor, now, this instant, and she should be in hospital. She's going to die if something isn't done quickly!'

He put a large firm hand on her arm. 'I'm a doctor, shall I take a look? Do you speak Portuguese?'

'No, but they speak English here, only there isn't anyone.'

'Coffee time. Shall I have a look at this girl? Your patient, is she?'

Phyllida nodded. 'Please. I'll give you an idea...' She started up the stairs fast, talking as she went.

She hadn't doubted that he was a doctor. He examined Gaby with careful speed while Phyllida stood beside him, watching.

There was a great deal of him and he was handsome too, with a patrician nose, a firm mouth and blue eyes beneath lazy lids. His hair was so fair that she wasn't sure if it was grey or not. He straightened up presently and looked at her. 'You're right, I'm afraid—I'll get the hospital, I happen to know someone there. There's nothing more to be done. You know that, don't you?'

'Yes. What shall I do about her parents?'

'When did they go? This girl's been dangerously ill for some time—surely they were told?'

'Yes, oh, yes. But they said that Gaby wanted to go on this cruise so badly and that's why I'm here, so that I could look after her. She got worse on our way here and the ship's doctor advised us to come ashore with her—he wanted us to fly home, but her parents wouldn't consent. They didn't want her to go to the hospital either...they wouldn't admit that she was ill, I did tell them, but they wouldn't listen. They came ashore with us and then went back on board—and that was the day before yesterday. They told me not to worry about an address if I should need them, they said it wasn't necessary, but I could radio the ship, couldn't I?'

His blue eyes hadn't left her face. 'Don't they love the girl?'

'I—I...it's hard to say; if they do it's not the kind of love most people have for their children—they gave her everything, though. They wanted to get away; her mother hates illness.'

They were in the foyer now and he had a hand on the telephone by the still deserted desk. He lifted the receiver, dialled a number as she spoke and spoke in his turn.

'They'll be here in a few minutes; you'll go with her and stay. I'll get a message to her parents. May I have their name?'

It didn't enter her head to argue with him. 'I'll get her things together and mine too. The name's de Wolff and they're on the *Blenheim*, going to Lanzarote and then Teneriffe and Las Palmas—they're expected back on Saturday.'

'Too late. Now go and get ready. I'll see you later.'

Packing furiously in Gaby's room, one anxious eye on her patient, Phyllida paused for a second. She didn't know the man's name; he might not have been telephoning the hospital, he might just disappear as suddenly as he had appeared; perhaps the ambulance wouldn't come. She shut the case with hands which still shook and then uttered a sigh of relief as she heard steady feet coming down the corridor towards the room.

She should have known better, she chided herself as she got out of the ambulance at the hospital. Her new-found friend was waiting at the entrance with a nurse and doctor and two porters. He wasted no time on greeting her, said merely: 'Follow us,' and led the procession along a corridor, past several wards and into a small room beyond them. Here Gaby was put to bed by Phyllida and the nurse while the two doctors talked together. Once she was asked if she had any notes about her patient and paused to fetch them from her case.

'They were given to me in case the ship's doctor wanted them,' she explained, 'and when he'd read them he pointed out that he hadn't the facilities for Gaby should she become worse. He couldn't understand why she had been allowed on the cruise in the first place. Nothing was said about her being ill when the cruise was booked, he was sure of that. Mrs de Wolff had told me that Gaby was expected to live for another year at least, perhaps longer, but she must have been mistaken.'

The two men nodded and after a minute of reading the big man said: 'She's recently completed her fifth course of chemotheraphy—Daunorubicin and Cytosine.' He glanced at Phyllida. 'Had she started the course of cytoreduction?'

'No, I understood it was to be started when we got back.'

'Well, it's too late to do anything about that now.' He handed back the notes. 'I've sent a radio telegram to the *Blenheim*; we should get an answer very shortly. And now that we know the name of the hospital where she has been treated, we can telephone them.' He paused at the door. 'You'll stay here.' His companion went ahead of him and he turned to say: 'My name is van Sittardt—Pieter van Sittardt.'

'Mine's Phyllida Cresswell.'

'We'll be in the building, ring if you want one of us—we'll be back.'

She was left with the unconscious Gaby and nothing to do but worry as to whether she had neglected to do something which might have saved her patient. Common sense told her that she hadn't; she had done exactly what she had been told to do. Moreover, she had warned Mr and Mrs de Wolff repeatedly that Gaby wasn't improving. They had taken no notice of her—indeed, she suspected that they had thought that she was being fussy and self-important. Or perhaps they hadn't wanted to know. And they couldn't have delivered the letter from the ship's doctor at the hospital…

Gaby looked beautiful lying there. She might have been asleep, only her pallor was marked and her breathing so light that it was hardly noticeable. It was inconceivable to Phyllida that her parents could have gone off so lightheartedly, knowing, as they surely must have done, that Gaby was very ill indeed. Tidying the already tidy bedcovers, Phyllida wanted to cry.

Gaby died two hours later and it was half an hour after that when the message arrived from her parents.

They would fly back on the following morning.

Phyllida had looked dumbly at Doctor van Sittardt when he had come to tell her. For once her self-possession deserted her and she was uncertain what to do. In hospital there was a fixed procedure, followed to the letter, but here, miles from home with no one to turn to, it was altogether a different matter.

But there was someone to turn to—Doctor van Sittardt. He suggested that she should return to the hotel and return again after breakfast the next day. 'You've had nothing much to eat, have you? I'll meet you in the bar at half past seven and we'll have dinner together.'

'Yes—well—thank you, but there's…'

'I'll deal with anything that comes up, if you will allow me. There are certain formalities, and her parents aren't here.'

'You're very kind.' Phyllida studied his face and saw its impersonal kindness, and because it was such a relief to let someone else cope, she had agreed, gone back to the hotel, bathed and changed and gone down to the bar to find him waiting for her. She was glad then that she had put on the blue-patterned crêpe and taken pains with her face and hair, for he was wearing a white dinner jacket—and very elegant too, easily the most attractive man there; on any other occasion she would have enjoyed the prospect of an evening in his company, but now she kept remembering Gaby. A shadow crossed her pretty face as he reached her and he said in a friendly, brisk voice: 'Now, Phyllida, no regrets. It was inevitable, and you did everything possible.' He took her arm and found stools at the bar. 'What will you drink?'

He talked about everything under the sun and never once mentioned the day's happenings. Neither did he tell her much about himself; he was staying at the hotel for a day or two and then going to visit friends, Dutch people who lived permanently on Madeira because of the wife's health, but that was all. By the end of the evening Phyllida still didn't know where he lived or anything about him save his name.

Not that there was any need to know, she told herself as she got ready for bed. After tomorrow they weren't likely to see each other again, as she would be going back with the de Wolffs to England and another job. She frowned at her reflection as she sat brushing her hair. Was this perhaps a sign that she should accept Philip after all? If it was she felt remarkably reluctant to take any notice of it. Philip, in the last few hours, had become strangely dim.

She slept soundly, although she hadn't expected to, and went down to breakfast, expecting to see the doctor. There was no sign of him and she ate hurriedly and then made her way in the early morning sunshine to the hospital, and met him at the entrance.

He gave her a businesslike good morning and turned her round smartly. 'I was coming to fetch you from the hotel, but since you're here we may as well go.'

'Go?' she looked at him without understanding.

'To the airport—to meet Gaby's parents.'

'Oh—yes.' She went pink, ashamed that she hadn't thought of that for herself; she should have hired a car to meet them.

The doctor went on placidly: 'I think that perhaps if there are two of us? It's a painful thing to have to do on one's own.'

She gave him a grateful look and got into the rather ramshackle car beside him and he set off without waste of time, travelling east from Funchal to the airport some twenty kilometres away. Half way there Phyllida said: 'I'm scared, having to tell them—you won't leave me, will you?'

His hooded eyes glanced sideways at her pale face. 'No. Tell me something, have the de Wolffs got money?'

She gave him a startled look. 'Well, yes, I think so. He owns several factories and has a big house in the country as well as a London flat. Why do you want to know?'

'It will help when it comes to making arrangements presently.' He overtook a bus with inches to spare. He said quietly: 'Even if I had been a pauper I would have chartered a plane as soon as I'd had that message yesterday.'

'So would I—I expect they feel terrible.'

They didn't have to wait long at the airport. The twice-weekly plane from Las Palmas arrived on time, and within a few minutes the de Wolffs were coming towards them. Mr de Wolff began speaking as soon as he was within a few yards. 'What's all this?' he demanded. 'I hope it's not a wild goose chase. I didn't telephone—no point. Luckily there was a plane leaving this morning, and heaven knows it's been inconvenient.'

And Mrs de Wolff added petulantly: 'Such a rush, and we've had to leave our luggage on board...' She paused and looked at Phyllida. 'What's wrong with Gaby this time?'

'She's dead,' said Phyllida, breaking all the rules of hospital training; bad news should be broken to relations in as gentle a way as possible...but it didn't matter, for the de Wolffs reacted just as she had feared they would. 'Why weren't we told sooner?' and 'I want to know what went wrong!'

It was here that the doctor took over; smoothly but with an edge to his cool professional voice. 'You were told. I sent a radiogram yesterday, asking you to get in touch with the hospital at once. Gaby was desperately ill—I told you that too. And nothing went wrong.' The edge had become a cutting knife. 'She received devoted care from Miss Cresswell and everything that could be done in the hospital was done.'

Phyllida looked at them both, searching for signs of grief, and could find none. Perhaps they were stunned; too shocked to feel anything. She said quietly: 'Doctor van Sittardt most kindly came to my aid yesterday…'

'Surely you knew what to do? We engaged you as a trained nurse.' Mrs de Wolff's voice rose sharply.

'Perhaps I haven't made myself clear,' said the doctor, his voice without expression. 'There was nothing to be done. Gaby was already a very ill girl. You knew that?'

Mrs de Wolff threw him an angry glance. 'Well, of course—the doctors told us she would die, but not as soon as this.'

'If she had stayed in hospital, or even quietly at home,' observed the doctor, carefully noncommittal, 'her life might have been prolonged for a short time.'

'We needed a break, we'd already booked on this cruise.' Mr de Wolff answered for his wife. 'We thought it would do her good, make her forget she was sickly.' He looked away from the doctor's stare and added uncomfortably: 'It isn't as though she were our own daughter. We adopted her when she was a baby—she was a gay little thing when she was a child, but she grew up so quiet and dull.'

The doctor didn't reply to this, neither did Phyllida, and after a moment Mr de Wolff said irritably: 'Well, we'd better go to the hospital, I suppose.'

He and his wife got into the back of the car and Phyllida settled herself beside the doctor, trying not to hear Mrs de Wolff grumbling behind her. 'I shall have to have this dress cleaned,' she complained, 'this is a dreadful car.' And then: 'I suppose we'll have to arrange to have Gaby taken back home, otherwise people might think it strange.'

Phyllida sat very upright, staring before her, her eyes wide so that she might stop her tears. Not that it helped; they tumbled silently down her cheeks and she wiped them away with a finger, stealing a glance at her companion to make sure that he hadn't noticed. He was staring ahead too, driving a little too fast, his mouth grim. He hadn't seen, she thought with relief, then went a slow red as his hand, large and cool, came down on hers and gave it a comforting squeeze. But he didn't look at her.

She wondered afterwards how she had got through that morning. Sorrow, regret, shock she could have coped with, but neither of the de Wolffs needed sympathy. Reluctantly they had conceded, in the face of the doctor's firm statement, that Phyllida had done all that she had been able to do, but they expressed no gratitude, only plunged briskly into the problems facing them, and when she asked them when she would be returning to England they told her that they would all fly back together in a few days' time, so that when Doctor Sittardt wanted to know if her future was settled, she was able to tell him that she would be leaving with the de Wolffs.

She helped Mrs de Wolff pack up Gaby's things after breakfast the next morning while Mr de Wolff was at the airport, making final arrangements, and when Mrs de Wolff suggested quite kindly that she might like to have a swim in the hotel pool before lunch, she went gladly, quite touched by her employer's consideration.

The water was warm and the sun shone. Phyllida swam lazily for a while, lay in the hot sunshine for a while and then went to dress ready for lunch. From her bedroom window she saw the *Blenheim* lying on the other side of the harbour; she would be sailing shortly and they should all have been on board by now, going home. Phyllida sighed, slipped into a cotton dress, brushed her hair smooth and went downstairs. Mrs de Wolff had told her to wait for them in the bar, and she chose a table in a corner and found herself wishing that the doctor had been there to keep her company. She hadn't seen him since they had left the hospital on the previous day and by now he would be with his friends. She occupied her time thinking about him because it wouldn't help anyone to think about Gaby and it was hard not to do that when she was on her own. It surprised her presently to find that she had been there for more than half an hour and, vaguely uneasy, she asked one of the barmen if there was a message for her and then, at his positive 'No', went to the reception desk and asked the same question.

She was surprised when she was handed a note, but not unduly alarmed. Something must have prevented Mr de Wolff from returning from the airport and probably his wife had gone out there to meet him. She opened the envelope and wandered out on to the terrace to read her letter. It was very hot now and the sea was a deep blue under the cloudless sky. The *Blenheim*, she noticed idly, was edging out of the harbour.

The letter was brief but its message was clear enough; the de Wolffs, their arrangements made at the airport concerning Gaby, had decided to sail home on the *Blenheim*. They were sure that Miss Cresswell would understand and she could follow in her own good time, taking whichever route she preferred. A cheque covering her fees was awaiting her at the Fred Olsen offices in the town.

Phyllida sat down abruptly on a stone bench and reread the letter. No mention was made of a return ticket. She supposed they had forgotten it; they must have also forgotten that there wouldn't be another boat for a week, and although there were two flights a day to England they went via Lisbon and would doubtless cost a good deal of money. And she hadn't a great deal of that with her; enough to buy presents and small necessities for herself, but she very much doubted if that and the cheque they had left for her would be enough to get her back home. And what about the hotel bill?

All thought of lunch escaped her. She went back to the reception desk and asked about the bill and heaved a sigh of relief to find that it had been paid, but only until the following day. She told the clerk that she would be leaving then and went to get her handbag. She was halfway down the hill to the town when she remembered that it was Saturday and the shipping office would be closed. The only thing to do would be to visit the Tourist Office and find out about hotels.

And when she got there it was to discover that they had shut for the afternoon siesta. At a loss, Phyllida wandered down the Avenida Arriaga and into the Jardim de Sao Francisco and sat down under the trees. There weren't many people about in the heat of the day although there was plenty of traffic, providing a background for her thoughts.

Good sense was taking over from the feeling of panic she had been struggling to ignore. It should be easy enough to find a small, cheap hotel for a couple of nights and surely her money would stretch to a flight home on Monday—perhaps the night flights were cheaper if she could get on one. And once she was back in London everything would be all right. She could cash a cheque at the bank, telephone home; go home. She closed her eyes and leaned back against a juniper tree.

'They were a little concerned about you at the hotel,' remarked Doctor van Sittardt quietly as he sat down beside her. He put out a hand and pushed her gently back as she started up. 'You left rather suddenly without your lunch.' He glanced at her. 'The clerk mentioned a letter.'

He obviously expected an answer and Phyllida realised that he was exactly what she needed—vast and calm and reassuring. She managed the shadow of a smile, dug into her handbag and handed him Mrs de Wolff's note. 'I always thought,' she observed in a small voice, 'that I was a capable person, able to cope with things when they went wrong, but it seems I'm not. I rushed straight out of the hotel to get a cheaper hotel and book a flight back to England on Monday, but of course everything's closed for the weekend or until four o'clock. So I thought I'd come here and think things out.'

He had been reading while she spoke, now he glanced up, his blue eyes studying her steadily from under their heavy lids. 'I suspected something like this would happen; if they could dismiss Gaby's death so easily they weren't likely to treat you any differently. I should have warned you, but as you say, you are a capable girl, quite able to cope.'

Phyllida nodded, her teeth clamped together to stop the trembling of her mouth. He thought her able to take care of herself and was doubtless thankful that he wouldn't have to put himself out any more on her account. All right, she would look capable even if it killed her!

'Well now,' went on her companion blandly, 'shall we go and have lunch, or would you like a good howl first? It's very pleasant here and not many people about, and I'll lend you my shoulder.'

Phyllida unclenched her teeth and let out a tiny wail. 'Oh, however did you guess? And you've just said I'm so capable!' She made herself sit up straight. 'But I'm all right now, really I am—it was having a surprise... Do please go and have your own lunch, I'm not hungry.'

He said patiently: 'I guessed because I've sisters of my own to plague me, and however capable you are, you have to let go sometimes. A drink is what you need, and a meal. You can weep to your heart's content afterwards if you still want to.'

He swept her to her feet and walked her briskly, despite the heat, back towards the heart of the city. Down a narrow side street he stopped in front of a small restaurant, its tables spilling out on to the pavement, its interior dim and cool. He must have been known there, for they were given a table in a corner by an open window and offered a menu.

'Sercial, I think, before we eat,' said the doctor, glancing at her still pale face. 'It's very dry but splendid before a meal. We'll have Malmsey afterwards. This is a fish restaurant, but if you don't like fish, there's chicken or omelettes.'

'I like fish.' Phyllida took a gulp of her Madeira.

'Good. We'll have *bifes de atum*—that's tuna steaks—and sweet potatoes in fritters and *pudim Mareira* to follow.'

'What's that?'

'A caramel flan with Madeira sauce. Very nice.'

She took another sip and began to feel better. 'You know Madeira well?'

'I come here from time to time.' And that was all he had to say, so that to break the silence she said awkwardly:

'It looks very beautiful. I must try and come back one day and explore.'

He didn't answer at once; the fish had come and she eyed it with pleasure, her appetite sharpened. It wasn't until they had made inroads into the delicious food that he spoke. 'How much money have you?'

She paused, her fork half way to her mouth. 'Oh, enough, I think. I'll find a small hotel until Monday and book a flight home then.'

'Do you know how much the fare is?' He mentioned a sum which made her catch her breath.

'That's the return, I expect,' she said hopefully.

'No, single. I think you should stay with my friends until the next ship calls on its way back to England.'

'Oh, but I couldn't—that's a week...besides, the fare...'

'I'll telephone their head office. The de Wolffs paid for your round trip, didn't they? So unless they've claimed a refund, your passage is already paid.'

Relief almost choked her. 'Oh, I hadn't thought of that. I can stay here until it comes—I'm bound to find an hotel.'

He finished his fish and leaned back in his chair. 'Phyllida, if you were me and I were you, would you offer to help me? And expect me to accept?'

'Of course I would!' She had spoken before thinking and he smiled.

'Well, that's all I'm doing. My friends will love to have you; Metha is rather crippled with arthritis and will enjoy your company.'

'Yes, but I can't...'

'We'll go back to the hotel presently and pick up your things and I'll drive you out there. I'll give them a ring while you're packing.'

She said weakly: 'But supposing they don't want me to stay? They don't know me.'

'How could they when they haven't met you?' he asked reasonably. 'Ah, here is our Madeira pudding—they do it very well here. There are some excellent restaurants in Funchal and quite a few scattered round the island. We must take you to some of them before you go back.'

They had almost finished their pudding when he asked: 'Do you want to telephone your family?'

She swallowed the last delicious morsel. 'Well, they're rather—I think they might worry; I thought a letter. If I send it today?'

He shook his head. 'No good, the *Blenheim* will get there long before the letter. Were you going straight home?'

'Yes.'

'Then telephone. You could say that plans have been changed and you'll be back a week later.'

The waiter brought two glasses of Malmsey and the doctor ordered coffee. Phyllida, who could think of no reason for disputing his suggestion, agreed.

They went unhurriedly back to the hotel presently, and she went up to her room to pack her things, leaving the doctor to tell the receptionist and telephone his friends. When she went down half an hour later, he was sitting on the terrace, his feet on a chair, reading an old copy of the *Telegraph*. There was a tall glass at his elbow, half full, and as he got to his feet he waved to a waiter and ordered her a drink. 'I'm drinking lager, but I've ordered you a lemonade and lime. Will that do?'

'Yes, thank you.' She sat down opposite him and he lounged back in his chair again.

'The de Meesters—my friends—are delighted to have you for as long as you like to stay. They want us up there for tea.'

'Do they live far away?' she asked.

He waved vaguely towards the mountains which swept up and away behind the town. 'No—in a village about five kilometres to the north—Monte. It used to be the island's capital and it's full of lovely old houses. There's a magnificent church too.'

He finished his drink and stretched out again, and Phyllida had the impression that if she hadn't been there he would have closed his eyes and had a nap. She sipped her own drink, relaxing under his casual calm, knowing that he didn't expect her to make conversation. When she had finished he sat up, all at once brisk. 'Right, did someone bring down your luggage?'

She nodded. 'Yes, it's at reception.' She hesitated. 'You've been very kind, Doctor van Sittardt.'

He smiled, a warm slow smile that transformed his rather austere good looks and made her feel safe and secure. 'The name's Pieter.' He got to his feet and stretched out a hand and pulled her out of her chair. 'Let's go and see if that car will start.'

The little car was certainly shabby, but there was nothing wrong with its engine. They went slowly through the town and then into the Rua 31 de Janeiro, and presently turned right into the Rua do Til. The drive might have been only five kilometres, but it was uphill all the way, and Phyllida, who had seen nothing of the island, was enchanted by the scenery as they climbed steadily up into the mountains. The doctor slowed down from time to time so that she could take it all in—the towering grey heights, the little green meadows tucked between them, with eucalyptus, mimosa and juniper trees, the small red-tiled houses, and from time to time a luxurious modern villa. He pointed Monte out to her before they reached it, to one side of the road, cloud hanging above it, its houses, and church clinging to the summit. The houses on its outskirts were modern, white-walled and red-tiled like the farms and each with its trailing vines and bougainvillea, with wisteria and the blue of the jacaranda trees adding splashes of bright colour. But once in the centre of the small place, they were back in the eighteenth century, for its square was lined with balconied houses of great age, overshadowd by the church and the mountains around them. The doctor turned the car down a narrow side street and then turned again through a wide arched gateway leading to a paved courtyard, enclosed on three sides by grey stone walls pierced by high narrow windows and with a massive door in its centre.

He stopped the car and leaned across Phyllida to open her door. 'We're here, and in case you find it rather forbidding, it's much nicer inside.'

The door was opened before they reached it by a small dark woman who smiled gravely at them and led the way across a wide dim hall to a door at one side. She flung this open, said something to whoever was inside, and stood back to let them pass.

The room was dim too with dark panelled walls and a plain white ceiling. The floor was tiled and covered by thin rugs in lovely colours and the furniture was dark and massive. There were two people in the room, a man and a woman, and the man got up at once and came towards them, his hand held out.

'Welcome, Miss Cresswell. You cannot know how glad we are to have you as our guest.' He engulfed her hand in his and beamed down at her. He was almost as tall as Pieter van Sittardt but inclined to stoutness, with a pleasant rugged face and fair hair already receding from a high forehead. 'You will forgive my wife if she doesn't get up.' He held her hand still and led her across the room to where a youngish woman was sitting in a high-backed chair. She was still very pretty with fair hair and dark eyes and she was dressed with great elegance. Only her crippled hands gave away the fact that she was an invalid. But that was forgotten when she spoke.

'I shall not call you Miss Cresswell,' she declared in a pretty voice. 'Phyllida is such a pretty name—mine's Metha,' she nodded towards her husband, 'and he is Hans. It is lovely to have you and I am so happy—these two talk about their work all the time and do not care for clothes.' She lifted a face to Pieter who bent to kiss her cheek.

'I should hope not indeed,' he declared, 'but you and Phyllida can talk to your hearts' content. I expect you miss the children.'

Metha nodded. 'Oh yes, very much—but now I have Phyllida and shall speak English all the time so that I will be occupied all the time and be happy.'

She smiled at Phyllida. 'You do not speak Portuguese, or Dutch?' and went on in a satisfied voice: 'No? That is splendid for me, for I shall improve my English and teach you a little besides.'

The solemn-faced woman brought in tea then, tea in a pot, Phyllida saw with pleasure, and plenty of milk in a jug, as well as a plate of little cakes and sugary biscuits. 'We like our tea,' explained Metha, 'it is for us a pleasant hour of the day, just to sit and talk.'

And very pleasant it was, Phyllida agreed silently, and how very at home Pieter looked, stretched out in one of the heavy tapestry-covered armchairs. It was evident that he was a friend of long standing but all the same, they all took care to include her in their talk, touching lightly on her reason for being there and then ignoring it to talk about Madeira and their life there.

Metha did most of the talking in her pretty English with her husband joining in frequently, only Pieter van Sittardt remained almost silent, looking, Phyllida decided, almost too lazy to open his mouth.

The pleasant little meal came to its leisurely end and Phyllida was taken upstairs by the solemn woman, who led the way along a corridor to a room at the back of the house, with a balcony overlooking a small paved yard with a fountain in its centre. Phyllida heaved a sigh of pure pleasure at the sight of it; things could have been so much worse—a small hotel and the worry of wondering if her money would hold out and business of getting a ticket for home. She would have to see about that on Monday morning; she couldn't impose on her new friends, whatever the doctor had said.

She unpacked and hung her things away, took a shower, changed her dress and went downstairs again.

CHAPTER FOUR

THERE WAS ONLY one occupant of the sitting room as she entered, the doctor, lounging back in a great armchair, his enormous feet on a convenient coffee table. He appeared to be asleep, but he wasn't, for he was on his feet before she had taken two steps into the room.

'Hullo,' he smiled disarmingly at her, 'the others will be down directly. Metha said I was to give you a drink.' He pulled forward a chair and she sat down. 'Have something long and cool; they dine rather later than we do at home.'

'Thank you.' Phyllida went on hurriedly: 'I've not had the chance to thank you properly for everything you've done—you've been simply super.'

'I think that we agreed that you would have done the same for me?' He dismissed her thanks with casual ease. 'Now, this drink—how about a Pimms with not too much gin?'

He mixed the drink, handed it to her, poured himself a whisky and sat down again. 'Metha thinks it might be fun if we drove round a bit tomorrow and showed you the sights. She wants you to see Cabo Girao—that's a very high sea cliff to the west of Funchal. It's a pretty drive there and afterwards we might go on to Ribeira Brava, it won't be crowded yet—we might even swim, but Metha's a bit shy of going into the water if there's anyone about. Hans carries her in; he swims on his back and takes her with him.'

'She's so pretty and young.' Phyllida's eyes searched her companion's face. 'Isn't there anything to be done?'

'Not much, I'm afraid. She had acute rheumatoid arthritis after the second child was born; she doesn't have much pain now, but it's left her with limited movement. She's a wonderful person, never complains and always looks so serene and marvellously turned out. She and Hans have the kind of marriage one hopes for and seldom achieves.'

'Are you married?'

He smiled slowly. 'No, I've always considered myself to be a dedicated bachelor. However, I think it very likely that I shall change my mind; there's something very appealing about a wife and children to comfort my old age.'

She looked a question, not quite daring to ask it.

'And I'm thirty-nine.' He glanced at her from under heavy lids. 'You, Phyllida? Are you married, divorced, engaged or having what I believe is called a close relationship with some lucky man?'

'Oh, I don't believe in that,' declared Phyllida. Her blue eyes met his candidly. 'And I'm not married or divorced.' She added after a pause: 'Nor engaged.'

'Thinking about it?' he asked lazily.

She shook her head. 'Not any more—it was just—well, we sort of slid into supposing that we might get married later on and then I discovered that I didn't love him at all, only liked him very much.'

'Now it's so often the other way round with me,' murmured the doctor. 'I fall in love with a girl and then discover that I don't like her.'

She wondered what kind of girls he fell in love with and then told herself that it was none of her business. All the same she was trying to think of a way of putting a tactful question or two when Metha and Hans came in. Metha was walking with two sticks, but she looked so pretty and happy that it went almost unnoticed; besides, she broke into lively chatter as soon as she was in the room.

'We'll have dinner in half an hour and then have coffee on the terrace,' she declared happily. 'It's such a beautiful evening and the sunset is always a delight. Phyllida, come over here and sit with me and tell me where you bought that pretty dress. There are one or two good shops here, but not very much choice. Twice a year we go to Holland for a visit and I do as much shopping as I can while we're there, but you know what men are; you put on a hat and they say: "that's fine, dear", and there you are saddled with something hideous, suitable for an aunt!'

They all laughed and Phyllida looked across at the doctor and found him staring at her, his eyes half shut, as usual. She pinkened faintly; he would think her horribly unfeeling to be enjoying herself so much, with Gaby…

He had read her expression unerringly. 'Now, Phyllida!' He shook his head at her and smiled so kindly that she had the sudden urge to run across the room and bury her face in his shoulder and howl her eyes out. But she wasn't given the chance; he went on: 'Why don't you two girls do some shopping tomorrow afternoon? We could go to Cabo Girao in the morning, lunch at Camara de Lobos at that nice place—the Riba Mar, isn't it?—and drop you both off at that boutique you go to in Funchal, Metha. Come to that, we'll park the car and come with you.' He grinned at Phyllida. 'I might even buy you a hat.'

The dinner was delicious, although Phyllida wasn't sure what they ate most of the time, and she was too shy to ask. The two men ate hugely, leaving most of the talking to the two girls and keeping their glasses filled with a light table wine which was presently replaced by Malmsey which they drank with their coffee.

It was still warm on the terrace and the view over the mountains and down towards Funchal and the sea was breathtakingly lovely in the late evening. The talk was quiet now, an effortless flow which Phyllida found very soothing. Presently the doctor got up and came over to where she was sitting. 'Come to the end of the terrace,' he suggested, 'we can see the sunset from there and with any luck you'll see the green flash.'

She got up willingly. 'What's that?'

He shrugged huge shoulders. 'I'm not sure—it sometimes follows a Madeira sunset.'

The back of the house overlooked a sloping garden which in turn led to a banana plantation, sweeping down to the ravine far below, and on the other side the mountains towered, but the valley between allowed them a clear view of the sun, setting in a blaze of colour. It was all so beautiful and Phyllida, looking at it, found to her horror that she was on the verge of tears. She muttered: 'Oh, poor Gaby, not to be able to see all this.'

A great arm was flung across her shoulders. 'There's no one but us,' he told her gently. 'Have your cry, my dear, you'll feel better for it.'

She sucked in her breath like a little girl. 'It's all such a waste,' she stopped to sniff, fighting the tears still, 'and I can't see why.'

'My dear child, I say that every day in my work, but I don't expect to be given the answer.' He turned her round so that her head rested comfortably on his chest and stood patiently while she sobbed, and presently he said: 'Feel better? Turn round, the sun's just going down.'

They stood together, his arm still round her, and watched the sky deepen its colour, and then as the sun sank from sight, they saw the green flash.

'That's something you can tell your friends about when you get back to the hospital.' He had fished a handkerchief from a pocket and handed it to her and she was mopping her face.

'I'm not going back. I—I left St Michael's just before I came on this trip.'

'Want to talk about it?' His casual voice invited confidence.

She hadn't realised how much she had wanted to talk to someone; it all came tumbling out and when she had finished: 'And the awful thing is I'm sure—at least, I'm not sure, but I think I may have made a frightful mistake; Philip's so—so safe.' She added quickly: 'I'm boring you.'

'No, you're not, and if I might offer my opinion for what it's worth; the frightful mistake would be if you were to marry Philip.'

He looked down at her thoughtfully, his eyes almost hidden under their lids. 'I think you're a girl who needs to marry for love and nothing else—you don't have any doubts if you love someone, you know.'

'I know you're right. I'm just being cowardly about looking

for another job—all those forms to fill in and the interviews and then getting to know everyone.'

'In your English you say: "Don't cross your bridges until you come to them". Such a wise piece of advice. Why do you not take a holiday?' He gave her shoulder a brotherly pat. 'You have a family?'

She found herself telling him about her home, her mother and father and Willy who was going to be a doctor like his father, and Dick who was in his last year at a veterinary college and Beryl, just twenty, who was at Bristol University. 'I think I will have a holiday,' she finished, 'just for a couple of weeks while I make up my mind where I want to go.'

'A splendid idea. And now as to the immediate future. I find that I shall be going back with the next ship too; we shall be fellow passengers, and in the meantime we may as well enjoy ourselves here. Metha and Hans love having guests and I know that she longs for more female company at times. Besides, we're an excellent excuse for sightseeing—she has a passion for picnics, too. When the children are on holiday she can arrange one every day, but they're in Holland and Hans is away all day she's very much alone. He's on holiday at the moment because I'm here.'

'It sounds wonderful, but are you sure—I mean, I just can't stay here for a week...'

'Metha would be heartbroken if you didn't. Besides, with you here, we can slope off on our own.'

Phyllida laughed a little. 'Of course, if you put it like that, I haven't any choice, have I?'

'None whatever.' He turned her round and deliberately studied her face in the twilight. 'Tears all gone? Good, we'll join the others, shall we? They'll want to make plans for tomorrow.'

They took her to Cabo Girao the following day, driving back to Funchal and along the coast road, climbing all the way, with the sea below on one side, and a scattering of villages on the other. There were flowers everywhere; nasturtiums, wisteria and echium jostled for a place, with jacaranda trees making great splashes of colour next the bougainvillea, and every wayside cottage and villa had a garden crowded with every sort of flower. Phyllida craned her pretty neck in her efforts to see everything which was being pointed out to her, sitting beside Pieter who was driving his friend's Mercedes, with Hans and Metha in the back.

'There's a dragon tree!' exclaimed Metha, and Pieter slowed the car so that Phyllida should get a good view of it before racing on, still climbing.

The cliff, when they reached it, was spectacular, but she was glad of Pieter's arm round her shoulders as they hung over the rail to stare down to the sea far below, and she was secretly relieved when they rejoined Metha in the car and drove down to Camara de Lobo, where they had lunch, and then, while Hans and Metha stayed on the restaurant's terrace, the doctor took Phyllida for a stroll on the beach to get a closer look at the gaily painted boats. Phyllida scuffed her sandalled feet happily in the shingle and wished the day would last for ever; it didn't seem possible that she had known her companion for such a short time; he was like an old friend, easygoing, goodnaturedly answering her questions, treating her like a sister. She stopped to examine a shell and wondered why she didn't really want him to treat her with such offhand ease. Yet, after all, they were only acquaintances, brought together by circumstances, and once she was back in England she wouldn't see him any more. She stole a look at him, meandering along beside her. He was already deeply tanned, so that his hair looked like silvered straw, and his eyes, when he bothered to lift the lids, were a quite startling blue. His face seemed haughty in repose, but that was because his nose was large and arrogant and his mouth firm. He was indeed a handsome man. He looked sideways at her, catching her unawares, and she went red and looked away quickly. But when she made to walk a little apart from him he caught her hand and didn't let it go. 'Enjoying yourself?' he wanted to know.

'Oh, yes, it's super. I didn't expect to see anything of Madeira, you know.'

'We'll take the toboggan ride tomorrow—that's something

everyone does when they come here. We'll go early before the tourists arrive.' He stopped to look at her. 'Can you swim?'

'Not very well, but I like it.'

'Good. We'll go to Ponta de Sao Lourenço, that's the only sandy beach there is. We can take Metha, of course, because there'll be no one much there and she can go in the water. We'll go over the Poiso pass and through Santo da Serra; it's a pretty run, you'll like it.'

'It sounds lovely, but I do have to go to the shipping office and collect my cheque and see about going back.'

'I hadn't forgotten. You and Metha can spend ten minutes in a boutique—it'll be open—and Hans and I will go and get your money and see about a sailing.'

'I can't bother you...'

'I'm not in the least bothered, I have to get a passage for myself too.'

'Oh, yes—of course.' She gave her hand a little tug and his grip tightened ever so gently.

'You haven't been around much, have you?' His voice was as gentle as his fingers.

She knew what he meant. 'No, I suppose not, there's not a lot of time for a social life—one comes off duty tired and only longing to kick off one's shoes and make a pot of tea. I used to go out more often before I met Philip.'

'You didn't go out with him?' He sounded surprised.

'Well, yes, of course—I meant we didn't go dancing or to shows or anything like that, just to a restaurant for supper or to his brother's house.'

There was no expression on her companion's face. 'It sounds cosy.' His voice was dry and she gave another tug at her hand.

'No, leave it where it is. You're a pretty girl, Phyllida, you should have your chance to play the field, meet people, and by that I mean men of your own age. Who knows if you go into the wide world and fall in and out of love a few times, you may go back to your Philip after all.'

She didn't fancy the idea somehow. Philip seemed far away, belonging to another world. The thought crossed her mind that it might be fun to fall in love with Pieter. Just a little, of course; he was a very attractive man and doubtless he had a girl at home. It was a pity that she didn't know him well enough to ask him; it struck her that he had asked her a great many more questions than she had done of him. Not that it mattered, he was a chance encounter...

She reminded herself of that several times during the day; just to be on the safe side, but it was a little difficult. Hans was a chance encounter too, but with him it didn't seem at all the same.

But she enjoyed herself, spending a pleasant half hour with Metha in the boutique, looking at bright cotton dresses and beautifully cut bikinis. She didn't dare buy anything, though.

The men came back presently and Pieter handed her an envelope. 'If you sign the cheque, I'll go across to the bank and get it cashed,' he told her. 'Have you any traveller's cheques with you?'

'No—they said I wouldn't need any money because they would be paying me. I've a few pounds, though, as well as some money I brought along just in case—it's not much, though.'

She opened the envelope. The cheque was for the exact number of days she had worked for the de Wolffs. No one had thought of her expenses, but all the same there would be enough to get her home now provided she didn't spend more than a pound or two in Madeira. She slid the cheque back into the envelope and Pieter, who had been talking to the others, turned round. 'You won't need any money for your fare,' he told her casually. 'They checked with their head office and you've been given a ticket—on the boat deck, a single cabin. The ship sails at two o'clock on Saturday.'

'And now you don't need to save your money,' interpolated Metha, 'we shall go right back into the boutique and you shall buy that Indian cotton sun-dress—and I think I shall buy one too.' She beamed at the men. 'And you, my dears, may come with us.'

They went in together and the shop owner surged forward,

produced a chair for Metha and whisked Phyllida away with an armful of dresses over her arm. The one she had liked, a vivid blue tied carelessly on the shoulders and with a deep scooped out neckline, was a perfect fit. Urged by the shop lady, she went back into the shop from the tiny fitting room and showed herself to the three of them. 'Beautiful,' said Metha at once. 'Smashing,' declared Hans, who prided himself on his up-to-date English, and: 'You'll need a bikini to go underneath that,' observed Pieter lazily.

So she bought a bikini too and for good measure a wide-brimmed straw hat, and while she was trying it on, the doctor, who had been prowling round on his own, came back with a silk dress flung over his arm. It was a delicate green patterned with the faintest of pinks.

'Try that on too,' he begged her. 'We're going dancing tomorrow.'

Which seemed a good enough reason for doing just that, and finding it to be a perfect fit, buying it too.

They spent the evening at the de Meesters' house and after dinner the doctor took Phyllida for a stroll round the little town and then up the path through the park to the church, and as they walked round its dim coolness he told her about Nossa Senhora do Monte, whose bejewelled statue held pride of place on the high altar.

'Rather lovely, isn't she?' he said very quietly. 'I'm not a Catholic myself, but she stands for a great deal to many people living on the island—they come each year, thousands of them, to see Our Lady of the Mountain.'

They strolled back presently through the cool evening and then once more indoors, spent the rest of the evening playing a noisy game of Canasta.

They went swimming the next day, but only after the doctor had kept his promise to Phyllida and taken her on the toboggan ride. He drove her away from Monte, up into the hills beyond, with Hans beside them, so that he could drive the car back to his house. It was still early and there weren't many people about. Leaving Hans and the car they took a narrow path which brought them out on to a cobbled lane where the toboggans were waiting, each with two men, dressed in their uniform of white suits and straw hats.

The journey took perhaps five minutes, the toboggan sliding at speed over the ridged cobbles, guided by the two men. Phyllida found it a bit alarming, especially on the frequent hairpin-bends, but it was fun too and she had Pieter to hang on to. 'You've done it before,' she gasped, half way down.

'Lord, yes—half a dozen times.' He didn't add with a girl, but she guessed that. 'Enjoying it?'

She nodded, her silky hair flying round her head, her eyes sparkling like a child's. 'But I'd hate to do it on my own.'

'I don't think there's any fear of that.'

The ride ended by the church they had visited on the previous evening, and tourists were already going in and out of its doors, stopping to examine and buy the embroidered handkerchiefs laid out neatly on large trays carried by the local man. But they didn't stop, going down the path again and back into the town and the de Meesters' house.

'Just time to put on the sun-dress,' remarked the doctor as they went inside, 'and don't forget the bikini!'

It was an hilarious day. Phyllida, lying awake at the end of it, went carefully over every minute of it. Pieter had driven the car, taking them up into the mountains through the kind of scenery she thought she would never see again, over the Poiso Pass, through the charming countryside past the golf course, tucked away on a small plateau and, she had considered, a bit inaccessible, and then on to Canical which she hadn't much cared for; it was dominated by a whale oil factory and looked forlorn. It was from here that they had to walk; not far, as it happened, for Pieter took the car to the very edge of the sand dunes which led to the beach. They had a light wheelchair with them for Metha and Pieter carried the picnic basket and no one hurried. The beach was almost deserted and the men went back to the car for airbeds, a huge sun umbrella, a basket full of tins of beer and lemonade and armfuls of cushions. Phyllida, remembering picnics at home—potted meat sandwiches and a thermos—got quite goggle-eyed at the lavishness of the food; delicate little sandwiches, potato fritters, cold, accompanying *espada* fish, cold chicken, tomato salad—there was no end. She had eaten a bit of everything with a splendid appetite and washed it down with lemonade. And it hadn't been hot, there had been a breeze from the sea and the water had been surprisingly cool. She had taken off the sun-dress rather shyly because there really hadn't been much of the bikini, but the doctor had barely glanced at her, and once in the water she had forgotten her shyness and after a few minutes close to the beach, she had struck out bravely, heading out to sea. She'd heard Metha laughing as Hans towed her through the water; Pieter she hadn't seen, not until he appeared beside her, swimming with no effort at all.

'They catch whales here,' he told her.

Phyllida, the kind of swimmer to sink like a stone at the least alarm, let out a small scream, swallowed a good deal of water and gurgled so alarmingly that the doctor flipped her over on to her back and slid an arm beneath her. 'When I said here,' he had pointed out unhurriedly, 'I meant some miles out to sea.'

He was paddling alongside her, looking at the sky. 'If you've finished spluttering, let's go back. Do you think you're strong enough to hold Metha up on one side, I'll hang on to the other. Then Hans can go for a swim.'

They had done that, with Metha, her thin arms on their shoulders, between them. It hadn't been quite like swimming, but it was the next best thing, and no one, unless they had looked very closely, would have known the difference; the water helped, of course, allowing her more movement, and Pieter acted just as though she were doing it all by herself. He was nice, thought Phyllida sleepily, and he had been even nicer that evening. True to his promise he had taken her down to Funchal after dinner, to the Hotel Savoy, where they had danced, watched the folk dancing and then danced again, and on the way back to Monte, at two o'clock in the morning, they had stopped at a noisy, dimly lit street café and had coffee and brandy.

Monte's narrow streets and old houses had been dark. The doctor stopped the car soundlessly and got out to open her door and then the house door. There was a lamp burning in the hall and the old house had seemed not quite real in the utter silence. She had thanked him for a lovely evening and wished him goodnight, and for answer he had caught her arm and walked her through the house to the terrace beyond. 'You can't go to bed before you've seen the view,' he had told her, and taken her to the very end of it.

It wasn't quite time for the dawn, but the sky to the east was already paling, and turning at the touch of his hand she had seen the dark outline of the mountains and the even darker ravines and beyond them the lights still burning in the outskirts of Funchal.

'All the years I've wasted in London,' she had said, talking to herself.

'Not wasted—and not so many—you can always make up for lost time.'

She had said: 'I'm not likely to come here again—not for a long time.' She didn't suppose that he had to worry overmuch about money and although she wasn't exactly poor, her salary hardly ran to the kind of holiday she was enjoying now. She turned away and gone back indoors and he had followed her, locking the glass doors after him. In the hall, at the foot of the stairs, she had said again: 'Thank you, Pieter,' and would have added a few conventional remarks to round off their evening, but she didn't have the chance. He had kissed her then—she turned over in bed and thumped her pillows, remembering it. She had been silly to think that it might be fun to fall a little in love with him. It wouldn't be fun at all, it would be disaster—a dead end affair with him bidding her a cheerful goodbye when they got to London, forgetting her the moment her back was turned. It had been an unexpected holiday, she reminded herself, and as so often happened on holiday, one met someone one rather liked and enjoyed a casual, short-lived friendship. She closed her eyes on this sensible thought; she was almost asleep when she remembered that Pieter had told her that she looked beautiful in the new dress.

After that the days flashed by, filled by picnics in beautiful remote spots and a drive to Ponta Delgada on the north coast, over the Eucumeada Pass, where they had stopped so that Phyllida might feast her eyes on the magnificent view from its top, and they had lunched at the hotel close by before driving on through the mountains. She would have liked to have stopped again, there was so much to see, but as Pieter explained, the roads were winding and precipitous and it wasn't always possible. Not that he seemed to mind the hazards; he drove with nonchalant ease whether they were going uphill, downhill or round hairpin bends which made her glad she wasn't driving. And that evening they had gone dancing again, only this time he didn't kiss her goodnight.

Saturday came too soon, she bade Metha and Hans goodbye with real regret for it seemed as though they had been lifelong friends, and then stood aside while the doctor made his own farewells, brief and cheerful, before he took her arm and hurried her on board.

Their cabins were next door to each other and very much to her taste, roomy and comfortable and spotlessly clean. She would unpack at once, she decided, but she had scarcely opened her overnight bag before the doctor thumped on her door. 'They'll wait on the quay until we leave,' he explained. 'We'd better go on deck.'

So she went with him, to hang over the rail and shout to Metha and watch the last-minute buying and selling going on round the little stalls set up alongside the ship, while Pieter lounged beside her, not saying much, watching her intent face with a half smile.

Once they had sailed Phyllida went back to her cabin to unpack. They wouldn't get back until Wednesday morning and she would need some clothes—evening clothes especially. She decided on her long evening skirt and a pretty top to go with it, put everything else tidily away and went along to the lido.

The doctor was there, sitting at a table by the swimming pool, a drink at his elbow, deep in a Dutch paper he had bought in Funchal before they sailed. She hesitated, wondering if she should join him; they weren't exactly travelling together, only fellow passengers. She started back the way she had come, only to be halted in her tracks by his: 'Hey, where are you off to?'

She approached the table slowly as he unfolded his length and pulled out a chair for her. 'Well,' she said carefully, 'I just thought we're only fellow passengers, not travelling together, if you see what I mean. You wouldn't want me hanging round your neck like a millstone.'

'Wouldn't I? Get this clear, love, I'm a shy man, I don't know a soul on board and I intend to cling to you like a limpet.' He added: 'During waking hours, of course.'

He was teasing her, she knew that, so she laughed back at him.

'Well, I don't know anyone, either. Only you must tell me if I'm in the way.' She grinned suddenly, at ease with him once more. 'I saw the most gorgeous blonde just now—she really is lovely.'

He lifted lazy lids and she blinked under his intent look. 'I must chat her up, I'm partial to blondes. Do point her out.'

'She doesn't need pointing out,' remarked Phyllida with something of a snap, 'you'll see her easily enough for yourself.'

He didn't answer her, only asked her what she would like to drink.

They went down to tea presently and then played Bingo, getting very excited when they nearly won, and then going along to the shop to browse around, buying postcards she would never send and a huge tin of toffees for Willy, who would appreciate them far more than anything foreign and unedible.

She was almost dressed when Pieter tapped on her door before dinner. 'Come in,' she called, 'I'm trying to find an evening bag.'

He sat down on her bed, watching her while she searched through the drawers and at length found what she wanted. He took up so much room in the cabin that it seemed to shrink as she stepped carefully backwards and forwards over his big feet before sitting down beside him to change things from one bag to the other.

He watched her lazily. 'You look very nice—we'll dance later, shall we?'

She nodded, finished what she was doing and got to her feet.

'The bar, I think,' he suggested, 'but let's go this way; I've an urge to play the fruit machines.' He handed her a handful of silver. 'Split fifty-fifty whoever wins.'

Phyllida had never played before. She had wanted to on the voyage out, but she had never had enough time to herself—besides, she had been afraid that she might lose too much money. She won two pounds now and screamed with delight. 'Here's your money, and your half of the winnings. Now you have a go.'

He won nothing and presently she cried: 'Oh, do stop, you won't have any money left—do have some of mine.'

He declined. 'My luck's out—let's go and have a drink, we can play later if we want to.'

The bar was crowded, but they found seats in a corner and bent their heads over the next day's programme. 'I don't think I'll go to the keep fit class,' said the doctor seriously, 'and definitely not the fancy dress—how about deck quoits and a nice long lie in the sun doing nothing?'

Phyllida agreed happily. And that was how they spent their days, swimming in the pool before breakfast, playing some deck game or other after breakfast and then lying side by side doing nothing, not even talking. Phyllida found it singularly restful; the sea was calm, even in the Bay of Biscay, and the weather stayed fine, although as they neared their journey's end there was a decided nip in the air, which made sweaters a necessity, and when they got too chilly, Pieter pulled her to her feet and made her play table tennis. They danced each evening too; the only fly in the ointment was the blonde girl. They had a table for two in the centre of the restaurant and the girl was seated close by in the doctor's direct line of vision. She was an eyeful, Phyllida decided vexedly on their first evening, and she couldn't compete with the white crêpe dress, cut low and with a long gored skirt which twisted and twirled as the girl walked the length of the restaurant. She had piled-up hair, dressed in a careless riot of curls and crowned with a tiny cap sporting a curling feather which curved round one cheek—absurd on anyone else, but on this girl, devastating. The doctor had studied her at length and with no expression.

'I told you I wouldn't need to point her out,' said Phyllida.

He gave her one of his bland looks. 'Oh, I do see exactly what you mean, love—she's a knock-out.'

She had agreed with chilly enthusiasm.

As far as she knew, he hadn't looked at the girl again that evening, nor the next morning. It was after lunch when he told her that he was going down to the purser's office, and strolled away.

He was still gone an hour later, and with nothing to do, she remembered that she had to press a dress for the evening. She was on her way to the ironing room when she saw them standing near the purser's office, deep in conversation. The girl was leaning back against the wall, her hands on either side of her, pressed against it, a beguiling attitude calculated to show her figure off to the best possible advantage. She was looking up at the doctor with a look which Phyllida had often tried before her looking glass, without much success because she had always giggled. She sped on down to the deck below, sure that she hadn't been seen, did her pressing and hurried back. They weren't there when she reached the purser's office.

She hung up the pink crêpe—really it had been a waste of time fussing with it, the doctor wasn't going to notice, was he? not with that creature making eyes at him—and bounced out of her cabin and back to the deck, to be waylaid at once by a young man with a lot of teeth and pebble glasses who asked her eagerly if she would like to use his binoculars. There was nothing to see, but she agreed with an enthusiasm which encouraged him to offer her a drink. It was nearly tea-time and not really warm enough for a cold drink, but he looked so anxious to please that she accepted a lemonade and stood at the rail with him, drinking it while he told her all about his job—something vague in the City.

She wasn't sure when she first felt that they were being watched; after a moment or two she looked round cautiously. Behind them, lying in a chair with his feet up, was the doctor. He grinned as she turned a shoulder to him.

She finished the drink slowly, aware that it was four o'clock and everyone was going down to tea, and trying to decide whether she should stay where she was and wait for Pebble Glasses to invite her to share his table, or excuse herself, ignore the doctor, and have tea on her own.

She knew that she was being childish and silly, which made it more difficult to decide. Luckily it was decided for her; the doctor tapped her smartly on the shoulder, smiled with charm at her companion and wanted to know if she was coming to pour his tea for him. Short of saying no, she wasn't, there had been nothing she could do about it. Out of earshot of Pebble Glasses he had observed placidly: 'Paying me back in my own coin, Phylly?'

'I don't know what you're talking about.' She tried to sound dignified, which was quite wasted on her companion, who sat her down in a quiet corner and fell to examining the plate of cakes on the table between them. Only when he had done this to his satisfaction had he said: 'Empty as a hot air balloon.' He looked at her, smiling faintly. 'What a pity—such beauty, and nothing—just nothing between the ears.' He sighed: 'But I found it interesting from a medical point of view.'

His voice was so silky that she shot him a suspicious glance. 'I don't believe it.'

He hadn't appeared to hear her. 'Now you, love, have good looks and a good brain to go with them—you'll make someone an excellent wife one day.' He added wickedly. 'Was Pebble Glasses all you could find?'

It had been impossible to be grumpy with him after that.

Phyllida packed with great regret before dinner on their final evening; she had been to the purser's office and got herself a seat on the coach which would take any passengers who wished up to Victoria Station, but she hadn't told Pieter. And he for his part hadn't said a word. She supposed that they would say goodbye after an early breakfast and she would never know where he was going. Somewhere in England? Holland? She had no idea.

They were watching a spirited entertainment after dinner when he said in a tone which brooked no denial: 'I've arranged for a car to be at the dock. I'll drive you home.'

She had been surprised at the delight which swept through her.

'But it's miles away...'

'Three hours run at the outside.'

'Well—but don't you want to go home?'

His smile told her nothing. 'I've two or three days to spare, I should enjoy the drive.'

Which really didn't answer her question.

CHAPTER FIVE

DISEMBARKING FROM the ship at Millwall Dock was smoothly efficient and swift. Phyllida found herself and her baggage on the road outside the dock with hundreds of others, only whereas they were getting on to a fleet of coaches, taxis or relatives' cars, she had been led to a corner and told to stay there while Pieter went to look for his car. He was back inside five minutes, driving a Ford Scorpio, and long before the buses had revved up their engines he had stowed the luggage, popped her into the front seat, got behind the wheel and driven away.

It was still barely nine o'clock in the morning and the traffic in the East End was dense; it got worse as they approached the city, but the doctor didn't allow that to irritate him, he kept up a gentle flow of talk weaving in and out of the traffic unerringly so that presently Phyllida asked: 'Do you know London well? You drive as though you did.'

'I come here from time to time. I'm aiming for the M3, I think it'll be best if we cut straight through, don't you, and cross the river at Chiswick. We can stop in Richmond for coffee, and what about Salisbury for lunch? Isn't there a place called the Haunch of Venison?'

'Yes, but I'm sure Mother would give us a late lunch, there's really no need...'

He shot her a quick smile. 'Oh, let's have a last lunch together, shall we?—Perhaps your mother will be kind enough to invite me to tea.'

It was while they were drinking their coffee in Richmond that Phyllida suddenly realised that she hadn't thought of Philip for days. She looked across at the doctor, scanning the headlines of the *Telegraph*, and thought how nice it was that they could sit together like this without making conversation because they felt that they should. Every now and then he read out some item which he thought might interest her, but he made no special effort to capture her attention; he might have been her brother. She wasn't sure whether to be annoyed about this or not. Upon due reflection she thought not, for although they hadn't known each other long they had an easy friendship, quite at ease with each other and enjoying each other's company. But that was all; he had never shown any signs of interest in her as a person. Indeed, the blonde on board had come in for more attention…

She frowned into her coffee. She wasn't a vain girl, but she was aware that she had more than her share of good looks and although she had no sophistication to speak of, someone had told her once that she was a wholesome girl. She had quite liked it at the time, now she wasn't so sure; she didn't think that Pieter would be interested in wholesomeness—he had, she considered, an experienced eye. She sighed and he put the paper down at once. 'Sorry—my shocking manners. Let's go.'

It began to rain as they started off again and by the time they got to Salisbury it was a steady downpour. But the Haunch of Venison was warm and welcoming; they ate roast beef and Yorkshire pudding and treacle sponge afterwards, and accompanied this nourishing meal with a bottle of claret. It was still raining when they got back into the car, and as they drove through the dripping countryside Phyllida felt a pang of disappointment that the first sight of her home should be marred by a grey, wet day. But her companion didn't share her view. As they went down the hill to the village and she pointed out her home on the opposite rise, he stopped the car to have a look.

'Early Georgian?' he asked.

'Partly. There's a bit at the back that's Queen Anne. It's a pity it's wet.'

'It's beautiful—rural England at her best.' He looked at her. 'Excited?'

She nodded. 'I always love coming home. I don't think I ever enjoyed living in London. I like pottering in the garden and going to the village shop and walking miles. That must sound very dull.'

She was surprised when he told her: 'I live in the country myself—not as lovely as this, but beautiful in a placid way. No hills like these.'

He started the car again, driving slowly now, and stopped again outside her home.

He was an instant success. Her mother, pottering around the window boxes along the front windows, turned at the sound of the car, crossed the narrow strip of pavement and peered through the window at them.

'Darling, how lovely, and you've brought someone with you.' She beamed at the doctor and added: 'How very nice,' because his smile held such charm.

He got out, opened Phyllida's door and when she had embraced her mother and introduced him, said in his placid way: 'I'm delighted to meet you, Mrs Cresswell. I hope it's not inconvenient…?'

Mrs Cresswell's smile widened. 'It's the nicest surprise, and how kind of you to drive Phylly home. Come in, I was just going to get the tea. There are rather a lot of us, I'm afraid.' She glanced at Phyllida. 'Willy's home again, he's been very under the weather, poor boy, and Beryl's home for a few days—so's Dick—half term,' she added vaguely, 'or whatever it is they have at these places.'

She paused to take a good look at her elder daughter. 'Darling, you're nice and brown, but you look—well—come inside and tell me about it.'

She glanced across at the doctor standing quietly by. 'There's something, and you'll know about it too, I expect. Come into the kitchen while I get the tea; the others won't be in for a bit. Willy's gone with Father on his visits and the other two went over to Diggs' farm.'

Mrs Cresswell had the happy knack of putting people at their ease and making them feel at home. The doctor was offered a seat at the kitchen table, given a pile of scones on a dish, a plate of butter and a knife, and asked if he would split and butter them. Phyllida, sitting opposite, making sandwiches, was surprised to see how handy he was; as far as she could remember he hadn't done a hand's turn at the de Meesters' house, although of course there he hadn't really needed to.

Her mother was taking a large cake from its tin. 'Well, darling?' she looked questioningly at Phyllida. 'Or shall Doctor—no, I shall call you Pieter—talk about it?'

Phyllida started to spread the sandwiches. 'Gaby died. We were put ashore at Funchal because the ship's doctor was worried about her and thought she ought to go home or into hospital. The de Wolffs left us at an hotel and went on with the ship. I—I found her unconscious and Pieter got her into hospital and fetched the de Wolffs back, then he took me to stay with some friends of his until there was another ship.'

Her mother received this somewhat bald statement calmly. 'Very distressing—poor Gaby, and poor you, darling. We have to thank Pieter for a great deal.' She glanced at the doctor's impassive face. 'Phylly, be a dear and run down to Mrs Brewster's and get some more cream—we haven't nearly enough for these scones.'

And when the door had closed behind her daughter: 'Neither my husband nor I will be able to thank you enough, Pieter. And now the child's out of the way, will you tell me exactly what happened?'

He sat back in his hard chair, his hands in his pockets. After a moment he began to tell her in his calm way, not taking his eyes from his listener's face. When he had finished Mrs Cresswell said again: 'Thank you, Pieter—just to say that isn't enough, but I don't know what else… Will you tell my husband when he comes in? After tea while we're washing up.' She added: 'Those wretched de Wolffs, what I'd like to do to them!'

The doctor nodded without speaking and then with his eyes on the door behind her: 'I can see that you're an excellent cook, Mrs Cresswell. Can you cook, Phyllida?'

'Of course she can,' Mrs Cresswell took her cue smartly. 'I taught her.' She took the cream from Phyllida and emptied it into a china dish just as the front door banged shut. 'Beryl and Dick,' she lifted her voice. 'We're in here.'

She had just finished introducing everyone when Doctor Cresswell came in too and it all had to be done again. 'And now we all know each other,' said Mrs Cresswell happily, 'let's have tea.'

It was a noisy meal with everyone talking at once, asking questions of Phyllida and not really listening to the answers, which was just as well, for she was quieter than usual. But they supposed her to be tired after her journey, although once or twice her father was on the point of asking her a question, but the doctor had intervened smoothly each time. It wasn't until the meal was over and Mrs Cresswell marched everyone into the kitchen to help with the washing up, bestowing a speaking glance at her husband as she did so, that Doctor Cresswell, left with his guest, observed: 'I gather there is something I should know. Am I right?' He got up. 'I think if we went to the study—Willy stayed out to tea, but he'll be back at any time—we might get interrupted here.'

His guest told him exactly what he had told Mrs Cresswell but without any glossing over of the harsher bits. Doctor Cresswell heard him out without comment.

'Poor little Gaby. I'll go and see the de Wolffs tomorrow. I'm deeply indebted to you for looking after Phylly and doing what was best for Gaby. And these friends of yours, I should like their address if I may, so that we can express our thanks to them as well.'

He got to his feet. 'You'll stay the night, of course—longer if you can manage it.'

'I should be delighted; I still have a few days before I need to go back.'

'Then spend them here. Do you suppose that Phylly wants to talk to me about this?' Doctor Cresswell's nice open face crinkled into a smile. 'We're the greatest of friends and I don't want to force her—perhaps she'd rather wait...'

'I think she would like to tell you herself. She was very upset about it, although she did everything possible in the most difficult of circumstances.'

'She shall drive me on my morning rounds.' Doctor Cresswell led the way into the hall and across it to the large, airy sitting room. 'Are you a G. P. like myself or do you specialise? I gather from the talk at tea that you live in the country...'

In the kitchen her mother said to Phyllida: 'Of course Pieter will stay the night. Beryl, run up and make sure that the cubbyhole is just as it should be.'

Beryl giggled: 'Mother, isn't he a bit big for it? Hadn't he better have the room next door? Phylly and I can make up a bed in no time.'

Mrs Cresswell nodded to her younger daughter, as dark as Phyllida was fair, small and pretty too. 'Of course, dear, he is rather big, isn't he—he might be a bit cramped.'

Phylly finished drying the tea things. The cubbyhole was kept ready for Willy's friends from school or the younger nephews and nieces. She smiled at the idea of Pieter trying to fit his bulk into the narrow bed. 'Very cramped,' she agreed. 'I'll come now, Beryl.'

They all sat down to supper later, and Willy, who should have been in bed because he still wasn't quite fit, somehow managed to persuade his mother that he was well enough to stay up. It was a nice old-fashioned meal, with cold meat and pickles and potatoes baked in their jackets smothered in butter, and a very large rice pudding with cream and raisins for afters. Phyllida watched Pieter a little anxiously, remembering the delicious food they had had on Madeira and on the ship, but she need not have worried. The doctor consumed a vast supper with every sign of content and enjoyment.

Going upstairs to bed later, it struck her that she had exchanged barely a dozen words with him during the whole evening, although his goodnight had been as friendly as it always had been. Tomorrow, she promised herself, she would find out when he was going.

Only she didn't. True, they met at breakfast, but by the time she had helped with the washing up and made the beds, her father was calling for her to drive him on his morning round, and Pieter and Beryl were at the other end of the garden, picking the rhubarb from under its forcing bucket, ready for one of her mother's super pies.

'I've heard it all from Pieter,' her father told her as they started off down the hill, 'but I'd like to hear it again from you, Phylly.'

It was a relief to talk about it, she felt better when she had told him about it, and better still when her father said: 'You did all you could, you have no reason whatsoever for blaming yourself. Put it behind you, my dear. Have you thought what kind of job you want?'

She hadn't; somehow she hadn't been able to put her mind to thinking about her future and she said so.

'Then take a holiday,' advised her father.

They got back a little late for lunch, and found the doctor in the kitchen, sitting in one of the old Windsor chairs by the Aga, his long legs stretched out on the rag rug at his feet. Willy was there too and Dick as well as Beryl and her mother. They looked as thick as thieves.

Everyone turned to look at her as she went in, and it was Dick who said: 'Hi, Phylly—we've hatched a simply super scheme.' He grinned round at the doctor, who was standing, staring at nothing. 'You tell her, Pieter.'

She looked at them in turn. Their expressions reminded her forcibly of Meg, their elderly spaniel, when she hoped for a biscuit, all except the doctor, who looked half asleep. Phyllida sat herself down on the edge of the table, picked up a raw carrot from the dish and began to crunch it, and asked: 'Well?'

The doctor sat down again. He looked quite at home in the rather shabby old kitchen, just as though he had been a family friend for years. 'I have been talking to your mother about the flowers in Holland at this time of the year. Bulbs, you know, fields full of them and a rather special park where one can go and see them all growing in a charming setting. I live quite near the bulb fields and I wondered if she might like a brief holiday so that she might see them for herself—Willy would come too, of course,' he sounded very bland, 'a few days' holiday might set him up ready for school again. Only there is one snag; Willy and I would like to go fishing and we don't feel that we can leave your mother alone while we fish, and as I'm told that if she accompanied us she would only remove the hooks from the fishes' mouths and throw them back into the water, I feel that it would be hardly conducive to our enjoyment.' He contrived to sound sad. 'She would be lonely.' He gave Phyllida a long look. 'We wondered if you would consider joining the party?'

It was a neat trap and she wondered which of them had thought it up. 'I must look for a job.'

The doctor's voice was all silk. 'You did tell me that you might take a holiday first.'

She bit into the carrot. 'Father…' she began.

He answered smoothly. 'We did—er—discuss it vaguely yesterday evening, after you had gone to bed.'

The trap had closed and she was amazed to find that she felt nothing but pleasure at its closure. All the same, she wasn't a girl to give in tamely. 'How will Father manage?' She looked at her mother.

'Beryl will be home for at least another two weeks—she doesn't get her exam results until then and the job she's after depends on those—she might just as well be here, and she'll love to look after him, and Dick can come down for the week-ends.' Her mother smiled so happily that Phyllida, peering at her from behind her fringe, knew that she couldn't disappoint her; she didn't have many holidays.

She said quietly, 'I'd love to come. When?'

There was a kind of concerted rush towards her, while her family, all talking at once, told her. When they paused for breath, Pieter said from his chair: 'In three days' time, if that suits everyone?'

Phyllida was sure that by everyone, he meant her; the rest of them would have already agreed happily to anything he might have suggested—even her father, who had just walked in, exclaiming: 'Well, is it all arranged? It's most kind of you, Pieter. My wife is a great gardener, nothing will give her more pleasure, but I do hope you know what you're taking on—three of them—you're sure you can house them all?'

The doctor answered him gravely. 'Oh, yes, I think that can be done. I hope you'll allow them to stay as long as possible—ten days? Two weeks?'

Willy looked anxious. 'If we're going fishing, two weeks would be super—I mean you have to work as well, I suppose?'

'I suppose I do,' he was gravely assured.

So Phyllida spent a good deal of the next two days unpacking and packing again, helping her mother to do the same, and going through Willy's wardrobe. Which left Beryl free to entertain the doctor, for Dick had gone again. She made a success of it too, judging by the way she made him laugh.

They left after breakfast to catch an afternoon Hovercraft from Dover, seen off by Doctor Cresswell, Meg the spaniel, an assortment of cats and Beryl, looking fetching in a large apron. She had flung her arms round Pieter's neck as she wished him goodbye and given him a hug and begged him to come back soon, and he had said something softly to make her laugh and kissed her soundly. Phyllida wondered why she was going and not Beryl. It should have been the other way round.

Their journey was a pleasant one, with a stop for an early lunch and a great deal of talk, mostly on Willy's part, concerning the joys of fishing, until they reached the Hovercraft, when he switched to engineering. Neither topic interested the two ladies of the party; they listened with one ear to make sure that Willy wasn't being rude or cheeky and carried on a desultory chat about clothes, the chances of Beryl remembering that her father couldn't stand lamb cutlets at any price, and what sort of presents they would buy to take back with them. But once on board, the conversation became general while they drank coffee and ate sandwiches and listened to their host explaining the rest of the journey to them.

It was well into the afternoon by now and it seemed that they still had a fair distance to go. They would land at Calais, travel up the French coast into Belgium and from these cross over into Holland at Sluis, then take the ferry to Vlissingen and from there drive all the way to Leiden on the motorway. He lived, explained the doctor, in a village bordering one of the lakes a mile or so from that city.

'Handy for your work, I expect,' chatted Mrs Cresswell. 'Do you have beds in a hospital there?'

'In Leiden, yes, also in den Haag.'

'Ah, yes,' said Mrs Cresswell knowledgeably, 'Leiden's a medical school, isn't it?'

So now we know, thought Phyllida, a thought peevishly, all this while and never a hint as to exactly where he lived—to her, at any rate.

They were actually disembarking at Calais when she wondered about the car. They had left the one he had hired in England and she hadn't given it another thought. She glanced round her and the doctor answered the question she hadn't asked. 'It's waiting for us, it should be over here.'

It was—a Bentley, not a new model, but a much cherished fifteen-year-old motor-car, sleek and gleaming and powerful. There was a man standing by it, a corpulent, middle-aged man, with a bald head and a round, cheerful face. The doctor spoke to him, shook his hand, and waved to a porter to load the luggage. The man had gone before that was finished and the doctor installed his guests without saying who he was.

'Such a nice car,' observed Mrs Cresswell, 'and what a lot of room!'

'Yes, I think so too—I've had her for a long time now and she suits me perfectly. She has a good turn of speed, too.'

Which proved to be the case. They went so fast through France, Belgium and then into Holland that Phyllida was hard put to it to know just where they were. Only as they crossed on the ferry to Vlissingen was there time to pore over a map while they drank coffee in the bar on board, and then she didn't take it all in, there was so much to see from the deck.

The spring evening was turning to dusk under a wide cloudy sky as they took the road northwards; Bergen-op-Zoom, Rosendaal, Dordrecht, by-passing them all, so that there was nothing to see of the actual towns. But there were plenty of villages, with their great churches and neat clusters of houses, and in between, wide water meadows striped with canals. Phyllida, sitting in the back with her mother, looked about her with interest. It was so very different from Madeira, from England even, but she liked it—it was calm, placid country and only as they skirted the bigger towns was she aware of factory chimneys and bustling industrial areas. It was nice when the doctor turned off the motorway on to a secondary road which took them across country to join another motorway just south of Leiden. He left this too after a few miles to turn down a country lane, brick built and with a canal on either side of it. They were back in the country again and presently she could see water; a wide lake stretching away into the dusk. The road ran beside it for some distance until they reached a village. 'Leimuiden,' said the doctor. 'The next one is Kudelstaart; I live just half way between them.'

There wasn't a village when he slowed the car presently, just a group of houses and cottages and a very small church, and then a high brick wall pierced by wrought iron gates, wide open.

The sanded drive was straight and quite long and the house at the end of it was so unlike anything that Phyllida had expected that she gave a gasp of surprise. It was a large square building, painted white, with single-storey wings on either side, connected by short covered passages. Its orderly rows of windows and all the ground floor ones were lighted, illuminating the great front door with its elaborate decoration of plasterwork picked out with gilt.

'How very grand,' observed her mother, who had a habit, sometimes embarrassing, of saying what came into her head. 'I'm quite overwhelmed—it's a good thing it's almost dark,' she added obscurely. But her host understood, for he assured her:

'It's not in the least terrifying, even in broad daylight, and I'm told it's wickedly inconvenient to clean.'

Willy hadn't said anything, but now, as they stopped on the

sweep before the door, he observed: 'I say, what a super place for a holiday—I'm glad I came!'

The doctor laughed and got out to open doors and usher his guests out of the car, and by then the house door had been opened too and a welcoming light streamed out to meet them from the hall beyond.

There was a tall thin woman standing just inside, looking so exactly as a housekeeper looked that there was no mistaking her; dressed severely in a dark grey dress, neat greying hair pulled back into a bun, a sombre face; but when she smiled she wasn't sombre at all, and she was delighted to see the doctor, who flung an arm round her as he introduced her.

'This is Lympke, my friend and housekeeper. She doesn't speak English but I'm sure you'll manage to understand each other. Her husband, Aap, who brought the car to meet us, will be here presently and he speaks it very well.'

He swept them all inside, through the wide hall and a pair of arched doors into a high-ceilinged room of vast proportions. It had wide windows at one end and at the other there were a few shallow steps which led to another, much smaller room, lined with books. The furniture was exactly right for its surroundings; glass-fronted cabinets filled with silver and porcelain, splendid wall tables carrying vases of flowers, a lacquered cabinet—and nicely arranged between these antique treasures were sofas, wing-backed armchairs and a variety of tables. The walls were white, the panels picked out with gilt and hung with paintings, mostly portraits, lighted by crystal sconces.

The doctor waved them to chairs amidst this splendour. 'Tea?' he enquired of Mrs Cresswell, unerringly guessing her one strong wish, and at her pleased nod, said something to Lympke who had followed them in. She went away and returned almost at once with a tea tray which she set on a small table by Mrs Cresswell's chair and while the two ladies drank their fill, the doctor gave Willy a glass of lemonade, pouring a whisky for himself.

'You have a very nice home, Pieter,' observed Mrs

Cresswell, passing Phyllida her tea. 'I had no idea—you told Ronald that you were a GP and I hardly expected...'

Phyllida stirred uneasily and hoped that the doctor wouldn't take umbrage. He didn't, only saying mildly: 'Well, I do have a surgery here in the house, you know, and quite a few local patients, but I must confess that most of my work is done in den Haag and Leiden, and sometimes abroad.'

'What do you specialise in?'

He smiled very faintly. 'Among other things, hearts.' He was looking at Phyllida, who knew what he was and kept her eyes fixed on a family group on the wall opposite her.

'Now isn't that nice?' asked Mrs Cresswell of the room at large. Neither of her children answered her because she had a habit of voicing her thoughts aloud and didn't expect anyone to reply anyway, but the doctor chose to do so.

'Well, I enjoy it; it's work I'm deeply interested in and it's a challenge.'

'Yes, of course.' Mrs Cresswell was well away. 'And you, you poor man, without a wife and children, you must be lonely.'

Phyllida gave her mother a look which that lady ignored, and the doctor's smile widened. 'I haven't been until now; just recently I have found that work isn't quite enough, though.'

He was still looking at Phyllida, who felt rather like a rabbit with the snake's eye upon it. She would have to look at him, she couldn't help herself; she withdrew her gaze from the family group, whom she now knew very well indeed, and met his eyes.

'You agree, Phyllida?' he asked blandly, then smiled so brilliantly that she found herself saying fervently:

'Oh, yes, I do! Work's very nice, but it—it...' She had no idea what she was going to say, but sat there with her pretty mouth open, praying for some witty, clever remark to come into her empty head.

It didn't, and his smile became the merest twitch of the lip.

'Would you like to go to your rooms?' He was the perfect host again. 'We'll dine in an hour's time if that's not too late for you, but do come down when you would like. I shall be around, but if I'm not, do make yourselves at home.'

Lympke led the way upstairs, up a handsomely carved staircase at the back of the hall, leading to a wide corridor above. Phyllida and her mother had adjoining rooms at the side of the house, while Willy, to his delight, was given a small room at the back of the house, well away from them. He could just see the gleam of water from his window even though it was almost dark now and came running back to tell them so.

'That's where we'll fish,' he told them importantly. 'I'm going down to talk to Pieter; someone's unpacked for me, so there's nothing for me to do.'

'You'll wash your face and hands, comb your hair and take a clean handkerchief,' decreed his mother, and when he had gone: 'How beautiful these rooms are, Phylly, and such heavenly bathrooms. Are you going to change your dress?'

'No, I don't think so, just do my face and hair and change my shoes.' Phyllida wandered over to the window and stared out into the evening, although she could see almost nothing by now. She said thoughtfully, 'It's a pity he's rich—I didn't know…' She sighed. 'And not just rich, he's—well…'

'Yes, dear, but he'd be that whether he had money or not, wouldn't he? And remember that your father's family is an old and honoured one.'

'Mother,' Phyllida's voice was rather high, 'I don't know what you're talking about.'

Her mother's reply was placid. 'No, dear, I often don't know either. Shall I back-comb my hair a bit in front? My head's as flat as a snake's after wearing a hat all day.'

They went downstairs presently and found the drawing room empty, but almost at once the fat man they had seen at Calais appeared at the door. 'Aap, madam, miss—the doctor's houseman. If you should want anything I will arrange it.'

They thanked him and Phyllida said: 'What good English you speak, Aap. Have you been in England?'

'Certainly, miss. At times I travel with the doctor, you understand. We also stay there from time to time—the doctor has many friends.' He smiled at them. 'The doctor and your brother have gone to look at the lake. It is now dark but Master Willy wished to see it for himself. It is not large, but there is a canal which leads to the *meer* beyond.'

He crossed to the windows and drew the heavy tapestry curtains, tended the log fire in the wide hearth, begged them to make themselves comfortable, and withdrew.

Mrs Cresswell sank into a deeply cushioned chair and sighed with pleasure. 'The last time I was in a house like this one was when I was ten years old—your Great-Aunt Dora at Weatherby Hall, dear. Such a pity she had to sell it.'

Phyllida had perched herself on a velvet-covered stool near the fire. 'Well, I like our house,' she declared a shade defiantly, 'it's beautiful and old and it's home.'

'Well, of course,' observed the doctor from the doorway, 'but home can be anywhere, can't it? A cottage or a semi-detached or an isolated farm—it's how one feels about it, isn't it?'

She had turned round to face him. 'I'm sorry,' she said quickly, 'I didn't mean to be rude; this is a lovely house and it's home for you, just as my home is for me.'

He smiled slowly. 'I hope that when I marry, my wife will love this house as much as I do. You must explore it one day.'

He had crossed the room to where a tray of drinks stood on a carved and gilded table. 'What will you ladies have to drink?'

He brought them their drinks and went back to get a Coke for Willy and a Jenever for himself. 'I don't need to go to the hospital until after lunch tomorrow,' he told them, 'and surgery should be over by half past nine. Willy and I thought we might do a little fishing, if you don't mind being left to your own devices. Lympke will be delighted to take you over the house and there's plenty to see in the gardens, please go wherever you wish.' He sat down in a great chair opposite Phyllida. 'I thought that we might go to the Keukenhof one day soon, it should be at its best now. It's not far from here and we could leave here after breakfast—I'm afraid I'll have to be back around tea time, though, for any evening patients I may have at my rooms in Leiden.'

They dined presently in a room a good deal smaller than the drawing room but still pretty large. It was furnished in mahogany, gleaming with endless polishing and age, and the table silver and glass almost out shone it. They sat at a round table, large enough to take a dozen people with ease, although they occupied only a part of it, sitting near enough to talk comfortably.

They ate splendidly; caviar for starters, salmon poached in white wine, chicken cooked in cream with a Madeira sauce. Willy hardly spoke, but ate with the deep pleasure of a growing boy who was hungry; it was left to the other three to carry on an undemanding conversation mostly about gardens and growing vegetables and the difficulties of protecting everything from frost. Phyllida, who was a willing but amateur gardener, marvelled at Pieter, who seemed evenly matched against her mother's expert knowledge. Surely it was enough, she thought a little crossly, that he was apparently a very successful man in his own profession, had a house like a cosy museum and the good looks to turn any girl's head; he didn't have to be a knowledgeable gardener as well.

Even the appearance of a honey and hazelnut bavarois, which tasted even better than it looked, did little to lift her spirits, although she did her best to look intelligent about greenfly and black spot while she ate it. She would excuse herself when they had had their coffee, she decided, on the grounds that she wanted to wash her hair before she went to bed, but in this she was frustrated. Pieter invited her mother to telephone her father, suggested that Willy might like to have an early night so that he would feel fit for a morning's fishing, and invited her to sit down and keep him company.

'For we don't seem to have exchanged more than a dozen words,' he observed pleasantly.

'Well, I'm not mad about gardening,' she said grumpily, and then remembering her manners: 'I'm sorry, I don't know what's the matter with me—I don't mean to be so beastly rude to you. I think...' she paused and looked at him with puzzled blue eyes, like a small girl with a problem. 'I think it's because all this is a surprise. I thought you'd have a house in a village, a bit like ours—and it's not.'

'You don't like it?' he asked in a gentle voice.

'Oh, I do—it's out of this world.' She added shyly: 'I feel as though I'm trespassing.'

'Oh, never that.' She wondered why he looked amused and it was on the tip of her tongue to ask why when her mother came back into the room, and soon after they went to bed, leaving him standing at the foot of his magnificent staircase. Her mother had already gained the corridor and was out of sight when he called Phyllida back.

'I forgot this,' he told her, and kissed her, hard.

CHAPTER SIX

PHYLLIDA WENT DOWN to breakfast after a somewhat wakeful night. Naturally enough, being a pretty girl and a perfectly normal one, she had received her share—rather more, perhaps—of kisses. She had enjoyed them too, but somehow Pieter had been different from the others. She had told herself several times during the night that it was because he was older and more experienced, but she knew that wasn't the answer. She had given up wondering about it then and gone to sleep.

The doctor wasn't at breakfast, nor was Willy, who had risen early, breakfasted with his host and then taken himself off to spy out the land around the lake. Phyllida assured her mother that she had passed a dreamless night, ate her breakfast under the fatherly eye of Aap and declared that she was going to explore the gardens; for some reason she felt shy about meeting Pieter and the gardens seemed an unlikely place for him to be in at that hour of the day; he had said something about morning surgery…

She had half expected her mother to accompany her, but Mrs Cresswell had found a splendid book on gardening in the library. 'I'll come out later,' she decided, 'when the sun's really warm.'

So Phyllida fetched a cardigan and found her way outside. Now that it was morning, and a bright one even if chilly, and she could see everything clearly, she had to admit that the house was charming; solid and unpretentious despite its size, fitting exactly into the surrounding formal lawns and flower beds and trees beyond. Moreover, everywhere she looked there was a blaze of colour; tulips and hyacinths and scilla and the last of the daffodils. She walked round the side of the house, peering into the wide windows of the wing she was passing. She supposed that it must be a ballroom, for it took up the whole area and its floor was waxed wood. The ceiling was painted, although she couldn't see it very clearly, and from its centre hung a chandelier, its crystals looped and twined into an elaborate pattern.

There were windows on the other side too and she walked on, rounded the wing and found herself facing a formal garden with a square pond bordered by masses of flowers and sheltered by a beech hedge. There was an alley leading from its far end and she went to look at it. It was arched by more beech, trained to form a tunnel, and that in its turn opened into a charming circle of grass, well screened by shrubs and with stone seats here and there. Right in the middle there was a wheelbarrow, loaded with earth and with a spade flung on top of it. It looked as though someone had just that minute left it there, and she looked round to see if there was anyone about, but she saw no one, neither in the alley from whence she had just come, nor on the neat brick path which led away from the grassy plot on its other side. She sat down on one of the seats and blew on her fingers. It might be the end of April, but it was still chilly unless the sun shone.

'It'll be pleasantly warm once the morning mist has gone,' observed the doctor from somewhere behind her.

She jumped. 'I thought you were taking your morning surgery.'

'My dear girl, we keep early hours here; surgery's from eight until nine o'clock and there are seldom more than a dozen patients, often less.'

He sat down beside her and she said doubtfully: 'But I thought you had a practice.'

'Well, I have, but I see most of my patients at my rooms in Leiden—this surgery is just for the villages close by.'

'Oh, I see—and you have beds in a hospital too?'

'In several hospitals.'

She gave him a searching look. 'I think you must be someone quite important.' And when he didn't answer: 'A consultant or a specialist—or do you teach?'

His eyes were smiling. 'Some of all three.' He picked up her hand and held it between his. 'You're cold. We'll walk down to the lake and see if Willy has fallen in, if he hasn't we'll bring him back for coffee before we get down to this business of fishing.'

As they started along the path, he added: 'I wondered if you would all like to come into den Haag this afternoon, you could look at the shops while I'm at the hospital. I shall only be a couple of hours and I'll show you where to go.'

She was very conscious of his hand holding hers; it was firm and warm and impersonal and she wondered again why he had kissed her on the previous evening. 'That sounds nice,' she said, her voice cool because she didn't want to seem too friendly.

They had come to the end of the path and were crossing rough ground at the end of which she could see the lake, and Willy, sitting on a log by it. Pieter had slowed his pace. 'My mother and father are coming to dinner this evening,' he said casually.

'Your mother and father?' Surprise made her repeat his words like an idiot. 'Oh, I didn't know—that is, do they live here?'

'They have a house on the coast near Scheveningen. My father is a doctor but retired now. I have two brothers and two sisters—my sisters are married, both living in Friesland, my youngest brother is in Utrecht, finishing medical school, and Paul, who is a year or so younger than I, is married and lives in Limburg—he's a barrister.'

He hadn't volunteered so much information in such a short time since they had met. Phyllida digested it slowly. Presently she asked: 'Then why do you live here, all alone in this great house?'

'When my father retired he and my mother went to live on the coast because the house—a charming one—is close to the golf course and he enjoys a game. It was always understood that they would go there eventually and it's like a second home to us all, as we spent our holidays there when we were children.' He sat down beside her. 'And as I'm the eldest son, I took over here. I don't regret it.'

'It's very large for one person.'

His eyes were almost shut. 'Yes, but it's surprising how a clutch of children fills even the largest of houses.'

'But you haven't any children.'

'Something which can be remedied.' He changed the conversation so abruptly that she was startled. 'I think you'll like the shops in den Haag—will Willy be bored?' He turned to look at her. 'I could take him with me; I'll get someone to take him round one or two of the more interesting wards until I'm ready—he's really keen on becoming a doctor, isn't he?'

She agreed, secretly put out. She would have been interested too, and she might have found out something of his life while she was there; his working life, but it seemed that he didn't want her to know. Well, if he wanted to be secretive, let him. 'I said I'd go and find Mother,' she told him.

They had a splendid afternoon wandering round the shops, buying inexpensive trifles to take home, drinking tea in a smart café and then walking back to the spot where Pieter was to pick them up. The journey home was occupied almost exclusively by Willy's observations about what he had seen, the doctor's mild replies and Phyllida's slightly cool ones, which she regretted when he asked her in the friendliest possible manner if she would go with him on the following day in order to choose a birthday present for his younger sister.

'I've no ideas at all,' he assured her, 'and if you would be so kind as to advise me…'

She agreed at once, and the rest of the ride was taken up with a lighthearted discussion between Willy and his host concerning the chances of them landing a good sized pike when next they fished the lake.

Phyllida was a little apprehensive about meeting Pieter's parents; while she dressed she tried to imagine what they would be like and failed; the doctor was an enormous man, probably his parents would be of a similar size, on the other hand, very small women quite often had large sons. She put together a mental picture of his mother, small and dark and terribly smart.

She combed her fringe smooth, put on a thin wool dress in a flattering wine shade, and went downstairs.

Her mother and Willy were already there, she could hear their voices through the half open drawing room door—other voices too. Aap, appearing suddenly, opened the door wide, and she went in.

The master of the house was standing against one of the display cabinets, one hand in a pocket, the other holding a glass, his long legs crossed, his shoulders wedged against the dark woodwork. He was talking to a very tall, very large lady, with elegantly dressed white hair, handsome features and what Phyllida described to herself as a presence. Across the room, talking to her mother and brother, was an elderly man, as large and powerfully built as the doctor and just as good-looking. The three of them made a formidable trio, and she wondered briefly if his brothers and sisters were the same size; no wonder they lived in such an enormous house.

The doctor came to meet her, his compelling hand urging her forward to where his mother was standing. That lady surprised her very much by saying mildly, before any introductions had been made: 'My dear, I'm sure Pieter didn't warn you about us—being so large, you know—when the whole family are together I've known people turn pale at the sight of us.' She laughed, a deep rich chuckle which transformed her austere appearance.

Why, thought Phyllida, taking the offered hand, she's just like Mother, only larger.

Pieter had been standing between them, now he said placidly: 'I don't think Phyllida is easily frightened, Mama.' He smiled a little. 'What will you drink, Phylly?'

He fetched her a sherry and took her to meet his father. It was like talking to Pieter, they were so very alike; the same hooded blue eyes, the same firm mouth and patrician nose, only his hair, still thick, was quite white.

She sat beside him on one of the vast sofas, while the others gathered together on the other side of the hearth, and he talked of nothing much in particular, putting her at her ease, and presently when Aap came to announce dinner, they went, still laughing and talking, to take their places round the beautifully appointed table. Phyllida, sitting beside the elder of the van Sittardts with Willy on her other side and Pieter's mother next to him, noticed with some amusement that her brother was getting on splendidly with his neighbour, which left her mother and Pieter, talking quietly together.

The evening was an unqualified success; the magnificent dinner helped, of course, and the glass or two of claret she drank with it, but even they wouldn't have been of much help without the easy charm of her host and his parents. She found herself quite anxious to meet the rest of the family.

Only one thing marred the evening for her. Sitting round the fire, drinking their coffee, Mevrouw van Sittardt took advantage of a pause in the talk to ask: 'And have you seen Marena yet, Phyllida? I feel sure that you must have, as she spends a great deal of her time here. She and Pieter are very old friends—lifelong, one might say, and he has grown accustomed to be at her beck and call at all times.'

The lady smiled as she spoke, but Phyllida had the strong impression that she would have preferred to have ground her teeth. She said that no, she hadn't met the girl in question yet, and glanced at the doctor, sitting with her mother. He looked as blandly impassive as usual, but she had no doubt that he had heard every single word, for his mother had a clear and ringing voice. She wished very much to ask about this Marena; it seemed strange that if she were such a close friend—perhaps more than a friend—Pieter should never have mentioned her. It wasn't her business anyway, she told herself sternly, and plunged into an account of their shopping expedition that afternoon; probably she would never see the girl.

She was wrong. They met the very next day, after Phyllida and the doctor had returned from a highly successful search for the birthday present. The afternoon had been fun although short, for he had had a number of private patients to see at his rooms in Leiden, and hadn't been able to pick her up until the middle of the afternoon. Nevertheless, the next hour or so had been delightful, especially when she discovered that there was no reasonable limit to the amount he might be called upon to spend. They chose a pendant finally, a dainty thing of gold with a border of rose diamonds, and then had tea before going back home, where Willy had immediately waylaid them and badgered them into a rather wild game with Butch, the nondescript old dog who was Pieter's devoted slave. Phyllida had cast off her jacket the better to run faster and was tearing across the lawn towards the house with Butch in hot pursuit when she saw a girl watching them from the terrace. She was small and slight, with large dark eyes and a pouting mouth, expertly made up; she made Phyllida feel tall and fat and untidy. Untidy she certainly was, for the sun had come out and was shining warmly so that her face was flushed and her hair blew wildly around her head, sadly in need of a comb.

The girl smiled charmingly as she crossed the lawn to join them, but there was malice with the charm and Phyllida sensed that the girl had already decided that there was no competition for her to fear. Her eyes spoke volumes for Phyllida to read—this guileless outdoor type with great blue eyes and a gentle mouth and a fringe like a little girl wasn't Pieter's type. The smile widened as she reached Pieter, tucked an exquisitely cared for hand under his arm and said in accented English: 'Darling Pieter, have you missed me very much? And how good it is that you have friends to amuse you while I am not here.' She gave his arm a little pat and gave a trill of laughter. 'But now I am.'

He smiled down at her. 'Nice to see you, Marena—how's the painting?'

She made a charming face. 'Not good, not good at all. I need your opinion, otherwise I shall destroy all that I have done. Will you come and look at them?'

'Yes, of course. Still at the studio, are you?' He turned to Phyllida. 'Phylly, meet Marena. She paints, and she's good at it, too.' His amused gaze swept over her untidy person and she flushed. She said politely:

'How interesting. I've never met an artist, it must be wonderful to be able to paint.'

'Anyone can learn,' Marena assured her sweetly, and dismissed her. 'Pieter, can I speak to you for one minute? It is important and private.'

Phyllida was at the door before she had finished speaking; she could take a hint as well as the next one and Marena clearly wanted her out of the way. 'I must tidy myself,' she muttered. 'I expect I'll see you again before we leave—so nice meeting you.' She wrenched open the door and ducked through it, casting a totally meaningless smile over her shoulder as she went.

Willy had melted away as only boys can, and Aap, crossing the hall as she stood a little uncertainly, offered the information that he and his mother had gone down to the lake to see if they could find the swan's nest there. There was still plenty of time before dinner; she flew upstairs and without bothering to do more than run a comb through her hair, flung on a cardigan, and using the back stairs, went out of the house. Somehow she couldn't bear to join the doctor and Marena again—indeed, she thought it unlikely that they would want her to. A good walk would do her good and if she returned with only enough time to change for the evening, the chance of meeting the girl again would be slight, although she might stay for dinner.

'And why should I care?' asked Phyllida loudly of the trees around her. 'Well, I do, anyway.' And indeed, to be quite honest, she had begun to think that Pieter had fallen a little in love with her, and she, moreover, had fallen a little in love with him. She stopped her brisk walking, struck by a sudden blinding thought. She wasn't a little in love with him; she was head over heels; no one and nothing else mattered in the world. Never to see him again would be a sorrow she wouldn't be able to bear, and it was a sorrow she wouldn't be able to share with anyone, least of all Pieter. At all costs she would have to hide her feelings. They would be going back home in ten days or so and she would have to be very careful. She walked on faster than ever, trying to escape the awful thought that she had allowed him to see that she liked him very much. Well, she could soon put that right. Cool friendliness and steering clear of anything personal when they were talking—that would leave him free to dote on his precious Marena. She ground her splendid teeth at the thought.

She turned for home presently, for she had been out too long already, and reached the garden door just as Pieter came out of it. He was looking preoccupied although he smiled when he saw her.

'Hullo there,' he said easily, and there was a glint of amusement in his eyes as he took in her flyaway appearance. 'You've been out and I thought you were still doing things to your hair. I've just left a message with Aap—I'm afraid I'll have to go out this evening and I do apologise to you all. I doubt if I'll be back until late.'

He held the door for her to go through. 'By the way, Marena wants us all to go over for drinks before you go back—may I tell her that you would like to?'

He was going to spend the evening with the horrid creature. Phyllida said in a cool little voice: 'Why, of course—we shall be delighted. How very kind.' She gave him a bright smile and hurried past him.

Mrs Cresswell made no comment when Phyllida told her that their host would be out for the evening, but Willy asked anxiously: 'Did he say when he'd be back? We're going fishing at four o'clock tomorrow morning.'

'Don't worry, dear,' soothed his mother, 'I'm sure Pieter wouldn't forget anything as important as that.'

But hours later, listening to the stable clock chiming twice, Phyllida wondered if he had, and she was sure of it when half an hour later she heard the Bentley whisper past her windows.

She slept after that, a miserable exhausted sleep which left her heavy-eyed and snappy, and when Berta the housemaid brought her her morning tea, she had no desire to get up. All the same, she went down to breakfast presently and found her mother and brother already there. Her mother wished her good morning and ignored her pale cross face, but Willy was less perceptive. 'I say, Phylly, you do look cross. We had a smashing time...'

'You went fishing? But Pieter...' She stopped herself in time. 'I didn't think Pieter would get up so early.'

'He wanted to,' said Willy simply.

'One can always find time to do what one wants,' observed her mother comfortably. 'Phylly, pass me another of those delicious rolls, will you? It's such a splendid morning, I think I'll take that gardening catalogue Pieter lent me and go and sit in that dear little summer house. What are you two going to do?'

'I'm going to the next village,' said Willy importantly, 'the one you can see across the fields from the side of the house. I have to deliver a note for Pieter; one of his patients has to go into hospital.' He buttered himself some toast with a lavish hand. 'We're all going to the Keukenhof the day after tomorrow, he told me so this morning.' He sighed with content. 'I caught two bream this morning and Pieter got four.' He wolfed down the toast. 'Phylly, are you coming with me?'

She agreed readily. Her own company was something she wished to avoid at all costs, and presently they set off into the bright morning, pleased with each other's company despite the dozen or so years between them, Phyllida rather silent and Willy talking non-stop.

'It was super of Pieter to come this morning,' he told her. 'He's been up most of the night, you know—that case at the hospital in Leiden.'

'What case?' asked Phyllida with instant interest. 'And how do you know?'

Her brother gave her a kindly, impatient look. 'He told me, of course—this boy had a relapse, so he was called in for a consultation. He's very important, you know.'

'Is he?' she asked humbly. 'I didn't know—he never said.'

'Well, of course not,' said Willy with scorn. 'I mean, a man doesn't go around boasting. But he's frightfully brainy—I expect he'd have told you if you'd asked—I did.' His chest swelled with pride. 'He knows I'm going to be a doctor when I'm a man, he says I'm a natural because Father's a doctor anyway and it's in the blood, like it is in his—he says you can't help yourself if it is and that I'll make a jolly good one. He talks to me just as though I'm grown up.'

Pieter loomed large in Willy's life, that was obvious, but then he loomed even larger in hers. She sighed. 'Oh, does he? What exactly does he specialise in, dear?'

They were almost at the village and had slowed their pace.

'Hearts—you heard him say so, didn't you? And leukaemia, didn't you know that either? And you're always talking to him…'

'Am I?' asked Phyllida sadly. But not, it seemed, about anything that really mattered. She wondered what Pieter really thought of her behind that calm, handsome face. Probably nothing much.

Willy discharged his errand and they walked back, having a one-sided conversation about fishing, with him in full spate about lines and hooks and flies and she saying yes and no and really, while she allowed her mind to dwell upon Pieter, so that she followed her brother in through the garden door rather dreamily, to bump almost at once into the master of the house, lying back in a large cane chair in the garden room, his feet on another chair, fast asleep.

They stood and looked at him for a moment and Phyllida saw how weary he was, with lines etched on his face which she hadn't noticed before, a faint frown between his brows. Willy wandered away, but she went on staring and then gave a squeak of surprise when the doctor asked softly: 'Why do you look like that, Phylly?'

'Like what?'

'Motherly and sad.' He unfolded himself and stood up, smiling.

'Oh—oh, I don't know. I'm sorry if we woke you up.'

'I'm not. Let's get Aap to bring some coffee to the summer house. I saw that your mother was there.'

So they all had their coffee together and he didn't say a word about where he had been or why, indeed, he presented the perfect picture of a man of leisure, only presently he went to sleep again and Mrs Cresswell and Willy crept away, leaving Phyllida sitting there with him. She wasn't sure why she wanted to stay, perhaps because it was wonderful just to be there; presently he would go off again and she wouldn't know where, or perhaps Marena would come frisking along to make him laugh. Two large slow tears trickled down her cheeks; she was only half aware of them and didn't bother to do anything about them and there was no one to see.

'Why are you crying?' asked the doctor softly.

She was so vexed with herself that she could hardly speak. She might have guessed that he wasn't asleep, but he had looked so tired. She didn't answer, only looked away from him, wiping the tears away with a finger.

'No job?' he persisted. 'An uncertain future? Not happy here, perhaps?'

'Oh, I am, I am. It's lovely—I thought when I first came that it was all so grand, but now I know just what you meant about it being a home, because it is.' She went on in a muddled way: 'Cats on the chairs and that nice old dog and the way you fling your jacket down on that magnificent table in the hall, and your mother and father...'

The doctor's eyes gleamed beneath their lids, but all he said was: 'Then you must be in love.'

She went red, and then, unable to stop herself: 'Yes, I am—I've only just found out, though I think that I knew days ago. It's funny...'

It was fortunate that she was interrupted, for she had flung caution to the winds and had actually started to tell him that she was in love with him. She froze with horror and for once was glad to see Marena crossing the lawn and smiling with the air of someone who was sure of a welcome. She flung her arms round the doctor's neck and kissed him with what Phyllida considered to be a sickening display of sentiment and then smiled at her. Her voice was gracious.

'Hullo—you look much nicer today, but I do not like your fringe. Fringes are for little girls, are they not? And you are no longer that.'

Phyllida tried to think of a suitable answer to this snide remark, but her head was still full of the things she had so nearly said; she felt sick just remembering them. The doctor answered for her: 'You're wrong, Marena, Phylly isn't grown up at all, not nearly as grown up as you are. And I like the fringe.'

'I am but nineteen,' declared Marena prettily, and perched on the arm of his chair.

'In years, in worldly knowledge, double that.'

She pouted and dropped a kiss on to his head. 'I do not know why I like you so very much, Pieter.'

'Nor I. Without wishing to be inhospitable, I should warn you that I am about to leave for my rooms. What do you want this time?' He sounded amused.

'Darling, I need some money and the bank say no more until my allowance is paid. If I could have five hundred gulden—just till then—I will pay back...'

He put a hand into a pocket and fished out a roll of notes. 'Here you are. A new dress, I suppose.'

Marena took the notes and stuffed them into her handbag, flashing a triumphant look at Phyllida. 'Of course—such a charming one. I shall wear it for you when you come.'

'I look forward to it.' He submitted to another embrace and with a careless wave of the hand for Phyllida, Marena skipped off. A moment later Phyllida heard a car start up and roar away.

'She's the world's worst driver,' murmured the doctor, and closed his eyes again.

Phyllida sat and looked at him, suspicious that he was only foxing again, but presently he snored, very faintly, but still a snore. She gave him ten minutes and then ventured: 'I say, you said you had to leave...'

He opened one eye. 'Did I really say that? Then I made a mistake—I have nothing to do until this evening, when I have to give a lecture at a hospital in Utrecht. You can come with me if you like.'

She sat up very straight. 'May I really—I'd like to.'

'Good. And now shall we finish that very interesting conversation we were having when we were interrupted? You were saying?'

'Nothing.' She couldn't get it out fast enough. 'It wasn't anything, really it wasn't.'

'No?' His tone implied disbelief. 'Ah, well, later on, perhaps.' He smiled at her and her heart bounced so that she caught her breath.

'I thought we might go to the Keukenhof the day after tomorrow,' he told her. 'It should be looking at its best; your mother is anxious to inspect the flowers.'

Phyllida was glad of the change in the conversation. 'Yes, she's a great gardener...' She babbled on for a few minutes and then stopped a bit abruptly; even in her own ears she sounded foolish.

They dined early by reason of the lecture and then drove the forty miles to Utrecht. The evening was fine and the country as they approached the city looked pretty and peaceful. 'But not as pretty as where you live,' declared Phyllida.

'Well, I do agree with you there, but I daresay I'm prejudiced.' He swept the car through the main streets, worked his way through some very narrow lanes and entered the hospital courtyard.

She was given a seat near the back of the lecture hall and made to feel at home by the young doctor who had been asked to look after her. She hadn't given much thought to the lecture. That it was delivered in Dutch really didn't matter; it was bliss just to sit there and stare at Pieter, elegant and assured and presumably amusing, for every now and again there would be a burst of laughter around her. He had a lovely voice, she thought, deep and a bit gravelly and unhurried. She sighed gustily and the young doctor gave her an anxious look which she dispelled with a beaming smile.

On the way home, later, Pieter observed idly: 'It can't have been much fun for you—did you go to sleep? I must have been out of my mind to have asked you in the first place.'

'Oh, but I loved it, and I didn't go to sleep—I listened to

every word,' and when he gave a great shout of laughter: 'Well, you know what I mean.'

'I like to think that I do.'

A remark which gave her plenty to think about until they got back.

She saw little of the doctor during the following day, though, surprisingly, Phyllida thought. His mother called in the afternoon and had tea with them, going round the gardens with her mother, enjoying a long talk about flower growing.

'I like her,' declared Mrs Cresswell when Mevrouw van Sittardt had been driven away in an old-fashioned, beautifully kept motor-car. 'She's a bit overpowering, but she's a woman after my own heart.' She added by way of explanation: 'She doesn't cut her roses back either.'

The doctor arrived home in the late afternoon, waved aside offers of tea and disclosed the fact that they were all going to Marena's studio for drinks before dinner. Phyllida instantly went into a flurry of hair brushing and fresh make-up, deploring the fact that the weather had turned quite warm and she really had nothing to wear. It would have to be the thin wool, which meant that after the first drink and with the central heating, she would be as red as a beet in no time at all.

Marena's flat was in the centre of den Haag, high up in a modern block, all black marble entrance and chromium fittings, and her studio was very similar—a vast room with paintings stacked along one wall and an easel under one enormous window. It was furnished in a modern style and its walls hung with Impressionist paintings, a fitting background for Marena who was wearing an outrageous outfit; a tunic slashed to the waist and tight velvet pants. Phyllida eyed her with real envy, wishing she dared to dress like that; it might capture Pieter's attention.

And it did, but not in the way she had expected. He took a long look and said slowly: 'If that's what you borrowed five hundred gulden for, my dear, it's been wasted.'

Phyllida saw the flash of anger in the girl's eyes although she laughed at him. 'It's not for you, Pieter—I've a new boyfriend.' She flashed a look at Phyllida, who looked back at her woodenly.

They drank a concoction in long glasses which Phyllida didn't like but didn't dare to say so, and yet it must have shown on her face, for while Marena was showing Mrs Cresswell her paintings, Pieter crossed the room and took the glass from her and gave her his empty one. He must think her an awful baby, she mused sadly.

They stayed a couple of hours, which gave Phyllida ample time in which to watch Marena at work on Pieter, who was treating her as one might treat a pretty child; goodnaturedly answering her preposterous remarks, praising her paintings, telling her that she was getting prettier each time he saw her. Phyllida, feeling a frump in the woollen dress, registered a firm resolve to go out the very next day and buy some new clothes. It wasn't until they were on the way home that she remembered that they were going to spend the whole of the next day at the Keukenhof.

CHAPTER SEVEN

THE KEUKENHOF WAS beautiful under a cloudless sky, although a chilly wind set the flowers nodding and swaying. They had left the house shortly after breakfast and driven the few miles there in no time at all, so that when they reached the park there were very few people about. They strolled round while the doctor and Mrs Cresswell exchanged Latin names and methods of propagation in an assured manner which left Phyllida and Willy quite at sea. But whatever they were called, the tulips and hyacinths and daffodils were a colourful sight, arranged in glowing patches of colour so that whichever way one turned there was something to delight the eye.

'Mind you,' remarked Mrs Cresswell, 'your own gardens are magnificent and must take a good deal of planning.'

The doctor laughed. 'I must plead guilty to leaving most of the work to Bauke, who has been with the family for so long I can't remember what he looked like as a young man. He's a wizard with flowers—I only study the catalogues and say what I like.'

'Do you ever garden yourself?' asked Phyllida, remembering the wheelbarrow and the spade.

'Oh, yes—the odd hour or so when I have the time; it's good exercise. And you, Phyllida?'

They had paused to allow Willy to investigate a stretch of ornamental water. 'Me? Well, I dig potatoes and pull carrots and cut the flowers if I'm home. What's that building over there?'

'A restaurant and café. If you won't get too chilly we might have coffee on the terrace before we go along to the glasshouses.'

Which they did, sitting near the water in the sunshine, and then wandering on again towards the great greenhouses. The gardens were lovely, but the display in the houses took even Mrs Cresswell's breath. She hurried from one spread of colour to the next, exclaiming over each of them, and: 'Oh, how I wish I could take them all home with me!' she sighed.

'Hardly possible, I'm afraid, but you must allow me to offer you a small memento of your visit—we'll pick out the bulbs you particularly admire and I'll order them—you'll get them in the autumn.'

'Oh, I couldn't!' and then at his gentle smile: 'Well, just one or two, perhaps.' She went happily all the way round again, trying to make up her mind which she would choose. 'Those Kaufmanniana hybrids for the rock garden, perhaps—or should I have that alium Moly, such a lovely colour.' Her eyes wandered to the display of parrot tulips. 'That blue and mauve one—if I might have one or two?'

'Do you care for the Mendel? I have them at home, if you remember—such a good colour in spring, I find.' The doctor was quietly leading her on. 'The clover pink goes so splendidly with the iris danfordiae—an unusual colour scheme, but you must admit that the pink and yellow made a splendid show.'

'Oh, yes—I did admire them in your garden. It's hard to choose—perhaps if I might have a few iris and one or two of the parrot tulips? And thank you very much.'

Mrs Cresswell looked quite flushed with pleasure.

'I'll go across and order them from the office there. Do go on looking around; I shall find you presently.'

Mrs Cresswell pottered off happily enough, pointing out what she would have if only she could afford them. Which gave Phyllida an idea. She would buy some bulbs for her mother too; if she went back to the little rustic hut where they took the orders she would be able to see which ones the doctor had ordered and get something to go with them. She muttered her plan to Willy and slipped away.

The doctor was still there and she was surprised to see the look of guilt on his face when he saw her. She didn't pause to consider this, however, but plunged at once into her idea. 'And if you'll tell me what you've ordered I'll get something else,' she finished.

Something in his face made her transfer her gaze to the clerk holding the order book. A whole page of it was filled and she turned a questioning look upon Pieter, who gave her a calm stare which told her nothing. 'It seems a pity,' he remarked blandly, 'that your mother shouldn't have something of everything she admired; I should like to think of your garden at home filled with flowers—she likes them so much.'

'The whole lot?' she gaped at him.

'Well, not quite all.' He smiled faintly. 'Now you're here, will you help me to decide which of the tulips to have in my own garden? That pink lily flowering one is charming—you were admiring it…'

'I think it's super, but why ask my advice? I mean, you'll be the one to see them, not me. But if I were choosing for my garden, yes, I'd have them. Where will you plant them?'

'In the beds on either side of the front door, under the windows. I'd better have two hundred.'

She gulped. 'That seems an awful lot,' she ventured.

'There's an awful lot of garden,' he pointed out, and took her arm. 'Let's find your mother and Willy—and not a word, mind.'

They had lunch presently in the restaurant and then a last stroll before driving back. At the house once more, Phyllida, wondering what to do with the rest of her afternoon was over the moon when the doctor suggested casually that she might like to go with him to his rooms.

'I'll be there a couple of hours,' he said. 'You can look round if you're interested and then while away the time at the shops until I'm ready.' He glanced at her mother, happily immersed in a pile of catalogues, and Willy, already on his way across the lawns with the dog. 'I don't think you'll be missed.'

His rooms were in a narrow street of elegant houses, with barely room to park a car before their doors. He stopped the Bentley half way down and got out to open her door. 'If you walk to the end and turn to the right, you'll be in the main shopping centre. This is Finklestraat and I'm at number ten. If you get lost, just ask the way back.'

He was on the ground floor; a richly comfortable waiting room, an office where his secretary sat and a consulting room beyond and beside it a small treatment room. There was a nurse there, a formidable middle-aged woman who greeted the doctor austerely and immediately took him to task for something or other. He listened meekly to her lecture, said something to make her laugh, and led the way into his consulting room. It was of a pleasant size and furnished in soothing shades of grey and soft browns, with comfortable chairs and a large desk. She looked round her slowly. 'You're a very successful man, aren't you, Pieter?'

His lips twitched. 'I work hard, Phylly.'

'Oh, I didn't mean to be rude—I only meant...'

He caught her hand. 'I know that. I wanted you to see where I work for a good deal of my day.' He bent and kissed her lightly. 'Now run along and enjoy yourself. You can have two hours.'

She found herself in the street, her head a muddle of thoughts and dreams. Perhaps he was falling in love with her, on the other hand he could be being just friendly, wanting her to enjoy her holiday. There was no point in brooding about it. She walked briskly to the end of the street and made for the nearest shops.

Egged on by the thought of Marena, she was tempted to enter a boutique presently, and once inside she cast caution to the winds and bought rather more than she had intended; a silk jersey tunic in a dusky pink, a pleated skirt in pale green with a matching jacket and a real silk blouse to go with them, and lastly a cotton jersey shirtwaister in pale amber; she hadn't meant to buy that, but the saleslady had pointed out, quite rightly, that it would be a most useful garment for the rest of the year.

Much lighter in the purse, and in the heart too, Phyllida found her way back to Finklestraat and poked her head round the waiting-room door. The room was empty and she had a sudden pang that everyone had gone home and left her behind; instantly dismissed as absurd, for the Bentley was still standing at the kerb.

She sat down with her packages around her and waited quietly until the nurse came out, followed by the secretary. They both smiled at her and the secretary said: 'The doctor is coming,' as they went out.

Pieter joined her a few minutes later, opened his sleepy eyes wide at the sight of her parcels, observed that she had put her time to good use, swept them up and ushered her out to the car. He seemed disinclined for conversation, so after one or two tentative remarks Phyllida gave up and sat silent until they stopped at his house. There was another car parked on the sweep and as he leaned over to open her door, he observed a little impatiently: 'And now what does Marena want, I wonder? Not another dress so soon?'

Phyllida received her parcels, thanked him for the outing and went ahead of him into the house; if Marena was there she didn't want to see her. Even so, she was illogically put out when the doctor made no attempt to delay her. He watched her make for the stairs, Aap behind with her purchases, before turning away and going into the drawing room.

Once in her room, Phyllida lost no time in trying on everything she had bought. The jersey tunic was certainly stunning. She decided to wear it that evening; it might possibly detract Pieter's interest from Marena. She had heard the car start up and leave, so she would have a clear field.

She went downstairs presently, feeling a little excited, aware that she looked her very best. It was a great pity that Pieter wasn't there. Aap tendered his excuses and begged that they would dine without their host, and offered no further information at all.

Phyllida received her mother's admiration of her new dress with a pleasant calm which concealed rage, carried on a spirited conversation with Willy about the size of the fish he might one day catch, and dinner over, declared that she had a headache and retired to her room, where she threw the new dress into a corner and cried herself to sleep.

The doctor, returning home presently to spend the rest of the evening with his guests, evinced surprise when Mrs Cresswell told him that Phyllida had gone to bed with a headache, but he said nothing beyond murmuring some civility or other, poured himself a whisky and sat down in his chair. Mrs Cresswell, studying him while he exchanged a bantering conversation with Willy, concluded that he looked thoughtful, but not in a worried way; more as though he was mightily pleased about something.

Phyllida went down to her breakfast the next morning with some caution. She didn't want to meet Pieter, not yet, not until her puffy eyelids were normal again. He should be gone, either to his surgery or to one or other of the hospitals he visited. All the same, she approached the breakfast room circumspectly and was about to peer round its half open door when his study door was flung open behind her. His cheerful: 'Ha!' uttered in a booming voice, sent her spinning round to face him.

She managed: 'Oh, good morning—I thought you'd gone?'

He leaned against the door frame, watching her. 'So who were you expecting to jump out on you?'

She had regained her breath and her composure. 'No one. I expect you're just off to the surgery.'

'Indeed I am. But I shall be back. It is unfortunate that I can't take Willy sailing as I'd arranged, but there are a couple of urgent cases I must see. Besides, I fancy this weather isn't going to last and the *meer* can be quite nasty if the wind rises.' He wandered towards her. 'Your headache is quite better?'

'Headache?' She remembered then. 'Oh, yes—yes, thank you—it wasn't a bad one.'

He said with faint mockery: 'I thought it wasn't. A pity that I should have returned home so soon after you had gone to your room.' And when she didn't answer: 'Well, I won't keep you from your breakfast. We shall meet at lunch, I hope.'

Her mother was too wise to ask after the headache. She launched into a rambling chat about a letter she had had from Doctor Cresswell, and Phyllida, listening with half an ear, wondered why Willy looked so glum. She wasn't kept in the dark for long.

'We should have gone sailing,' declared her brother. 'I was looking forward to it no end, and now Pieter says he can't—not today.' He made a hideous face. 'And you'll see, it'll be raining tomorrow and if it's fine he'll have more patients to see...'

'Well, he is a doctor,' Phyllida pointed out reasonably, 'and you've had a lot of fun—fishing and so on.'

Willy buttered toast and spread it with a slice of cheese. 'Yes, I know—it's been super, but there's only another week.'

'Well, let's do something else,' suggested Phyllida. 'Any ideas?'

'I think I'll borrow the bike in the garage and go for a spin.' The look he gave her was so angelic that she instantly suspected that he was up to something, but surely a bike ride was harmless enough.

'OK, I've got some letters to write. How about you, Mother?'

Mrs Cresswell looked vague. 'There was something— Oh, yes, I remember now, Bauke is going to take me round the glasshouses and the kitchen garden. We shan't understand a word each other's saying, but I don't see that it will matter.'

So they all dispersed to their various morning activities and it wasn't until a few minutes before lunch time that Phyllida, wandering into the garden room, wondered where everyone was. Her mother arrived just as she was thinking it and burst at once into an account of the delightful morning she had spent with Bauke. 'A taciturn man,' she observed, 'but a most knowledgeable one. We're going to spend another hour or two together before we go back. Where's Willy, dear?'

Phyllida had one ear cocked for the doctor's firm tread. 'I don't know, Mother—still cycling, I expect.'

'Not at all likely,' remarked his parent sapiently. 'He'll be near home; it's too near lunch time.' She sat down and sighed contentedly. 'See if you can find him, Phylly, he's sure to be grubby.'

There was no sign of him in the gardens near the house.

Phyllida went further afield, exploring the shrubbery paths, peering in the summer house and garden sheds, even the garages behind the house. The bike was still there and she frowned at the sight of it and went on down to the lake, its waters ruffled by a chilly little wind coming in gusts, shivering as she went, for the watery blue sky was clouding over rapidly. It took her a minute or two to register the fact that the yacht which had been moored to the jetty by the boathouse wasn't there, and another minute to find Willy's school blazer flung down carelessly beside the path.

He'd taken the yacht. That accounted for the innocence of the look he had given her at breakfast; he had meant to all along. Phyllida ran along the narrow path bordering the lake and then followed it beside the canal which led to the wide *meer* beyond, and presently reached its edge.

Quite close inshore was the yacht, just ahead of her, bowling merrily along—much too fast, she thought—before the blustery wind, and she could see Willy quite clearly in it. As she looked he caught sight of her and shouted something and waved, then turned away so sharply that she thought the boat would heel over. Surely Willy would have enough sense to hold the rudder steady? Apparently he hadn't, for the yacht was careering towards the centre of the *meer* and he was getting further away with every second.

She looked around her, seeking inspiration, trying not to feel frightened. There was a promontory half a mile further along the bank, standing well out into the water. If she could reach it before Willy she might be able to guide him towards it and beach the yacht. It was to be hoped that they could tie the yacht up; she worried for a minute about Pieter's reaction if they damaged it and then dismissed the thought; it was more important to get Willy out of his fix. She began to run, urged on by the rising wind and the first few drops of rain.

She reached the spit of land ahead of Willy, now heading away from it once more, and she hurried to its very edge, filled her lungs and bawled at him to steer towards her. 'Turn the rudder slowly,' she counselled at the top of her lungs, and almost before she had finished the yacht swung violently towards her, its sail almost touching the choppy water. 'Gently!' she called, and waited anxiously as the boat came towards her, much too fast. It wasn't like Willy to behave in such a way; he could do most things well and he had a solid common sense which had got him out of any number of awkward situations. Now he was waving at her and calling, but before she could catch what he was shouting, the yacht careered off again, only to turn in a few moments and come towards her once more, this time within hailing distance.

'What's up?'

'The rudder's broken.' He didn't sound too upset. 'I've got an oar and I'm trying to steer with it, but it's not much good.'

Phyllida had kicked off her shoes and tossed her cardigan onto the grass bank. 'Keep her steady if you can, I'll come out to you.'

She wasn't a strong swimmer and the water was very cold. And worse, Willy wasn't having much success in keeping the yacht on the same course. It was pure luck that the boat swerved towards her, coming so close that she was able to cling to its side, to be hauled aboard with a good deal of difficulty.

She subsided on to the deck, wringing wet, smelling of weed. 'Willy, I'll wring your neck!' she said forcefully, and then: 'What do we do first?'

Willy ignored her threat. 'If we both hang on to the oar—or perhaps we could tie it with something?'

'What?' She looked around her; the yacht was immaculate with everything in its place, but she didn't dare touch the ropes arranged so neatly in case something came adrift and they were worse off than ever.

'We'll hold it,' she decided, 'and try and steer to the bank somehow.' She looked up at the sky, shivering. The wind, freshening fast, had brought the rain with it.

She said suddenly: 'Willy, is there a horn?'

He gaped at her. 'A horn? Yes, of course—it's used when you go through a lock. Why?'

'Can you remember the Morse Code?'

'Yes, of course I can.'

'Well, do it on the horn. Is it three short, three long, three short, or the other way round?'

Her brother gave her a withering look. 'Girls!' he uttered with scorn. 'Can you manage the oar for a bit?'

Her teeth were chattering now; she was already so wet that the rain made no difference, except to make her feel worse. 'I'll have to, won't I? Willy, why did you do it? Have you any idea what Pieter is going to say when he discovers that you've taken his boat?'

'He's going to be angry—I daresay he'll ask us to go home.'

'Oh, you wretched boy! Go and blow that horn, for heaven's sake!'

Mrs Cresswell waited for ten minutes or so and then wandered to the window and looked out. There was no sign of either of her children; it was fortunate that Pieter was late for lunch; they might get back before he did. But after another ten minutes she became uneasy. She drank the sherry Aap had poured for her in an absent-minded fashion and wondered why they were so long—perhaps they could all come in together.

But presently the doctor came in alone, took one look at her face and asked: 'What's worrying you, Mrs Cresswell?'

'Well, I'm not exactly worried. I daresay I'm just being a fussy old woman...' She explained simply, adding: 'Willy did say that he was going to borrow the bike in the garden shed.'

The doctor went to look out of the window. 'We can check that easily enough,' he assured her, and pulled the bell rope by the fireplace, and when Aap came spoke briefly to him.

Aap went away and returned within a few minutes. The bicycle was still in the shed, he reported impassively.

'So he's fishing.'

Aap shook his head. All the rods were in their rightful places; he had looked on his way back from the garages. The doctor frowned, took another look at the rain and wind outside, then opened the french window and glanced around. It was while he was doing this that he became aware of the insistent blast of the horn.

He listened for a moment. 'Someone is sending out what I presume to be an SOS,' then: 'My God, it's the *Mireille*—that young devil's got her out on the *meer*!' He swung round. 'Aap, get me a jacket. Mrs Cresswell, don't worry, I'll be back with Willy and Phyllida very shortly.'

He took the anorak Aap was holding out to him, gave a satisfied grunt when he saw that Aap was putting on a similar garment, and made for the garden. Mrs Cresswell watched the pair of them walking briskly across the lawn, to disappear presently behind the shrubs at the far end.

The moment they were out of sight they broke into a run, the doctor covering the ground with his long legs at a great rate, and Aap, for all his stoutness, close on his heels. They followed the path Phyllida had taken and reached the edge of the *meer* in time to see the yacht veering away towards the opposite shore.

'What the hell...?' began Pieter furiously. 'Aap, I believe they've lost the rudder, and why don't they get the sail down?' His face was coldly ferocious. 'We'll get the speedboat out and get alongside her. Stay here—I'll pick you up.'

He went back, running fast, to the boathouse by the lake, and within a very short time came tearing through the canal, to pick up Aap and then roar out into the choppy water.

Phyllida, wrestling with the oar, watched his rapid approach with mixed feelings—relief, because she didn't want either Willy or herself to drown, and she could see no alternative at the moment, the way they were careering around and the weather getting nastier at every moment—and apprehension as to Pieter's reaction to seeing his lovely yacht exposed to some of the worst handling he might ever witness. Willy, hanging on to the oar beside her, gave a gusty sigh.

'It's like one of the gods coming to wreak vengeance! I'm scared. Are you, Phylly?'

'Not in the least,' she screamed at him above the wind, and

felt her insides turn to ice with fright. Pieter, she decided, was going to be far worse than the storm.

It looked as though she were right as the speedboat drew near. The doctor was standing, his face like a thundercloud, tearing off his anorak and then stooping to pick up a rope. If he threw it, she thought miserably, she would never catch it, she was rotten at catching things—Willy would have to do it; presumably they were to be towed in. The yacht, caught in a gust of wind, made a sweeping turn and started off merrily in the opposite direction so that she lost sight of the speedboat. But only for a moment; it roared into view once more, almost alongside, and she gave a gasping shriek as Pieter, the rope in his hand, jumped into the water. He was a powerful swimmer; before the yacht could turn again he had pulled himself on board and was tying the rope, turning to shout to Aap, still in the speedboat, taking no notice at all of her or Willy.

Aap shortened the distance between them and when he was alongside Pieter said: 'Over you go, Willy, into the boat with Aap, and look sharp!'

There was no question of disobeying him; he might be sopping wet, his hair plastered on his head, water dripping off him in great-pools, but that made no difference to his air of command. Willy did exactly as he had been told without so much as a word, landing awkwardly beside Aap, who grinned at him and nodded directions to sit down. Phyllida, expecting to go next, clutched the oar to her as though it were an old familiar friend and had it taken from her, none too gently.

'I would expect Willy to play those schoolboy pranks,' said the doctor in a voice which did nothing to reassure her, 'but you, Phyllida, what the hell possessed you?'

He had dumped her down on the deck and was reefing the sail with swift expertise, and she didn't bother to answer. Let him think what he liked, she thought furiously; she was cold and still frightened and wet and smelly and nothing mattered any more.

Aap was sidling away from the yacht, going ahead of her and turning slowly in the direction of the canal, and presently

Phyllida felt the yacht turn too, obedient to the pull of the tow rope. Pieter was hanging over the rudder, examining the break which had caused all the trouble. He turned his head to say: 'Well, you haven't answered my question. Why did you let Willy get on board in the first place?'

She pushed her soaking fringe out of her eyes. 'I didn't,' she raged at him, 'he was already in the middle of the *meer*. I had to swim out to help him.'

She choked at his amused smile. 'Swam, did you? Brave girl!' He turned away to do something to the tow rope and she said angrily to his enormous back: 'I certainly wouldn't have got on to your rotten old boat for any other reason.' Her voice shook. 'I thought Willy would drown!'

The yacht was dancing along through the rough water, the speedboat ahead, and they were almost at the canal. Pieter finished what he was doing and squatted down on the deck beside her. 'Are you very angry?' she asked in a small voice.

He flung a heavy wet arm round her shoulders. 'When I was ten—eleven, I did exactly the same thing, only the rudder didn't break. I got quite a long way before my father caught up with me. I was punished, of course, but the next day he took me out and taught me how to sail a boat.' His rage had gone, the smile he turned on her was very gentle. 'I think we'd better teach Willy how to sail too before he sinks everything in sight.'

'I'm sorry—we'll pay for the damage...' She had forgotten her rage. 'And I didn't mean it—about it being a rotten old boat.'

'I didn't think you did. Can you sail?'

'No.'

'Then I shall have to teach you too.'

'There won't be time.'

He had got to his feet, as they were entering the canal. 'All the time in the world, love.'

They were at the boathouse and he was shortening the tow rope, calling to Aap. 'And don't do that again, Phylly.'

She was on her feet too, relieved to see the jetty and dry land but reluctant to leave him. 'Do what?'

'Terrify me to my very bones.' He said softly: 'You could have drowned.'

He lifted her on to the jetty, fetched a blanket from the boathouse and wrapped her in it. 'Whose idea was it to send an SOS on the horn?' he wanted to know in an ordinary voice.

'Phylly's,' said Willy, 'and I did it.'

'Next time, boy, get it right. OSO isn't quite the same thing, only I happened to recognise the *Mereille's* horn. Off to the house with you, tell your mother you're safe and get dry and into other clothes—you can have fifteen minutes. After lunch you and I have to talk.'

Willy went red but met the doctor's eye bravely enough. 'Yes, you'll want to punish me. I'm sorry I did it.' He darted off, and the doctor spoke to Aap, busy with the boats, and took Phyllida's arm. 'And a hot bath and dry clothes for you, too.' He was walking her along so rapidly that she had to skip to keep up with him.

Steadying her chattering teeth, she asked: 'Am I to be talked to too?'

'There's nothing I should enjoy more,' he assured her, 'but we'll keep that until a more suitable time.' A remark she didn't take seriously.

They lunched at last, the doctor making light of the whole episode so that Mrs Cresswell shouldn't be upset. And afterwards he and Willy went along to the study, leaving Phyllida sitting uneasily with her mother in the drawing room.

'It was most considerate of Pieter to treat the whole thing as a joke,' remarked Mrs Cresswell. 'I hope he's giving Willy the talking-to of his life. Is he angry with you, too, dear?'

Phyllida glanced at her mother. She had thought they had done rather well at lunch, glossing over the whole adventure, but for all her vague ways, her parent was astute. 'I don't think so,' she said slowly.

'I should be very surprised if he were,' observed her mother. 'That girl—what's her name? is coming to tea—I heard Pieter on the telephone while you were upstairs.'

'But Mother, you can't understand Dutch.'

She was treated to a limpid stare. 'No, dear, but I happened to be sitting near him and he's far too well-mannered to speak Dutch when he knows I don't know a word.'

'Mother,' began Phyllida, 'you could have walked away.'

'So I could—I never thought of it. She's coming at four o'clock. Why not go and wash your hair properly, darling? You did it in a great hurry before lunch, I expect. It looks so soft and silky when it's just been done.'

'Mother!' said Phyllida again, then laughed. 'All right, I'll go now.'

She was glad presently that she had taken such pains with her hair and her face and that she had kept on the jersey shirt-waister. Its soft amber gave her a nice glow and contrasted favourably with Marena's flamboyant striped dress. Not that the girl didn't look quite wonderful—how could she help it with looks like hers?

Marena had driven herself over, greeted Pieter effusively, turned her charm on to Mrs Cresswell and smiled at Phyllida, dismissing her as not worth bothering about, just as she ignored Willy. A rather quiet Willy. After tea, when the other three had gone into the garden Phyllida asked him: 'Was he very cross, Willy? Did he suggest that we went back sooner, or anything like that?'

He shook his head. 'No—he gave me a good lecture.' Her brother swallowed. 'He's great, Phylly, and I like him a lot, but he can make you feel an inch high…when he'd finished he said he'd take me on the lake tomorrow if the weather was right and show me how to handle a boat.' He sighed loudly. 'I wish he was my brother.'

'You don't need any more brothers,' declared Phyllida crossly, and added severely: 'And don't you dare do anything else silly!'

The others came back then, Marena with her arm through Pieter's, looking like a sweet little kitten who'd found the cream jug.

They sat about talking for a little while longer and Phyllida did her best not to look at Pieter and Marena. The girl was at her most tiresome, talking about people only the two of them knew, leaning forward to touch his arm, smiling into his face. It was really more than Phyllida could bear. If only something would happen, she mused, something to change Pieter's manner towards her. He had always been friendly and kind and teased her a little, but she had been wrong in thinking that he was even a little in love with her. That had been wishful thinking on her part. Trying not to see Marena's lovely little hand patting Pieter's sleeve while she talked to him, Phyllida guessed that the next few days before they went home weren't going to be either easy or happy ones for her. She pinned a smile on her face now, and listened to Marena being witty about her holiday in Switzerland. To add to everything else, it seemed that she was expert on skis and even better on ice skates, and the horrid girl, drawing Phyllida into the talk, asked her the kind of questions that showed her up as a perfect fool on skates and an ignoramus when it came to skiing.

In the end, sick of the girl's barbed witticisms, Phyllida said a little too loudly: 'I'm no good at anything like that, but at least I can drive a car.' Which was a palpable hit because Marena, when she had arrived that afternoon, had knocked over a stone urn by the sweep, gone into reverse by accident, hit a tree, dented her bumper and then left all her lights on. Everyone had laughed it off at the time, but Phyllida, her gentle nature aroused, didn't see why she should get away with it.

Marena glared at her when she got up to go and ignored her as she said her goodbyes and went to the door with the doctor. When they were out of earshot Mrs Cresswell whispered, 'You were very rude, darling, but she deserved every word!'

Phyllida felt better about it then, but the feeling didn't last long, for when Pieter came back it seemed to her that his manner towards her was a little distant. Not that she cared about that in the very least, she told herself.

CHAPTER EIGHT

IT WAS disappointing that Phyllida didn't see Pieter all the next day until the evening. She had been shopping with her mother in the morning, lunching out and shopping again afterwards; they hadn't bought much, small presents for family and friends, but they had spent a good deal of time gazing into the enticing windows. By the time Aap had picked them up at the agreed rendezvous it was late afternoon, but there was no sign of their host as they sank into comfortable chairs in the small sitting room behind the drawing room and drank their tea, soothed by the peace and quiet of the old house.

'Bliss!' observed Mrs Cresswell on a contented sigh. 'I could hear a pin drop.' She took a sip of tea. 'When is Willy coming back?'

'Well, Pieter said he'd be staying to tea at the *dominee's* house.'

Mrs Cresswell ate a biscuit and followed her train of thought. 'Five more days. What a wonderful holiday we're having—I shall never forget it.'

'Nor shall I,' agreed Phyllida; she was going to remember it for the rest of her life, although perhaps not for the same reasons as her mother. 'I wonder where Pieter is—he's usually home just about now.'

Her mother darted her a look over her tea-cup. 'Well, dear, he's a busy man. Besides, he must have any number of friends—after all, we don't know a great deal about his life, do we?' She took another biscuit. 'I shall get fat, but these are so delicious. A pity we aren't likely to meet again once this holiday is over. I expect we shall exchange Christmas cards and I daresay Willy will write to him.' She sighed. 'The world is full of nice people one never gets to know.'

Phyllida, surveying a future without Pieter, felt like weeping.

'The minute I get back,' she told her mother with entirely false enthusiasm, 'I shall start looking for a job. I'll try for something in Bristol, it's not far from home and it'll make a nice change.'

'Yes, dear. Have you heard from Philip since you left?'

'Philip?' Phyllida looked blank. 'Oh, Philip—no, but I didn't expect to.'

Willy came in then, full of his day and all he had done and what he intended to do the next day. He was looking very well; the holiday had done him good at any rate, thought Phyllida; it had done her mother good too—she wasn't sure about herself.

She was pouring second cups when she heard the front door close, a murmur of voices in the hall and then Pieter's firm tread. Her colour was a little high as he sat down beside her mother, although she replied to his enquiries as to her day with composure.

It was her mother who brought up the subject of their return home. 'Ought we to book our places?' she asked, 'and will you tell us which is the best way to go, Pieter?'

He took a large bite of fruit cake. 'With me, of course—in the same way as we came, in the car.'

'Oh, but we couldn't—to take you away from your work...'

He got up and handed his cup to Phyllida, and when she had refilled it, sat down beside her. 'Well, you know, Mrs Cresswell, I am able to arrange my work to suit myself to a large extent, and it so happens that I've been asked by a colleague to see a patient in London within the next week or so. I can combine business with pleasure.'

Mrs Cresswell beamed at him. 'Won't that be nice—and of course you'll stay at least one night with us—longer if you can manage it.'

He glanced sideways at Phyllida's charming profile. 'That depends on circumstances, but I hope that I shall be able to accept your invitation.'

He uttered this formal speech with such blandness that Phyllida looked at him, to be met with a sleepy gaze which told her nothing at all. She occupied herself with the teapot and left him and her mother to make conversation.

But her mother got up presently, with a murmured observation that she was to visit the rockery with Bauke before it got too late, and since Willy was bidden to accompany her, Phyllida was left with the doctor. She sat for a minute or two, thinking up plausible excuses for going away too, and had just settled on the old and tried one of having to wash her hair, when her companion spoke.

'No, Phylly, your hair doesn't need washing, nor do you wish to write letters or take them to the post. Just relax, love, I shan't eat you.'

He lounged back beside her, his eyes half closed, contemplating his well-shod feet. He looked placid and easygoing, and if truth be told, sleepy, and yet Phyllida was aware that underneath all that he was as sharp as a needle, ready to fire awkward questions at her and make remarks she couldn't understand.

'Any plans?' he asked casually.

She hesitated. 'Vague ones—well, not so vague, really. It's time I got back into hospital again.'

'London?'

Her unguarded tongue was too ready with an answer. 'No, Bristol, I thought,' and then, furious with herself for having told him that: 'Probably not—I haven't decided.'

He had moved closer, one arm along the back of the sofa, behind her. 'That's good; I rather wanted to talk about your future, Phylly. We haven't seen as much of each other as I should have wished, all the same...' He paused and she held her breath, her heart thumping nineteen to the dozen while common sense told her that she was being a fool. In a minute she would know...

Aap propelled his cheerful rotundity through the door with a lightness of foot which made the doctor mutter something forceful under his breath.

'A gentleman to see Miss Cresswell,' announced Aap, ignoring the mutter.

Phyllida, brought down from the improbable clouds where she had been perched, said quickly: 'But I don't know any gentlemen,' and Pieter laughed. 'Ask him to come in, Aap,' he said in such a casual voice that she wondered if she had imagined the urgency in his voice not two minutes earlier.

Aap went away, to reappear almost at once, ushering in Philip Mount.

Phyllida caught her breath and jumped to her feet. 'Philip—why ever are you here? How did you find out where I was? What's the matter?'

Philip wasn't a man to be bustled into making hurried answers; he didn't say anything for a moment, only stood in the doorway, looking first at her and then at the doctor, standing beside her. At length he said: 'Hullo.'

The doctor stepped smoothly into the awkward silence. 'A friend of Phyllida's?' he wanted to know pleasantly. 'How delightful.' He crossed the room and shook Philip's hand. 'Pieter van Sittardt. I've heard of you, of course.'

His visitor shook hands cautiously. 'Oh, have you?'

'You'll want to have a talk—I'll get someone to bring in some coffee—do make yourself at home, and I hope you'll stay to dinner.'

He waved Philip to a chair, smiled benignly at him, beamed at Phyllida, standing there as though she were stuffed, and went away so quickly that no one else had a chance to say a word. Phyllida gnashed her teeth; there had been no need for Pieter to be quite so hospitable; he had almost flung Philip at her—perhaps he felt that providence, in the shape of Philip Mount, had saved him in the nick of time from saying something to her which he might have regretted. She sat down rather abruptly and Philip asked sharply:

'Who's he?'

'You heard—our host.' She had found her voice at last. 'Why on earth are you here?'

He took no notice of her question. 'He said he'd heard of me—from you?'

'Well, I suppose so.' She felt as though she had been blindfolded, turned round three times and abandoned. She asked again: 'Why are you here, Philip?'

'To see you, of course.'

'But why?'

He answered with a smugness which made her seethe. 'I knew you wouldn't forget me—and you haven't, have you? talking about me to what's-his-name.'

'Doctor van Sittardt. And I haven't been talking about you. I may have mentioned you by name, that's all.'

She broke off as Aap came in with the coffee tray, walking slowly so that he could get a good look at the unexpected guest. Phyllida poured coffee for them both, asked Philip if he wanted a biscuit in a snappy voice and waited. Philip had always been deliberate, now he was maddeningly so.

'I had a few days off,' he told her. 'I telephoned your home and your sister told me where you were. I've come to take you back with me.'

'Whatever for? I don't want to go. You're mad, Philip!' She had got to her feet. 'I'm not staying to listen to any more of your nonsense!'

He put his coffee cup down and got up too. 'It's not nonsense, Phyllida; just because you've been living it up for the last few weeks, you've lost all your good sense. I suppose you think you're in love with this fellow—well, stop your day-dreaming and be your sensible self again. Come back with me and we'll start again.'

'I don't want to start again!' Her voice rose several octaves. 'Can't you understand? I don't want...' He had crossed the room and caught her clumsily in his arms.

'Don't be a silly girl,' he begged her. 'Once you're married to me...'

He was facing the door and she felt his arms slacken around her. Someone had come in, and she knew at once who it was.

'So sorry,' said the doctor with loud cheerfulness. 'I should have remembered. You really must stay to dinner, Mount, and spend the night too.'

Philip's voice sounded stiff and sullen. 'Thanks—I'd like to stay to dinner; I've already booked at an hotel for the night.'

'Splendid!' Pieter smiled, his eyes icily bright beneath their lids. 'Aap shall show you where you can freshen up presently, but while Phyllida changes we'll have a drink. You're a doctor, are you not? What do you specialise in?'

He barely glanced at Phyllida as he opened the door for her, and when she peeped at him, she could see a mocking little smile on his face.

Her mother and Willy weren't to be found. She bathed and dressed in the new tunic, did her hair and face with tremendous care and sat down to wait until the very last minute before dinner. The idea of spending even a few minutes with Philip made her feel quite sick. Somehow she would have to get Pieter alone and explain...

She had no chance; when she eventually went downstairs it was to find not only Pieter with his unexpected guest, but her mother, Willy, Pieter's mother and father and Marena, grouped around the log fire, having what appeared to be a high old time over drinks.

Pieter crossed the room to her as she stood, quite taken aback, just inside the door. The nasty little smile was still there, she saw uneasily, and he observed just as nastily: 'A new dress? Very charming—kept for Philip, I suppose.'

'You suppose wrong,' snapped Phyllida very quietly so that no one else could hear. 'It's a new dress, but I bought it for...' She couldn't tell him that she had bought it for his benefit; she closed her mouth firmly and glared at him.

'You didn't know that he was coming?' His soft voice held incredulity.

'Of course I didn't! Pieter—oh, Pieter...'

'Oh, Phylly!' His voice mocked her. 'What will you have to drink?'

Hemlock would have been a good choice, she thought silently, but aloud she settled for a dry sherry and went to speak to his parents.

Marena was talking to her mother and neither of them looked over-happy. Phyllida smiled emptily at them both and drank her sherry far too quickly, plunging into an animated conversation with Mevrouw van Sittardt and puzzling that lady considerably by answering her questions with a series of random replies, engendered by the sherry and her chaotic thoughts. Out of the corner of her eye she had seen Marena leave her mother and go and stand by Pieter, so close that she was almost in his pocket. No one, she thought bitterly, had warned her that there was to be company for dinner. Which was hardly surprising since the doctor had made lightning telephone calls to his guests at the last minute, intimating that a close friend of Phyllida had arrived to see her and it seemed a good idea to invite a few people to meet him.

His parents had arrived full of curiosity, although to look at their dignified calm, no one would have guessed it; Marena had accepted gleefully, wanting to see Phyllida's close friend. Only Mrs Cresswell had accepted the situation with placid calm, apparently doing nothing about it, merely waiting to see what would happen. She had greeted Philip with well concealed surprise, asked kindly after his well-being and engaged Marena in conversation. But now, seeing her daughter looking quite distracted, Mrs Cresswell wandered over to Pieter and Marena, prised her away from him with a ruthless charm which made his blue eyes sparkle with appreciation, and wandered off again, Marena in tow, beckoning to Philip and talking to Willy as she did so.

'Philip, I don't know if Pieter told you, but Marena is an artist—so clever of her, because she's far too pretty to do anything at all, don't you agree?'

Her listeners swallowed this barefaced flattery with no trouble at all; Marena had such a good opinion of herself that she found it not in the least unusual that other people should share it, and as for Philip, he had been staring at her ever since she had entered the room and had longed to talk to her, something his host hadn't seemed to think he might want to do, for he had stationed Philip in front of him so that he had had no more than a glimpse of her from time to time because the doctor's broad person had quite blocked his view.

Mrs Cresswell, standing between them, listened with interest to Philip, usually so staid, letting himself go. The pair of them, she considered, were ideally suited. She sipped her sherry and glanced around the room, to encounter the doctor's hard stare. She returned it with a vague smile and presently he strolled over and invited her to admire the charming view from the window. They stood for a minute admiring the riot of colour outside.

'Mother love is a wonderful thing,' observed the doctor silkily.

'Oh, indeed, yes,' agreed Mrs Cresswell imperturbably, 'it should never be underestimated.'

'How right, Mrs Cresswell. The pity of it is that it is so often called into action when none is required.'

She turned to look at him. 'Interfering?' she asked. 'Now that's something I never do, Pieter.' She gave him one of her vague, sweet smiles. 'What a lovely girl Marena is.'

He didn't answer her, only smiled a little, and a moment later Aap appeared to bid them to dinner.

Later, during a mostly sleepless night, Phyllida reviewed the evening. It had been pure disaster for her; Philip had been placed next to her at table and Pieter had treated her with the politeness of a good host with whom she was only slightly acquainted, and was bent on giving her every opportunity to be alone with Philip. And the awful thing had been that Philip, although he had stuck to her like a leech, could hardly take his eyes off Marena. And when she had tried to get him alone—really alone where they could talk without anyone overhearing them—it had been impossible; Pieter might have contrived in the most ostentatious manner possible that they should be in each other's company, and yet each time she had sneaked off into a quiet corner with Philip, he had materialised like an evil genie and swept them back with the other guests.

Of one thing she was fairly sure—Philip might have come with the intention of asking her to marry him, under the impression that he loved her, but now that he had actually seen her again, he'd gone off her completely. An arrangement which suited her very well if only Pieter hadn't foiled her every chance to tell Philip that. He had even insisted that Philip should call round on the following morning: 'For I'm rather booked up myself,' he had observed urbanely, 'but do consider yourself at home—I hope to be back for lunch, and I'll see you then.' He had added blandly: 'I had arranged to drive Phyllida back, but if she wants to, by all means take her with you.'

And he hadn't even asked her what she had wanted to do! fumed Phyllida, sitting up in bed, choking with temper at the mere memory. 'If he wants to get rid of me, he can,' she cried loudly, 'then he can spend all the time he wants with his beastly Marena. I can't think why he asked me in the first place...'

She had cried then and gone to sleep with puffy red eyes and a pink nose. Her eyes were still puffy when she went down to breakfast, but she hadn't bothered to find her dark glasses; Pieter had said he had a busy morning—at the hospital, she supposed, or Marena, of course.

He was occupied with neither. He was sitting at his breakfast table, chatting pleasantly to Mrs Cresswell and discussing the chances of another fishing trip with Willy. He stood up as Phyllida went in, wished her a cheerful good morning, asked her if she had a cold and added: 'Your eyes are puffy,' before begging her to help herself to anything she fancied.

She didn't fancy anything. She crumbled toast on her plate and drank several cups of coffee and had great difficulty in not throwing a plate at his head when he suggested that she should take a couple of Panadol tablets. 'So that you'll feel up to young Mount's company. Have you decided if you are going back with him, Phylly?'

'If Phylly can bear it, I'd much rather she went back with us,' interposed Mrs Cresswell. 'I really cannot manage by myself,' she explained plaintively. She wasn't going to have to lift a finger, everyone knew that, but Phyllida couldn't agree fast enough, the relief in her voice so obvious that Pieter's mouth twitched and his eyes danced with laughter. But all he said, and that seriously, was:

'Of course—I should have remembered that. Mount will be disappointed.'

'No, he won't,' she snapped, tossing her fringe with a pettish shake of her head. 'I can't think why he came in the first place.'

'My dear Phylly,' his voice was very smooth, 'isn't it obvious why he came?'

She went a fiery red, a dozen furious words on her tongue waiting to be uttered, but she had no chance. Willy said in a matter-of-fact voice: 'He's such a saphead I never thought he'd come after you, Phylly—I mean, he's not really stuck on you, is he?' He added with brotherly candour: 'I daresay he fancied you for a bit—you're not bad to look at, you know.'

This remark was received in silence. The doctor's face was impassive and he had dropped the lids over his eyes so that no one could see their expression. Mrs Cresswell buttered a roll with deliberation before remarking: 'I do not like to curb the young, Willy, but I think that you have rather overreached yourself.' And Phyllida stared at him and then burst out laughing, only half way through the laughter changed to tears. Pieter jumped to his feet, but before he could reach her, she had rushed out of the room.

Pieter sat down again. He said thoughtfully, looking at Mrs Cresswell: 'I can but guess at the reason for that; I can only hope that I have guessed correctly.'

Neither of his two companions answered him; Willy for the obvious reason that it might be better to hold his tongue for a while, and his mother because she could see that the doctor required no answer.

He went away presently and as soon as the Bentley had disappeared Philip arrived in the local taxi and Phyllida came downstairs, greeted him quite cheerfully, explained that she was wearing dark glasses because she had a slight headache, and agreed readily to go for a walk.

She had had a good cry upstairs and time to think. She would have to pretend that she intended to marry Philip because that was what Pieter wanted. They had got a little too friendly, but only through force of circumstances; now he wanted to get back to his Marena. She hadn't been able to understand his bad temper of the previous evening, nor guess at what he had been going to say just before Philip arrived, but it couldn't have been what she had hoped and now she would never know. Besides, he had fairly flung her at Philip... She had stopped thinking about it, otherwise she'd cry again, and had allowed her mind to dwell on their first meeting on Madeira. He had been so easy to like...to love...

She took Philip for a long walk, following the narrow brick roads between the canals, carefully pointing out anything of interest as they went. They had walked for more than half an hour before Philip, abandoning the threadbare theme of the weather upon which she had been harping, said: 'You met this fellow on Madeira, didn't you? I suppose he turned your head and now you fancy you're in love with him, just as I was saying when he interrupted us. He's got a girl anyway, that little beauty who came to dinner.' He added, not unkindly: 'You haven't a chance; you're pretty enough in a nice open-air way, but she's gorgeous.'

Phyllida had stopped so that she might steady her breath and answer him with calm. She would have liked to have screamed at him, but that would have done no good—besides, she had realised something in the last few moments.

She said with an entirely false enthusiasm: 'She's terrific, she's known Pieter van Sittardt for simply ages and I suppose they'll marry sooner or later, but I don't know—I'm not sure if she's in love with him, or he with her.' She added distractedly: 'It's hard to tell, isn't it? Philip, all this time while you thought you were in love with me you weren't, you only thought you were, and now you've discovered you aren't. We get on well, I told you that, but you wouldn't listen, and that's not the same as loving someone. I'm not saying you're in love with Marena, but she excites you as I never did, doesn't she? One day you'll find a girl like her.' She stopped because it had just occurred to her that she would never find a man quite like Pieter, even if she searched for the rest of her life.

'She's wonderful,' said Phillip. 'Why can't I meet a girl like that? Clever and stunning to look at...' He went on awkwardly: 'I say, Phylly, I didn't mean to say that—I mean, you're very pretty and no end of a good companion, but you're right—I came over here intending to ask you to marry me, but now...' He paused and she finished for him:

'And now you've seen me, and you don't want to. Well I don't want to either, so don't waste time on me, Philip; there must be hundreds of girls like Marena—you'll just have to look for them. Why don't you ask her out to dinner? She might have sisters or friends or—or someone...'

They had turned for home once more, not hurrying. 'Well, as a matter of fact I did ask her if she'd have dinner with me. I'll have to go back tomorrow some time, but I can catch the night ferry. She wants to show me her paintings.'

Phyllida stifled a giggle. Marena must have heard that one about men asking girls up to see their etchings—only hers were paintings.

Philip gave her a look of suspicion. 'Why are you giggling?'

'Oh, I'm not,' she denied hastily. 'Philip, don't get too serious, will you? It wouldn't be fair to cut out Pieter.'

He gave an angry laugh. 'Good lord, I've never met a man more capable of getting his own way! I thought his mother was a bit of a tartar, too.'

'She's a darling,' said Phyllida warmly, instantly up in arms. 'She's a bit—well, large, but she's kind and—and...'

'Oh dear,' his voice mocked her. 'I had no idea you were so keen on her, but I suppose that's natural.'

They could see the house now, through the trees. 'It's a wonderful place he's got here. We had quite a chat yesterday evening. Can't say that I like him, though.'

She thought it very likely that Pieter didn't like him either, but she didn't say so. There was no point in stirring things up; heaven knew that the muddle was bad enough as it was. But at least she and Philip could part finally and on friendly terms. She would go back home, start all over again and forget Pieter and his family and those nice friends of his on Madeira and the brief period of happiness she had had.

'You're not listening,' complained Philip. 'I was telling you about this new job I've applied for.'

Phyllida said she was sorry and gave her full attention to him prosing on about senior registrars' posts and getting a consulting job in a few years' time and his expectations from an elderly grandparent which was going to make his future a decidedly better one. It lasted until they were within a few yards of the garden room, where they paused.

'I've enjoyed this walk,' said Philip in a voice which implied that he hadn't expected to. 'You're an easy person to talk to, Phylly. You don't mind? Us splitting up, I mean.'

Just as though they hadn't split up weeks ago, only he hadn't accepted it then. 'No, I don't mind, Philip, truly I don't—I hope you find a smashing girl and carve a splendid career for yourself, you've started that already.'

'Yes, I haven't done so badly,' he answered her complacently, and put his hands on her shoulders. 'No hard feelings, then?'

He bent to kiss her just as she became aware that the doctor was standing at the open door of the garden room, watching them.

She wriggled free of Philip, muttering that she must tidy herself for lunch and ran indoors, passing Pieter without looking at him, only to be halted by a large hand on her arm. 'So sorry,' he said softly and sikily, 'I always turn up at the wrong moment, don't I?'

She didn't answer, only ducked her head and rushed across the room and out into the hall, to pound up the staircase as though the devil were after her, not stopping until she had reached her room and shut the door. But there was no time in which to have the good howl she ached to have. She did her face, combed her silky hair and went downstairs again, this time at a sedate pace, to find everyone in the drawing room drinking sherry.

Afterwards, she couldn't remember what she had eaten at lunch, nor did she remember a single word she had spoken; presumably she had been quite normal, as no one had stared at her. And after lunch Philip had gone, but only after the doctor had wished him goodbye and then pointedly swept her mother and Willy out into the garden leaving her and Philip together in the hall. It was a pity that there had been no one there to see them shake hands.

There was just one day left now before they were to return home. She spent the night dithering between wishing that Pieter would spend the whole of it at home, and praying fervently that she wouldn't have to see him again until they left. As a consequence she went downstairs to breakfast in the dark glasses again, with a splitting headache and in a frightful temper.

Pieter was at breakfast, although he left within a few minutes of her arrival at the table. During those few minutes he had been his usual placid self, touching only briefly on their journey and reminding them that they would all be dining with his parents that evening. 'And I'm free for a couple of hours after lunch,' he told Willy. 'We might have a last try at catching a pike.' With which he left them, looking so cheerful and normal that she could have thrown something at him.

She mooned about after breakfast, packing for herself and for Willy, strolling round the garden with her mother, and then at her brother's request, walking down to the village for some last-minute trifles he simply had to have. It seemed an age until lunch time and even Lympke's offer to show her the kitchens, semi-basement but still kitchens which a woman might dream of and never have, wasn't sufficient to take her mind off her own troubles. All the same, she admired their size and old-world charm and all the well-concealed modern gadgets. She hoped that when Marena married Pieter, she would appreciate it all. Somehow she doubted that.

When she went into the drawing room, Pieter was already there although her mother and Willy were nowhere to be seen, which seemed strange because she had heard them go down earlier.

'They're down at the lake,' his voice was disarmingly casual. 'The swans are taking the cygnets for their first swim. What will you drink?'

'Sherry, thank you. Have you had a busy morning?'

'Yes, very. And what have you been doing?' He shot her a glance from under his brows. 'You must miss young Mount.'

She didn't answer that. 'I've been for a walk with Willy and then Lympke took me round the kitchens. They're very—nice,' she finished lamely.

His firm mouth twitched slightly. 'Yes, aren't they? Is there anything you would like to do this afternoon? Shopping? Aap can drive you into Leiden or den Haag.'

They were like two polite strangers and she thought with longing of their easy comradeship. 'No, thank you—I think we've got everything. I expect Mother will want to go round the gardens just once more and I'll go with her, I expect.'

He said carelessly: 'Oh, by all means. Willy and I will be at the lake until tea-time, we don't need to leave for den Haag until seven o'clock.'

He had arranged things very well; she would see almost nothing of him for the rest of the day.

And she didn't, not until the evening, when clad in the jersey tunic, she went downstairs. Pieter and Willy had gone back to the lake after tea and she was reasonably sure that no one would be down yet, as they hadn't returned until almost half past six.

She was wrong. As she reached the hall, Pieter's study door was opened and he came out, dressed for the evening in one of his dark grey, beautifully cut suits; another man entirely from the rubber-booted, sweatered figure which had come hurrying in not half an hour earlier.

He greeted her smilingly and set her teeth on edge with the remark: 'You shouldn't waste that pretty dress on us, you know. What will you drink?'

Phyllida astonished herself and him by asking for whisky, a drink she loathed, but somehow the occasion called for something strong. She sipped it cautiously, trying not to pull a face, and didn't see the amusement in his eyes.

'Was Mount going back today?' asked the doctor casually.

'Yes—on the night ferry. Did you have a busy morning?'

He was kind enough not to remind her that she had asked him that already before lunch, but sketched in his activities at the hospital until Mrs Cresswell and Willy joined them.

The short ride to den Haag was fully taken up with lighthearted talk of the next day's journey, and the other three didn't appear to notice Phyllida's silence. Between her 'yeses' and 'noes' and 'reallys' she was wondering if Marena was going to be there too. Very likely, although it didn't matter any more now. If only she could have had five minutes alone with Pieter while she explained about Philip and herself in the lucid language one always thought of in bed in the dead of night. At least it would clear the air and they could part friends, but he had given her no chance to talk—really talk—while they had been waiting for her mother and Willy, and even if he had, she thought mournfully, she would quite likely have burst into tears.

With an effort she stopped thinking about it and arranged her features into a suitable expression of pleasure at meeting Pieter's parents again.

The evening lasted for ever, with leisurely drinks in the magnificent drawing room, preceding an equally leisurely dinner in the sombre Biedermeier dining room. Marena wasn't there and her name wasn't mentioned until very shortly before they left, when Mevrouw Sittardt asked her son: 'And have you seen Marena, Pieter? She telephoned here earlier today, thinking you might be with us.'

'I saw her this morning, Mama.' Mother and son exchanged a long look and Mevrouw van Sittardt nodded her elegant head, smiling a little. Phyllida, her ears stretched to hear everything Pieter said, had heard the brief conversation but hadn't seen the look. She gazed unseeingly at Pieter's father, telling her a gently meandering tale about something or other, not hearing a word of it, wishing she were anywhere other than where she was; as far away from Pieter as possible, and wishing at the same time that she could stay for the rest of her life near him.

But the doctor appeared to have no such feeling of reluctance at the thought of seeing the last of her. He chatted amiably about her future prospects as he drove home at speed, saw them all safely indoors, bade them a cheerful goodnight and took himself off in the car again.

He got back at two o'clock exactly. Phyllida, who had been lying awake listening for his return, had heard the great Friesian wall clock in the hall boom twice in its majestic voice as Pieter's quiet step mounted the stairs and crossed the corridor to his own room.

Of course he had been with Marena. She stayed awake for another two hours, her imagination running riot, until sheer exhaustion sent her finally to sleep.

CHAPTER NINE

THE RETURN TO England went smoothly. To Phyllida, sitting in the back of the Bentley with her mother, it went far too quickly too. Pieter had hardly spoken to her beyond polite enquiries as to her comfort, observations upon the weather and the remark that she looked tired. It wasn't until they were speeding in the direction of Shaftesbury with the greater part of their journey behind them that she found herself sitting beside him. She wasn't sure how this had happened; they had stopped because Willy had been thirsty and she had found herself propelled gently into the front seat without being able to do much about it. She sat silent, turning just a little sideways, so that she could watch his large capable hands on the wheel. They had covered quite a few miles before he spoke. 'Will you be seeing young Mount?'

'No.' She added hastily: 'Well, not straight away.' It would never do for him to discover that she and Philip, although they had parted friends, were unlikely to meet again.

The doctor grunted. 'It seems a long time since we first met.'

She was breathless. 'Yes, ages.'

'The de Meesters asked after you in their last letter—they would like you to visit them again.'

'That's very kind of them, but I don't suppose I shall ever go back to Madeira.'

'What's happened to us, Phylly?' he asked softly. 'Or rather, what's happened to you?'

It was difficult to get the words out. 'Me? Nothing—what should have happened? I've had a lovely holiday and now I've got to find a job.' She added for good measure: 'I can hardly wait!'

His voice was casual. 'And Philip—he won't mind you working?'

'It's no busi… He won't mind in the least.'

He slid the car past a coach load of tourists. 'I must confess I'm puzzled, Phylly—I understood you to say that you weren't going to marry young Mount. But of course when he turned up unexpectedly like that, you probably realised that you'd made a mistake.'

She muttered something or other, longing to tell him just how she felt, wondering what he would say if she told him that she loved him to distraction. He would be very nice about it, but it was hardly likely that it would alter his feelings for Marena. She sighed, a sad little sound which caused him to glance at her quickly and then again, a little smile lifting the corners of his mouth. When he spoke he sounded very matter-of-fact. 'We shan't be long now—half an hour, I would think.'

Home looked lovely as the car swooped gently down the hill and up the other side, and when they stopped before the door there was Beryl to welcome them and a moment later Doctor Cresswell. Everyone talked at once, unloading luggage, urging the travellers to go indoors, offering refreshment. They all surged into the sitting room finally, still talking and laughing, and Phyllida, watching her family clustered round Pieter, suddenly couldn't bear it any longer. He would be gone soon; she had heard him say only a moment ago that although he had hoped to spend the night with them, he had discovered that it wouldn't be possible after all. She slid out of the room and into the kitchen, where the kettle was boiling its head off beside the waiting teapot. She made the tea, put on the lid and then stood looking at it, willing herself not to cry. She didn't hear Pieter come in and it wasn't until he spoke that she whisked round to face him.

'Well, I must be on my way, Phylly.' He smiled at her and her heart rocked. 'I had hoped…' he paused and sighed gustily. She felt his hands on her shoulders and his light kiss on her cheek.

'I'm not a great lover of poetry,' he told her, 'but there's a verse by John Clare which seems appropriate to the occasion; it goes something like this: ''Last April Fair, when I got bold with beer—I loved her long before, but had a fear to speak.'' I don't know how it ends, but I hope he was luckier than I.'

He had gone as quietly as he had come, out of the room, into the hall, out of the house. Out of her life.

She stood exactly as he had left her for the space of several seconds while the verse rang in her ears. Suddenly she gave a small scream, galloped out of the room in her turn and flung herself at the front door which she banged behind her, to slide to a shaky halt by the Bentley.

Pieter was behind the wheel and the engine was ticking over nicely.

'Pieter—Pieter, don't go. You can't go!' Her voice rose to a wail. 'Can't you see, it's not me and Philip—you thought it was, didn't you? and I pretended it was because I thought it was you and Marena, but it's not, it's you and me, Pieter. Pieter darling!'

He switched off the engine, got out of the car unhurriedly and opened his arms. They were gentle and strong around her, crushing her to his great chest so that it was hard for her to breathe.

'My own dear darling, you've got it right at last.' He smiled down at her and her heart, already doing overtime, leapt into her throat so that she couldn't speak. Not that it mattered. He bent his head and kissed her, soundly and at length, and she kissed him back.

'My darling girl, I love you,' said Pieter in the kind of voice which left her in no doubt about it. And Mrs Cresswell, happening to glance out of her bedroom window at that moment, had no doubts either. She hurried downstairs to tell her husband, talking to herself as she went. 'I thought they never would—at least, Pieter knew, but Phylly—dear child, so dense sometimes!' Her thoughts kept pace with her hurrying feet. 'I shall wear one of those large flowery hats—the bride's mother always does…' She broke off to say to Willy, coming upstairs towards her: 'Wash your hands, dear. I think Pieter and Phylly have just got engaged.'

'Oh, good—now I can go and stay with them and fish. Pieter will like that.'

It was hardly the moment in which to tell the boy that his future brother-in-law might not share his enthusiasm, at least not for the first few months. She said: 'Yes, dear, won't that be nice? Don't forget your hands,' and hurried on down to the study.

Phyllida, being kissed again, found the breath to mutter: 'I thought you were in love with Marena. Oh, Pieter, I'm crazy about you,' and then: 'You were going away.'

She felt his chest heave with laughter. 'No, my dearest girl, I wasn't going away. I thought that if I came and sat in the car you might think that I was…'

She stared at him and then began to laugh. 'Pieter, oh, Pieter!' and then seriously: 'You won't do it again, will you?'

'Leave you? No, my darling, I'll never do that.'

They didn't notice when the milkman stopped his float alongside the Bentley; they didn't notice as he squeezed past them, nor did they hear his cheerful good morning. He left his bottle on the doorstep and wriggled past them once more.

'All I can say is,' said the milkman to no one in particular, 'it's a very good morning for some of us, and that's a fact.'

THE COURSE OF TRUE LOVE

by

Betty Neels

CHAPTER ONE

MARCH was doing exactly as it should; it had come in like a lamb, now it was going out like a lion. An icy rain driven by a roaring wind was sweeping the streets clear of all but those unfortunates who had been forced to go out. And these, needless to say, were scuttling along, anxious to get within doors as fast as possible.

There was a long queue half-way down the street, an impatient line of people under umbrellas, jostling for position, ready to rush forward when their bus arrived. The girl at the end of the queue edged away from the drips running down the back of her neck from the umbrella behind her and sighed resignedly. It had been a long day and she was tired and home was still a bus ride away; she could not even tell if she would be lucky enough to get on to the next bus…

It came, sending great splashes of water from the gutter as it slowed to a halt. The queue surged forward. The owner of the umbrella gave her a vicious poke in the back as the slow-moving elderly man in front of her stepped back and planted a foot on her instep. She gave a gasp of pain and came to an involuntary halt, to be instantly swept aside by those behind her. Which meant one foot, the injured one, in the muddy water of the gutter.

The bus went, taking with it almost all the queue, leaving the girl to lift a dripping foot back on to the pavement and hobble to join it once more. But she didn't reach it; the car which had drawn up behind the bus edged forward and stopped beside her and the driver got out.

He looked even taller than he actually was in the light of the street lamps and she couldn't see him very clearly. He said with decided impatience, 'Are you hurt? I saw what happened. Get into the car, I'll drive you home.'

She looked up from the contemplation of torn tights and a trickle of blood. 'Thank you; I prefer to go by bus.' Her voice was a pretty as her face but there was a decided chill to it.

'Don't be a fool, young woman, I've no intention of kidnapping you. Besides, you look hefty enough to take care of yourself.' He ignored her outraged gasp. 'Don't keep me waiting, I have an appointment.' The impatience was even more decided.

Still smarting from having her Junoesque and charming person referred to as hefty, the girl took his proffered arm and allowed herself to be settled beside him. 'Where to?' he asked, and slid into the stream of traffic.

The girl gave a delicate sniff; the car was a Rolls-Royce and smelled of leather and, faintly, of cologne. She said in her nice voice, still chilly though, 'You should have asked me before I got into the car, which I wouldn't have done if you hadn't been so impatient. Meadow Road, a turning off Stamford Street. That's…'

'I know where it is. Which number?'

'Fifteen.' She added, 'It's quite a long way. You could drop me off at a bus-stop; I shall be quite all right.'

He didn't answer, and after a moment she realised that he wasn't going to. She glanced at her foot; it had left a muddy, watery mark on the car's splendid carpet and it was bleeding sluggishly. Nothing serious, she decided.

They crossed the river and he turned the car into the busy streets around Waterloo station and then, without being told, into Meadow Road, a dingy street which didn't live up to its name for there wasn't a blade of grass throughout its length. Its houses were bay-windowed with steps leading to shabby front doors, and iron railings concealed the semi-basements. Her companion stopped before number fifteen and got out. It surprised her when he opened her door and offered a hand. She stood on the pavement, looking up at him; she was a tall girl but she had to look quite a way.

'Thank you, you were most kind. I hope you won't be late for your appointment.'

'What is your name?'

She answered matter-of-factly, 'Claribel Brown. What's yours?'

'Marc van Borsele. And now that we are introduced, I will come in with you and see to that foot.'

She saw then that he held a case in one hand. 'You're a doctor?'

'Yes.'

There seemed no point in arguing with him. 'Very well, though I'm perfectly able...'

'Let us waste no more time in polite chat.'

Claribel opened the gate to the basement with rather more force than necessary and led the way down the worn steps to her front door. In the sombre light of the street lamp its paint shone in a vibrant red and there were tubs on either side, holding the hopeful green shoots of daffodils. She got out her key and had it taken from her and the door opened. He switched on the light, too, and then stood aside for her to enter.

There was a tiny lobby and an inner door leading to the living-room, small and perforce dark but very cosy. The furniture was mostly second-hand but had been chosen with care, and there was an out-of-date gas fire under the narrow mantelshelf. The one easy chair was occupied by two cats, one black and white, one ginger, curled up together. They unrolled themselves as Claribel went in, muttered softly at her, and curled up again.

'Do come in,' said Claribel unnecessarily, for he was already right behind her.

They stood for a moment and studied each other. Claribel was a pretty girl, almost beautiful with golden hair drawn back rather too severely into a knot, green eyes and a straight nose above a generous mouth. She was tall and magnificently built and looked a good deal younger than her twenty-eight years.

She stared back at her companion, frowning faintly because he was staring even harder. He was well over six feet, she supposed, and big with huge shoulders. He was also good-looking in a formidable way, with dark hair, sprinkled with grey, an aggressive nose, a firm thin mouth and dark eyes. He might be any age between thirty-five and forty, she guessed, and he had a nice taste in dress: conservative but elegant.

'Be good enough to take off your tights or whatever and let me see that foot.' He glanced at his watch. 'I can spare five minutes.'

The arrogance of the man! Someone should take him in hand, Claribel thought as he turned to undo his case. She whipped off her tights, sat down on a small upright chair and held her foot out.

There was more mud and blood; he poked and prodded, remarked that she would have a bruised foot but nothing worse and suggested that she should wash it. 'That's if you have a bathroom?'

She bit back what she would liked to have said in reply and went through the door at the back of the room and shut it behind her. The bathroom was a pokey little place reached through her bedroom; she cleaned her foot and whisked back to find him standing before the watercolour hanging over the mantelpiece.

'Your home?' he wanted to know.

'Yes.'

'The west country?'

'Yes.' She had sat down and was holding her foot once more. 'You said you had five minutes...'

He sat on his heels, used penicillin powder, gauze and strapping and then stood up. 'You don't like me,' he observed.

'I don't know you. Thank you for your help. You were kind.'

'I am not a particularly kind man.' He closed his case and she opened the door and held out a nicely kept hand.

'Goodbye, Dr van Borsele.'

He shook it briefly. 'Goodbye. You live alone?'

She was surprised. 'Yes. Well, there are Enoch and Toots...'

'I trust that you don't open your door to strangers or accept lifts from those you don't know.'

Her pretty mouth dropped open. 'Well! You insisted on bringing me home and here you are telling me...' She strove to keep her voice at a reasonable level. 'I never accept lifts and I certainly don't open my door. Whatever do you take me for?'

'The most beautiful girl I have seen for a long time.' He didn't smile. 'Goodnight, Claribel.'

She bolted the door after him and stood listening to him driving away.

'What an extraordinary man,' she observed to her cats, 'and much too sure of himself.'

She went into the kitchenette and began to get her supper, all the while considering ways and means of deflating his arrogance. 'I dare say he's quite nice,' she mused out loud, 'once one gets beneath that cold manner. Perhaps he is crossed in love. Or unhappily married. And what's he doing here in London if he's Dutch?'

She dished up her omelette and sat down at the table in the living-room to eat it. 'I wonder what he does? Private practice, or just on a visit, or at one of the hospitals?'

She finished her supper, fed the cats and washed up, turned on the gas fire and got out the sweater she was knitting, but somehow she couldn't settle to it. Presently she bundled it up and took herself off to bed, where, to her annoyance, she lay awake thinking, much against her will, of the man she had met that evening. 'A good thing we'll not meet again,' she observed to the cats curled up on the end of her bed, 'for he's too unsettling.'

It was still raining when she got up the next morning, dressed, breakfasted, fed the cats and tidied up her small flat. The physiotherapy department opened at nine o'clock and Miss Flute, who was in charge, had put her down to do a ward round with Mr Shutter, the orthopaedic consultant, at half past that hour. She needed to go through the notes before then.

The bus was jammed with damp passengers, irritable at that hour of the morning. Claribel wedged herself between a staid city gent and a young girl with purple hair arranged in spikes, and reviewed the day before her.

A busy one. Mr Shutter had the energy of two men and expected everyone to feel the same way; she had no doubt that by the end of his round she would have added more patients to the already overfull list Miss Flute brooded over each morning. Besides that, she had several patients of her own to deal with before lunch, and in the afternoon Mr Shutter had his out-patients clinic. It crossed her mind that she had more than her fair share of that gentleman; there were, after all, four other full-time physiotherapists as well as several who came in part-time. There were other consultants, too, milder, slower men that Mr Shutter, but somehow she always had him. Not that she minded; he was a youngish man, an out-of-doors type whose energy was very much in contrast to his broken-limbed patients, but he was kind to them and she had never minded his heartiness. Some of the girls she worked with found him intimidating, but it had never bothered her; she had a peppery man of the law for a father.

Jerome's Hospital was old; it had been patched up from time to time and there were plans afoot to move it, lock, stock and barrel, to the outskirts of London, but the plans had been mooted so often, and just as often tidied away again, that it seemed likely to stay where it was, surrounded by its dingy streets, its walls grimed from the traffic which never ceased around it, its interior a maze of passages, splendid public rooms and inconvenient wards. Claribel, who had trained there and stayed on afterwards, surveyed its grim exterior as she got off the bus with a mixture of intense dislike and affection. She loved her work, she liked the patients and the people she worked with, but she deplored the endless corridors, the dimness of the various departments and the many annexes where it was so easy to get lost. Her kind heart went out to patients who, for the first time, arrived for treatment and wandered in bewilderment all over the place, despite the little signposts none of them ever saw, until someone took pity on them and showed them the way, to arrive, hot and flustered, late for their appointment.

Claribel wished the porter on duty a good morning and went down the short staircase at the back of the entrance hall. It led to a narrow passage used by the electricians, porters and those going to the theatre serving casualty; it was also a short cut to the physio department. She opened the door and went in with five minutes to spare.

Miss Flute was already there, a middle-aged, grey-haired lady with a sharp tongue and a soft heart who led her team with unflagging energy and didn't suffer fools gladly. She smiled at Claribel as she wished her a brisk good morning. 'A busy day,' she observed. 'There's a huge out-patients.'

Claribel paused on her way to the cloakroom they all shared. 'Are we all here?' she asked.

'No. Mrs Green phoned to say that she had a bad cold—we'll have to share out her patients.'

Claribel got into her white overall, gave her reflection a perfunctory glance and went into the office to con the notes. It was indeed going to be a busy day.

The orthopaedic wing was right at the other end of the hospital and Mr Shutter was doing his rounds in both the men's and women's wards. Claribel poked her pretty head round Sister's office door, announced her arrival and joined the social worker, a nurse burdened with charts and, at the last minute, Sister herself. Just in time, the ward doors swung open and Mr Shutter strode in, bringing with him a great rush of energy and fresh air. Also with him was the man who had given Claribel a lift on the previous evening.

Although she had thought about him a great deal, she hadn't expected to see him again, but if she had she would have expected him to at least give some sign of recognition. As it was, his dark eyes looked right through her. She was conscious of annoyance. Of course, it wouldn't have done at all to have spoken to her, but he could have smiled…

She took her place in the group surrounding Mr Shutter and the round started. There were sixteen patients in the ward but not all of them were having physio. It wasn't until they reached the fourth bed that Mr Shutter said, 'Claribel, how's this leg shaping? Is it going to need much more massage? It looks pretty good to me.' He glanced at the man beside him.

'What do you think, Marc?' He didn't wait for an answer. 'This is one of our physiotherapists, Claribel Brown. Claribel,

Mr van Borsele has joined us for a period—he'll be taking over for a week or two while I'm away. Well, what do you think, Marc?' Mr van Borsele had barely glanced at her; only by the slight nod of his handsome head had he acknowledged that she was there. He studied the limb at some length, smiled nicely at the young man lying in the bed and said, 'Might Miss Brown put this lad through his paces? There's considerable muscle wastage.'

He and Mr Shutter studied the X-rays and they watched Claribel as she exercised the boy's fractured leg; it had been taken out of the plaster, the pin taken from the knee and the extension removed only days before, but thanks to her daily visits there was quite a lot of movement. Of course there was muscle wastage, she reflected silently. If Mr van Borsele should ever break one of his legs and she had the task of exercising it... She looked up to catch his dark eyes upon her and a knowing light smile curled his lip. So he read people's thoughts, too, did he?

By a great effort of will she managed not to blush.

The round wound to a close and presently she was able to leave the ward, armed with a great many instructions, and make her way back to the physio department. The waiting-room was full but it always was: people waiting patiently for their turn, holding crutches or walking aids, nursing arms in slings. She uttered a general good morning and went through to the office where Miss Flute was on the phone—admonishing someone severely by the sound of it. She put the receiver down and remarked, 'I have very little patience with some people. Well, I suppose you've collected another bunch of patients. Your Mrs Snow is waiting.' She studied Claribel's face. 'Have a cup of coffee first. Heaven knows when you'll get another chance.'

Claribel sipped thankfully. 'Five more—two discharges to come here three times a week and three on the ward—all extensions. There's a new man taking over from Mr Shutter—did you know?'

'Met him yesterday. Dutch—well thought of, I believe. A bit terse, I thought.'

Claribel put down her empty mug. ‘I’ll say. Mr Shutter introduced us; he looked right through me.’

Miss Flute said drily, ‘How could that be possible?’

Claribel frowned. She was a sensible girl, aware that she had more than her share of good looks, and she was accustomed to people remarking on that, but she had no vanity and was quite uncaring of the admiring glances she drew. All the same, for some reason Mr van Borsele’s lack of interest in her had irked her. ‘Perhaps he hates blondes…or he’s a misogynist.’

Miss Flute gave a hoot of laughter. ‘My dear girl, the grapevine has it that he is out and about at all the best restaurants with various lovelies.’

‘Good luck to him,’ said Claribel and went off in search of Mrs Snow. Mrs Snow was elderly, stout and chatty; Claribel rather liked her. She had tripped in her own kitchen and broken an arm and, having passed through Casualty, X-ray and Mr Shutter’s Out-patients, was now in the hands of the physio department. She was a chatty soul and at each session related an instalment of her home life while Claribel massaged her and egged her on to do the exercises she was so loath to do.

‘I seen a nice young man as I come in,’ she observed as Claribel began on the arm. ‘Getting out of ’is car, ’e was—one of them Rolls, ever so posh. ’E went into Outpatients.’

She fixed Claribel with a beady eye; having set a sprat to catch a mackerel, she was hopeful of a good catch.

‘He’s taking over from Mr Shutter for a week or two. You’re due to see him next week, aren’t you? Mr Shutter is having a holiday.’

‘’E deserves it. ’E must be sick ter death of other people’s bones.’ Mrs Snow cringed away from Claribel’s gentle fingers. ‘Ow, that ’urts. Is ’e nice, the new man?’

‘I’m sure he will be very good at his job,’ said Claribel sedately. ‘Now, Mrs Snow, let me see you lift that arm.’

The day wore on with its unending stream of patients. By five o’clock Claribel was bone-weary. Not that she minded; she liked her work and it was satisfying to see arms and legs returned to normal. Of course there was a hard core of elderlies with arthritis who were more or less permanently on the books, but they still benefited, even if they made little progress.

There was a general rush to go home once the last patient had gone, and a good deal of cheerful chatter since it was Friday and the department closed down until Monday morning. They left in a cheerful bunch, pausing to say goodbye to Miss Flute as she got into her Mini and then streaming across the hospital forecourt, intent on getting their various buses. Claribel, intent on getting home for the weekend, raced away to the nearest bus stop, her mind already dwelling happily on the peace and quiet of her parents' home in Wiltshire, so that she failed to see Mr van Borsele's Rolls at the entrance, waiting to join the rush of traffic in the street. She had in fact forgotten all about him.

She went home once a month, an undertaking which called for a strict routine the moment she got into her flat. Shower and change, feed the cats, stow them in their travelling basket, snatch up her already packed weekend bag and get a taxi, not always easy, especially in her unfashionable corner of London. Waterloo station wasn't all that distance away, but too far to walk with the cats and her bag, and this evening she was later than usual.

She reached the end of Meadow Road and not a taxi in sight, although there was more chance of one in Stamford Street. She paused on the corner by the few rather tatty shops and looked hopefully in either direction. Traffic streamed past but every taxi was occupied; she would have to try for a bus if one came along, although the nearest stop to the station was several minutes away from the station itself.

She didn't see the Rolls, going the other way, slow, do a U-turn and slide to a halt beside her.

'Get in quickly,' begged Mr van Borsele, 'I'm breaking any number of regulations.' He had nipped out smartly, taken the basket from her and put it on the back seat, and hurried her round the car into the seat beside his. 'Where to?'

Claribel caught her breath. 'Waterloo Station. My goodness, you do pop up in unexpected places, don't you?' She added quickly, like a small girl who had forgotten her manners, 'Thank you very much. I haven't much time to catch my train.'

Mr van Borsele grunted and joined the steady stream of traffic, weaving in and out of slower vehicles in a rather unnerving fashion.

'You're going very fast,' Claribel pointed out severely.

He said irritably, 'I was under the impression that you wished to catch a train, or was that just an excuse to get a lift?'

Claribel drew such a deep breath she almost exploded.

'Well, of all the nerve…' She remembered suddenly to whom she was speaking; one showed a proper respect towards consultant surgeons. 'You stopped the car and told me to get in.'

'Indeed I did. I don't remember inviting you to criticise my driving.'

She gave his unfriendly profile an almost motherly look. He was touchy; had a tiff with his girlfriend, perhaps. With a brother only a few years younger than herself she was familiar with the sudden snappish reply.

She said reasonably, 'I'm not criticising you at all, Mr van Borsele—I'm very grateful to you.'

He grunted again. Hardly a sparkling conversationalist, she reflected, and prepared to get out as he pulled in at the station's main entrance. She still had almost ten minutes but there would be a queue for tickets. She had a hand on the door handle when he said, 'Wait,' and got out and opened the door, retrieving the cats and her bag from the back of the car and strode into the station. Outside the vast ticket office he asked, 'Where to?'

'Oh, Tisbury.' She put out a hand for the basket and her bag and found she was holding them both and watching his vast back disappearing into the queue. Her protesting, 'Mr van Borsele,' fell on deaf ears.

He was back within five minutes, which left three minutes to get on to the train. He took the cats and her bag from her, bustled her past the platform gate, found her an empty seat opposite two respectable matrons, put the cats on the floor beside her with her bag on the rack, wished her a coldly polite goodbye and had gone while she was on the point of thanking him yet again. She remembered then that he had paid for her ticket and she had forgotten to repay him. What must he think of her? She went pink at the thought and the matrons eyed her with interest, no doubt scenting romance.

She would have to pay him when she got back on Monday; better still, she could put the money in the consultant's letter rack with a polite note. Not that he deserved any politeness. Not a man to do things by halves, she mused as the train gathered speed between the rows of smoke-grimed houses; she had been handled as efficiently as an express parcel. And with about as much interest.

She occupied the train journey composing cool observations to Mr van Borsele when next they met, calculated to take him down a peg.

Less than two hours later she was on the platform at Tisbury station being hugged by her father and then hurried to the family car, an elderly estate car in constant use, for he was a solicitor of no mean repute and much in demand around the outlying farms and small estates. Enoch and Toots were settled in the back with Rover, the family labrador, and Mr Brown, without loss of time, drove home.

His family had lived in the same house for some considerable time. It was a typical dwelling of the district: mellowed red brick, an ancient slate roof and plenty of ground round it. A roomy place, with a stable converted to a garage and a couple of rather tumbledown sheds to one side, it stood a mile outside the little town, its garden well tended. It had never had a name but was known locally as Brown's place.

Its owner shot up the short drive and Claribel jumped out to fling open the door and hurry inside, leaving her father to bring in the animals. Mrs Brown came out of the kitchen as she went in; a smaller version of Claribel, her fair hair thickly silvered but with a still pretty face.

Mother and daughter embraced happily and Claribel said: 'Oh, it's marvellous to be home again. What's for supper?'

'My potato soup, shepherd's pie and upside-down pineapple

pudding.' She eyed her daughter. 'Been working hard, darling? We'll have a glass of sherry, shall we? Here's your father.'

Enoch and Toots were used to their weekend trips; they ate the food put ready for them and sat themselves down before the Aga while Rover settled close by and Claribel and her parents sat at the kitchen table drinking their sherry and catching up on the news.

'Sebastian has a new girlfriend,' said Mrs Brown. 'She's a nurse, not finished her training yet. He brought her down for the weekend—we like her, but of course he's young yet...'

'He's been qualified for a year, Mother.'

'Yes, dear, I know, but he seems so much younger than you.'

'Well, he is—three years, almost.'

There was a small silence. Claribel had had her share of young men but she had never been serious with any one of them; her mother, without saying a word, nevertheless allowed her anxiety to show. Her beautiful daughter was twenty-eight years old and it was inconceivable that she wouldn't marry. Each time Claribel went home, her mother contrived to bring the talk round to the young men she had met and always Claribel disappointed her.

To change the trend of her parent's obvious thoughts, Claribel said cheerfully, 'I almost missed the train. Luckily the orthopaedic man who is standing in for Mr Shutter happened to drive past and gave me a lift.'

'Nice?' asked her mother hopefully.

'No. Very terse and rude. He's Dutch.'

'What does he... Is he nice-looking?' asked Mrs Brown.

'Very. In an arrogant sort of way.'

'I don't see that his looks matter as long as he got Claribel to the station. Very civil of him,' observed her father.

He hadn't been civil, but Claribel let that pass. She finished her sherry and they went across the stone-flagged hallway to the dining-room, handsomely furnished in a shabby way with massive pieces inherited from her mother's family. The talk was all of local events while they ate and when they had washed up and had coffee, Claribel took herself off to bed; it had been a long day, rather more tiring than usual.

'I wonder what that Dutchman's like?' mused her mother over her knitting.

Mr Brown had a good book. 'I don't see that it matters; Claribel doesn't like him.'

Mrs Brown did a row in silence. 'We'll see,' she said. 'She hadn't a good word to say for him—a good sign.'

Her husband sighed. 'Mr dear, how you do run on. Besides, he's a consultant. Presumably hardly likely to take up with a physiotherapist.'

'Claribel is beautiful,' said her mother simply, as though that put an end to the argument.

The weekend went too fast; it always did. Claribel biked into Tisbury in the morning on various errands for her mother and to waste a good deal of time chatting with various friends she met there. In the afternoon she and her father took Rover for a walk along the bridle paths, which were short cuts leading to the villages around the little town. The weather had improved but it was wet underfoot. Claribel, in wellies, an old tweed skirt and an even older quilted jacket, had tied a scarf round her golden hair and borrowed her mother's woolly gloves. They got back for tea glowing with fresh air.

Sunday morning was taken up with church and leisurely chats after the service. Claribel had a lot of friends, most of them married now, and several with weddings in the offing. She was to be a bridesmaid at two of them and wandered off into the churchyard with the brides-to-be, to sit on a handy tombstone and discuss clothes.

The day wasn't too long enough. She collected Enoch and Toots, packed her bag and in the early evening was driven to Tisbury once more, very much inclined to agree with her mother's remark that it was a pity that she couldn't stay at home. But there was no hospital nearer than Salisbury and no vacancies there. Besides, she had to stand on her own two feet and make her own life. She might not marry; she had had chances enough but none of them had been right for her. She wasn't sure what kind of man she wanted for a husband but she supposed that she would know when she met him.

Meadow Road looked more dingy than ever as the taxi drove down it, and her little semi-basement seemed unbearably small and dark even with all the lights on. She made tea, fed the cats and turned on the gas fire. She always felt like this when she came back after a weekend at home; in a day or two she would settle down.

She got out paper and envelopes, and wrote a stiff little note to Mr van Borsele, enclosing a cheque for her railway fare. In the morning she would take it to the lodge and ask a porter to put it in the pigeonholes reserved for the consultants and that would be the end of that.

She went to bed presently and fell asleep at once, to wake in the night and wish that it wouldn't be the end; he was such a thoroughly unpleasant man that it would be a pleasure to reform him. She thought of several ways of doing this before she slept again.

CHAPTER TWO

CLARIBEL was disappointed that she wouldn't be doing a ward round during the week; Mrs Green was back and there was a backlog of patients to deal with. The first few days of the week flew by and not once did she cast eyes on Mr van Borsele. She had handed in her note and the cheque and if she had expected an acknowledgment she was doomed to disappointment. Not that she had any wish to see him again, or so she told herself.

Not only was it a busy week, but the hospital was to hold its bi-annual bazaar at the weekend. It seemed a most unsuitable time for this, but since for very many years it had taken place on that particular Saturday, no one had considered changing it. Everyone was expected to help in some way. Minor royalty would be opening it, and the lecture hall would be turned into an indoor fair, the more expensive goods well to the forefront, the jumble and secondhand books at the back. Claribel was helping at the jumble stall; only the young and active were asked to do so for the local inhabitants relied upon it for a large proportion of their wardrobes and there was keen and sometimes ill-natured competition for clothes contributed by the patrons of the hospital.

The bazaar opened at two o'clock sharp and Miss Flute, marshalling her staff, reminded them to be there at one o'clock and not a minute later. Which meant that Saturday morning was rather a rush, what with having to shop for the weekend, clean the flat and do the washing. Claribel got into a needlecord skirt and a knitted jumper—the jumble stall caught all the icy draughts—tied her hair in a scarf, put on a quilted jacket, and went to catch her bus. It was a dreadful waste of a Saturday afternoon; she would have preferred to stay home with the cats, reading and making scones for tea.

The lecture hall was a hive of activity; she went straight to her stall and began to sort clothes into suitable piles. They wouldn't last long like that but the first bargain hunters would be able to snap up their choice without too much tossing of garments to and fro. There were two other girls on the stall, both good friends of hers, and, ready with ten minutes to spare, they had a pleasant gossip until a sudden subdued roar told them that the doors had been opened.

No one could buy anything until the bazaar had been officially opened. Minor royalty arrived exactly on time, made a brief speech, received the bouquet the hospital director's small daughter had been clutching, and declared the affair open, the signal for a concerted rush to the various stalls. Trade was brisk; the more élite toured the hall in the wake of royalty, buying beribboned coat hangers, lace pincushions and homemade jams, while the rest surged towards the jumble and secondhand books.

Claribel did a brisk trade; the mounds of clothing, hats and shoes disappeared rapidly. She knew a good many of her customers and wasn't surprised to see Mrs Snow edging her way along the stall, her arms already full of garments and a couple of hats.

'There you are, ducks,' said that lady cheerfully. 'Got a nice haul 'ere. 'Ere, I say, that nice young feller I told you about—'e's over there with the nobs.' She waved a cluttered hand towards the centre of the hall and Claribel perforce followed its direction. Sure enough, there was Mr van Borsele, head and shoulders above everyone else, talking to one of the hospital committee. He looked at her across the crowded hall and, although he gave no sign of having seen her, she turned her head at once. She took great care not to look around her again and indeed she had little time; by four o'clock she longed for a cup of tea but trade was too brisk for any of them to leave the stall. When the last customer had gone, an hour later, there was almost nothing to pack up and they made short work of it, grumbling among themselves in a good-natured way because their precious Saturday had been infringed upon. But as Miss Flute had told them, it had been well worth it; they had made a good deal of money and the hospital would be the richer by another kidney machine. They trooped off to wash their hands and do their faces and dispersed in a chorus of goodbyes. Miss Flute was standing by the door talking to Mr van Borsele as Claribel and several of the other girls reached it. She stretched out a hand as Claribel went by so that she had to stop.

'Claribel, Mr van Borsele has kindly offered to give me a lift home; he will have to go past Meadow Road and says it's no trouble to drop you off.'

Claribel said quickly, 'Oh, please don't bother—there will be plenty of buses.'

'No bother,' said Mr van Borsele smoothly. 'Shall we go? I'm sure you must both want your tea.'

She found herself sitting behind him, watching Miss Flute chatting away with surprising animation. They were on the best of terms, she reflected peevishly, and only occasionally did Miss Flute address some remark to her over a shoulder.

Miss Flute lived alone in a tiny mews flat behind Charing Cross station and Mr van Borsele got out and opened the door for her and saw her safely inside before coming back to his car.

He opened the door and studied Claribel. 'Come in front?' he enquired so pleasantly that she had no choice but to get out and get in again beside him. He shut the door on her with the air of a man who had got his way, got in beside her and drove back along the Embarkment, over Waterloo Bridge and into Stamford Street. It had turned into a dull afternoon and Meadow Road, when they reached it, looked drab. He stopped outside her flat and turned to look at her.

'Are you going to invite me in for tea?'

It was the last thing she had expected. 'Well, I hadn't intended to but if you'd like to come in, do.' That sounded rude; she amended it hastily, 'What I mean is, I didn't imagine you would want to come to tea.'

He said gravely. 'You shouldn't let your imagination run away with you, Claribel—and I should like to come to tea. That was an infernal afternoon.'

She laughed then, quite forgetting that she didn't like him.

'Yes, it always is, but it's only twice a year. Such a pity it has to be on a Saturday, though.'

They got out of the car and he opened the door and stood aside for her to go in. The cats rushed to meet them and he bent to tickle their heads and then stood up; his size made the room even smaller. She said, 'Do take off your coat—there's a hook in the lobby. I'll put the kettle on.'

She threw her coat on the bed and changed her shoes, decided her face and hair would have to do and went into the tiny kitchen. There was a cake she had baked that morning and one of her mother's homemade loaves. She sliced and buttered, cut the cake, added a cup and saucer to the tray and made the tea.

Mr van Borsele was sitting in the largest of the chairs with a cat on either side of him. He got up as she opened the door, took the tray from her and set it on the small table on one side of the fireplace and went to fetch the cake. The cats followed him in what she considered to be a slavish fashion and when he sat down again, resumed their places on either side of him.

'You like cats?' Hardly a conversational gambit, but they would have to talk about something.

'Yes. My grandmother has two—Burmese.' He accepted his tea and sat back comfortably and she found herself wondering what his grandmother was like—somehow he was such a self-contained man, obviously used to getting his own way, that it was hard to imagine her—a small, doting mouse of a woman, perhaps? And his wife? If he was married.

He was watching her, his dark eyes amused. 'I have two of my own,' he told her. 'Common or garden cats with no pedigrees, and two equally well-bred dogs who keep them in order.'

She passed him the bread and butter. 'And your wife? She likes animals?'

The amusement deepened but he answered gravely, 'I am not yet married.' He took a bite. 'Homemade bread. Are you a cook, Claribel?'

'Well, I can, you know, but my mother is quite super.'

She watched him consume several slices and made polite conversation. She didn't like him, she reminded herself, but there was something rather pathetic about a very large man eating his tea with such enjoyment. As she offered him the cake, she wondered briefly where he was living while he was in London.

'Do you go home frequently?' He sounded casually polite and she found herself talking about Tisbury and her friends there and how she loved her weekends. He led her on gently so that she told him a good deal more than she realised; she was telling him about Sebastian and how clever he was when the phone rang.

She was going out that evening—one of the girls she worked with was getting engaged and there was to be a party; she wanted to make sure that Claribel would be there.

'Yes, of course. I haven't forgotten. Eight o'clock. I'll be ready at half past seven.'

'I'm so happy,' burbled the voice at the other end.

'Well, of course you are.' Claribel smiled at the phone as she put down the receiver.

Mr van Borsele was watching her with an expressionless face.

As she sat down again he said easily, 'A date this evening? I'll be on my way. A pleasant hour, Claribel, between this afternoon's tedium and the evening's pleasure.' He added thoughtfully, 'Surprising, really, for you still aren't sure if you like me, are you?'

He stood up and she got to her feet, facing him. She gave him a clear look from her beautiful eyes. 'No, I'm not sure, but it doesn't really matter, does it? There must be any number of women who—who admire you!'

'Probably.' He spoke without conceit. 'But I'm really only concerned with one girl, not untold numbers.'

'Oh, well in that case it doesn't matter what I think about you, does it, Mr van Borsele?'

He shrugged into his coat, offered a gentle hand to Enoch and Toots and went to the door. He didn't answer her, only wished her the politest of goodnights as he left.

Several times during the evening she found herself wishing

that Mr van Borsele had been there, which, considering she didn't like him, seemed strange.

Back in her flat, lying in bed with the cats curled up at her feet, she decided it was because he was so much older than the young men who had been at the party, mostly newly qualified housemen or final-year students. 'After all, I am getting a bit long in the tooth,' muttered Claribel to her unresponsive companions.

Of course she knew other older men. There was one in particular, Frederick Frost, the junior registrar on the orthopaedic wards, a serious man who had given her to understand that he had singled her out for his attention. She had gone out with him on several occasions now, and liked him well enough although she found him singularly lacking in romantic feeling. He would be a splendid husband; he would also be very dull.

Sometimes she lay in bed and wondered if she had been wise to refuse the offers of several young men who had wished to marry her. She hadn't loved any of them; liked them well enough, even been fond of them, but that was all. Somewhere in the world, she was convinced, was the man she could love for always; she had no idea what he would look like but she supposed that when she met him she would know that he was the one. Only here she was, the wrong end of the twenties, and it looked as though she would never meet him.

Frederick had asked her to spend Sunday afternoon with him; she came back from church in the morning, ate her solitary lunch and took a bus to Hyde Park where they were to meet. Frederick believed in good fresh air and exercise; he walked her briskly from the Marble Arch entrance to Green Park and thence to St James's Park, talking rather prosily all the way. Claribel, brought up in the country and fond of walking, nonetheless was relieved when they finally reached the Mall and Trafalgar Square and entered a modest café for tea and toasted teacakes.

Frederick was on duty at the hospital at six o'clock. He saw her on to a bus, assuring her that she looked all the better for the exercise they had taken that afternoon, and invited her to repeat it on the following Sunday.

Claribel's feet ached and her head buzzed with the various diagnoses he had been entertaining with her; she said hastily that she would be going home, thanked him prettily for her tea and sank thankfully on to a seat in the bus.

The cats were pleased to see her and her little room looked cosy as she went indoors. She kicked off her shoes, took off her outdoor things and turned on the gas fire. She would sit and read for an hour before getting her supper.

It was barely ten minutes before the knocker on her front door was given a sound thump. She got up reluctantly, dislodging the cats, and went to open the door.

Mr van Borsele loomed over her. 'I thought I told you never to answer the door without making sure that you knew the caller,' he said testily. 'Well, won't you ask me in?'

'Why should I?' she snapped. 'Banging on my door... Next time I shan't open it.'

'What makes you think there will be a next time?' he asked smoothly.

Only by a great effort did she stop herself from grinding her teeth. 'There won't be if I can help it,' she assured him coldly.

'Having cleared up that knotty point, may I come in? There's something I wish to discuss with you.'

'Could it not wait until Monday?' She added crossly, 'It's Sunday, you know.'

'Monday will be too late.' He suddenly smiled at her with great charm. 'If I might come in?'

She stood back reluctantly and remembered that she wasn't wearing her shoes. At the same time Mr van Borsele observed, 'Been walking? Don't bother to put your shoes on for me.' He studied her stockinged feet. 'You have nice ankles.'

He was impossible! She said stonily, 'You wished to say something urgently, Mr van Borsele?'

'Ah, yes. There is an orthopaedic clinic in Whitechapel; it seems there is a flu bug there which has laid low the visiting consultant and three of the physiotherapists. They have asked us for help, and Miss Flute suggested you might accompany me—she can get a part-time girl in to do your work at our clinic for the morning, and I happen to be free until the afternoon. The clinic starts at eight o'clock and lasts until about noon.'

'Why me?' asked Claribel.

'You seem to be a sensible young woman, able to cope.'

'Am I given any choice?'

'Not really. It's a busy clinic; takes fringe cases from several hospitals; I believe the patients come quite long distances.'

Claribel eyed him carefully; he didn't appear to be anything else but serious but one couldn't tell. She said slowly, 'Very well, Mr van Borsele.'

'Splendid. One does appreciate a willing volunteer.' His voice was all silk so that she darted a suspicious look at him. He met her eye with a look of bland innocence and she was sure that he was finding something very amusing behind it.

'I am not a willing volunteer,' she protested. 'You yourself have just said...'

He interrupted her in a soothing voice, 'No, no, of course you're not; merely doing your duty, however irksome. I will call for you at seven o'clock precisely; that will give us time to find our way around.'

He had been standing all this time and so had she. 'You have had a pleasant afternoon? A few hours in the country, perhaps?'

She thought of her aching feet. 'Hyde Park and Green Park and St James's Park.'

'Delightful in pleasant company.'

She thought of Frederick. 'I dare say,' she sighed.

'Never alone, Claribel?'

'No,' she added, forgetting to whom she was talking. 'I would have liked to be at home.' She looked up at him with her lovely eyes and was startled at the look on his face, gone so quickly that she supposed that she had imagined it.

He said casually, 'One can be lonely even with companions. Do you suppose we might dine together this evening? I had to cancel a date so that I could get arrangements made for the morning and I'm sure we could remain polite towards each other for a couple of hours; we don't need to talk unless you want to.'

While he spoke he contrived to look lonely and hungry and in need of companionship; Claribel was aware that he was doing it deliberately, but all the same it would be heartless to refuse. Besides, there was only cold ham in the fridge... She said quickly before she thought better of it, 'Very well, Mr van Borsele, I'll dine with you, but I have to see to Enoch and Toots first.' She remembered her manners. 'Do sit down, I'll only be ten minutes.' At the door she paused. 'Nowhere posh—I'm not dressed to go out.'

He cast an eye over her person. 'You will do very well as you are. Only put your shoes on.'

He took her to Chelsea, to a restaurant just off the Kings Road: English Garden, quite small but pleasantly surrounded by a conservatory full of greenery and flowers. They ate traditional English food, beautifully cooked and served, and rather to Claribel's surprise she found herself enjoying not only the food but her companion's conversation. Not that she discovered anything much about him from his talk; he talked about Holland, touched lightly on his work, went on to discuss several West End plays he had been to and then led her on, ever so gently, to talk about herself. It was only later that she realised this, annoyed with herself for telling him so much, especially as she hadn't found out anything at all about him. She had asked, in a roundabout way, how long he would be in London, but somehow he hadn't answered her. Lying in her bed, thinking about it, she promised herself that she would have another go in the morning.

Perhaps he wasn't as bad as she had first thought, she decided sleepily; he had driven her back to her flat, opened her door for her and then bidden her a cheerful goodnight. She had been debating whether to ask him in for a final cup of coffee as they drove, but the very briskness of his manner decided her against it.

She was ready and waiting for him when he arrived the next

morning. They exchanged good mornings but, beyond a few civil remarks about the weather, which for early April was chilly and damp, they had nothing to say to each other, and once at the clinic they each went their own way, to meet again presently on a strictly professional basis.

Even if they had felt inclined, there was no opportunity to talk. The clinic bulged with patients of all sorts, a good-natured crowd with its crutches and slings and neck braces, sitting patiently and rather noisily in the waiting-room. There were two physiotherapists there besides Claribel. They shared out the work between them and long after Mr van Borsele had seen his last patient, they were all hard at it. It was after one o'clock when they began to clear up and tidy away the apparatus.

He'll be gone, reflected Claribel as she got out of her overall. I'll have to get a bus—it'll take hours. She dragged a comb through her hair, dabbed powder on to her nose and got into her coat. The other two girls were waiting to leave. She said goodbye and went out through the side door and saw the Rolls parked in front of it. Mr van Borsele was at the wheel, looking impassive. He got out and opened the door, and ushered her in without a word.

'There was no need to wait,' protested Claribel, faintly peevish, and was taken aback when he replied,

'Well, of course there wasn't, only I chose to do so.'

'Well, really…'

'I have found,' remarked Mr van Borsele blandly as he sent the car smoothly to join the traffic, 'that the English language is littered with useless phrases.' And, while she was getting over that, 'Unfortunately there is not sufficient time to have lunch, but one of the registrars assures me that Nick's Diner, just round the corner from Jerome's can offer a sound beef sandwich and good coffee. We will go there.'

He had no more to say and for the life of her Claribel could think of no conversation suitable for the occasion. She knew very well that if she raised any objections she would be either ignored or talked out of it; she held her tongue.

The streets were comparatively empty; she got out, still

wordless, when Mr van Borsele parked tidily in the consultant's car park and walked beside him as he strode out of the hospital forecourt into the dingy street beyond. Nick's Diner was down a side street, one side of which was taken up by St Jerome's looming walls. It was small and rather dark and the plastic tables were crowded close together, but it was clean and the aroma from the coffee machine caused Claribel to wrinkle her pretty nose.

The little place was full but as they went in two medical students got up from a table near the door. 'Over here, sir,' they chorused and ushered Claribel into a chair, accepting his thanks with a kind of reverence which made her smile a little, and rushed out. Probably they had skipped a lecture.

The proprietor, a small wizened man who had been there so long no one could remember when he first appeared, joined them at once, gave the table a wipe and bent a differential ear to Mr van Borsele's request for beef sandwiches and coffee.

'Couldn't 'ave chosen better,' he assured them. 'Nice bit o' beef I've got—cuts like silk—and good 'olesome bread to go with it, too; none of that white flannel stuff from a factory. Be with you in a couple of shakes, sir.'

Sir sat back and looked around him and then across the little table at Claribel. 'Hardly a place I would like to bring anyone. You're not feeling insulted or having injured feelings, I hope?'

'Me? Heavens, no.' She added waspishly, 'I'm not a snob.'

'I hardly imagined that you were. Nor am I, although I can see that you think that I am. But one would normally choose a rather more fitting background for a girl as pretty as you are, Claribel.'

He watched her blush.

'Why are you called Claribel?'

'My mother liked—still likes—historical romances. Just before I was born she was reading a tale where the heroine was called Claribel—so I was christened that. She rather wanted Mariabella, which is another version of it, but Father put his foot down.'

'And your brother?' The question was put casually.

'Sebastian? Oh, Mother was into Shakespeare in a big way.' She bit into a sandwich. 'Why were…' she began, but stopped just in time and took another bite; she must remember that he was a consultant and, from what Miss Flute had let drop, an important one in his own field.

'My name, as you know, is Marc, spelled with a C, and, since the conversation tends to be rather more personal than usual, I am thirty-six years old. At the moment I am not prepared to divulge more details of my life.'

She chocked on some of the wholesome bread. 'I am not in the least interested in you, Mr van Borsele.' She spoke with a cold dignity marred by having a mouthful of sandwich.

He laughed. 'What a touchy girl you are! How old are you, Claribel?'

She said indignantly, 'Don't you know that you never ask any girl how old she is?'

'Yes, I know, but you aren't any girl, Claribel. You look about eighteen, but of course, you're not.' He waited for her to reply, his eyebrows raised.

He was utterly impossible and getting worse all the time; she couldn't imagine Frederick saying a thing like that. Come to think of it, she couldn't imagine Frederick… He had become so vague she could barely remember what he looked like. 'I'm twenty-eight.' She added coldly, 'Is there anything else you want to know?'

'Oh, a great deal, but unfortunately we are pressed for time.'

She put down her empty coffee cup. 'I really have to go. Thank you for my lunch, Mr van Borsele.'

He got up with her, paid the bill, and followed her into the street. 'What's his name, this young man who walks you through London parks until your feet ache?'

She said quickly, 'Oh, you wouldn't know him.' She spoke so hurriedly and loudly that he had his answer and smiled to himself. 'I'm not being nosey, just making polite conversation,' he assured her blandly. 'Are you—what is the term?—going steady with him?'

They were crossing the forecourt and in a few moments she

would be able to escape his endless questions. 'No, of course not.' She was an honest girl, so she added, 'Well, I suppose I could if I wanted to, only I don't. It's just that he wants someone to go for a walk with.'

Mr van Borsele gave a chortle of laughter and she said crossly, 'Don't you dare laugh.'

'No, no, my dear girl, I'm laughing for all the wrong reasons. You have too kind a heart; I suspect you don't discourage this young man with no name. I suspect also that you get dates enough and can pick and choose.'

She said seriously, 'Well, yes, I suppose so, but I'm not very, well—modern.' She stared up at him with a grave face. 'You won't know what I mean.'

'On the contrary, I know very well.' He smiled suddenly and she discovered that he was a kind man after all. 'If ever I should invite you out again, Claribel, it will be on the strict understanding that you have no need to be modern. Being well past my first youth, I'm not modern, either.'

They had reached the side door leading to the physiotherapy department. He opened it for them and with a brief nod walked away.

She scuttled down the covered way, already late. Perhaps she liked him after all, she thought confusedly; well, some of the time at any rate.

Miss Flute was surprisingly mild about her lateness; someone had covered for her and Mrs Green had gone to the wards. 'Mr van Borsele had a round on Women's Ward,' she observed. 'I didn't dare wait for you for I wasn't sure how long you would be. Were you very busy?'

Claribel, tearing into her overall, told her.

'You've had no lunch?' asked Miss Flute worriedly.

Claribel went faintly pink. 'Well, Mr van Borsele gave me a lift back and I—we had a sandwich in Nick's Diner.'

'Very civil of him,' answered Miss Flute briskly. 'There's that nervous old lady with the hip—will you take her on? She's so scared, she needs someone gentle and unhurried.'

'Unhurried?' Claribel cast her eyes to the ceiling. 'Miss Flute, I'll be lucky to get away by six o'clock.'

'Well, you've had a nice morning, haven't you, dear?' suggested Miss Flute and went back into her office.

Claribel, pacifying her elderly patient, decided that, yes, she had had a nice morning. It was a pity that she had been too late to go to the ward for Mr van Borsele's round; perhaps Miss Flute would send her to Men's Orthopaedic for the next consultant's round; she had been treating several patients there.

But Miss Flute, it seemed, had other ideas. Claribel spent the next two days in Out-Patients with the senior registrar and Frederick and didn't so much as catch a glimpse of Mr van Borsele. Life was really rather dull, she reflected, getting her supper while Toots and Enoch sat and watched her; it might be a good idea if she were to go home at the weekend. 'It would be a nice change for all of us,' she assured the cats as she sat down to her solitary meal.

She bumped into him—literally—as she crossed the courtyard to go home on the following day. He put out a had to steady her and said without preamble, 'I'm going to Bath for the weekend. I'll drop you off at Tisbury and pick you up on the way back.'

'Oh, but I…' She caught his eye and stopped then began again, 'I really hadn't intended…' Under that dark gaze she faltered again. She said slowly, because she felt compelled to, 'I should like that very much, Mr van Borsele.' She added hastily, 'To go home, I mean.' She wondered why he grinned suddenly. 'Shall I meet you here, and at what time?'

'Haven't you forgotten your cats? I'll pick you up—half past six at your flat, and mind you are ready.'

He nodded his goodbye and had gone before she could frame so much as a single word.

She told Enoch and Toots when she got home and, mindful that she might get away late on Friday afternoon, put her overnight things in a bag and decided what she would wear; before she went to work in the morning she would put her clothes ready. Mr van Borsele might have offered her a lift, but he was quite capable of going without her if she kept him waiting for more than a minute or so.

Friday's clinic was overflowing and, to make matters worse, Mrs Green went home during the morning, feeling, as she put it, not at all the thing. That meant Claribel would have to take on several more patients as well as her own, for two of the other girls were at the ante-natal clinic and the other two were only just qualified and needed an eye kept upon them.

Claribel got home half an hour late. To have sat down, kicked off her shoes and drunk the teapot dry would have been bliss; as it was, she fed the cats, showered, changed into a short jacket and plaid pleated skirt, got her aching feet into her rather smart boots, popped the cats into their basket and opened the door to Mr van Borsele, looking as composed as if she had spent the entire day doing nothing much.

He ran a knowledgeable eye over her person. 'Tired? You can doze in the car.'

A remark which incensed her after her efforts. But she hadn't noticed the shadows under her eyes or the lack of colour in her cheeks.

She wished him a good evening, adding that she had no desire to doze. 'Besides, you might want me to map-read for you.'

He took her bag from her and stowed it in the boot and then put the cat basket on the back seat. 'Straight down the A303, once I'm on it. You can wake up when we're nearby and tell me where to go from there.'

She said huffily, 'Well, if you want me to sleep all the way I'll do my best. There's no need for you to talk.'

He shut the door and made sure that it was locked. 'In you get,' he urged her. 'You're a bit edgy but I dare say you've had a hard day with Mrs Green away.' He got in beside her and turned to look at her. 'You thought that I wouldn't wait if you weren't ready? I am an impatient man, Claribel, but for some things I am prepared to wait—if necessary, for ever.'

She puzzled over this and found no clear answer. 'Have you had a busy day?' she asked politely.

'Very. A quiet weekend will be delightful. You know Bath?'

'Quite well—we go there to shop sometimes. You—you said you had friends there?'

He was driving west out of London in heavy traffic. 'Yes, they live at Limpley Stoke—not friends; my young sister and her husband.'

'Oh, she's Dutch, too…' It was a silly remark and she waited for him to say so. But he didn't.

'She spent some years over here at boarding school. She's happy here and of course they go to Holland frequently.'

Claribel tried to imagine his sister. Tall, short; thin, fat?

'She's not in the least like me: small, fair and very slim.' He glanced sideways at her. 'Close your eyes, Claribel, you are tired.'

She frowned. Tired so often meant plain. The thought didn't stop her doing as she was told; she was asleep within minutes.

CHAPTER THREE

THEY were racing past Stonehenge when she awoke, feeling much refreshed.

'Feel better?' asked Mr van Borsele.

'Yes, thank you. There's a turning on the left once you've got to Wylye; it's a side road to Tisbury. You can get back on to the A303 if you go through Hindon. If you go via Warminster it's the quickest way to Bath.'

'Oh, dear, oh, dear. You can't get rid of me quickly enough, can you, Claribel?'

Any sleepiness she might have felt evaporated in a trice. 'I am merely trying to be helpful; you're coming out of your way to take me home and I am grateful but I don't wish to impose upon you.'

'Very commendable, Claribel, your thoughtfulness does you credit.' She could hear the laugh in his voice. 'Let me hasten to assure you that no one has, or ever will, impose upon me. I do what I like and I contrive to get my own way.'

'How very arrogant. I am surprised that you have any friends, Mr van Borsele.'

'Ah, but I am also cunning; I hide my arrogance under a smooth exterior.' He contrived to sound ill-done-by. 'I am in fact both soft-hearted and lovable when you get to know me.'

Claribel felt laughter bubbling up inside her. She gave a little chuckle. 'What a good thing that we're almost there or I might begin to feel sorry for you. The gate is on the left; it's just a short drive to the house.'

Light shone through the downstairs windows and as he drove slowly up to the door Mrs Brown flung it open. She hadn't got her spectacles on, so she blinked short-sightedly as the car stopped. 'Darling, you got a lift? How nice—bring them in, whoever it is.' She came a little nearer and saw Mr van Borsele move from the car. 'My goodness!' she observed cheerfully. 'What a large man, and isn't that a Rolls-Royce?'

Claribel skipped round the car and embraced her parent. 'Mother, this is Mr van Borsele from the hospital. He kindly gave me a lift home—he's going to Bath.'

She tucked an arm through her mother's. 'My mother, Mr van Borsele.'

He shook hands gently, smiling down at her. 'How do you do, Mrs Brown?'

'Come inside,' invited Mrs Brown, beaming up at him. 'Have a cup of coffee—something to eat? Sandwiches?'

'You're very kind, but I am expected at Bath this evening.'

'My husband would like to meet you. Are you taking Claribel back?'

He glanced at Claribel, standing silently. 'Sunday evening, about six o'clock? Perhaps I shall have the pleasure of meeting Mr Brown then.'

'That will be delightful. Supper?'

He shook his head and if he didn't feel regret he was pretending very well indeed. 'I've a late evening date—I must be back in town by nine o'clock at the latest.'

He shook hands again, gave Claribel the briefest of smiles and got back into his car.

They watched him drive away and Mrs Brown said, 'What a very nice man. Is he a friend, darling?'

'No, Mother, he's not. We argue whenever we meet, which is seldom. He has a nasty caustic tongue.'

'Most unpleasant.' They were inside the house, the door shut. 'His patients must detest him?'

Claribel had been brought up to be fair and not to fib unless she really had to. 'Well, as a matter of fact, they all dote on him; he's quite different with his patients.'

She had tossed her jacket on to a chair and they had gone into the sitting-room. Mrs Brown shot a quick look at her. 'So he must be nice. It was kind of him to bring you home, darling. A pity he didn't stay for a cup of coffee.'

Claribel shook up a cushion and let Toots and Enoch out of their basket. 'Yes, I suppose I should have suggested it.'

Her mother went to the door. 'Well, he's coming on Sunday. Supper is ready, darling, and there's plenty for you—your father won't be back just yet. He's over at Bradshaw's Farm advising them about selling the ten-acre field. It's a lovely surprise having you back for the weekend.'

Her father came in just as they were sitting down in the panelled dining-room across the hall. He helped her to a portion of one of Mrs Brown's excellent steak and kidney pies with the observation that it was a treat to see her and how had she got home, anyway?

'One of the orthopaedic consultants was going to Bath for the weekend; he offered me a lift. He'll pick me up on Sunday evening, Father.'

'One of your beaux?' Mr Brown wanted to know. It was a long-standing joke in the family that she was choosy and would end up an old maid. No one believed it, but just lately Claribel had had moments of anxiety that the right man wasn't going to turn up and the joke wouldn't be a joke any longer.

She laughed because he expected that she would. 'Oh, not likely, Father,' she said brightly. 'He's a consultant; they live on a higher plane than any one else. Besides, we don't get on very well.'

'No? The more decent of him to give you a lift. I look forward to meeting him.'

She consoled herself with the thought that the meeting would be brief. She even forgot Mr van Borsele for quite long periods at the weekend—there seemed so much to occupy her: gardening, driving her mother into Salisbury to shop on Saturday morning, taking the dog for a walk, and going back to the vicarage after church on Sunday because the vicar's eldest son was home on leave from some far-flung spot. They had grown up together, more or less, and she thought of him as another brother; it was mid-afternoon before he walked her back to her home and, naturally enough, stayed for tea. Claribel just had time to fling her things into her bag and make sure that the cats were safely in the kitchen ready to be scooped into their basket before Mr van Borsele arrived.

She had expected that he would spend an obligatory five minutes talking polite nothings to her father and mother, settle her and the cats in the car with dispatch, and drive away to his evening date. She might have known it; he was a man who did what he liked when he liked, and it seemed that he liked to stay an hour, drinking her mother's excellent coffee and discussing international law with her father. She sat quietly, handing coffee cups when called upon, feeling vaguely sorry for whoever it was he was taking out that evening. A girl, of course; and if I were that girl, reflected Claribel, I wouldn't go out with him; I'd have a headache or go to bed or something—or find someone else to have supper with.

She glanced up and found his dark eyes resting thoughtfully on her so that she felt as guilty as though she had spoken her thoughts out loud. He smiled suddenly and she smiled back before she could stop herself.

He got to his feet. 'We should be going.' He made his goodbyes with a grave courtesy which she could see impressed her parents and then ushered her out to the car. Toots and Enoch were handed in, final goodbyes were said and he drove away.

'You're going to be late for your evening out,' said Claribel as they left Tisbury behind.

'I think not. It's half past seven; we can be back soon after nine o'clock; my date is for ten o'clock. The road should be pretty clear at this time of the evening.' He added, 'I imagine you don't want to be too late back.'

The roads were almost empty; it was a wet evening and until they reached the outskirts of London there was nothing to hinder them. Claribel, who had allowed herself to wonder if they might stop for coffee, realised that her companion had no such intention. She was deposited inside her front door with the cats and her bag very shortly before half past nine, bidden a casual goodnight and had her politely phrased thanks dismissed just as casually. He had had little to say during the drive, and that of a general nature; she was left with the strong impression that, having done his duty, he was only too glad to be shot of her. She wished him a pleasant evening in a voice which belied her words and closed the door on his departing back.

'And that's the last time,' declared Claribel, not quite clear what she meant.

She woke to a lovely morning: sunshine and blue skies and a breathy little wind with warmth in it. It being April, it was liable to rain before she got home, but that didn't stop her from wearing a knitted suit with a matching blouse. It was in chestnut brown which went very nicely with her pale hair and, since it was a Monday morning and her spirits needed a boost she wore a pair of high-heeled shoes, deceptively simple and, for that reason, expensive. She left for work feeling pleased with her appearance and attracted several wolf whistles as she went to catch her bus. Vulgar, but good for a girl's esteem.

Mr van Borsele, passing her in the hospital forecourt, didn't whistle, although he slowed the car as he went past her and took a good look. She gave him a pleasant smile and walked on, feeling a deep satisfaction, although she wasn't sure why.

It was several days before she saw him again. Miss Flute had kept her in the department, dealing with the regular patients, most of whom came at least once a week, and often twice. They were all hard work, some harder than others, and she was glad to get back to her little flat in the evening and cook her supper and go to bed early. Frederick had wanted her to go with him to a concert and one of the housemen had suggested that they might go to a disco, but she found herself singularly lacking in enthusiasm for either suggestion.

All the more surprising then that when Mr van Borsele, towards the end of the week, thumped on her door, she should admit him with something like pleased anticipation. And not without reason; he had tickets for *The Phantom of the Opera*, and took it for granted that she would go with him.

'Why me?' she asked.

He sat himself down in the easiest chair and the cats got onto his knee.

'I suppose that you have had a busy day—so have I. I don't

want to make small talk and I don't think you would want that either. On the other hand I don't want to go alone.'

'How charmingly put,' said Claribel, her breast heaving with indignation. 'Just the sort of invitation any woman would jump at. No, I won't come.'

'Supper afterwards?' coaxed Mr van Borsele in his most beguiling voice. 'I believe the music is a delight, just right after a tiresome day. Was your day tiresome, Claribel?'

'Yes, very. And I'm tired; I was just going to get my supper.'

'Make coffee instead, jump into something pretty and we'll be off. We have an hour.'

She had wanted to see *The Phantom of the Opera*, but Frederick wasn't the man to waste his money on anything so frivolous as the theatre, certainly not a man to bang on the door and take it for granted that she would go anyway. She said, 'There isn't enough time—I haven't fed Enoch and Toots.'

He heaved himself out of the chair. 'Go and dress; I'll see to the coffee and the cats.' He wandered off into the kitchen and she went to her bedroom and poked about in her wardrobe. Only when she had showered and changed into a pretty patterned dress did she remember that she hadn't said she would go with him. Impulsively she padded into the sitting-room with her shoes in her hand. 'I haven't said I'll go...' she began.

'Well, you can't sit around all evening in that dress. I've fed the cats and the coffee is ready. What a pretty dress, and I like your hair.'

She stared at him. 'But I haven't done it yet.' It was hanging down her back, a golden damp tangle. She had forgotten it when she had gone into the sitting-room; now she felt very self-conscious about it. 'If you wouldn't mind pouring the coffee I'll only be a few minutes.'

She did her face rapidly, swept her hair tidily into a chignon and went back to join him. He was standing by the window, a mug in his hand; he handed her hers and told her to drink up and not waste any more time.

She took a heartening sip. 'What a most unfair thing to say,' she pointed out. 'I had no intention of going out and I'm only coming with you because...well, because...'

'You want to?' He smiled at her and she gulped her coffee and burnt her tongue.

The show was marvellous; Claribel sat spellbound, her eyes on the stage listening and watching, afraid to miss a single moment of it. Mr van Borsele sat back in his seat, watching her. During the interval he took her to the foyer for a drink and listened to her rather breathless remarks about the show, agreeing gravely, the perfect companion. When the curtain came down for the very last time, he led her out to the car and drove to the Savoy Grill and gave her a delicious supper: lobster thermidor, with a mouthwatering salad, *chaudfroid* of raspberries and endless coffee and petits fours.

'Working tomorrow?' he enquired casually.

'Yes. There's an ante-natal clinic in the morning and Outpatients' Department in the afternoon. The orthopaedic registrar takes it, but you know that, of course.'

She nibbled a petit four. 'When does Mr Shutter come back?'

'Next week.'

She waited for him to say more but he remained utterly silent. Presently she asked, 'Do you leave then?'

'Within a day or two of his return, yes. Will you miss me?'

'Mrs Green has been working with you...'

'I asked if you would miss me, Claribel.'

For something to do she poured more coffee. 'Well, yes, I think I shall.'

'You will doubtless have as many dates as you can cope with?'

'Yes.' She was quite serious. 'But they're not like you.'

'God forbid! Tell me, Claribel, what do you intend to do with your life?'

The wine she had drunk at supper had loosened her tongue. 'I like my work—it's very rewarding, you know—but I'd like to get married and have children, only I'm getting a bit...'

'But you must have had offers of marriage?'

'Several, only they've never been...I'm not sure... How will

I know when I meet the right man, if I ever do? And perhaps it's too late.'

'You'll know, and it's never too late. But most of us make do with what we get offered and make a success of it, too.'

'You mean we don't always meet the right person?'

'I don't mean that at all; almost all of us do, but we don't always realise it.'

'Oh.' She thought about that. 'Don't you think that people should marry because they fall in love?'

'Well, of course I do, but there are a dozen other excellent reasons for marrying and none of them have anything to do with falling in love. And they make for sound marriages, too.'

She eyed him across the table, faintly muzzy from the wine. 'Are you going to get married, Mr van Borsele?' A question she wouldn't have dreamed of asking, only the wine was talking now.

He smiled a little, 'Yes, Claribel, I have the urge to settle down and become a family man.'

'In Holland, of course?'

'Of course.'

'I hope you will be very happy.' The wine had taken over with a vengeance. 'She'll be small and dainty and agree with everything you do and say and she'll do exactly as you wish. I can't imagine you marrying anyone else.'

'You're letting your imagination run away with you, dear girl.' He gave her a mocking smile which acted like a shower of cold water, drowning the rest of the wine.

She muttered, 'I'm sure you will be very happy, Mr van Borsele.'

'I'm sure I shall be, too.'

She was very conscious of having been rude. 'I'm sorry I said that,' she told him. 'I didn't mean a word of it. Do you mind if we go now? It's quite late…'

He asked for the bill and his smile wasn't mocking any more. 'You have no need to apologise, although I don't think I shall take your advice.'

He talked of everyday things as they drove back, and having

seen her safely indoors, bade her a cheerful farewell and good-night and got back into his car, barely giving her time to thank him for the evening.

She didn't see him the next day, but she hadn't expected to. The following Tuesday she spent the day in Intensive Care, helping one of the patients to adjust to breathing normally again. It was on Wednesday in the clinic at the end of a busy morning, with only Mrs Snow between her and a brief lunch, that that lady came trotting in.

'There you are, dearie,' she began as she started to peel off a variety of woollen garments. 'Wot a week I've had—there's me youngest out of work again and the old man with toothache and me 'aving to look after young Claude while 'is mum goes to the ante-natal...'

Claribel arranged her on a stool by a low table, put a cushion under her arm and ran a gentle hand over it. 'Been doing your exercises?' she wanted to know.

'Well, now, love, I 'aven't 'ad much time, wot with the ironing and that.'

Claribel was massaging gently. 'No, I don't suppose you do have much time,' she agreed. 'Could you manage to do a few exercises before you get up? Just lifting your arm like I showed you and swinging it a bit?'

'Anything to please yer, ducks. Where were you last week? I 'ad a cross old dragon, got real narked 'cause I couldn't touch me 'ead.'

'I had to go to an outside clinic—they were short of staff.'

'All on yer own?'

'Oh, my, no, there were other staff there.'

'That nice young man I saw—'e's gone back to Holland. Ain't it a shame? I rather fancied him. I just 'appened to be passing as 'e was shaking 'ands with Mr Shutter and I 'eard him say, "Well, I'll be off—I plan to catch the evening ferry from Harwich."' She breathed a gusty sigh, redolent of onion, all over Claribel. 'Silly ter say I'll miss 'im,' she observed and Claribel, rather to her surprise, agreed with her silently. So silly really; she hardly knew him and she still wasn't quite sure if she liked him, but here she was regretting his departure. And without so much as wishing her goodbye. He could at least have mentioned it when he had brought her home from the play; he had said within a day or two of Mr Shutter's return and Mr Shutter had returned only that morning…

'Tired, ducks?' asked Mrs Snow kindly. 'All that rubbing you do…I can come next week; perhaps you'll be feeling more the thing.'

'I never felt better, Mrs Snow.' Claribel resumed her massage and the soothing chat with it.

As they ate their sandwiches together she said to Miss Flute, 'Mr van Borsele didn't waste much time in going back to Holland. Perhaps he didn't like it here.'

Miss Flute bit daintily into a sausage roll. 'Didn't you see him? He came in to say goodbye. Said he'd enjoyed every minute of being here; hoped to come back some day. He and Mr Shutter were students together, you know.'

Claribel said lightly, 'Oh, were they?' It seemed that Miss Flute knew more about him than she herself did. But then, why should he have told her anything about himself?

She felt cross for the rest of the day and when Frederick met her on her way out of the hospital and asked her to go to a concert with him on the Sunday evening, she agreed, instantly regretting it. Frederick no longer interested her in the slightest.

But a promise was a promise. She was dressed and waiting for him when he called at the flat on Sunday and listened with every appearance of interest to the account of the week's work with which he regaled her as they walked to the nearest bus-stop. The concert was in a rather pokey hall and given by an ensemble who played modern music which she didn't like. Frederick sat back with his eyes closed, enjoying it, while she sat beside him, making a mental list of the groceries she would need for the following week and brooding over the patients she would be working on. She clapped when everyone else did and finally rose with well-concealed thankfulness and filed out in to the late April evening. It would be glorious to be at home now, she thought, but here in the busy London street there was only a strip of sky and stars to be seen. She sighed and agreed with Frederick that a cup of coffee would be very nice.

There weren't many cafés open in that part of London on a Sunday evening; the one they entered was small and rather dark and almost empty, but the coffee was good. She accepted a second cup and waited for Frederick to tell her what he so obviously was longing to say. Finally she said, 'There's something on your mind, Frederick. Do tell.'

He said rather pompously. 'Have you ever taken me seriously, Claribel?'

He sounded anxious and she said soothingly, 'No, Frederick, but I don't think you ever led me to suppose…' she paused delicately, hoping that he would explain.

'Oh, good'. His relief was so obvious that she almost laughed. 'You see, I like you very much, Claribel—at one time I actually considered asking you to marry me—but I met Joyce when I went home a couple of weeks ago.' He added solemnly, 'I'm not a man to play fast and loose.'

'No, of course you aren't,' she told him warmly. 'I've always considered you as a friend, Frederick, nothing more.' Which wasn't true, but it was what he wanted to hear. 'Tell me about her—does she love you, too?'

'Well I think so, but it's too soon to ask her…'

'Rubbish,' cried Claribel. 'How will you ever know if you don't ask? When are you going home again?'

'I've a couple of days due next week.'

'Oh, good. Get after her fast, Frederick, before someone else snaps her up. What is she like?' It took a considerable time to tell her. They had to have a third cup of coffee while he enlarged on the subject nearest his heart.

'Of course, we'll still be real friends?'

She put down her cup for the last time. 'Of course—why ever not? But do let me know what happens, Frederick. I think it's marvellous for you.'

Back in her flat she got supper, fed the cats and sat down to write a letter home. She wouldn't miss Frederick in the least, so why did she feel so out of spirits?

The cats, when questioned, had no answer; she made a pot of tea and went to bed.

Normally a contented girl, sensible enough to accept her lot in life and be happy with it, for after all, it wasn't so bad, Claribel found that her spirits didn't rise. The week went by, busy as it always was, but there were things which should have made her happy. The weather, usually unpredictable in April, had been steadily warmer and sunnier each day so that going to work was a pleasure, even though her way led her through rather shabby streets. Besides, the early tulips in the tubs she had so carefully cherished by the front door had bloomed and gave a nice splash of colour to her little home, and, over and above these small pleasures, she had been given an unexpected free afternoon and had gone shopping. She hadn't intended to buy anything but the sight of a cotton jersey ensemble in a pale toffee colour sent prudence to the winds. She bought it, knowing that its colour did all the right things to her eyes and hair, and this despite the doubt as to when she would be able to wear it. It was too elegant to wear to work and she supposed that she would wear it when she went home for the weekend. Strangely, when one of the house doctors waylaid her on the following afternoon and asked her to spend the following Sunday afternoon with him—an excellent opportunity to air the new outfit—she refused; he was quite a pleasant man but when he suggested that they might go to an absent friend's flat for tea, she prudently said no.

Squashed on the bus going home after this encounter she supposed that she was getting prudish, certainly old-fashioned. Perhaps she should have tried harder with Frederick and made sure of a secure future. She frowned at the thought and an elderly man on whom she had bent her unseeing gaze looked the other way. She wasn't a very nice girl, she reflected, and sighed loudly, right down the neck of the woman pressed against her. The woman turned an indignant face to her. 'Do you mind?' she asked aggressively.

'So sorry,' said Claribel and brought her thoughts back to the present. She got off at the next stop, walked briskly down

Meadow Road and unlocked her front door. She felt better once she was inside, with the cats there to welcome her and the prospect of tea.

She cast about her for ways in which to fill the approaching weekend. She could have gone home, but the outfit had cost far too much money; it was pay day during the next week; she would go on the following weekend. She cheered up at the thought and decided to wash the sitting-room net curtains; they were necessary to keep prying eyes from staring in, but they didn't stay clean for more than a week or so. And she would recover the little chair in the bedroom. She had bought the velvet weeks ago and there was webbing and tacks and a hammer somewhere in the kitchen, and while she was at it she could use the rest of the velvet to cover a couple of cushions.

'I'm getting to be a real old maid,' she told the cats.

The weekend came; she had the curtains washed and dripping over the bath and, fired with a sudden energy, had upended the bedroom chair and was ripping off its old cover when there was a thump on the door knocker. It was the kind of thump Mr van Borsele gave. Just for a split second she felt delight surge though her, to be instantly quenched by common sense; he was in Holland.

Only he wasn't. He was on her doorstep, looking impatient when she opened the door.

She stared up at him, conscious of vexation because she was wearing an old dress and a plastic pinny with 'Work Hard' printed on its bib.

'You're in Holland,' she greeted him.

'No, I'm here waiting to be asked in.'

She mumbled, 'Oh, sorry.' How like him to turn a situation to his advantage. 'Do come in, I'm having a weekend turn out.'

He stalked past her. 'Have you nothing better to do?' he asked testily. He poked at the chair. 'Do you know how to upholster chairs as well as get bones working again?'

'No, and I'm not upholstering, only covering. Sit down, Mr van Borsele.'

It would hardly do to ask him why he had come. Instead she asked, 'Would you like some coffee?'

'Yes. I came on the night ferry to Harwich. For some reason there was a hitch and there was no breakfast car on the boat train and I didn't stop on the way.'

Her motherly instincts were aroused. 'Just you sit there and I'll get you a meal. Bacon and eggs and mushrooms and toast and marmalade and tea—no coffee.'

'Since I am in England, a pot of your strong tea and with luck while you are getting it I will see to this chair. It seems as if you are not making a very good job of it.'

She rounded on him indignantly. 'Well, you really are the limit! You come here for breakfast—and there's no reason why I should cook it for you only I've got a kind heart—and then you mock my work. I'd like to see you do it better.'

'And so you shall, Claribel. But I do beg of you, give me a meal before you deliver the lecture which I feel is hovering on your tongue.'

'Oh, you are impossible!' she told him. But she went into the kitchen and got out the jar of fat and the frying pan, and presently the delicious smell of bacon frying filled the little flat.

When she went back into the sitting-room to lay the table she was surprised to see that he had taken off his jacket and was making a splendid job of covering the chair. 'There's no need,' she cried. 'I've all the weekend in which to do it.'

'No you haven't. We're going to Richmond Park after lunch—I need a good brisk walk—and this evening I thought we might go dancing after dinner.'

She stood goggling until he said briskly, 'Don't burn the bacon, Claribel.'

She dished up a plateful, carried it in and set it on the table.

'I don't know what you are talking about,' she began.

'Well, for a start, for heaven's sake stop calling me Mr van Borsele—my name's Marc. You know that already.' He pulled the velvet tight over the chair and tacked it neatly.

He polished off his breakfast and returned to the chair. Claribel, speechless, for she had no idea of how to deal with the situation, cleared away the remnants of his meal, washed the dishes and went back into the sitting-room. The chair was finished, and very nice it looked, too.

'Do passers-by always stare in so rudely?' he wanted to know.

'I've washed the curtains. They're almost dry.'

'Let us hang them up at once then.' Still bemused, she fetched them and watched him hang them up once more. 'And let us hope that is the extent of your activities for the day,' he commented.

She said feebly, 'I'm going to cover some cushions...'

'Surely not urgent?' He had settled into an easy chair. 'Get yourself dressed, Claribel, while I take a nap.'

She knew exactly how a rabbit felt when it was face to face with a snake. 'But I'm not going out—I told you...'

He stretched out his legs and closed his eyes. 'I haven't come all this way just to watch you do the housework,' he pointed out. 'You have no need to demonstrate your capabilities in that field.'

She stood and looked at him, mulling over a number of things she intended to say, but was stopped from doing this by the quite genuine snore which, while not detracting in the least from his dignity, bore witness to the fact that he was sound asleep.

She stood uncertainly, studying his sleeping face. Very handsome, she conceded, and somehow rather endearing; she almost liked him. She corrected herself: she did like him. His ill-humour didn't mean a thing to her; behind that bland mocking façade there was quite a nice man, she felt sure. She couldn't for the life of her imagine why he had come back to London, but then she knew nothing of his life, did she? And a walk in Richmond Park would really be rather nice...

She slid away to her bedroom and got into the new jersey outfit.

CHAPTER FOUR

MR VAN BORSELE was wide awake when she went back into the sitting-room, with the cats on his knee and a rather smug look upon his handsome features. He got up as she went in, remarking that there she was, and that she had been rather a long time, in the manner of someone who had been waiting with impatience, his eye on the clock.

'You were asleep,' said Claribel, quick to point out the fact, 'so don't try and pretend that I've kept you waiting.'

'My dear Claribel, you are the very last person I would pretend to. Are we ready?'

He arranged the cats on the chair he had just vacated and opened the door for her. The Rolls was outside, looking rather out of place in the shabby little road. She cast her eyes back at her windows and was pleased to see the pristine whiteness of the curtains and the tubs of flowers. He followed her look. 'Very nice,' he observed. 'I like your outfit. Did you buy it to wear when you come out with me?'

This perfectly preposterous suggestion left her speechless. She allowed herself to be ushered into the car and the door closed, but she was still speechless when he got in beside her. She said, finally and coldly, 'I bought it because I needed something to wear and I liked it. I had no idea that I should see you again.'

'You hoped you would?' He smiled at her slowly, his head a little on one side.

Claribel opened her handbag, looked inside and closed it up again. 'Well, it's always nice to renew acquaintance with people one has met.' That sounded pompous and affected. 'It's nice to see you again.'

Mr van Borsele let out a long sigh. 'Oh good. Let's have lunch.' He took her to Boulestin's where she ate a delicious lunch which she allowed him to choose for her: chicken mousseline for starters, brill with lobster sauce and chocolate ice-cream in a pastry case.

They didn't linger over their coffee; the bright, sunny afternoon reminded them that they were to visit Richmond Park. On the best of terms, they got back into the car and drove the short distance to the park, left the car and started their walk. They had left the car at the southern edge of the park and were making for Richmond Hill when they paused to admire the view.

'It's nice here,' observed Claribel. 'London seems far away.'

'You don't like London?' He was leaning on a rough wall beside her.

'Well, I like theatres and going out, but only now and again. Life's always such a rush. At home the days seem twice as long.'

She glanced at his face, half turned away from her. 'Do you like London?'

'Just as you do—not too often; but of course, I go where my work takes me.'

'Surely you can choose. Miss Flute said that you were at the top of the tree.'

He laughed. 'It's not much use perching at the top if you're wanted in the branches, is it?'

'So you can't live exactly as you would like?'

'Perhaps not. My work is important to me, of course, but I dare say once I settle down I shall draw in my horns a little.'

They started back presently, and when they were within sight of the car Claribel asked, 'Would you like to come back for tea? It's been a lovely afternoon.'

'Delightful, and yes, I'd like to have tea with you.' He sounded casually friendly.

She offered him the easy chair again, fed the cats and laid the tea tray. A plate of very thin bread and butter, some of her mother's homemade jam and a cake she had baked the previous evening. She carried the tray into the sitting-room and found him asleep again, and waited patiently for several minutes before he opened his eyes.

'Didn't you go to bed last night?' she asked. 'On the ferry, I mean.'

'Oh, yes, for an hour or so. I've had several busy nights and they've caught up with me.'

She gave him tea and a plate and offered him the bread and butter.

'You should have gone to bed and slept the moment you got to London,' she told him severely. 'Do you have to go to Jerome's tomorrow?' She frowned. 'It's Sunday.'

'Certainly not. I've given myself the weekend off.' He made short work of the bread and butter. 'We'll go out to dinner this evening and go dancing.'

'Don't be silly,' she cried. 'You're worn out—I must have been mad to agree to walking all those miles this afternoon. Mr van Borsele...' She caught his dark gaze. 'Marc, then—you must drive straight to your hotel and sleep the clock round.'

'I haven't a hotel, and if I sleep the clock round I won't be able to go out this evening, and just now and again, dear girl, it's good to be a little mad.' He sat back in his chair and smiled at her. 'Did you make that cake?'

'Yes, of course I did. Why haven't you a hotel to go to?'

'I have a small flat I use when I come over here.'

She offered him a slice of cake, biting back the questions on her tongue; where was the flat and was it his or lent to him, and was there someone there to look after him? A housekeeper? A girl perhaps? But he had said that he was looking forward to being a family man...

His dark eyes were filled with amusement. 'You should learn to disguise your thoughts, Claribel. This is excellent cake. May I call for you at eight o'clock?'

'Well, all right.' That sounded ungracious so she added, 'Thank you, but somewhere quiet, and no dancing. You should have an early night.'

'You're a bossy young woman, Claribel; with a name like that you should be soft and clinging and agree with every word I utter.'

She nodded. 'I told you that was the kind of wife you needed.'

He smiled a little and got to his feet. 'I'll be here at eight o'clock; we'll dine at the Savoy and dance afterwards.' The smile turned to a grin. 'Perhaps it will be my last fling before I marry.'

He paused at the door. 'A delicious tea. Many thanks, Claribel.'

He closed the door quietly behind him and she stood at her window, looking up into the street and watched the Rolls slide away. She began to tidy away the tea things, voicing her thoughts to the cats. 'I can't think why he came here—he must know heaps of girls. And why come to England when he's got a perfectly good country of his own? And where's this girl he's going to marry?'

She began to wash up, stopping to think from time to time until a glance at the clock sent her scurrying to her wardrobe to find a suitable dress.

There was no time after that; Enoch and Toots wanted their suppers and she stood for ages trying to decide what to wear.

Finally she decided on the newest of her three long dresses, a pearly grey crêpe-de-Chine with a flowery pattern of palest pink and equally pale green. There was no time to wash her hair; she took a shower and dressed and then sat down before her dressing-table and put on her make-up very carefully. She didn't use much. She had a lovely clear skin and thick dark brown lashes which everyone believed she had dyed; cream and powder and a pale pink lipstick were all that she needed. She spent much longer on her hair, arranging it in a coil at the nape of her neck. It added dignity to her appearance, or so she believed.

She was transferring her keys to her evening bag when Mr van Borsele thumped the door knocker. She padded across the room into the tiny hallway and opened the door, to be met by his frosty, 'How many times must I tell you not to open the door unless you have put up the chain? And why are you not wearing any shoes?'

She eyed his magnificent person; she doubted if the inhabitants of Meadow Road had ever seen such dinner-jacketed elegance. She said kindly, 'Goodness, you are cross—but it's your own fault if you won't go to bed and have a good sleep.' She led the way into the living-room. 'And I haven't forgotten my slippers; I'm quite ready.'

She poked her feet into green slippers and picked up the short velvet evening coat, inherited from an aunt who no longer wore it—its old-fashioned cut had gone full circle and it was once again in the forefront of fashion. Mr van Borsele took it from her and helped her into it and then touched her hair lightly.

'Nice hair,' he commented; Claribel had the depressing feeling that he would have used such a tone of voice if he had been admiring a friend's dog.

There was a good deal of curtain-twitching as they got into the Rolls, but Claribel wasn't disturbed by that. On the whole, she was liked by her immediate neighbours; she was quiet, was meticulous about putting out the rubbish on a Monday morning and never stock-piled empty milk bottles. Nor did she complain when the noisy family across the road gave one of their frequent all-night parties, and when the old lady next door lost her cat it was Claribel who gave up her evening to search the nearby streets and find it. All the same, she found herself reflecting, there would be gossip; Mr van Borsele was becoming a frequent visitor.

The thought became a question. 'Just why did you come to London? You said you had been busy and yet when you get a weekend free you waste half of it travelling.'

He turned to look at her, his eyebrows lifted, a faintly mocking smile on his firm mouth and she went a bright pink. 'Sorry,' she said breathlessly, 'it's none of my business.'

'No, it isn't, Claribel.' He started the car and they purred the length of the dreary road; he didn't speak until they were on the other side of the river. 'Tell me,' he asked, 'do you begin to like me?'

She said crossly, 'You do ask such awkward questions, but

since you ask, yes, most of the time I like you.' She drew a deep breath. 'Though why that matters I can't think.'

'Pretty girls like you shouldn't think too much. Shall we agree to like each other just for this evening? Such a pity to come all this way...' He left the rest of his remark in the air.

She smoothed her silken lap. 'Why not?' She felt bewildered. She was a level-headed girl, leading a well-ordered life, but now, suddenly, she felt reckless. 'I—I think I'm going to enjoy my evening.'

'I know I am.' He ran the car down the entrance to the Savoy, handed it over to the doorman and ushered her inside.

The River Room was almost full, but their table was one of the best in the room, in one of the windows, overlooking the Embankment. Claribel, more than ready to enjoy herself, beamed at her companion. 'This is simply super,' she told him. 'Have you got hotels like this in Holland?'

'In the big cities, yes. Where I live there is very little night life, though Holland is a small country and it is possible to spend an evening out without having to drive too far.'

She chose smoked salmon, chicken cooked in a cream sauce and an omelette filled with strawberries and awash with a wine sauce and thick cream. Mr van Borsele ate his fillet steak and then suggested that they might dance.

Claribel was a good dancer, but then so was he; they suited each other perfectly and although the omelette was delicious she got to her feet at once when he suggested that they might dance again. He had contented himself with the cheeseboard, and when they got back to their table coffee was brought at once. Claribel poured out. 'Oh, I am enjoying myself,' she declared, and presently they danced again. They danced until late, but not too late to stop quite a few curtains twitching as he pushed open her door for her and bade her goodnight.

'I'll be here at ten o'clock tomorrow,' he observed as she paused uncertainly in the doorway. 'Goodnight, Claribel.' He edged her gently inside, shut the door on her, got back into his car and drove away.

'Well, whatever next?' asked Claribel of the cats. 'Ten

o'clock indeed, and just what did that mean? For two pins I'll be in bed... Anyone would suppose that he was anxious to be rid of me.' She began to undress slowly. 'I don't have to go out with him again, do I?' she wanted to know, but both cats had curled up at the end of the bed and took no notice.

A brilliantly sunny morning melted her stern resolutions of the night before. She was up early to feed the cats, eat her breakfast, tidy her small home, and dress with care in the new outfit once more. She was sitting, apparently doing nothing, when Mr van Borsele arrived, to bang on her door with his customary vigour. His 'Hello—coffee?' quite put her off her stroke. She had planned to be cool and casual and here he was demanding coffee the moment he poked his commanding nose around her door.

'Do sit down,' she begged him coldly, 'while I make the coffee.' She swept into the kitchen and filled the kettle with a good deal of noise and clattered the mugs on to the tray.

'The peace of domesticity,' he observed from the comfort of his chair. The cats were squashed on to either side of him and he had his eyes closed.

Claribel peered at him round the kitchen door. 'Domesticity has two sides to it,' she pointed out rather sharply. 'You have overlooked the cooking and washing up and clearing away side of it.'

'No, no.' He opened an eye to look at her. 'There is pleasure in the sight of some little woman bending over the kitchen sink.'

Claribel said 'Huh!' Had he noticed that she wasn't a little woman and she loathed washing up? She retired to the kitchen before he could answer that.

She offered him his coffee and passed the sugar without speaking and went to sit on the little spinning-chair by the window.

'The Cotswolds?' He sounded almost humble, although she suspected him of being nothing of the sort.

'Too far.'

'Nonsense.. We'll go through Twyford and Didcot and

through the White Horse Vale and have bread and cheese in Adlestrop...'

'But that's almost in Cheltenham—it's miles away.'

'A change of scene is good for one.' He finished his coffee. 'Drink up, Claribel. Feed your cats and bolt your windows and turn off the gas and do the hundred-and-one things women do before they go out.'

She rounded on him. 'The first thing you said when you got here was "Coffee?" and now I'm expected to rush and tear around at the drop of a hat.'

He got up, his head almost towering to the ceiling. 'I'll see to these mugs and feed the cats; you go and comb your golden hair.' And, when she put a hand up to her hair, 'I speak metaphorically.'

There wasn't a great deal of traffic once they had shaken off London and its suburbs, and Mr van Borsele kept to the secondary roads as far as possible, driving with a nonchalant ease which Claribel, a rather nervous driver herself, envied.

They talked comfortably and sometimes lapsed into companionable silences, while the Rolls sped effortlessly towards Adlestrop which when they reached it was quite delightful, with its houses of golden stone and the cottages lining the main street with dormer windows and weathered slate roofs. Mr van Borsele slid to a halt in the courtyard of the village pub and helped Claribel out of the car.

'I've been here before,' he told her. 'I think you will like it.'

She did. The bar was long and rather dark, held together by crooked beams and yellowed plaster walls; there was a darts board at one end, but thankfully no fruit machines or taped music. There were a lot of people there; church was over and it wanted ten minutes before the one o'clock Sunday dinner would be dished up in almost every home in the village. She was settled at a table, asked what she would like to drink and given the menu card from the bar, unaware of the admiring glances sent her way. Mr van Borsele came back with her drink and a tankard of beer for himself and they discussed what they should eat. 'You said bread and cheese,' she glanced at him, smiling, 'so I'll have a ploughman's lunch—with stilton.'

The food when it came was delicious: homemade bread, a little pat of butter in a pot and a generous wedge of cheese with an array of pickles. They ate with appetite and finished with coffee before Mr van Borsele suggested that they might stroll through the village and take a look at the church.

They wandered round, looking at the numerous monuments to the Leigh family who had lived in the great house nearby for hundreds of years. Some of the inscriptions were very old and Mr van Borsele obligingly translated their Latin text. Claribel, listening to his deep voice, reflected that if he had been Frederick she would have been bored; as it was, she wished the day to last for twice its usual length.

A wish she was not granted. They had wandered out of the church into the sunshine again and Mr van Borsele said, 'Ah, well, a delightful interlude—now for home.'

Claribel had allowed her thoughts to dwell on tea at some wayside cottage and perhaps dinner that evening, but she agreed at once; perhaps he had had enough of her company, even though he had made such a point of spending the day with her. The thought caused her conversation to become rather stiff and her companion smiled once or twice, remarking casually that they would go back through Chipping Norton and join the road to Oxford. 'We can pick up the motorway there,' he explained. 'It's barely an hour's run from there to London. Will you give me tea when we get back?'

'Of course.' She spoke in her best hostess voice and his dark eyes gleamed with amusement.

It was just after five o'clock when he opened her door and she went into the living-room. The cats rushed to meet them as she opened the kitchen window to let them into the tiny back yard before she put on the kettle. There were the biscuits she had baked earlier in the week and the rest of the cake; she got the tray ready and carried it through and poured the tea.

'Thank you for my lovely day,' she said politely. 'I really enjoyed it.'

'But you are wondering why I have brought you back without so much as stopping for tea—you may even have wondered if I was going to ask you out to dinner?' His voice was bland. 'Unfortunately I have to go back to Holland this evening.'

She tumbled her cup on to its saucer and almost broke it. 'You what? This evening? But it's almost six o'clock now; why didn't you tell me?'

'You sound like a wife.' He was laughing at her. 'If I had told you it would altogether have spoilt your day; you would have been looking at your watch every ten minutes.' He sat looking at her for a long moment. 'You know, Claribel, you are the only girl I know who doesn't bore me; you eat bread and cheese and inspect churches and don't fidget with your hair and make-up and you make an excellent cup of coffee and yet you make any man proud to take you out to dinner.'

She stared back at him. 'Why did you come?'

He got to his feet. 'My dear Claribel, I have just told you. Thank you for my tea. Your biscuits melt in the mouth. *Tot ziens.*'

She was at the door with him. 'What does that mean?'

'In this case, until I see you again.'

'Don't be too sure of that.' She gave him a frosty smile and offered a polite hand. It was disconcerting to have it held gently and then kissed.

She watched him drive away, shut the door smartly and poured herself another cup of tea. 'I didn't like him when we met,' she told the cats, 'and then I did, or I thought I did, but I don't. And if he thinks I'll give him biscuits next time he comes, he's in for a disappointment—dry bread and water.' Her voice rose indignantly. 'I shan't open the door.'

But while washing up it crossed her mind that it wasn't very likely that he would come again. She had been far too easy with him; she should have refused his first invitation. He was unsettling—not her type... She said it twice out loud to make sure that she believed it.

So she should have been glad that there was no sign of him, let alone mention of his name, during the ensuing week. She had decided to go home for the weekend but instead of going on the Friday evening, she told herself that there was no rush; she caught a mid-morning train on the Saturday, refusing to admit to herself that she had been hoping for Mr van Borsele's imperious thump on her door.

'You're pale, dear,' observed her mother. 'You've been working too hard, cooped up in London; I hope you get into the parks at the weekends. Does that solemn young man—Frederick wasn't it?—still walk you miles on Sundays?'

'No, Mother—he's going to marry a girl he met when he went home a month or so ago.'

'Oh, do you mind, darling?' Her mother was bending over the tapestry frame she worked at with religious persistence.

'Not a bit.'

'Oh, good. I never thought that he was quite the right man for you. Do you see anything of that nice man who gave you a lift here?'

'He is Dutch, mother dear; he lives in Holland. He comes over to Jerome's to operate from time to time.'

Her mother eyed her narrowly. Dear Claribel wasn't fibbing, but she was holding something back. Mrs Brown allowed herself a small smug smile. She was a firm believer in motherly instinct, and so far it had never let her down.

She made no demur when dear Claribel decided that she would have to go back to Meadow Road by an earlier train than usual. Things to do, she had said vaguely, smalls to wash and she simply *had* to turn out the kitchen cupboard. Her mother agreed soothingly, packed up a pot of homemade marmalade and a rich fruit cake and begged her not to work too hard. 'Have fun, too,' she advised. 'I'm sure you get lots of dates.'

Claribel agreed, as indeed she did—but she didn't always accept them.

Monday morning began all wrong; she woke late, her hair refused to go up with its usual smoothness, the cats didn't want to come in from the yard and she broke a plate, then to crown it all she missed her bus. She got to Jerome's out of breath, a little peevish and with a heightened colour.

'Late,' observed Miss Flute, 'but not too late to go the men's ward—Mr Shutter's round.'

Claribel cheered up at once. The wards were interesting; the patients she had to treat there were suffering from complicated broken bones which it gave her great pleasure to straighten out again. She sped through the hospital and reached the group of people gathered round Sister just as the clock struck the hour.

They were just inside the ward doors and as they swung open Sister stepped forward; it was her prerogative to say good morning before anyone else. But it wasn't Mr Shutter who answered it. Mr van Borsele, followed by another group, this time the registrar, houseman and students, strode through the door, acknowledged her greeting with a courteous smile and cast his eyes over her entourage. Claribel had gone a good deal pinker than she already was by reason of her haste and his gaze paused momentarily at her astonished face and then swept on without any sign of recognition. Not that he could have said anything, but a smile would have been quite permissible. The day had begun badly, she reflected, and it looked likely to continue so. She submerged herself among the nurses and the lady social worker, no easy task since her splendid person made the rest of them look like midgets, and she followed dutifully in the wake of Mr van Borsele and his team. She wasn't left long in obscurity, though; she had been treating several of the patients and Mr van Borsele wished to see what progress had been made, so she lifted arms and legs, demonstrated the head traction on one unfortunate young man who had had a fracture of his cervical spine, and then assisted an elderly man to demonstrate his walking powers.

'Very nice,' commented Mr van Borsele in measured tones. 'Shall we see this patient Mr Shutter has told me of? He's for theatre this afternoon. Miss Brown, you will begin passive exercises as soon as he is conscious—he is unfortunately a chronic bronchial but if we are to save that leg we must operate immediately. So breathing exercises and hourly coughing, if you please.' His glance was impersonal.

He left the ward presently and, after a brief consultation with

Sister, Claribel went back to the physio department, where she poked her bright head round Miss Flute's door. 'May I come in? I say, I've been given that man who came in last night with the compound fracture of the left leg. He's a chest as well; I have to give him hourly treatment starting when he's in recovery coming round from the anaesthetic—that'll be late afternoon, I suppose. And I'm booked solid down here.'

Miss Flute looked unworried. 'Yes, dear, I'll have to transfer your patients for a day or two. Someone will take over for night duty? What hours have you got, did anyone tell you?'

'Sister asked me to stay until eight this evening; she said she'd be seeing you.' Claribel paused. 'It's a bit awkward—the cats, you know.'

Miss Flute, who had an elderly moggie herself, nodded sympathetically. 'Suppose you go home about three o'clock—you can be back before five o'clock? The list doesn't start until three o'clock; I should think you won't be needed for a couple of hours.' The phone rang and she stopped to answer it, nodding her head and saying yes, yes, several times.

'Sister,' she told Claribel. 'Would you like to do eight in the morning till half past four; she can have Mrs Down from then until eight o'clock and I'll do the night shift.' And, when Claribel lightly protested, 'No, don't argue, Miss Brookes can hold the fort here until midday, when Mrs Green can come on duty here until she relieves you. It will only be for a few days; once we've got him going it will be a TDS job. We've done this before, there's no reason why it won't work again.'

Miss Flute's word was law. Claribel, after a hurried return to her flat to see Enoch and Toots, presented herself in Intensive Care to wait for the arrival of the patient. He came from the recovery room with two nurses in attendance and for the first hour there was nothing for her to do except watch the nurses hoist the plastered leg on to a Balkan beam and apply the weights. A very nasty compound fracture, one of them told her; bits of bone all over the place, but Mr van Borsele had assembled them with infinite patience, pinned them neatly, nailed the bone together and was of the opinion that the leg would be quite useful in a few months' time. The leg, at the moment, looked of no use at all, with toes sticking out of the foot end of the plaster and a long window cut so that the big incision which had been made could be examined frequently.

Presently the man opened his eyes and Claribel started her work. He certainly had what she would have described as a nasty chest, but he had no wish to cough.

'Oh, come now,' said Claribel at her most beguiling. 'You're going to feel so much better, and that's a promise. It's no good you arguing, for I have to do this every hour, but the more you cough the quicker I'll stop plaguing you.'

The man swore softly but he did as she asked and presently lay back on his pillows while the nurses made him more comfortable.

'Everything all right?' asked Mr van Borsele in her ear. 'If you can keep that up for a couple of days he'll be OK.' He went past her to bend over his patient and then went away again as quietly as he had come.

Miss Flute came just as quietly at eight o'clock, nodded briskly to Claribel, exchanged a few knowledgeable remarks and bade her go home just as Mr van Borsele returned, so there was a small delay while Claribel gave her report and, when she would have gone, 'Wait for me, if you please, Miss Brown.' His voice was pleasant but held a note which she didn't care to ignore. She went to stand with Miss Flute while he conferred with the night nurse and Sister, took another look at his patient and rejoined them to wish Miss Flute goodnight and urge Claribel through the door.

In the corridor he said briefly, 'I'll be outside the physio department entrance in five minutes. I'll run you home.'

'Thank you, but there is no need. I'm perfectly able…'

'Don't argue, Claribel; we're both tired and you need a night's sleep—I want that man fit in the shortest possible time.'

She said, 'Very well, Mr van Borsele,' in such a meek voice that he opened his eyes wide although he said nothing. They went down in the lift to the ground floor and parted without a word.

She was tired; she hadn't realised that until now. The patient was a heavy man and unwilling, and he had been hard work; supper and bed would be delightful. She changed and locked the door after her and found the Rolls waiting. Mr van Borsele, lounging over its bonnet, opened the door for her, got in and drove away without speaking. There wasn't a great deal of traffic and Meadow Road when they reached it was deserted. He got out when she did, took her key and opened the door and followed her inside.

'Coffee?' asked Claribel, anticipating what he was going to say.

'No, tea, I think. And a sandwich?' He went past her and put the kettle on. 'Hello, Claribel.'

She turned to stare at him. 'But you saw me this morning…'

'So I did, but that was—how shall I put it?—a professional meeting. Now we are just you and me.'

He watched her face, reading her thoughts. 'The last thing I would wish to do would be to lay you open to the hospital grapevine.' He took the teapot from her and poured hot water into it. 'I value your friendship too much.'

She stood there watching him empty the teapot, spoon in tea and pour on the boiling water. 'You don't seem like a friend,' she muttered. 'Oh, you're very kind, giving me lifts and—and a day out and dinner…but I don't understand you. Sometimes I'm not sure if I like you.'

'I know that. Don't let it worry you.' He smiled suddenly at her and she saw then that he was tired. She said quite sharply, 'Do sit down; I'll make those sandwiches. Do you have to go back to Jerome's?'

'In an hour or so, yes.' He lounged back in his chair and closed his eyes and she felt a sharp pang of pity as she got out the bread and butter and started on the sandwiches. He hadn't stirred when she had finished so she fed the cats and carried the tray noiselessly into the living-room. He needed a good hot meal, she thought worriedly; probably he hadn't had lunch and would forget about his dinner if he was worried about his patient. He was a man who drove himself too hard.

She piled sandwiches on a plate and poured the tea, and when she turned round he was watching her closely; there was nothing sleepy about his gaze.

She said tartly, 'I thought you were asleep.'

'I was. What is in the sandwiches?'

'Cheese and pickles, ham, lettuce and tomato.'

He munched contentedly. 'Tell, me, Claribel, when you marry will you be prepared to offer your husband refreshment at whatever hour he comes home?'

'Well, of course, provided he's been working and not just gallivanting around.'

He said seriously, 'I can't imagine your marrying a man who gallivanted. These sandwiches are delicious.'

'Didn't you have any lunch?'

'No.' He took another sandwich and bit into it.

'But you'll get dinner when you get back to Jerome's?'

'Probably. It depends on how that man is doing. You take over in the morning?'

'At eight o'clock. What kind of a chance has he?'

They talked comfortably about the case and presently he got up to go.

He wasted no words on polite observations that he would see her in the morning or anything similar, merely bade her goodnight, adding a laconic, 'Thanks for the food, Claribel.'

Leaving her, as he usually did, feeling cross.

She saw him frequently during the next day or two but only on the ward, and then to do no more than pass her report to whichever nurse was on duty.

The patient was hard work, but he was responding at last; by the third day Claribel no longer needed to be with him continuously. Miss Flute went back to her office and Claribel and Mrs Green shared a complicated schedule of duty for another thirty-six hours before he was pronounced out of danger and needed physiotherapy only morning and evening, so that he could be fitted in with her other ward cases.

It would be nice to be back to normal working conditions, Claribel assured Miss Flute, while at the back of her mind there was regret at not seeing Mr van Borsele again. And when the following day she went to the ward for a round, it was Mr Shutter who arrived to take it. Gone back to Holland, ruminated Claribel, busy showing Mr Shutter just how nicely a boy with cut tendons of the hand had regained very nearly its full powers. Not that she missed him, but he could have said goodbye.

She was going home for the weekend; she raced to the flat as the buses were slow, gobbling her tea, showered and changed, fed the cats and ushered them to their basket. With luck she might just catch the train before her usual one. She was dashing about on a last-minute check when the door knocker was thumped. The sound brought her up short; only one person used such force and he, to the best of her knowledge, was in Holland.

He was on the doorstep. She drew a breath. 'I'm just leaving...'

'The warmth of your welcome leaves much to be desired,' he observed mildly. 'All the same, I shall come in.'

Which he did, shoving her gently ahead of him until they were both in the living-room.

She turned to face him. 'Look, I'm catching a train home—I shall miss it!'

'I'll drive you down—I'm going that way.' He gave her a beguiling smile. 'We could have a cup of coffee now and I'll give you dinner on the way.'

'Mother's expecting me.'

He lifted the receiver off the cradle and handed it to her. 'I'll put the kettle on.' He went into the kitchen, unfastening the cat's basket as he went, leaving her speechless. She put the receiver back and followed him into the kitchen. 'Look, this really is too much; you walk in here and tell me what to do, and now I've missed my train!'

He was spooning coffee into two mugs. 'We'll get there before the train or very soon after.' He added blandly, 'Shouldn't you let your mother know?'

She went back to the telephone and rang her mother, aware that she was taking the line of least resistance. Her temper wasn't improved by her mother's cheerful voice. 'How nice, dear. Your father and I both hoped that we'd meet your nice young man again...'

'He's not my young man.' She spoke in a cross rather loud voice and put the receiver down quite sharply.

'Is it so refreshing,' remarked Mr van Borsele from the kitchen, 'to be referred to as a young man, even when the speaker is now in a nasty temper.'

He handed her a mug of coffee with a disarming smile and she found her peevishness evaporating. She said, half laughing, 'Doesn't anything upset you?'

'Oh, yes.'

He was quite serious. He sat down in the easy chair and sipped his coffee and, because she found the silence a little awkward, she asked, 'Are you over here to work again?'

He nodded. 'We shall change that plaster—I think I may close the wound; he's doing extremely well. And there's a rather complicated case Mr Shutter has asked me to discuss.'

'Don't you mind going to and fro so often? Don't you want to be at home?'

'Do you not have a saying, ''Home is where the heart is''?'

She looked at him, puzzled. 'Do you mean that you can't settle down?'

He smiled a little. 'At the moment it would be premature.'

She picked up the mugs and took them to the kitchen. 'You're going to get married, Mr van Borsele?'

'The name is Marc, and yes, that is my intention.'

'Then you won't come over to England so often?' She turned to look at him and met his dark eyes and felt the colour flooding her face when she saw his raised eyebrows. She said gruffly, 'I didn't mean to be nosey.'

She scooped up the cats and put them back into their basket. 'I'm ready when you are.' Her voice was wooden with embarrassment. 'It's kind of you to run me home.' She took a quick peep at him and saw that he was smiling. 'What's so funny?'

He took the basket from her. 'You know, you really are rather a dear girl—you'll make a splendid wife.' He opened the door and she went past him, her question unanswered.

CHAPTER FIVE

In her efforts to appear quite at ease, Claribel plunged into talk, trivial stuff to which her companion replied politely without contributing any conversation of his own. After a time her chatter petered out and she sat silent.

Mr van Borsele gave a deep sigh and observed blandly, 'There's no need to try so hard, Claribel. You may not like me overmuch but at least you know me well enough by now to be able to keep silent if you wish. Where shall we stop for a meal?' he asked, but didn't wait for her to answer.

They were almost on to the M3 which would take them nearly as far as Andover. 'Once we are off the motorway we can stop at Middle Wallop—there's a good restaurant there, the Old Drapery Stores, run by a Dutch family.'

He began to talk easily about the place in a placid voice so that presently Claribel began to relax again. By the time they reached the restaurant she was her usual self, able to enjoy the good food set before her. But they didn't linger over the meal; they were on their way again within the hour, speeding towards Salisbury.

'I'll take the A30 and turn off it at Fovant,' observed Mr van Borsele, and he put down his well-shod foot.

It was dark by now but the sky was starlit and the moon was rising; the road leapt ahead of them in the car's powerful headlamps and Claribel, quietly content without quite knowing why, sat back in her seat, watching Mr van Borsele's masterly handling of his car.

They turned off at Fovant, travelling along a narrow country road full of unexpected twists and turns. 'Tell me if I go wrong,' said Mr van Borsele placidly. 'I don't know this road.'

There were no villages, only the odd farmhouse or row of

farm cottages and the occasional isolated house standing well back from the road.

Mr van Borsele slowed for an S-bend and as they came out of it slowed still more; there were blue lights flashing ahead of them and a police road sign. A few hundred yards down the road they were stopped by a policemen.

Mr van Borsele opened his window. 'Anything I can do to help, constable?' he asked. 'I'm a doctor.'

'We are waiting for the ambulance, sir—there's a badly injured man and an elderly couple with cuts and shock and a young lady apparently uninjured. If you'd care to take a look at the man? We—we aren't sure...' He glanced at Claribel, hesitating.

'This lady is hospital staff and unshockable.' If Mr van Borsele heard her indignant breath he gave no sign. 'I'll have a look if you wish.'

He got out of the car, took his bag off the back seat, said, 'Stay where you are,' to Claribel and walked off with the constable.

He had been gone perhaps ten minutes when the ambulance arrived, but it was a good deal longer than that before he returned. He stuck his head through the window to address her.

'The man is dead. The ambulance will take the other two into Salisbury, but the girl's unhurt and she is desperate to get to Bath as quickly as possible. I'll give her a lift—her family live there.'

He went away again before Claribel could ask any questions and presently returned with the girl, small and slim and dark with an elfin prettiness and an air of helplessness. As they reached the car she stared up into Mr van Borsele's face with what Claribel uncharitably considered to be a sickening look of adoration.

'You're so very kind,' she uttered in a wispy little-girl voice. 'I don't know what I would have done...' Her voice faltered and a small sob escaped her. 'I simply must get back home this evening—my parents will be so worried.'

She allowed him to settle her in the back of the car and Mr

van Borsele said briskly, 'Claribel, will you get in with this young lady? She's had rather a shock. Do you suppose your mother would give her a cup of tea before I take her on to Bath? She's had a bad time.'

Claribel got out and got in again beside the girl, who threw her a quick look and smiled charmingly.

'Of course,' she agreed at once. 'We could put her up for the night if that would be a good idea.'

She was interrupted instantly by the girl saying urgently, 'No, no, I must be taken home as quickly as possible.' The girl's voice was so urgent that Claribel looked at her in surprise. She said kindly, 'Well, I'm sure if it's urgent that you should go home, Mr van Borsele will take you.'

He had been conferring with the road traffic police but now he came back to his own car.

'The police will contact you in the morning,' he told the girl in what Claribel considered to be far too soothing a manner; couldn't he see that the girl was acting up? She had shown no concern for her dead companion or the couple in the other car and Claribel didn't think she was in a state of shock, either; her colour was good, her hands were as steady as rocks and she had taken out a pocket mirror and was studying her face in it.

Mr van Borsele gave her a long, considering look and got into the car.

'We turn off somewhere here?' he asked Claribel over his shoulder.

'Left at the next signpost.' She sat looking out of the window, worrying a little about the dead man and the elderly couple. 'They'll be all right?' she asked.

He understood her at once. 'Yes. They were on their way to Wilton; they have a son living there. The police will take him to them.'

'And the poor man?'

'His people come from Bath; the police have the address.'

'His poor mother and father,' muttered Claribel. Mr van Borsele didn't answer; the girl ignored her.

Her mother needed only the briefest of explanations before ushering them into the sitting-room, offering a bed to the girl to rest upon, hot tea and the telephone. 'Your parents will be worried,' she said kindly.

'I don't want to phone.' The girl sounded uneasy. 'If I could just have some tea, the doctor has kindly offered to drive me home—I have to get back as soon as possible.'

She flashed a smile at Mrs Brown and allowed herself to be settled in Mr Brown's easy chair. When Claribel came in with the tea tray presently she was talking animatedly to Mr Brown and Mr van Borsele.

As Claribel poured the tea and offered biscuits, Mr van Borsele asked casually, 'This young man who was killed, you knew him well?'

The girl shrugged. 'I've lots of friends. He always drove too fast.'

Claribel saw the shocked look on her mother's face and made a great business of passing teacups.

Mr van Borsele got up the minute he had finished his tea. 'We'll go, shall we?' he asked and the girl jumped up and hurried to the door, barely pausing to utter thanks. She flashed the smile at Mrs Brown again, another one at Mr Brown, wasted no more than a nod at Claribel and caught Mr van Borsele by the arm. 'I do feel shaky,' she told him in her little-girl voice, and gave him a limpid look.

He bade Mrs Brown goodbye and thanked her without any appearance of haste, shook Mr Brown by the hand and paused by Claribel. 'Have a pleasant weekend,' he advised her. 'I'm sorry it had to start like this.'

Then they had gone. Claribel watched the car's tail-lights disappear into the lane and came in and shut the door. She didn't go back into the sitting-room at once but went to let out the indignant cats and feed them. It was in the kitchen that her mother joined her.

'Tell me about it, love. I know Mr van Borsele gave us the facts but I want the trimmings.' She sat down at the table. 'I didn't like that girl.'

'Nor did I.' Claribel cut a slice of bread from the loaf on the table and began to munch it. 'Mother, she didn't utter one word of concern for that poor man who was killed, and all that "poor little me" act she put on just for Marc's benefit... Men!' said Claribel with feeling. 'They can be so dim.'

Mrs Brown had felt a certain satisfaction when Claribel had said 'Marc', but just now it was overshadowed by the memory of the girl. Men, the most sensible of men, fell for that helpless wistful look; it was unfortunate that her darling Claribel had never looked either wistful or helpless; indeed, she was usually the first to come forward with a practical suggestion of help or matter-of-fact solving of a problem. She sighed. 'Perhaps she was in shock', she suggested half-heartedly.

'Oh, pooh!' said Claribel.

Mr van Borsele hadn't said a word about taking her back and, since he hadn't phoned by Sunday morning, she packed her overnight bag again, had lunch with her parents and told them she would go back by train. 'If you wouldn't mind taking me into Tisbury, Father? There's the five-fifteen that'll get me back in nice time for supper.'

Mr Brown had his mouth open to observe that surely Mr van Borsele was calling for her when he encountered his wife's eloquent look. He closed his mouth, coughed and said, 'Of course, dear. That's a good train.'

There was time to go for a quick walk along the bridlepath after lunch. Claribel took Rover with her and tried not to think about Mr van Borsele. Of course, she had never liked him, she reminded herself; it was highly likely that he had only taken her out because there was no one else available. She would, she observed to Rover, accept the invitation she had had from one of the medical housemen to accompany him to a disco at the club the following weekend and in the mean time, if Mr van Borsele should knock on her door, which seemed unlikely, she would on no account open it.

Her mother had tea ready when she got back. She made brisk work of it, reminding her father that he was to drive her to the station and went upstairs to get her bag. She was stowing the cats into their basket when the phone rang. Her mother was standing with her, and Claribel said urgently,

'You answer it, Mother. Just tell Marc if it's him that I've gone back by train,' and, when her mother hesitated, added fiercely, 'Please, Mother. Look, I'll go outside; Father's already in the garage, so you won't be fibbing...' She kissed her doubtful parent and darted through the door with the cats and her bag.

To her father's surprised, 'You could have waited indoors, my dear,' she said airly, 'I thought it would save you a minute or two and we haven't all that much time, have we?'

It was absurd, but she didn't feel safe until she was on the train on the way to Salisbury and London. Safe from what? she asked herself. The possibility that Mr van Borsele might have that girl with him? Or that his phone call could have been made from a nearby call-box and he was even now listening to her mother's only too obviously trumped-up excuses.

Claribel sat staring out of the window. Perhaps it hadn't been him at all, in which case there was no harm done. The more she thought about it the more certain she felt this to be the case, and by the time the train got into Waterloo station she had managed to dismiss the whole business from her mind. She took a taxi to the flat, an unwonted luxury, but the buses were full and she had the cats.

Meadow Road was a cruel contrast to the peace of the Wiltshire countryside. She unlocked her door and went inside quickly; at least her own little flat looked cosy and welcoming.

She freed the cats and, since they were grumbling, fed them before she did anything else, but half an hour later she was laying the table for her supper—scrambled eggs on toast and a pot of tea, and since the evenings were still chilly she lit the gas fire, pulled the curtains and turned on the radio—it was something wistful and romantic and suited her mood exactly. She had the saucepan with the butter and the milk heated ready for the eggs when there was a knock at the door. Only one person thumped it in that ferocious manner—Mr van Borsele—and she had promised herself that she wouldn't let him in. A second thunderous knock changed her mind for her; the neighbours, already deeply interested in his comings and goings, would be at their windows twitching their curtains. She went to the door and flung it open, the saucepan still in her hands.

Mr van Borsele scooped her to one side and went past her into the living-room. He said in an admonitory voice, 'Must I remind you yet again not to open the door unless the chain is in position?'

The remark wasn't what she had expected; she gaped at him, speechless. He took the saucepan from her, turned off the gas and set it tidily on the stove.

'Your mother,' he observed in a silky voice, 'is a charming woman—I like her immensely—but she's a very poor fibber. Besides, you banged the front door as you went out.'

Claribel found her voice. 'Go away,' she said loudly. 'I don't know why you're here...'

'You fib as badly as your mother. Of course you know why I'm here and I'm not going away. I've driven at risk to life and limb in order to get here before you locked up for the night. Why did you run away?'

'I didn't.' Her voice came out too loud and she tried to keep it cool and dignified. 'I have to go to work in the morning which means that I have to get back here this evening. I caught the train...'

His smile disquieted her for it held mockery. 'Now let me guess—I didn't say that I would take you back; indeed, I went on my way with a charming fairylike creature whose antics were calculated to arouse male chivalry to its highest pitch. Naturally, with two days in which to embroider your imagination to the full, you felt yourself cast off, rejected for a slip of a girl half your size; you probably went for a long walk, vowing never to open your door to me again...'

Claribel glared at him; he was so exactly right. She said frostily, 'Don't be so conceited; I've other things to think about,' and added loftily, 'Now do go, I want to cook my supper.' However, she was unable to prevent herself from saying, 'I'm not a bit interested in how you spent your weekend.'

She took a quick look at him. His face was impassive but his eyes were gleaming with amusement. She hadn't liked that bit about the girl being half her size, it made her feel a size eighteen at least, and she wasn't; she was a nicely curved twelve.

His smile had lost its mockery. 'May I stay to supper?' he asked. 'And will you empty that head of yours of the fairy stories you've been thinking up?' He went past her into the kitchen, broke eggs into a bowl and began to beat them with a fork. 'I'll do the eggs if you make the toast.' And, when she began to slice a loaf, still wordless, 'That girl had gone off with the young man who was killed; they were evidently intent on a weekend together and she had told her parents that she was staying with friends. Hence her anxiety to get to Bath—heaven knows what story she cooked up for them. Just as well I didn't accept her invitation to go in provided I said nothing about the accident. I was already late.' He poured the eggs into the saucepan and stirred them very gently. 'I went to see my sister—she had a son on Sunday morning. We were up all night with her, and by the time I got back from the hospital it was early morning, too soon to phone you. I slept for a bit and then went back to see her.'

Claribel stood, her knife poised over the bread, her pretty face the picture of contrition.

'Oh, Marc, I'm a witless fool. I'm so sorry. You've had almost no sleep and now you've come racing back without your supper.'

He said placidly, 'I like driving and I'm going to have my supper and I can always catch up on my sleep. May I use all these eggs?'

'Yes, of course. What would you like to drink?' She had forgotten her peevishness, bent on feeding him, seeing, now that she really looked at him, that he was tired to his bones.

'Tea. Is there anything to drink before supper?'

'Father gave me a bottle of claret months ago. I'll find it.'

She rooted around in the cupboard in the living-room and held up the bottle for his inspection. He nodded approvingly.

'Rather unusual before a meal, but we must celebrate with something.'

'Celebrate? What are we celebrating?'

'Why, that we are back on our old footing, Claribel. If you'll find a corkscrew I will open this.'

While he was doing that, she laid another place at the table, feeling suddenly light-hearted.

They drank their claret—not quite at the right temperature for Mr van Borsele, who was a stickler for such things—buttered quantities of toast, and dished up the eggs. When they had eaten, Claribel fetched the fruit cake her mother had given her and watched her companion eat several large slices, washed down with tea. Finally, he sat back.

'A delightful meal, Claribel.' He glanced at his watch. 'But unfortunately I must go. Forgive me if I don't wash the dishes?'

He had got up and she stood up too, disappointed but determined not to show it. The vague idea that they might have spent the rest of the evening together, sitting comfortably before the fire, talking about nothing much, had taken root in her head; she told herself now that there was no reason why he should do so. On the face of things, she was a bolthole convenient for a quick meal, a kind of younger sister… She disliked the idea very much.

'Don't be late,' she said brightly and wondered where he was going—it was almost ten o'clock and a Sunday…

He grinned suddenly. 'Claribel, you're making up fairytales again. Why not ask me where I'm going?'

She said severely, 'Certainly not. And in any case I have no wish to pry into your life.'

He tapped her cheek with a gentle finger. 'But we are friends again?'

She said peevishly, 'If by that you mean may you come here for coffee and a meal when you have nowhere better to go, then yes.'

'That's my kind, forgiving girl.' He put out a hand. 'Friends?'

His grip was firm and brief, his nod of goodbye even briefer.

When he had driven away she slowly cleared the table, washed up and put her breakfast ready. It was obvious to her that, whether she liked it or not, he regarded her as a sister; the thought was very depressing.

In the morning she viewed things in a different light; common sense asserted itself. There was no reason why Mr van Borsele shouldn't consider her in the light of a sister. He was at liberty to do so if he wished, only somehow she was finding it difficult to look upon him as a brother…

She saw him thrice during the week. On the first occasion it was on the ward, during his round, when she was called upon to demonstrate the progress of the patients she had been treating, and two days later there was a lengthy session with the chesty man, now making steady progress despite his wheezing. The third occasion was a rather different one. On Saturday morning she was window-shopping in the Burlington Arcade, looking for a suitable birthday present for her father. She had turned away from a tasteful display of ties, all beyond her means, when she saw Mr van Borsele walking down the arcade in her direction. He hadn't seen her, and no wonder: the fairy-like creature from the car accident was tripping along beside him.

Claribel, driven by some strong feeling she didn't stop to analyse, opened the door of the exclusive men's shop whose window she had been looking at and hurried inside. She emerged ten minutes later, having purchased a tie with almost all the money in her purse, but nevertheless cheap at the price for it had enabled her to avoid Mr van Borsele.

She walked to Piccadilly Circus, turned down Haymarket and caught a bus to Stamford Street with the rest of the weekend looming emptily before her. It was providential that within half an hour of her return a junior surgical registrar at Jerome's should ring up to invite her to his birthday party.

'We're having it at the Dog and Thistle—' the pub frequented by the medical staff at Jerome's. 'Someone will fetch you and take you back. Miss Flute's coming, and Tilly and

Pat—' both girls from the physio department. 'You know everyone.'

It turned out to be a pleasant, noisy evening: far too many people crammed into the private bar of the pub, eating potato crisps and drinking beer or tonic water; it was too near pay day for anything more expensive. It was almost eleven o'clock when Miss Flute edged her way over to where Claribel was at the centre of a group of several of the young doctors and signified her intention of going home.

'Pat's got the car here, she says she'll run us back if we'd like to go now.'

So Claribel eased her way to the door, calling goodbyes as she went, and got into Pat's elderly Austin with Miss Flute and presently was back in the flat, opening a can of soup, giving the cats a meal and getting ready for bed.

One of the more senior housemen had suggested that they might spend the next afternoon together and have tea. He was a serious young man, and she had been out with him once or twice; he was given to visiting museums and art galleries and they had enjoyed a casual acquaintance. She had said that she would go, for it would fill her day nicely. As he was on call after six o'clock, they had agreed to meet at two o'clock outside the National Gallery, so after a morning cleaning the flat and doing the chores, she got into a jersey dress, covered it with a raincoat since it was drizzling and caught a bus to Trafalgar Square, where she found him waiting for her.

He was a nice young man, undemanding, polite and able to talk well; they spent an hour or so in the National Gallery and then found a small café where they had tea. It was a pleasant afternoon and, back at the flat feeding the cats, she wondered why she hadn't enjoyed it more. Nicky was a serious, steady young man, her own age; she was aware that he liked her and that if she encouraged him he would more than like her. It was therefore surprising that she didn't really care if she never saw him again.

Miss Flute sent her to the wards on Monday morning. It would give her a chance to give Mr van Borsele a cool stare if he so much glanced at her, Claribel thought. It was a great pity that there was no sign of him; Mr Shutter took the round, remarking as they paused by a patient so that she might put him through his exercises, 'A pity Mr van Borsele had to return to Holland. He would have liked to see the results of his work here.'

Claribel murmured a reply. The feeling of disappointment she felt she put down to not having a chance to snub the man. She wasn't quite clear as to why she wished to do this; he had, after all, come and gone in her life and she would forget him completely—well, almost completely. He had made life interesting, even though they had argued each time they had met, and she had enjoyed his company.

The week seemed longer than usual. Several new patients came for treatment, a number of them very hard work, for they were naturally timid about exercising a painful arm or leg, and by Friday evening Claribel was tired and dispirited. The weekend loomed emptily before her. She could, of course, go home and as she got her supper she decided that she might do that, only it would have to be in the morning; she could go out early and do what shopping she had to do, and catch a late morning train; twenty-four hours at home might improve her mood. She decided against telling her mother, though; that could be left until the morning. Much cheered, she cleaned the flat, saw to Enoch and Toots, washed her hair, did her nails and went to bed.

She was out early. There were a few shops at the other end of Meadow Road; she bought what she needed and hurried back to pack a shoulder bag and put away her groceries, then telephone her mother.

The hearty thump on the door caused her to drop the bag of sugar she was emptying into her storage jar. Mr van Borsele was in Holland; Mr Shutter had told her so. A second thump sent her to the door which she prudently opened with the chain up.

'Hello,' said Mr van Borsele, at his most placid. 'I'm delighted to see that you have taken my advice at last. Now open the door, there's a good girl.'

Claribel peeped at him through the narrow opening. 'I'm just leaving,' she pointed out. 'So sorry, but I had no idea that you would be calling.'

'Well, of course you hadn't.' He looked down his nose at her. 'I shall stand here and thump the knocker until you let me in; there are curtains twitching already.'

She opened the door and he went past her into the living-room. 'I want to talk to you,' he observed, briskly businesslike. 'The most sensible thing seems for me to drive you down to Tisbury and we can talk on the way; in that way I shall have your full attention.'

He went into the kitchen and filled the kettle. 'Coffee?'

She followed him. 'Have you been in London all this time?'

He bent over the stove so that she didn't see the gleam in his eyes. 'No, in Holland. I crossed over last night.'

'So why have you come here?' She put two mugs on a tray and got the milk from the fridge.

He turned to look at her. 'We're still friends?'

She said huffily, 'I suppose so, although I don't see why…'

'Ah, you're still peevish,' he observed blandly. 'Did you buy anything in that shop with all the ties in the window?'

Claribel dropped the spoon she was holding. A slow blush crept up her face, contributing a delightful prettiness to her already very pretty face.

'You saw me! How mean can you get.'

He spooned instant coffee. 'Dear girl, mean because I didn't come into that shop and help you choose a tie? Or because I was with Irma Cooper?'

She said crossly, 'Is that her name?' then added icily, 'Not that I'm interested.'

'Why should you be?' He handed her a mug of coffee and smiled into her frowning face. 'I thought we might have luncheon on the way—the Old Drapery Stores again if you would like that? Go and do whatever you have to do while I stuff these cats into their basket.'

It was obvious to her that he had no intention of telling her anything until they were on their way. She tidied her hair and whisked herself into the new three-piece, reflecting as she did so that she spent a good deal of her free time making coffee and then being rushed to wherever Mr van Borsele desired to go. It would have to stop, but first she would find out what he wanted of her.

He was in no hurry to tell her; they talked trivialities as he drove westwards, falling into friendly silence from time to time, and even when they stopped for lunch at the Old Drapery Stores, he gave her no hint as to what he wished to discuss with her.

Claribel, a sensible girl, dismissed the matter for the more important one of enjoying her lunch: homemade soup, trout caught that morning and rhubarb tart which melted in the mouth, accompanied by a great dish of clotted cream. They drank tonic water since Mr van Borsele was driving and she had no wish to drink alone, and when they were having their coffee she ventured a question.

'This—whatever it is you want to talk about, what is it?'

'Presently.' He sounded remote and rather cold; for the life of her she felt unable to pursue the matter and was forced to contain her curiosity while he finished his coffee and presently ushered her back into the car.

Even then he said nothing. it wasn't until they had turned off at Fovant and Tisbury was only a few miles away that he slid the Rolls to the side of the road and remarked, 'I want your attention, Claribel, and no interruptions.'

She said pertly, 'You sound as though you were going to deliver a lecture, but I'll listen—I can't do anything else, can I?'

She turned to look at him and saw that he was frowning. 'It's about that Irma, isn't it? Before you start, let me guess. You've fallen for her, but you've got a girl in Holland—perhaps you are engaged—and you don't know what to do. Though I should have thought you were the very last man to need help with anything.'

'Did I ever tell you that you have a splendid imagination Claribel? Yes, it is concerning Irma, and you are near enough the mark, but there is more to it than that. I left her at home in Bath and as far as I was concerned that was the end of it, but it seemed she wished to see me again. She discovered who I was and where I lived and worked. She has been a most unwelcome visitor ever since. I've treated her as I would treat any other woman of my acquaintance but she seems bent on plaguing me; I told her that I was going to be married but she refuses to believe me.' He turned to look at Claribel, and something in his face made her sit up straight. He went on, his voice silky, 'If I could produce a fiancée she would be convinced. It crossed my mind that you might consent to, er, take on that role in a temporary and nominal fashion...'

Her voice came out a squeak. 'Me? You must be mad! What about...I thought you were going to be married to a girl in Holland.'

'You may have thought that, but I believe I never actually told you so.' He smiled thinly. 'Your imagination again, Claribel.'

'Yes, well... It's ridiculous.'

'Of course it is. And trifling, but of course if you are going to magnify the whole matter out of all proportion then there is nothing more to be said.'

'What will you do?'

'Why, as to that, it's a simple matter for me to return to Holland. A pity, though, for Mr Shutter and I work well together and have several worthwhile projects we intended to set up.'

He spoke quietly, staring ahead of him, and Claribel, glancing at him, thought how grim his profile looked. She knew that his work was important to him and that he had done some splendid surgery at Jerome's; to have to give all that up because of some tiresome girl pestering him seemed unfair to him. She said, 'What exactly have you in mind?'

She watched his face as he turned towards her; one look of triumph at having got his way and she would refuse to help him. But there was no expression on his face at all, although he smiled at her.

'I'll explain and you can think about it over the weekend. Irma is staying in London with friends. I haven't met them and I don't know where they live. She contrives to meet me when I get back in the evening and when I leave the flat in the morning; at times she has attached herself to me when I've been out—in the Burlington Arcade on one occasion; you saw that for yourself. She phones and leaves messages and is generally a nuisance. I rashly told her that I was engaged to be married but she refused to believe me. If I can produce a fiancée, however, it might discourage her...'

'Don't you know any other girls more suitable than I am?'

'I know any number of people in London, but if you think about it you must agree with me that you are exactly right—you are free in the evening and at the weekends, we can arrange to go out on the town without difficulty, you can come to my flat and I can go to yours.'

She said coldly, 'It all sounds very convenient for you.' She heaved an indignant breath; she was to be at his beck and call, was she? Her own social life was to be neglected to suit him. 'What about me?'

'It won't be for more than a week or so,' he told her soothingly. 'A few evenings out. Dinner and dancing or the theatre, places where we're likely to be seen by her or her friends—they haunt them at night, she told me; we are bound to meet them at one place or another. I'll drive you back with me in the evenings so that there is a good chance of her seeing you then.'

He fell into a placid silence and she said snappishly, 'You've got it all worked out, haven't you?'

He said blandly, 'But of course.'

'It would make a lovely plot for a romantic novel,' she snapped again.

He agreed in a voice which reminded her forcibly of a grown-up pandering to a child's tantrums. 'Though I don't read them myself,' he added.

She had nothing to say to that but, after a few moments, 'The whole idea is ridiculous. I'm surprised at you for thinking it up in the first place.'

He laughed then. 'Well, let's get on, shall we?' he observed easily. 'Your people will be wondering why we are late.'

Most aggravatingly, he began to talk about the charms of the English countryside at that time of year, a subject which he maintained until they arrived at her home.

They were welcomed warmly and Claribel was surprised when Mr van Borsele accepted her mother's invitation to stay for tea. They had it in the sitting-room, around the fire, for the day had turned chilly. To the casual visitor the scene couldn't have been more convivial; the talk was general as Mrs Brown's sandwiches and cakes disappeared rapidly, and if Claribel was more silent than usual, no one remarked upon it. Mr van Borsele got up to go eventually and she reflected how quickly he had made himself at home with her parents as he bade them goodbye. At the door he told her, 'I'll collect you about six o'clock tomorrow, Claribel,' and gracefully refused Mrs Brown's invitation to have tea with them.

Watching the car's lights disappear, Mrs Brown said slowly, 'What a very nice man he is, and such beautiful manners.'

Her daughter eyed her stormily. 'Mother, when he wants something he is quite ruthless...'

'Well, dear, I suppose a clever man such as he, performing small miracles of surgery almost every day of his life, is entitled to have his own way sometimes.'

'Always, Mother, always.'

'Such a pity you don't like him,' murmured Mrs Brown. She stole a look at her daughter's cross face. 'That friend of Sebastian's is staying at the refectory; he was wondering if you would be at home this weekend. How about giving him a ring?'

'Him? Malcolm something or other? He's so young, Mother!'

An answer which pleased her parent mightily.

CHAPTER SIX

THERE wasn't much of Saturday left, and although Claribel would have liked to confide in her mother she could see the good sense of saying nothing. Mr van Borsele could change his mind. Besides, if he went back to Holland within a day or so, there would surely be no need for his hare-brained scheme to be put into action. She spent the evening sitting cosily by the fire with Rover and the cats at her feet, listening to her mother's gentle gossip about the village and giving in her turn a faithful account of her week at Jerome's, although she had little to say about Mr van Borsele. To her mother's carefully casual enquiries she replied airly that he had returned unexpectedly from Holland and she had no idea how long he would be in England.

Sunday, comfortably filled by walking Rover, going to church, passing the time of day with various friends at the church door and going home to Sunday lunch, flew by too fast. She had stuffed her bag with her overnight things and one of her mother's mouthwatering fruit cakes, and was sitting round the fire eating buttery muffins, when Mr van Borsele arrived.

He apologised for being early and, at her mother's invitation, sat down beside her father's chair and started on the muffins, falling into easy conversation with Mr Brown. He had left his sister's home rather earlier than he had intended, he explained, and he hoped that he wasn't putting Claribel out in any way.

As though he hadn't put her out enough, she thought indignantly and told him in a cool voice that half an hour or so made no difference to her. She went on to remark about the rather chilly weather. 'It probably spoilt your weekend,' she observed and got up to pour second cups.

'There are so many things other than weather which can spoil a weekend,' he remarked blandly, 'just as it can turn out completely successful when it is least expected to.'

She eyed him uncertainly, wondering if he was referring to his scheme, and met his bland stare. 'One lump or two?' she asked him, so sharply that her mother looked at her in surprise.

He seemed in no hurry to go. Her mother's cake, a Victoria sponge, and a slice of gingerbread were sampled in turn with enjoyment and a well-phrased compliment or two which delighted her mother. When they finally left it was well past six o'clock.

It was frustrating of him to remain silent for long stretches of time and when he did speak it was on some trivial topic. They were on the motorway, rapidly approaching London, before he asked, 'Are you doing anything this evening? I thought we might have dinner somewhere?'

'The cats,' she reminded him, aware of pleasure warming her chilly thoughts.

'Shall we go to the flat first? You can feed them or whatever and we can go on from there.'

She agreed readily enough; to dine out would make a pleasant end to a weekend which hadn't been altogether pleasant. She debated with herself as to whether she should bring up the subject of his scheme and decided not to say anything about it. She had more or less refused to have anything to do with it and he hadn't pressed her for an answer. It was a pity if the girl was being a nuisance, but surely he could think of something...

At the flat she saw to the cats, did her face and her hair and pronounced herself ready. 'There's no need to dress up, is there?' she asked anxiously.

'None at all; you look very nice in that thing.'

The kind of remark Sebastian might make. She got into the car and tried not to smile when Mr van Borsele gravely saluted the inquisitive face peering from the next door window.

He drove to the Savoy. It was only as she got out of the car that she was struck by an unpleasant thought. 'Is this one of the places Irma comes to?'

He nodded to the doorman to get the car parked before taking her arm and marching her through the imposing doors. 'Yes. Shall we have a drink first?'

She said softly in a fierce voice, 'No, I'd like to go back to my flat, now.' She gave him a look to wither him up completely, only it didn't appear to make any difference to him. 'You planned this, didn't you? I told you it was a silly idea…'

'The word was ridiculous. I was so sure that you would have second thoughts, Claribel, and agree to help me. You're a sensible girl, there's no romantic nonsense about you, and after all it is such a trifling little matter for you.'

They had paused on the way to the bar and she gave him a long deliberate look. His opinion of her was galling to say the least.

'I don't really see why I should allow you to make use of me just to get you out of a hole.'

He had never looked more patiently reasonable. He said gently, 'You're just about the nicest person I know, Claribel, and certainly the most beautiful. Irma will take one good look at you and know that she hasn't got a chance.'

She went faintly pink. 'You have no need to say that. Anyway, she's seen me already.'

'That's why you're so exactly right.' He smiled. It was a charming smile, warm and reassuring; she reflected idiotically that if she was one of his patients and he had just told her that he was going to amputate an arm or a leg she would accept the horrid news with complete trust.

'All right. But just as soon as she leaves you alone or goes home it's to stop.'

He raised his eyebrows. 'But of course, Claribel.' He dug a hand into a pocket and put something into her hand. A diamond ring, three large stones surrounded by circles of smaller stones. She opened her mouth to protest but his hand closed over hers. 'Put it on…'

'It's not real?' she half whispered.

'Of course it's real. It belonged to my great-grandmother. Shall we have that drink?'

They went into the bar and she tried not to gape at the magnificent jewels on her finger while she drank her sherry, an excellent one which as far as she was concerned could have been tap water. They went into the Grill Room presently and she felt disquiet at their table: in a prominent position in the centre of the room.

'Just right,' murmured Mr van Borsele. 'Put your hand on the table and flash the ring; Irma is sitting quite close by with a party of people.'

She had the good sense not to look around her and buried her pretty nose in the menu while she steadied her breath. Mr van Borsele's calm voice was suggesting that caviare might be good to start with, and how did she like the idea of chicken *à la* king?'

They had ordered and he was telling the wine waiter to bring a bottle of champagne when Irma arrived at the table. Claribel, mindful of her companion's wishes, laid a hand on the cloth so that the ring was in full view, arranged her features into an expression of friendly surprise and watched Mr van Borsele get to his feet.

Irma spoke before anyone else had a chance. 'Where have you been?' she demanded. 'I haven't seen you for ages. You must know...' Her eyes caught the sparkle of the diamonds on Claribel's hand and she stopped.

Claribel returned her glare with a sweet smile. 'Hello,' she said with every appearance of pleasure. 'Do you remember me? When you had that accident—we took you to my home before Marc drove you to Bath.'

She turned a dazzling smile upon Mr van Borsele. 'We've often talked about it, haven't we, darling?'

'You are engaged?' Irma looked at them in turn. 'So it's true. I didn't believe you, but it's true.' Her eyes fastened on the ring. 'Not that it's important; engagements don't mean much these days.' She tossed her head and smiled at Mr van Borsele, who smiled back thinly.

'Ours does,' he told her. 'Now if you would excuse us, we have a great deal to discuss—plans for the wedding and so on.'

He glanced over to the table she had left. 'I think your friends are waiting to leave.'

Irma left without a word and presently departed with her companions without looking at them again. Claribel, spreading caviare on toast with a hand which shook very slightly, couldn't quite suppress a sigh of relief.

'Women,' observed Mr van Borsele, 'never fail to surprise me. Just for a few minutes I actually believed that you and I were engaged.' He smiled at her in what she considered to be a smug fashion. 'You should call me "darling" more often; it does something to my ego.'

She choked on a morsel of toast. 'Your ego doesn't need any propping up. You're Mr van Borsele, and Mr van Borsele you'll remain, as far as I'm concerned.'

'Marc?' he suggested. 'We're bound to meet the tiresome girl again and you might slip up.'

'I should imagine you're rid of her after that little scene.' She studied the chicken *à la* king which had just been set before her; her appetite had in no way been impaired by her acting. 'How fortunate that we should meet her so soon; we can call the whole thing off.'

'Certainly not; she's badly adjusted mentally, and spoilt and selfish and uninhibited; it will take more than one encounter with us as a devoted engaged couple to convince her.'

'Oh, will it? Aren't you going back to Holland?'

'What I like about you, Claribel, is your plain speaking. I am aware that you have a poor opinion of me, but I beg that you will endeavour to overcome that until I can, as it were, sink without trace.'

She remained unmoved. 'So you're not going back to Holland?'

'For the moment, no. Mr Shutter and I are joining forces over a child who sadly needs extensive surgery; we hope to get to work on her next week. Which means that you and I will be free to show ourselves as a loving couple on several evenings.'

'Which evenings?' she wanted to know. 'I have plans as

well.' Her glass had been filled for a second time and she took a defiant sip of champagne.

'It's hard to say at the moment. I expect I shall be at the hospital until quite late tomorrow evening; I'll call in on my way home and let you know if Tuesday evening will be free. So if you have a date for tomorrow evening, go ahead.' He spoke in a kindly voice which annoyed her very much. 'Only don't go anywhere you are likely to be seen by Irma.'

She said coldly and crossly, 'How am I to know where she will be? Anyway, I never go out on a Monday evening; I wash my hair.'

'I'll dry it for you while we make our plans.' And, at her outraged look, 'Quite permissible by Meadow Road standards. After all, we are engaged.' He smiled his sudden beguiling smile. 'Now, shall we bury the hatchet and enjoy ourselves?'

Which, surprisingly, she did.

Monday was always a busy day and she got home rather later than usual. She got her supper, fed Enoch and Toots, washed the smalls, prudently set the coffee tray ready and washed her hair. It was almost ten o'clock and she was sitting in her dressing-gown drying it when the door knocker resounded with the familiar thump. She unlocked the door, leaving the chain up, and Mr van Borsele said, 'Good girl. Open up.'

She stood aside as he went in and followed him into the living-room.

'It's rather late,' observed Claribel.

'Not so late that the neighbours aren't peering at me through their curtains.' He stood looking at her. Her abundant hair hung in a golden stream down her back, not quite dry. 'Come and sit on this stool and I'll finish that for you.'

There seemed nothing strange in sitting down at his feet while he settled in the armchair, took a towel from her and began a vigorous rubbing.

'Had a busy day?' she asked through a tangle of hair.

'Very, but I think we've got it right. If it all goes as it should we'll be able to lengthen her legs by six inches; she'll still be on the short side when she has grown, but at least she won't be grotesque.'

'Oh—is it that operation where someone has to turn a key each day?'

'Well, something like that, yes. Daily manipulation enables the bone to lengthen gradually. We've dealt with one leg; if it's a success we'll do the other in due course.' He took up a length of her hair and began on it. 'What a mass of hair you have, Claribel. They should have called you Rapunzel.'

'I've been wondering if I should have it cut.'

'Don't you dare. You'll probably get the child for physio. Have you been busy today?'

'Not nearly as busy as you. Are you going back to Jerome's?'

'Yes, but if it goes as it should I thought you and I might have an evening out tomorrow. Remind me to give you the ring again.'

She mumbled behind her hair. She had given it back on the previous evening, growing shy and awkward doing it—stupidly, as he had taken it from her in a matter-of-fact way. She tossed her hair out of her eyes and took the towel from him. 'Thanks; that's dry enough to plait. Would you like a cup of coffee before you go?'

'I've only just got here,' he complained mildly, 'but, yes, I'd like that.'

She made coffee for them both and they drank it in a companionable silence before he got to his feet.

'Tomorrow then,' he said. 'Now, let me see—you'd better dine at my place and we can go on from there. A bit dressy, I think. I'll call for you at seven o'clock unless you get a message to the contrary.'

To all of which she agreed meekly enough. She had agreed to help him; in for a penny in for a pound. And there was no denying that he was a delightful companion with whom to spend an evening, even if they did argue most of the time. She saw him to the door and wished him goodnight, and was quite unprepared for his kiss.

The following morning Miss Flute told her that she would

be treating the little girl Mr van Borsele and Mr Shutter had operated on. 'She is still in intensive care. You're to give her breathing exercises for the first few days, ten-minutes sessions, TDS. She'll be going to Crispin Ward once she is fit enough. They want you at ten o'clock.'

The intensive care unit was on the top floor of the hospital, next door to the theatre block, a daunting place to the layman, full of technical apparatus, yards of tubing and computer screens, and manned by teams of nurses round the clock. There were several patients there, but the little girl was the one Claribel had to deal with. The child was small, with a white face and enormous dark eyes.

Claribel knelt down by the bed. 'Hello, poppet. I've come to help get you well again. We're going to play some breathing games; I'm sure you'll win every time.' She talked to the child for a little while and then pulled up a chair and began the exercises which had been ordered, going cautiously. Each day they would be stepped up but just at first she had to gain the little girl's confidence. Ten minutes wasn't long; they parted the best of friends. Claribel slipped quietly away and started for the stairs. Half-way down she met Mr van Borsele going up. He stopped by her.

'Ah, good morning, Miss Brown. You've been with Rita?'

Her cool, 'Good morning, Mr van Borsele,' was uttered in her best professional manner and the corners of his mouth twitched. 'Rita has been very good, although she is apprehensive. I think we'll have to keep to the simple breathing exercises for a couple of days until I have her complete confidence.'

He nodded. 'Good, good. I'll leave that to your capable judgement.'

With a nod he had gone on his way, leaving her vaguely annoyed, although she wasn't sure why.

She was kept busy for the rest of the day with a snatched sandwich lunch and a cup of tea gulped down during the afternoon. As she dressed that evening she thought about her dinner—a substantial one, she hoped; she was famished.

She had chosen to wear a long-skirted dress of green crêpe

which exactly matched her eyes. It was discreetly simple in cut, elegant and severely plain, suitable she hoped for whatever evening Mr van Borsele had in mind; he had, after all, told her to wear something dressy. She put on her very best slippers—bronze kid with very high heels, a wicked extravagance she had been unable to resist—and from the depths of her wardrobe hauled out a mohair wrap, a long-ago gift to her mother who had handed it over to Claribel, quite rightly observing that such a garment could only be seen to advantage on a tall, queenly figure. Claribel had accepted it with delight, telling her indignant parent that it was just the thing to cover her buxom person.

'You are not buxom,' Mrs Brown had declared, 'and you never will be. You work too hard.'

'I might marry,' Claribel had said flippantly, 'and live a life of sloth.'

Her mother had snorted indignantly. 'If you marry, love, a husband and children won't give you any chance to idle.'

Mr van Borsele was punctual, but then he always was. He had been home first, that was apparent as soon as she cast eyes on the elegance of his attire. He looked more handsome than ever in a dinner-jacket; no wonder the tiresome Irma found him irresistible.

She said, 'Hello, or should I say good evening, Mr van Borsele?'

He came to stand in front of her. 'Don't be pert; there is a time and a place for everything. You look charming.' He bent and kissed her, adding, 'If you see what I mean.'

He picked up the wrap. 'Must we cover your charms?' he wanted to know, and Claribel, for once feeling shy, said, 'Well, it is chilly in the evening,' and swathed the garment around her.

'We'll have to go via Jerome's,' he told her as they went out to the car. 'I want to check on Rita.'

'She's not so well?' Claribel turned a concerned face to him.

'She's splendid, but Shutter's out of town and I want a word with Night Sister about her.'

Sitting in the car, waiting for him, Claribel thought idly that being married to a doctor or a surgeon was, to say the least, a life of unexpected happenings: late meals, no meals at all, broken nights, difficult patients, and, in the case of an eminent surgeon such as Marc, a good deal of travelling. As he got back into the car she asked, 'Is everything going well?'

'It's early days, my dear, but I'm hoping so. Another day or two and we'll feel more certain of it.'

'Have you done this particular operation before?'

He was going over Westminster Bridge, and the overhead lights showed his rather stern profile. 'Half a dozen times.'

'And all successful?'

'Yes, to date.'

She said in a worried way, 'You know, I think I'm a bit in awe of you—you're clever, and you do things that few other people would dare to do.'

He laughed. 'If I were asked to cut out and make one of your dresses I wouldn't have the faintest idea where to start. Perhaps others don't dare to pick up a scalpel, but *I* don't dare to let myself pick up dressmaking scissors.'

He gave her a quick glance. 'What is it you say in English? "It takes all sorts to make a world".' He drove along Whitehall and turned into Trafalgar Square, into Pall Mall and then began to work his way through the one-way streets until they were in Wigmore Street where soon he turned into one of the quiet streets close by and stopped before a terrace of Regency houses, with handsome porches and well-tended window-boxes. There was only the muted sound of traffic and there were trees lining the pavement.

'Very nice,' said Claribel, taking it all in as she got out of the car.

He had her arm. 'London can be delightful,' he observed, 'and it is convenient for the rooms I share with Shutter.'

They were mounting the three steps which led to the front door and he took out his keys. 'Oh, do you have private patients as well?' She answered herself. 'Of course you do.'

'Well, yes.' He opened the door and ushered her into a vestibule opening on to a fair-sized hall. A porter was standing there who bade them good evening and went towards a lift to open its gates. Mr van Borsele flapped a large hand. 'We'll walk thanks, George—healthy exercise.'

They went unhurriedly up the stairs to the next floor and he opened one of the doors on the carpeted landing. The lobby they entered was square with a number of doors leading from it. Mr van Borsele took her wrap and threw it over an English elbow-chair, calling at the same time, 'Tilly, come and meet Miss Brown.'

Tilly was small and round and brisk with grey hair and twinkly blue eyes; she bounced into the lobby almost before he had finished speaking and fetched up in front of Claribel.

'Claribel, this is Tilly, my housekeeper and old friend; she cooks like a dream, rules the cleaning lady with a rod of iron and keeps a firm hand on me.'

The housekeeper grinned at him as Claribel said, 'How do you do' and shook hands. 'Don't you believe a word, miss,' observed Tilly. ''Is lordship does just what 'e wants, bless 'is 'eart.' She eyed Claribel. 'You're as pretty as a peach—all that lovely 'air. A sight better than that nasty little piece 'oo comes poking her nose in where she's not wanted.'

She whisked away again, saying as she went, 'You can 'ave ten minutes, then I'll dish up.'

Mr van Borsele hadn't said a word; he pushed open a door and stood aside for Claribel to go into the room beyond: a charming room, high ceilinged with a bow window at one end. The walls were panelled and it was furnished most comfortably with armchairs and with a large sofa on either side of the fireplace. Small wine tables, some with lighted lamps, were scattered around, and a mahogany break-front bookcase with glass doors stood against one wall. There were flowers, too, and some charming pieces of china; a beautiful room, she decided, admiring the brocade curtains at the window.

'Do sit down,' advised Mr van Borsele. 'We have time for a drink before Tilly dishes up.'

Claribel was still getting over her surprise; she hadn't expected such a lovely home and certainly she had been taken aback by Tilly and her down-to-earth Cockney manner. Mr van

Borsele handed her a glass and said thoughtfully, 'You are surprised...' He was interrupted by the telephone on the table at his elbow. He lifted the receiver, listened for a moment without speaking and then beckoned Claribel and handed it to her. Mystified, she took it from him silently. It was Irma.

'Who is that?' she demanded.

'Claribel Brown,' said Claribel in her sweetest voice. 'Can I help you?'

'I want to speak to Marc.'

'I'm afraid he is in the shower,' said Claribel. 'Can I give him a message?'

'I might have known you'd be there,' said the sharp voice into her ear. 'Are you really going to marry him?'

'Oh, yes. We're deciding the date this evening.'

'It's so sudden,' said Irma suspiciously.

'Love at first sight, you know,' said Claribel in what she hoped was a convincing voice. 'I must go,' she finished naughtily, 'I haven't finished dressing!'

She put down the receiver and looked across at Mr van Borsele, who was watching her with a thoughtful expression. 'I could hardly believe my ears! If I didn't know you better I would have believed every word you uttered.'

She had the grace to blush. 'Well, I had to say something on the spur of the moment.'

'I would be interested to hear what you might tell her if you had the time to consider...'

She took a heartening sip of sherry. 'Well, you really are too bad. There was no earthly reason why I should be made to answer the phone.'

'My apologies, Claribel, but you must admit that it was effective.'

He smiled so disarmingly that she found herself smiling too.

Tilly was a splendid cook. They dined in an atmosphere of cordiality, doing justice to her watercress soup, Dover sole and rhubarb pie and cream. Over coffee they decided where they should go next.

'Now, where do you suppose a newly engaged couple, very much in love, would go?' asked Mr van Borsele.

She considered. 'Somewhere to dance.'

'The London Hilton. Not quite my choice, but sooner or later I believe that one meets everyone there.' He fished in a pocket and gave her the ring. 'Put that on, there's a good girl.' He raised his voice. 'Tilly, show Miss Brown where she can tidy herself.'

Claribel was beginning to enjoy herself; she had no idea that Marc could be such fun. It surprised her, on thinking about it, that she had ever disliked him or thought him cold and reserved. Of course, she mused as she did her face in the splendidly equipped cloakroom, once she had fulfilled her role of fiancée and Irma had been dispatched for good, he might possibly revert to his old manner, but in the meantime it was a nice change from her little flat.

The Hilton was crowded but they were given a good table. Mr van Borsele ordered champagne, but they didn't drink it at once, taking instead to the dance floor. They danced well, the pair of them, not talking until he said softly to the top of her head, 'The gods are with us; Irma is here, sitting at a table with half a dozen others. Could you look up at me in an adoring manner when I give you a dig?'

She gave a little splutter of laughter and then, at a sharp poke in the ribs, smiled up at him. She was quite unprepared for the look on his face; tender and loving and somehow exciting. It was gone almost as soon as she saw it. When she looked again he was looking over her head, his features austere; she must have imagined it, she thought uneasily.

They went back to their table presently and he said, 'About tomorrow: I've seats for the theatre—*Starlight Express*. We'll dine at the Connaught first. And on Friday we'll drive out of town. I must be at Jerome's on Thursday evening so I'll come round to your place. Saturday I'll get a table at the Ritz; we can dance there.'

'And when do I get the chance to wash my hair?' added

Claribel with a slight edge to her voice. 'Or for that matter have a few hours to myself?'

'On Sunday, I'll fetch you about ten o'clock and take you to Tisbury.'

'And supposing I don't wish to go?'

'Don't be silly. You can sit and drowse in your father's delightful garden and mull over the week. I'll pick you up at about seven o'clock.'

'What happens when people don't want to do what you have planned?'

He gave her a bland look. 'But, my dear, they do, and if by any chance they don't, I persuade them.'

She said slowly, 'You know, when I first met you…'

'You didn't like me!' he finished for her. 'You're still not sure, are you?' He gave her a little mocking smile. 'Shall we dance again?'

Presently he took her home, refusing nicely enough to go in and bidding her a cheerful goodnight without any reference to the evening they had spent together.

Of course she saw him the next morning for she had to go to the intensive care unit to start little Rita on her exercises, but beyond a civil good morning they didn't speak and when she returned at midday and later again in the afternoon, he was operating. It was Miss Flute who gave her his message.

'You're to be ready for six-forty-five,' she told Claribel. She looked as though she wanted to ask questions but she didn't.

It was Claribel who said, 'It's all right, Miss Flute, I'm helping Mr van Borsele with a small problem, that's all.'

Miss Flute eyed the pretty face smiling so nicely at her. She was fond of Claribel, who worked hard and didn't grumble, and she cherished a secret passion for Mr van Borsele; she had been hoping that she was taking a small part in a romance between them, but neither of them had evinced the least sign of it. She sighed and reminded Claribel that Mrs Snow was waiting.

Luckily it was a day when the physio department finished its work on time. Claribel, home in good time, spent ten minutes or so deciding what she was going to wear. A short dress, she decided, dark blue crêpe-de-Chine, pleated from a yoke, with long tight sleeves and an important belt which emphasised her slim waist. It was especially good as a background for her golden hair and green eyes and proved to be exactly right for the evening. In bed, hours later, she thought with satisfaction of Mr van Borsele's quick look of approval. The evening had been a success, too. She had never been to the Connaught before; its quiet elegance had pleased her and, besides, Mr van Borsele had put himself out to be an interesting companion. Best of all, *Starlight Express* had been better than she had expected. A heavenly few hours, she had to admit, and then fell to wondering if he expected supper on the following evening. He had warned her that he might be late—after seven o'clock. Sandwiches, she decided drowsily, or, if she had time, sausage rolls. Or had she better cook a hot meal? She slept on the problem.

They saw nothing of each other the next day. Mr van Borsele was in theatre for hours on end and there was no sign of him when she went to put little Rita through her exercises. Back at the flat she made tea for herself, saw to Enoch and Toots, made a batch of sausage rolls and, after a little thought, another batch, this time of apple turnovers.

By seven o'clock she had the table set with plates and coffee mugs, a bowl of fruit and the apple turnovers; the sausage rolls were keeping hot in the oven. By eight o'clock she was getting restless; she was also getting hungry. About then she ate a sausage roll and sat down to read, only to give that up presently to ponder if he was coming after all. Presumably not, she decided, as the clock struck nine. In ten minutes, she promised herself she would have her own supper, lock the door and get ready for bed.

She was actually on the way to the kitchen when the door suffered its usual hefty thump. She went to let him in, prudently leaving the chain up and taking her time about undoing it. But she was sorry about that when she saw his face. He was tired, weary to his bones, and somehow it was all the more obvious because he was his usual immaculate self. The kind of man, she reflected, who would shave in the middle of the Sahara.

She answered his terse, 'I'm late,' with a soothing murmur.

'Coffee first?' she asked and drew the armchair nearer the gas fire. She handed him his coffee and sat down quietly opposite him. Only when he had drunk almost all the coffee did she ask, 'A bad day? Not little Rita, I hope?'

'She's fine. And nothing went wrong; it was a long list...'

'That girl with the fractured pelvis?'

He told her about it and she listened quietly. Finally he said, 'What a good listener you are, Claribel.'

'I'm interested. When did you last eat?'

'I had a sandwich around lunchtime.'

She fed him the sausage rolls and then the apple turnovers washed down with more coffee, and when he had finished she said, 'Now you must go home and go to bed. Have you a list in the morning?'

'No, only rounds and Out-patients at two o'clock.' He smiled a little. 'You sound like my old nanny. Shall we go somewhere quiet tomorrow evening? Shutter will be taking over for twenty-hour hours so I should be free by six o'clock. I'll come straight here from Jerome's and you can come back to the flat with me; we'll go from there.'

It was remarkable what food and drink had done for him; he looked quite his old self again. She agreed willingly enough. 'No dressing up?' she wanted to know.

He shook his head. 'We'll find a restaurant somewhere and eat whatever they've got.' He stood up and stretched hugely. 'Thank you, Claribel, you're a good girl.' He bent and kissed her cheek lightly. 'Goodnight.'

When he had gone she tidied away the plates and mugs, ate another sausage roll and went finally to bed, with the cats lying comfortably on her feet. They weren't supposed to do that but somehow she was glad of their company.

She was in the physio department all the next day except for her short spells with Rita. Mrs Green went to Out-patients in the afternoon and Claribel was kept busy until it was time to go home. Once there, she saw to the cats, put everything ready for the morning, showered and changed into a jacket and a skirt with a plain silk blouse, did her face with care, patted her golden hair to pristine tidiness and sat down to wait.

Not for long; it was barely six o'clock as she got into the car. Traffic was heavy and it took longer than usual to reach Mr van Borsele's flat. As he drew up before the door Claribel said sharply, 'That's Irma—coming down the steps.'

He thrust his hand into a pocket and gave her the ring, opened her door and got out himself to come round and take her arm as she got out, too.

'Remember that you love me to distraction,' he said softly as they crossed the pavement.

Irma stood watching them. Mr van Borsele greeted her without any sign of embarrassment and after a moment Claribel said, 'Hello, Irma. Did you want to see us?'

Irma said nothing but flung away to where an MG sports car stood. She got in and drove off without a word.

'Do you suppose she is tiring?' asked Claribel with interest.

'Let us hope so. Come in; you can have a drink while I change.'

Tilly welcomed her with a beaming smile as he settled her in an easy chair in the sitting-room, poured her a drink and disappeared, to reappear very shortly with a brisk, 'Well, are you ready?'

For all the world as though I had been the one who had kept him waiting, thought Claribel with a touch of peevishness.

The peevishness disappeared, though, as they drove out of London. He took her to the Waterside at Bray, elegant and charming and overlooking the river, and even on a rather chilly summer evening, it was a delight to have drinks and watch the countryside. They dined presently: a pâté of fish followed by duck with stuffed vegetables and, to finish, lemon tart for her while Mr van Borsele contented himself with the cheeseboard. They lingered over coffee and Claribel allowed a feeling of well-being to sweep over her; life, after all, was really rather nice and her companion was rather nice, too. She rose reluctantly when he suggested that they had better return. 'I've a list as long as an arm tomorrow,' he observed. 'I want to get as much done before I go back.'

'Go back?' She was startled. 'Are you going back to Holland?'

'Well, yes. I only come here from time to time, you know...'

She did know; he specialised in several techniques which meant that he was in demand in countries other than his own. All the same, she said, 'So you don't need to bother about Irma once you've gone back home.'

They were in the car now, already on the motorway on the way to London.

'I'm not sure about that. She's bored and spoilt and has nothing better to do than follow her own inclinations. If she feels like it she could follow me wherever I choose to go. And I'm sorry if that sounds conceited. My hope is that she will set eyes on some other man and develop a fancy for him.'

He threw her a sideways look. 'Claribel, when I go back to Holland I should like you to come with me.'

She gaped at him. 'Me? Go with you? Whatever for?'

'It would, I think, clinch the matter. You can stay with my grandmother.'

'I don't know your grandmother,' snapped Claribel, much put out, 'and I refuse, so please don't mention it again.'

He said silkily, 'I imagined that would be your reaction, but just let the idea simmer, will you?'

'It's impossible. I've no holiday due, and what about Enoch and Toots?'

He didn't answer, which was most unsatisfactory. Nor would he come in when they reached her flat. He saw her to the door, reminded her that they were to go dancing on the following evening, held out his hand for the ring and drove away, apparently quite unconcerned at her refusal.

CHAPTER SEVEN

CLARIBEL spent a good deal of the night worrying away at Mr van Borsele's strange request. Well, it hadn't really been a request, rather a statement of something which he had taken for granted. And for once he had gone too far. All he was thinking of was his own convenience. And if his grandmother was half as bossy as he was, the visit would be nothing less than sheer misery. She lay picturing herself sitting between the pair of them, two haughty noses and two pairs of dark eyes boring into her, organising her days to suit themselves... And more than likely Granny wouldn't speak a word of English; she had no intention of letting the ridiculous idea simmer.

She spent Saturday shopping and cleaning her little home and composing cool, logical speeches to make to Mr van Borsele when he came. It was a great pity that when he did, he gave her no opportunity to say a word about it. His talk was of ordinary things as he whisked her off to the Ritz to dine and dance until the small hours. After a brief period of deciding coolness on her part, he wanted to know if she was sulking about something. 'And if you are, you are to stop it at once, for Irma has just come in.'

They were sitting at a table which had a splendid view of the restaurant, and where they could be seen. She had promised to play a part for him and she was an honest girl; she gave him a dazzling smile just in time. Irma was passing their table and stopped.

She said sulkily, 'Together again? Have you moved in with him, then?'

A faint pink covered Claribel's cheeks. 'Oh, hello, Irma.' Her voice was sugary-sweet and Mr van Borsele's mouth quivered ever so slightly.

'Well, no, I'd love to but I work at a hospital, you know; it would take me too long to get to and fro each day. But that won't be for much longer...'

Mr van Borsele's voice was very smooth. 'I shall be going back shortly and of course Claribel will go with me.' The bland expression didn't alter when Claribel gave him a sharp kick under the table; on the shin and painful. She was still smiling but only for Irma's benefit.

'Back to Holland?' asked Irma.

Mr van Borsele gave her a look of well-bred surprise. 'Naturally. That is my home.'

'Whereabouts?'

Claribel chipped in, 'How long are you staying in London?' Her smile was wide; there was nothing in her quiet voice to suggest the violence she would like to do to the wretched girl.

'What you mean is,' said Irma rudely, 'that there is no point in me trying to get Marc away from you.'

'Something like that,' agreed Claribel. She turned her green eyes upon him. 'Darling, could we order? I'm famished.'

She suspected that behind his impassive politeness he was amused, but his, 'Of course, dearest. I'm sure Irma will excuse us,' couldn't be faulted.

Irma flounced away to her own table. He sat down again and, just in case she should turn round to look at them, took Claribel's ringed hand in his. 'You would be a splendid receptionist for a busy man,' he observed. 'Would you consider giving up your job and coming to work for me?'

'Certainly not,' Claribel spoke a shade tartly. 'And anyway, I've not got the slightest idea how to be a receptionist.'

'It's a gift one is born with: the ability to tell whopping great fibs with the voice of a dove and to smile like an angel at the same time.' He added blandly, 'I'd pay you handsomely.'

She withdrew her hand from his and studied the menu she had been handed. 'For two pins I'd get up and go back to the flat.'

'By all means, but do eat something first. What about *duo de langoustines*, and ragout of salmon and scallops to follow, and I think champagne, don't you? After all, we have something to celebrate.'

'What?' asked Claribel. Her thoughts were on the delicious dinner suggested to her and she had forgotten to be tart.

'The future,' said Mr van Borsele at his blandest.

That sounded harmless enough; she settled down to enjoy her dinner. It was every bit as good as it had sounded, and the iced curacao mousse with strawberries, which followed the scallops and salmon served with watercress sauce, mushrooms and truffles, left her in a pleasant state of repletion which, however, didn't prevent her getting up to dance at his suggestion with every sign of pleasure.

Just before she went to sleep that night she thought drowsily that Marc van Borsele certainly knew how to take a girl out in style. She smacked her lips at the memory of the mousse and went happily to sleep.

On their way to Tisbury the following morning she asked him rather diffidently if he would like to lunch at her home, but he declined with reluctance; she was told his sister was expecting him and, since she wouldn't be seeing him for some time, he had promised to spend the day with her and her husband and the baby, adding that he intended leaving towards the end of the week.

'And you are still adamant in refusing to come with me?' he asked.

'Well, of course I am. I can't leave my job at a moment's notice.'

'In that case, give in your notice tomorrow and I'll come over for you.'

She turned in her seat to look at him. 'Just for once,' she told him severely, 'you're not going to have your own way. I've helped you because I said I would, but that's the lot.'

He said mildly, 'You could take your holidays; I'm sure dear Miss Flute could contrive to let you go—family affairs, or something like that.'

She said stubbornly, 'It's no use; it's a good job and I have to work.'

It was very disconcerting when he agreed cheerfully and suggested that they should stop for coffee.

He didn't say another word about his suggestion, but spent ten minutes talking to her mother and father, warned her to be ready by seven o'clock that evening and drove away, leaving her feeling dreary and deprived, but of what she had no idea.

That Claribel was *distraite* was obvious to Mrs Brown but she didn't remark upon it; her beautiful daughter was up to something or other, and Mrs Brown hoped fervently that the something was to do with Marc van Borsele. It was most fortunate that Sebastian was coming home for the day: the brother and sister were close and she might unburden herself to him.

But she didn't. She was delighted to see him, they exchanged outrageous stories, teased each other and argued amicably, but somehow Mr van Borsele wasn't mentioned. Not until the afternoon as they sat at tea did Claribel let fall the information that she was being given a lift by someone from the hospital.

'Who?' asked Sebastian. 'Some callow medical student?'

'Well I dare say he was years ago, although it's hard to think of him as such. He's one of the consultants; divides his time between Jerome's and some hospital or other in Holland.'

Sebastian sat up. 'He's not by any chance called van Borsele?'

'Yes. Why?'

'Only, my dear sister, you've hooked one of the cleverest and most famous orthopaedic men there is around. I say, is he coming here?'

'Well, of course. Why all the fuss? He's got a bad temper and he likes his own way.'

'Don't we all? He's a real workaholic, too.'

'He dances very nicely,' observed Claribel demurely.

To all of which conversation her mother listened with the greatest satisfaction.

Mr van Borsele arrived punctually, accepting a mug of coffee from Mrs Brown, shook hands with Mr Brown and Sebastian and nodded casually to Claribel. There was nothing loverlike about the nod, nor did Claribel evince any sign of delight at the sight of him; Mrs Brown was quite put out. She felt better after they had gone, though; Sebastian, sitting on the kitchen table while she got the supper, remarked idly, 'So our old Clari has succumbed at last.'

Mrs Brown stopped beating eggs to look at him. 'What do you mean, dear?'

'Why, Mother, it's as plain as the nose on my face; they're in love.'

Mrs Brown brightened visibly. 'You really think so? But he hardly speaks to her when she is fetched and Claribel is quite offhand.'

'Clari hasn't discovered it yet and he's far too clever to do anything about it.' He helped himself to a slice of bread from the loaf on the table. 'You mark my words, Mother dear, we've got a romance on our hands.'

There was nothing romantic about Mr van Borsele's manner as they drove back to London. He talked intermittently about nothing much, and as for Claribel, she said hardly a word. She had given the matter a good deal of thought and was feeling, surprisingly enough, mean. Mr van Borsele had treated her generously, even if for his own ends, and she had refused to listen to his plans. They were silly plans, she considered, but she could have refused nicely, let him down gently... She waited for him to mention them again but he had nothing to say on the subject; he saw her and the cats into the flat, declined her offer of coffee with friendly casualness, and drove off. Not a word about meeting her again. She told herself that that was just what she wanted; she was sick and tired of him turning up at all hours and demanding coffee... That this wasn't in the least true didn't bother her; she wasn't in the mood to feel well disposed towards him.

'I hope I never see him again,' she told the cats, happily unaware that fate was about to take a hand in her affairs.

Physio was busier than usual in the morning and, besides, there were several more patients on the wards to be treated, but other than her usual morning session with little Rita, Claribel was kept in the department. Mrs Green had gone to Out-patients, and Miss Flute had gone to the orthopaedic wards to accompany Mr van Borsele's round. Claribel worked her way steadily through a variety of broken limbs, frozen shoulders and arthritic knees while Tilly and Pat, at the far end of the department, dealt with an enormously stout and heavy man learning to walk after a severely fractured leg.

Claribel, bidding goodbye to a tough young man with a torn knee ligament, heaved a sigh of relief; Miss Flute would be back in another ten minutes and so would Mrs Green, unless Mr van Borsele chose to be extra long-winded; they would take it in turns to have their coffee and get their breath before working on until their lunch break. Mrs Snow, still cheerfully unable to use her arm as she should, was her next patient. She came trotting in, chatty as ever, and began peeling off the various garments she still found necessary despite the fact that it was quite a warm day and summer was well advanced. But presently, with her felt hat still firmly on her head, she sat down, put her arm on the cushioned table and settled for a cosy chat while Claribel took her through her exercises. She was in the middle of a saga concerning the neighbour's daughter and her goings-on when Claribel caught a movement out of the corner of her eye. Pat and Tilly were disappearing through the far door, supporting their patient to the waiting ambulance; the movement had come from the other end. She turned to look sideways to the waiting-room in time to see a man stoop to put a carrier bag between the benches.

'Just a tick,' she begged Mrs Snow, then hurried into the waiting-room, but the man had disappeared and there was no one else there. The bag was, though, wedged so that she couldn't get at it. Someone leaving something quite harmless for a patient who had perhaps not yet arrived? One of the workmen around the hospital leaving tools for later on? Or a bomb?

It seemed a bit silly to telephone the porter's lodge; perhaps she was over-reacting, and she was going to look an awful fool if it turned out to be someone's shopping. All the same, she explained to Begg, the head porter, and asked if he would notify whoever ought to know.

Mr van Borsele, head and shoulders thrust though the lodge's small window, writing a note to his registrar, looked up at Begg's worried, 'Does it look like a bomb, Miss Brown?'

He removed his head and shoulders and went to stand by Begg. 'Trouble?' he asked without any appearance of anxiety.

'There's Miss Brown, down in physio, says she glimpsed a man go into the waiting-room and leave a parcel. She went to investigate and can't move it. It's a plastic shopping bag; she says it's wedged tightly, and should anyone be told?'

Mr van Borsele took the phone from him. 'Claribel? Have you any patients there with you? One? Get out, both of you, as fast as you can. It may be nothing at all to worry about, but let us take precautions. Warn anyone nearby to get well clear. I'll see that the right people know. Now leave, fast.'

'Begg, give the alarm then get the police; you know the drill.' Mr van Borsele was already disappearing at a rippling pace through the hospital entrance. Once outside he ran; the physiotherapy department was to one side of the hospital, built on to one wing. He went to the far door and saw Claribel, hurrying Mrs Snow towards him…

Claribel had wasted no time; Marc had sounded urgent but unflurried. She had shot back to Mrs Snow, sitting at her ease, with her shoes off, in order to ease her corns.

'We have to leave at once, Mrs Snow,' she had said as calmly as she could. 'There's a suspicious parcel in the waiting-room.' She had no need to explain; everyone knew about bombs in plastic bags these days. 'We must be quick…'

Mrs Snow had bent to her shoes. 'Oh, if you say so, ducks. You'll 'ave ter wait while I get my feet back in, though.'

Claribel had caught up the various garments scattered around her patient. 'Never mind putting them on,' she had said urgently. 'We can do that outside.'

Her voice had been drowned by the hospital alarm sounding the pre-arranged signal in case of dire emergency, and at the same time she had seen Mr van Borsele racing towards them.

He was within feet of them when the bomb went off, so that she didn't hear his roared warning to get down. She wasn't sure, thinking about it later, if it was the explosion or Mr van Borsele's considerable weight on top of her and Mrs Snow which knocked the breath from her and left her head spinning. It seemed to her that the entire hospital was disintegrating about them, although, since the bomb had been a small one, it was only the physiotherapy department which was torn apart, subsiding into piles of debris. By some miracle they escaped the worst of it. True, lumps of ceiling plaster, torn and twisted equipment, tattered remnants of curtains and broken chairs and stools and landed on them, but their effect had been deadened by the burst pillows from the couches which had more or less smothered them.

Mr van Borsele rose cautiously to his feet, his beautiful suit covered by feathers, bundles of curtain bits and a great deal of plaster. He was rather pale but his voice was calm. 'Let's get out of here, shall we?'

He pulled Claribel to her feet and put an arm around her. She was white and dazed and all she wanted to do was to cling to him and bury her head in his shoulder. 'Hold hard,' he told her in a matter-of-fact voice, and stopped to help Mrs Snow to her feet.

'Me 'at,' said Mrs Snow urgently, 'and me shoes! Drat them blessed bombs.'

Given some chance she would have searched for them but Mr van Borsele said firmly, 'Out of here, as quick as you can,' and caught her by the arm and urged her over the rubble towards the further door.

Claribel was feeling peculiar; she had lost her shoes and there was a warm trickle of something down one leg; she had a fearful headache and all she really wanted to do was to lie down somewhere and go to sleep. She muttered such wishes aloud, to be answered by Mr van Borsele's, 'Later. Let's get you outside first.' He added sternly, 'And do remember that we have a patient with us.'

'Heartless brute,' Claribel mumbled, but she stumbled along beside him, half listening to the rumblings and grumblings of the ruin around her as it settled.

She became aware that there were other people around them. Deft hands reached out to help them and she was dimly aware of Mrs Snow's indignant voice going on about her hat. Mr van Borsele's voice, unhurried and quiet, penetrating her dimmed wits. 'Mrs Snow, tomorrow I promise I will gladly call upon you and take you to buy a hat and shoes. You are a very plucky lady; I'm proud to know you.'

At this point Claribel was regrettably sick, and was conscious of Mr van Borsele's firm hand on her forehead. 'I bet you're not so proud to know me,' she said loudly, and hardly noticed when he picked her up and laid her on one of the trolleys being rushed from the accident room.

She was dimly aware once more of people doing things, but their voices were far away and she couldn't be bothered to open her eyes and look at them while they peeled off her clothes, cleaned her up, examined the long scratch on one leg and warded her. She slept soundly once she had been put to bed and, being young and strong, when she woke up some hours later she felt perfectly all right.

'I'll go home,' she told the nurse who came to look at her. 'You must be busy enough and there is nothing wrong with me.'

'I'll fetch Sister.' The nurse smiled at her and slid away and a moment later Sister came, and with her Mr van Borsele, looking immaculate, not a hair out of place.

He stood looking down at her. 'Feeling better? I'm afraid I knocked all the wind out of you. You want to go to your flat? There's no reason why you shouldn't but be good enough to stay quietly there tomorrow, in bed if you wish. Miss Flute asked me to tell you that she'll be round to see how you are in the morning. Don't worry about coming to work—they are arranging to transfer the physio patients to Clem's and St Giles.'

'No work,' she repeated. Despite her pale face she looked quite beautiful sitting up in a theatre gown several sizes too large for her, her hair in a golden tangle. 'Oh. I suppose I'll go to either Clem's or St Giles'...'

He smiled. 'I believe the physio staff are to go on protracted leave.' His smiled widened and she stared up at him. 'So you'll be able to come to Holland with me after all, Claribel.'

She gaped at him, taken by surprise and conscious of Sister's interest. Before she could say anything, he said to that lady, 'Claribel has been invited to stay with a member of my family in Holland. It will be an ideal break for her—just what she needs now after this—er—upheaval.'

Claribel cast him a fulminating look which he returned with a bland smile. He had her cornered; to manage to explain to Sister was impossible and now, in less than no time, the entire hospital would know that she was going to Holland with him. Perhaps there would be no snide asides; he was respected and liked and the general opinion was that he was a widower. He was aware of this surmise and had never chosen to correct it. Now the hospital grapevine would conclude that he intended to take a wife, and who better than Claribel Brown, who was a nice girl anyway?

She watched him go with a smouldering eye while Sister tripped along beside him, dying to spread the news.

Angry tears filled her eyes, but she brushed them away as Miss Flute came briskly down the ward and stopped beside her bed.

'Pat has gone to your flat to get you some clothes, dear. You are sure you feel all right? You had a very bad shock.'

'It was rather. Miss Flute, were there many people hurt, and is the damage bad?'

'Half a dozen with cuts and bruises—a miracle that there wasn't more damage. Physio's wiped out though.' She repeated what Mr van Borsele had already said and added, 'They don't want us at Clem's or St Giles', at least not for some weeks—they plan to put up a temporary extension for us. Our place will have to be re-built and equipped of course—it will take months.'

She patted Claribel on the shoulder. 'We're to have paid leave for at least a month; by then they will have sorted things out. I'm coming to see how you are in the morning, so don't go rushing around, there's a dear girl. We found your bag, or rather the remains of it. Pat took your keys; she'll be along soon.'

'Is Mrs Snow all right?'

'She was taken to the accident room and given a check-up and then driven home. She was keen to know if you were all right and was full of Mr van Borsele's promise that he would buy her a hat and shoes. What a kind man he is, and so resourceful.' She glanced at Claribel's face. 'Well, I'll be off home; everyone's settled down again. There's a frightful mess outside, of course, but the hospital itself is back to normal. They're looking for the man; the police want to see you after you get to the flat. Will you be all right?'

Claribel nodded and Miss Flute left.

Pat came up with her clothes very shortly afterwards. Claribel dressed and, with Sister as an escort went down to the entrance. Almost there she said hesitantly, 'I think I'd better have a taxi, Sister, if someone could phone for one?'

'No need, you are being taken home, my dear.'

They had reached the entrance hall and Claribel saw Mr van Borsele sitting on a windowsill, reading a newspaper. He folded it up, put it away and came to meet them. 'Quite ready?' he asked in a voice nicely balanced between casual and concerned.

She stopped beside him. 'Yes, but I'm quite able to go home in a taxi...'

'I'm sure you are, but the police want to interview you and I think it might be a good idea if someone from this hospital was there as well.'

She stood undecided. 'Oh, I hadn't thought of that.'

Sister said firmly, 'You go along with Mr van Borsele, dear—he is quite right, someone ought to be with you.'

Claribel said, 'Yes, Sister,' meekly and got just as meekly into the Rolls. To tell the truth, she still felt not quite herself and the idea of having to answer a host of questions filled her with quite unreasoning fright.

Mr van Borsele didn't utter a word as he drove her to Meadow Road. When they reached the flat he took her key from her, opened the door, urged her inside and then followed her.

The cats rushed to meet them and she bent to stroke them, and then sat down quickly because she felt giddy.

Mr van Borsele had gone at once to put on the kettle and, still without speaking, he fed the cats, made the tea and brought her a cup. She took it with a hand which she was ashamed to see still shook a little, which made her so cross she said snappily, 'It doesn't seem to have bothered you at all, being bombed.'

He said mildly, 'Well, you know, men aren't supposed to show their feelings on these regrettable occasions.' He added with a smile, 'I was scared stiff.'

Her peevishness dissolved. 'Oh, were you? No one would have known.' And then, 'How much do you weight?'

'Very nearly fifteen stones. I hope I didn't hurt you too much.' He sat opposite her, very much at his ease, sipping his tea.

She shook her head. 'Heaven knows what would have happened to us if you actually hadn't protected us. I—I haven't thanked you, but I do, with all my heart.' To cover up a sudden shyness she added, 'Mrs Snow was marvellous…'

'Ah, yes. We have a date for tomorrow, she and I.' He put down his cup. 'The police will be here in an hour. Go and take a bath, Claribel, and get into your nightie and dressing-gown while I make some sandwiches for our supper. The moment they have gone you'll get into bed and stay there, and don't get up tomorrow until I've been to see how you are.' And, at her look, 'Delayed shock,' he observed smoothly.

It was easier to do as he said than argue with him. The bath soothed her; she washed her hair, too, and presently went back into the sitting-room. Mr van Borsele glanced up, his look impersonal. 'Good. I'm going to go next door for a few minutes. If I let the good lady know a little of what has happened there'll be no speculation among the neighbours.'

He disappeared and she sat down to finish drying her hair. She felt much better and her headache was bearable now. Enoch and Toots came to sit by her, pleased because she was home early.

'What shall I do?' she enquired of them. 'I expect we'd all better go home until something is arranged. I suppose someone will let me know...'

Mr van Borsele came back looking amused. 'I like the old lady next door. She will, of course, spread the tale far and wide; you'll not lack for neighbourly interest. She was concerned about you being alone tonight, but I was able to set her mind at rest. I would prefer to stay here myself, but that would hardly do, would it? So I've arranged for Tilly to sleep here. I'll fetch her in a while and collect her in the morning.'

Claribel said a little wildly, 'But there's no bed. I'll be quite all right, really I will.'

'Yes, I know that. She'll bring a sleeping bag with her and bedding; and don't argue, please, Claribel.'

She said weakly, 'But how will you manage on your own?'

'I've boiled an egg before now, and if I know Tilly there won't be any need for me to do even that.' He went through to the bedroom and came back with a brush. 'The police will be here shortly. May I use your phone?'

He talked for a few minutes to his registrar and then put the receiver back. 'I phoned your mother,' he observed, 'but I expect you'd like a word with her.'

She felt guilty. 'Oh, thank you, Marc. I should have thought of that—I feel awful about it.'

'No need. You see, you were badly shocked. I'll get your home now; there is time before the police arrive.'

He came across the room with the phone. 'Your mother was very upset,' she was told as she picked up the receiver.

She forced herself to be her normally matter-of-fact self and was relieved to hear both her mother and her father relaxing as she talked. When she had finished, Mr van Borsele said, 'Good girl. It's worse for them; they'll feel better now you have talked to them.'

The police arrived then to take a statement, a quite unfrightening business done over more cups of tea, and when they had gone Mr van Borsele fetched the sandwiches, went out to his car and came back with a bottle under his arm. 'Claret,' he remarked. 'Just what you need. I'm going to fetch Tilly in half an hour or so, but shall we talk first?'

'What about?' asked Claribel as, very nearly restored to normality, she bit into an apple and a cheese sandwich.

'You had a number of reasons why you shouldn't accompany me to Holland. None of them exist any more. On the contrary, a brief holiday is just what you want. I'm going back on Friday. I'll drive you down to Tisbury tomorrow evening and you can take the cats and leave them there while you are in Holland. I'm sure Miss Flute will help you pack tomorrow before the evening.'

Claribel stared at him, her mouth full of sandwich. She gobbled hastily before she spluttered, 'Well, of all the...I never did!'

'Neither of which remarks is to the point,' he observed calmly. 'Just for once can you not argue, Claribel; just accept my invitation gracefully.'

'You're only asking me because of Irma, though I don't see that it makes a scrap of difference if I'm with you or not.'

'I must admit that your company should give her the *coup de grâce*, for I shall make no secret of your going with me and the wretched girl seems to have ears and eyes everywhere. I must add, though, that I shall enjoy your company, although you won't see much of me; indeed, I dare say I shall be away for most of the time.' He added silkily, 'But, of course, you won't mind that, will you?'

He got up and washed their supper things, saw to the cats, made sure that the windows were closed and picked up his bag. 'Goodnight, Claribel. I'll go and fetch Tilly and I won't come in when I bring her back. Will you let me have your key? I'll see her safely in. You go to bed; she won't disturb you.'

He dropped a kiss on top of her golden hair and went away before she had framed a single word.

After a few minutes she got up and wandered around the little room. He had taken it for granted that she would do as he suggested and if she hadn't known that it was for his own ends, she might have been glad to accept.

'I won't go,' she told the cats, and got into bed, prepared to think the thing out in peace and quiet. She fell asleep at once and never heard Tilly creeping soft-footed around the living-room, arranging her makeshift bed.

Claribel slept soundly and indeed didn't waken until Tilly brought her a cup of tea. She sat up in bed, feeling quite herself again, and declared her intention of getting up and cooking their breakfast. 'And thank you very much for spending the night here,' she added. 'I didn't hear you come in. I only hope you weren't too uncomfortable.'

'Not a bit of it, miss. Jus' you 'ave yer bath and dress while I get us a bite ter eat.' Tilly nodded her head quite severely, standing small and round, arms across her ample bosom. 'The boss said as 'ow I was ter cherish you, and that I'll do.' At the door she turned to ask. 'These 'ere cats, shall I feed 'em?'

They had had their breakfast and were washing up together when Mr van Borsele arrived. His laconic, 'OK this morning?' wasn't quite what she had expected, but she was aware of shame at having expected anything else; she hadn't been hurt, only frightened, and here he was, immaculate as always, looking as though he had slept for at least twelve hours and never been near bomb in his life. She was getting very sorry for herself, which wouldn't do at all. And he had been kind and thoughtful...

She said brightly, 'I had a marvellous night. Thank you for letting Tilly stay, it was nice having company.'

He nodded. 'Miss Flute will be coming presently. I'm going to run Tilly home now. I'll be here about six o'clock. Pack enough to see you through a couple of weeks in Holland; I doubt if there will be time to come back here on Friday while you pick over your wardrobe.'

She began, 'I don't...' and then stopped. It would be pointless to argue; he was doing exactly what he wished to do and if she raised objections she had no doubt that he would ride rough-shod over them.

When he and Tilly had gone she made another pot of tea and sat down to consider her immediate future. It was largely in the hands of Mr van Borsele and, thinking about it, she decided that a holiday would be rather nice anyway, even if Granny was an old tartar, which was more than likely if she and her grandson were alike. He had said that he would see very little of her and after all there was no need. The idea was for her to go to Holland with him in order to convince Irma that she might as well give up pursuing him. She had no doubt that he would find some means of letting the girl know that they were going and give her the opportunity of actually seeing them leave the country if she had a mind to do so.

She drank the rest of the tea, and the began to get the flat ready for her departure. When Miss Flute came they emptied the pantry, handed the old lady next door the perishable food that was in it, and then started to pack.

'I have no idea what to take,' declared Claribel pettishly.

'Wear that nice suit—that knitted one you bought; you can travel in it and wear it every day if you've a mind. A couple of jersey dresses; skirts, blouses and jumpers; and take that nice blazer you had last summer. Oh, and a pretty dress in case you go out in the evening—two, perhaps?'

'I don't even know where I am going...'

'What fun,' declared Miss Flute. 'I wish I was in your shoes.'

'Are you going away, Miss Flute?'

'To my sister's in Cornwall. We shall be notified when they've got something planned for us, but that will be a couple of weeks at least. They have Mr van Borsele's address so they can reach you wherever you are.'

Claribel paused in folding her blouses. 'Miss Flute, do you think I'm a bit mad to go?'

'Not in the least. I understand from Mr van Borsele that you are doing him a favour in doing so, and the change of scene is just what you need.'

They sat down to a snack lunch presently and Claribel was very tempted to tell Miss Flute all about Irma, but it wasn't her problem and Mr van Borsele was known to be a reserved man who seldom allowed details of his private life to emerge. All the same she thought she would tell her mother...

Strangely enough it was Mr van Borsele who suggested just that as they drove to Tisbury. 'We have nothing to hide,' he observed coolly. 'I may say I think you have been making a great fuss over nothing, Claribel.'

'Fuss? Fuss! I haven't been fussy at all. I've agreed to your hare-brained schemes like a half-wit.'

He said soothingly to infuriate her, 'Now, now, don't malign yourself, Claribel. I have never thought of you as half-witted.'

'I should jolly well hope not! If I'd known what I was letting myself in for…'

He chose to misunderstand her. 'Oh, you'll enjoy your stay with Granny.' There was no way in which she could ruffle his complacency.

'I shall take Mother's advice; probably she will tell me not to go to Holland.'

'As to that, we have to wait and see, don't we?' Then suddenly he wasn't mocking any more. 'Don't worry, my dear. Let life happen; don't try to alter it.' He sounded kind and reassuring; she found herself relaxing. Perhaps she had been making mountains out of molehills after all.

CHAPTER EIGHT

RATHER to Claribel's surprise, when they arrived at her home, Marc showed no sign of wishing to hurry away. Instead, when her father suggested that they might go to his study so that he might be shown a rare hand-drawn map of the village, he agreed with alacrity, so that she, rather at a loss, followed her mother into the kitchen to help with the supper.

'He can stay the night if he wants to,' observed her mother, prodding the potatoes.

Claribel had been so wrapped up in her own problems she hadn't thought about that. 'Oh—well, I expect he's going to his sister. I didn't ask.'

Her mother shot her a quick look; it was obvious that her daughter had a lot on her mind and moreover it apparently had nothing to do with the bomb. That had been exclaimed over and talked about at some length, and as far as she could see Claribel, once over the shock, had recovered nicely. It had been a very nasty thing to happen. She spoke her thoughts out loud, 'What a good thing Mr van Borsele was there.'

Claribel paused on her way to the dining-room with the plates. 'Yes, well, you see he was with the porter when I phoned—I did tell you.'

'I forget so easily, love.' A remark Claribel took with a pinch of salt; her mother never forgot anything.

When she went back into the kitchen the men were there, whisky glasses in their hands, and her father was pouring the best sherry into two more glasses for her mother and her. 'There you are, darling. Marc will stay to supper; he can't drive all the way back to London without a meal.'

Claribel put her tray down on the table. 'Do you mean to tell me,' she asked in a high voice, 'that you have to go back this evening? It's well after nine o'clock.'

He returned her icy green stare with a look of such innocence that she almost laughed. 'I enjoy driving at night,' he said placidly, 'and something smells delicious.'

Mrs Brown beamed at him. 'Watercress soup, my own make,' she told him happily, 'bacon and egg pie, and baked apples and cream for afters.'

Claribel, feeling that she was in the dark about something but not sure what it was, began cutting bread at the table. She very nearly dropped the knife when her father said, 'It really is most kind of you to invite Clari—a short break after that most upsetting incident is just what she needs.' He turned to smile at her amazed face. 'You'll enjoy it, my dear, won't you?'

The villain, she thought furiously, going behind my back and settling everything. She swallowed rage and said flatly, 'I expect I shall. I don't even know where I'm going.' She shot Mr van Borsele a look to burn him up, if that had been possible.

'Surprises are always nice,' he said smoothly, 'but I'll tell you. My home is in Friesland, the northern province of the Netherlands; still unspoilt, mostly farmland and lakes. The peace and quiet will do you good.' His voice was silky. 'You are rather uptight, only to be expected after your unpleasant experience.'

Her parents nodded approvingly and she turned away from his mocking gaze, aware that he was enjoying himself. Well, she wouldn't give him the pleasure of seeing how angry she was. 'It sounds delightful.' She spoke sweetly, although it was an effort. It would have pleased her mightily to have thrown the loaf at his head.

The talk was general during supper, ranging from bomb outrages to the Friesian landscape, the easiest routes to Holland, and vague, very vague, replies on Mr van Borsele's part to Mrs Brown's gentle questions about his life. It was almost eleven o'clock when he left with the assurance that he would be back at the end of the week to fetch Claribel.

They were standing in the hall and she said tartly, 'And what about Irma? Will you be able to find another girl to take out while I'm here?'

'Tut, tut,' he reproved her in a kindly tone to set her teeth on edge. 'You're being peevish. If it makes you any happier I shall be at the hospital each evening. There's a good deal of work still to do and this bomb has thrown the theatre lists rather out of line. Mr Shutter and I will be operating each evening; very awkward for all concerned, but the only solution. If I should see our friend Irma I shall tell her that you and I will be travelling together to Holland.' He bent and kissed her quickly. 'Don't worry, Claribel, no one shall take your place.'

'Much I should care. And another thing.' She was whispering, for her parents were in the drawing-room and the door was half open. 'How dared you go behind my back and tell Mother and Father about—about us? I haven't said I'll go with you...'

'Oh, yes you did. I expect this bomb business has curdled your wits a little.' He gave her a wide smile and went out to his car and, without looking back, drove away.

Claribel shut the door with something of a snap, wishing that just once she might have the last word. 'I shan't go,' she muttered, all the while knowing that, of course, she would. It would be interesting to see his home, even if he wasn't going to be there for most of the time. She hoped that he would drive back carefully...

The few days passed peacefully. The weather was pleasantly warm, even if it was chilly towards evening. She combed through her wardrobe and got her father to take her and her mother into Salisbury so that she might add to it. She found just what she wanted: a pale blue pencil-slim wool skirt, a matching top in cashmere and a loose light cardigan, edged with satin ribbon, all more than she intended to spend. However, as her mother pointed out, good clothes were more economical because they looked good until they fell apart. Uplifted by this sensible remark, Claribel bought a short-sleeved silk dress which exactly matched her eyes, and which would, as she was careful to point out to her mother, come in very useful. Mrs Brown agreed; any dress likely to catch Marc's eye and increase his interest in Claribel would be useful. Claribel had thought exactly the same thing, though, of course, she didn't say so. Indeed she wasn't actually conscious of thinking it.

Mr van Borsele arrived shortly after lunch on the Friday, accepting coffee from Mrs Brown, enquiring casually after Claribel's health, passed the time of day with her father and signified his intention of leaving as soon as she was ready.

'We'll look in at my flat as we go,' he told her. 'Tilly will have my bags ready. We're going from Harwich. I went to Meadow Road, by the way, and talked to your neighbour; she'll keep an eye on your place while you're away. Miss Flute sends her love; she's off today as well. They're still clearing rubble away at Jerome's; it will be some time before they have put up temporary buildings and there's almost all the equipment to install.'

Claribel, looking very pretty in the knitted outfit, went to say goodbye to her cats and collect her overnight bag. She felt excited now; she had tried to drum up some ill feeling against Marc during the week, but somehow it had been difficult. He had behaved very badly, but he had been kind, too, and he had undoubtedly saved her from injury when the bomb had exploded. She told herself that she owed him something for that; by the time she came back to England Irma would have tired of him and she would have paid off her debt to him.

She said goodbye to her mother and father and got into the car, reflecting as she did so that it was surprisingly easy to get used to comfort and luxury—travelling in a Rolls Royce, for instance.

Mr van Borsele had gone back to speak to her father and she wondered why; he had already said goodbye. Whatever it was was briefly spoken, then he got in beside her and they drove away.

He had nothing to say; she peeped sideways at his profile and found it a little stern. Perhaps he was thinking about the patients he had operated upon during the week, or the work waiting for him in Holland. She searched her head for something to say, but, since she couldn't think of anything, stayed silent, too.

Presently he broke the silence. 'We'll stop for tea at Oakley. Is there any need for you to do anything at the flat?'

'No. If you're in a hurry there's no need for us to go there.'

'Not as hurried as all that. We'll just check that everything is all right there, and we'll have a meal at my flat; we don't need to get to Harwich until round about ten o'clock.'

She was a little puzzled; he sounded friendly enough, but somehow remote. Perhaps he was regretting his invitation. She was a level-headed girl but given to impulsive acts upon occasion. 'If you're having second thoughts, do say so,' she begged him. 'You can drop me off at the flat and I can catch a train in the morning.'

He gave a crack of laughter. 'Claribel, you're letting your imagination run riot again. Here we are at the end of a most successful campaign to shake off Irma and you suddenly choose to behave like a teenager who doesn't know her own mind.' He added bracingly, 'You, a grown woman of twenty-eight, with a mind of your own.'

'There's no need to bring my age into it,' said Claribel crossly. 'I only wondered.'

Just for a moment he put a hand over hers. 'Just remember that I'm glad to have you with me.'

Which was reassuring. On the other hand, of course he was glad; she was a necessary buffer between him and the wretched Irma. If the girl got her claws into him, he would get what he deserved. She was ashamed of the thought the moment it had flitted through her head, and she frowned, trying to understand why she thought of him in such a muddled way. They had started off on the wrong foot, of course...

Meadow Road looked dingier than ever in the afternoon sunshine, and her flat, even with its brave show of flowers in the tubs and its cheerfully painted door, looked shabby. They went inside together, checking that everything was as it should be, and as they left, a few minutes later, Claribel wondered how she would feel when she returned to it. London, that part of London anyway, seemed at that moment the worst possible place in which to live.

That couldn't be applied to Marc's flat, she admitted to herself as he ushered her through its dignified entrance. No neighbours peered through grubby net curtains as they went in and, with the door shut, no noise from the street spoilt the quiet.

Tilly had been on the look out for them. She had the door open as they reached it. ''Ere you are then,' she exclaimed cheerfully. 'I got a nice tasty meal all ready. Just you tidy yerselves up, the pair of yer, while I dishes up.' She turned away to go back to the kitchen, saying as she went, 'An I've packed yer things like you asked, an' that young woman 'oo's always pestering you, she rang up, wanted to know where you were.'

'What did you tell her?' asked Mr van Borsele.

'Like yer says—out of town and leaving for 'olland this evening.'

'Good girl. What a treasure you are, Tilly.'

'Go on with yer.' She gave him a wide smile and went.

Sipping her sherry in his beautiful sitting-room, Claribel observed, 'Well, that's the last of Irma. I don't really need...' She caught his eye. 'Oh, well, I suppose just to be on the safe side.' She frowned. 'But do you have to tell her so much?'

'Dear girl, just think for a moment. Do you not remember as a child being forbidden something you wanted very much and for that very reason wanting it all the more, and if by some chance it was available to you, you lost all interest? The same idea applies very roughly to the tiresome Irma.'

They dined deliciously with Tilly trotting in and out, making sure that they ate what she put before them. As she put a magnificent Bavarian cream on the table by way of dessert she admonished them to eat it up. 'For it's something I don't fancy, meself, not with me figure being what it is. But it'll do you good, the pair of yer; yer need to keep plenty of flesh on them big bones of yours, sir, and as for you, miss, another ounce, or so won't 'urt them nice curves.' A speech which caused Mr van Borsele to smile and Claribel to blush.

He had timed their journey very well; the bulk of the passengers were already on board and the queue of cars waiting was a short one. Mr van Borsele sat back in his seat, his eyes half closed, so it was all the more surprising when he said in a tone of satisfaction, 'I have been hoping that she would come.'

Claribel sat up straight. 'Irma—she's here? She's not going to Holland, too?'

'Ah, no, I think not. Merely making sure that we are, together. Try and look a little loving if you can, Claribel.'

Claribel arranged her features into what she hoped was a suitably moony rapturous expression, and just in time. Irma rapped on the window and Marc lowered it. There were two men with her, both looking sheepish, as well they might, thought Claribel, beaming with false sweetness at Irma's face peering at them both.

'You meant it,' she cried. 'You really are going away. You're not married?'

'Not yet.' Mr van Borsele sounded patiently civil. 'But take my word for it, it won't be very long now.' He smiled at Claribel, his dark eyes gleaming with amusement. 'Just as soon as arrangements can be made. Isn't that so, darling?'

Just as well be hanged for a sheep as a lamb, thought Claribel and heard her voice, revoltingly gushing, 'Yes, dear.' She turned the gush on Irma. 'You would be so surprised at what a lot there is to do even for a quiet wedding.'

Irma said huffily, 'I shall have a big wedding with bridemaids and a train and dozens of presents.'

'Why, of course,' agreed Claribel sweetly, 'but Marc and I aren't exactly young, you know, we're rather past all that.' She looked ahead and exclaimed, 'Oh, look, we're going aboard at last. Goodbye, Irma. When you marry do let us know; you'll make a lovely bride.'

Mr van Borsele turned a snorting chuckle into a cough. 'Yes, do do that,' he urged and started the car. 'Enjoy your drive back. London or Bath?'

'Oh, London now, but I suppose I might as well go home tomorrow.'

He swept the car onto the ship's car deck and Claribel took the smirk off her face. 'Now that is the last time,' she declared.

'I hope so. I must say you were superb, Claribel. Had you ever thought of going on to the stage? You know, just for a moment I quite believed that you were looking forward to our wedding...'

It was a pity that the business of parking the car and getting out of it interrupted the white-hot remark ready on her tongue. When they met in the bar later after going to their cabins he silenced her with a bland, 'I do think you were rather severe about our approaching middle age, Claribel. Maybe you feel your years, but I can't say that I feel all that elderly.' He sat her down at a table. 'A drink before we part for the night? I hear it's quite choppy out at sea; a brandy might be a good idea for you.'

She said strongly, 'What a perfectly horrid thing to say. And I hate brandy.'

'If I apologise handsomely, will you please have the brandy?'

He could be charming when he wanted. She said rather ungraciously, 'Oh, well, all right,' and, when her glass had been put before her, sipped at it. It warmed her nicely and she sat back and look around her.

The ferry was fairly full. There were a good many people milling around laughing and talking and she asked, 'Do you always come this way?'

'Usually; it gives me a night's sleep. Sometimes I fly, but that means I haven't got the car and have to rent one. I use the hovercraft occasionally.'

'Don't you want to stay in one place—your home?'

'Frequently.'

It was obvious that she wasn't going to make much progress in that direction. She realised that she didn't know where he lived. In the morning she would ask him, but not now. She tried a different approach. 'How did you find Tilly? She is a dear, but not a bit like a housekeeper.'

'She was a patient of mine some years ago. I had just bought the flat and she told me one day that she hadn't got a job, her husband had died and she had no family, no one who mattered at any rate. So she has been housekeeping for me ever since. You like her?'

'Very much. I expect she looks after you beautifully.'

'Indeed she does. Are you sleepy, Claribel?'

'No, not in the least.'

'You've never asked me where I live. Are you not interested? I have of course told your mother and father. Either you are very naïve or you have a touching trust in me.'

She said gravely, 'Well, I do trust you, and you said you lived in the north somewhere. But I don't know much about you, do I? I know that you have a sister...'

'Three sisters—the other two are married and live in Holland; they're all a good deal younger than I. There are aunts and uncles and cousins, too, scattered around but my grandmother is the only member of the family I see frequently. She lives in Leeuwarden but I live in a small village to the south of the city. The motorway to the south is close enough to be able to drive down to Amsterdam, about ninety miles away—I go there once a week to operate. I go to The Hague, too—that is a hundred and twenty miles—but I do most of the work in Leeuwarden and Groningen. I have beds in the hospitals there, and consulting rooms.'

'You aren't at home very often. Do—do you live alone?'

He didn't smile but his eyes gleamed with amusement. 'Yes. I have a housekeeper and her husband sees to the garden and the odd jobs and in fact looks after things when I'm away.' He did smile then. 'Now you know all about me, Claribel.'

'Yes. Thank you for telling me.'

'You are entitled to know. Are we not friends?'

She nodded. 'I'll go to bed, I think. Where do we meet in the morning?'

'I've asked the stewardess to bring you tea and toast when she wakes you—we'll stop for breakfast on the way. I'll knock on your door just before we get in.'

She got to her feet and he got up with her. 'Goodnight,

Marc.' She was taken by surprise when he bent to kiss her cheek. 'So hard to break a habit,' he murmured.

She had been remarkably silly, she thought drowsily. She had agreed to everything he had suggested without finding out how long she was to stay with his grandmother. A few days? A week? Longer? As far as she could see there was no reason why she shouldn't go back to England within a day or so. Irma, having seen them actually board the ferry, would most certainly have gone back to Bath, and she would be able to go back home until the hospital had got something sorted out... Her thoughts became more and more muddled and she fell asleep in the middle of them.

She slept all night; if the crossing had been rough the brandy must have acted as a splendid soporific. As she ate her toast and drank her tea she hurried to dress, and she was just ready when Mr van Borsele knocked on the door.

She called him to come in, wished him a friendly good morning and collected up her gloves and handbag. 'Are we there?'

'About ten minutes to go. Come on deck and take a look.'

It was a fine morning, but cool. The Hook lay before them, surprisingly busy for that early hour, and Claribel looked around her with interest. It looked, rather to her disappointment, rather like any English port but there wasn't much time to inspect it for car owners were asked to rejoin their cars.

Going ashore proved both brisk and easy; they were waved past the last official and Mr van Borsele took the road north. They were on the main road almost immediately, bypassing Delft, racing along until they were almost at Amsterdam and then changing to the Alkmaar road. Half-way there, Marc pulled in to a petrol station.

'We can get breakfast here,' he told her and left the car to be filled up as they crossed to a small café, with flagpoles before it and neat gingham curtains. It was just as neat inside, with tablecloths to match the curtains and a great many pot plants on the windowsills. They sat at a window and the café owner brought them coffee and a basket of rolls and croissants, thinly sliced cheese and ham, boiled eggs and small pots of jam in a dish.

Claribel, who was famished by now, enjoyed every morsel and presently, much refreshed, they got back into the Rolls.

'Is it much further?' she asked.

'Over the dyke and then about twenty-five miles.'

'Where's the dyke?'

'A good thirty miles from here and then the dyke—that is about sixteen miles. We shall be at my grandmother's in about an hour.'

He had been a pleasant companion as they drove, pointing out anything which he thought might interest her, answering her questions patiently, and now, on a cross-country road, he was at pains to tell her something about Leeuwarden. Not a very big city, he assured her, but with some beautiful old houses and any number of peaceful little streets if one knew how to find them.

They reached the Afsluitdijk, the high sea dyke on one side of the wide road, the Ijsselmeer on the other, and raced across it, and presently Claribel could see the land ahead of her: Friesland. Marc's home.

On the mainland they joined the main road again although when they reached Franeker Marc turned off and drove quite slowly through the town so that she might glimpse the narrow gabled houses by the canal and take a quick look at the *Gementehuis*—Dutch Renaissance at its best, he pointed out. 'And the Planetarium is close by. Perhaps you will have the chance to come and see it while you are here; it is unique: the man who built it, Eise Eisinga, worked each evening by candlelight—it took him seven years.'

'I wish I understood Dutch,' sighed Claribel, suddenly apprehensive.

'No need—almost everyone speaks or understands a little English. Besides, we speak Fries among ourselves.'

'Oh—like the Welsh speak Welsh?'

'Exactly. Here is Leeuwarden.'

The outskins were sober middle-class red-brick houses, each

with a small garden, but soon they gave way to shops and old houses leaning against each other in a mass of small streets.

Marc had turned away from the heart of the city and presently joined a street lined with large houses set behind high walls or glimpsed through gardens, well away from the street. Half-way along he drove between gateposts and along a short semi-circle of gravel, and stopped before a fair-sized house with a flattened gable, a very large front door reached by a double pair of steps, and three rows of large windows. There were trees encircling it and formal flower beds cut into a pattern, which extended as far as the high wall shielding it from the street.

Mr van Borsele got out to open Claribel's door and they reached the steps just as the door was opened and a white-haired man greeted them.

'Domus—Granny's butler; been with her man and boy, and runs the place.' Mr van Borsele clapped the old man on the back very gently. 'Domus, this is Miss Claribel Brown.'

Claribel shook hands and smiled and was ushered into the hall, long and narrow and lofty, its walls almost covered by paintings and with an outsize chandelier hanging from the ceiling. Mr van Borsele had a firm grip on her arm and Domus went ahead of them to open arched double doors.

It was a very large room with enormous windows draped in red velvet and a good deal of large furniture, too. The lady who came to meet them across the polished floor suited her surroundings very well: she was tall and rather stout, with a very straight back; Claribel was reminded of Queen Mary, King George the Fifth's wife. The hairstyle was the same, too, and the rather severe expression…her heart sank. But only for a moment. Marc's hand slid from her elbow to take her hand in his while he flung the other arm round the old lady. 'Grandmother, my dear…' He bent to kiss her. 'Here is Claribel, as I promised.' He pulled Claribel gently forward. 'Claribel, this is my grandmother, Baroness van Borsele.'

Claribel and the old lady shook hands; they were of a similar height and surveyed each other gravely, each liking what she saw. 'Dear child,' murmured the baroness, 'such a pretty name and such a pretty girl. I am so delighted to have you here. I lead a very quiet life, you know, but we will contrive to give you some amusement and it will be delightful for me to practise my English.'

Claribel murmured something; the old lady's English was every bit as good as her own; there was only the hint of an accent, just as Marc had.

'Let us sit down and drink our coffee. Marc, you will stay to lunch?'

'Thank you, Grandmother, but I must go home this afternoon, there's a good deal of work waiting for me.'

'Of course, my dear.' His grandmother had seated herself in a tall chair by one of the wide windows. 'Such a pity that we shan't see more of you, but to have a glimpse of you is delightful. I only hope that you don't work too hard.'

He said casually, 'I enjoy my work, my dear.' He had seated himself opposite Claribel. 'You will actually have a peaceful time here, Claribel, with no patients to worry about and no one to remind you of Jerome's.'

She said doubtfully. 'Don't you come here? To operate in the hospital, I mean?'

'Indeed I do. I shall be in Leeuwarden tomorrow, but I shall be too busy to come here. A good thing,' he added blandly. 'As I have just said, there will be no one to remind you of Jerome's.'

She was nonplussed. 'Oh, yes, of course, and naturally you have your friends to see.' There was a faint waspishness about her voice.

'That, too, but don't worry, I'll let you know when we're going back, and you can always phone me. The hospital has this address so that you will be in touch with them.'

She took a sip of coffee, feeling that she needed it badly. She hadn't expected to see him every day but she had supposed that they would have spent some time together; now she realised that he had no intention of doing anything of the sort. He had indeed told her when he had first suggested the whole thing that she wouldn't have to see much of him, but she hadn't taken him seriously; now she saw that she should have done. He had invited her to Holland for exactly the reason he had told her in the first place: to get rid of Irma once and for all. As usual, he had arranged things to suit himself. She gave him a charming smile while her eyes flashed green temper at him. 'How nicely you have arranged everything. I'm sure I'm going to love being here.' She turned to her hostess. 'It is so kind of you to invite me, Baroness.'

The old lady has been sitting quietly listening to Marc and chuckling silently; the girl was delightful, and capable of managing her much-loved grandson, and yet, she was sure, unaware of his real purpose in bringing her to stay with her. He had always had his own way, never arrogant about it, just silently going ahead with what he intended to do, listening politely to advice and ignoring it for the most part, looking after his sisters in an unobtrusive manner until they married, ignoring their hints that he should get himself a wife. But here was someone he would listen to... She smiled kindly at Claribel. 'My dear, I believe that we are going to have a most enjoyable time together. There is a great deal to see in Leeuwarden and we can drive out to the surrounding country, too. Domus shall drive us.'

Claribel smiled with suitable enthusiasm and reflected that she would much prefer Marc to drive her, and then felt mean at the thought. Sensibly she applied herself to giving civil answers to the baroness's questions while Mr van Borsele sat back in his chair looking amused.

Domus came in presently, addressing himself to the lady of the house and then he turned to say something to Marc. When he had gone, Claribel said diffidently, 'Why did he call you Baron? Aren't you just mister?'

'Er, no, but I don't bother with that in England. Domus is rather a stickler for titles and so on. I hope you don't mind.'

'Mind? Why should I mind?' She had gone rather pink and both grandmother and grandson studied her appreciatively; she looked quite lovely when she was put out about something. 'I mean,' she added with chilly politeness, anxious not to be rude, 'it really doesn't matter, does it?'

'Not in the least.'

Domus came in again and murmured briefly and the baroness said briskly, 'Lunch is ready. I arranged for it to be served early, Marc, for I know you are anxious to get back to your own home.'

A remark which gave Claribel a distinctly forlorn feeling.

They lunched in a room at the back of the house, overlooking a surprisingly large garden laid out with shrubs and trees and with a small fountain at its centre. The table was covered by a thick white damask cloth and the silver was heavy and old. Claribel, eating soufflé off Delft china, wondered briefly what Marc had thought of the Woolworth's mugs from which he had drunk his coffee at her flat. Besides the soufflé there were cold meats on a big silver dish and side dishes of salad, and more coffee afterwards.

Marc got up to go very shortly after they had finished their meal, kissed his grandmother, patted Claribel on a shoulder in a casual manner, saying carelessly that he would doubtless see her at some time or other, and took himself off.

'Such a dear boy,' said his grandmother as they stood at the window watching the car disappear down the drive. Claribel didn't say anything; she was struggling with an overwhelming sense of disappointment.

Any qualms she might have had about being welcome in the baroness's house were quickly dispelled; she was cosseted from the moment she woke each morning until she went to bed at night. Her hostess, despite her eighty-one years, carried her age lightly; the pair of them went sightseeing each day, driving at a stately pace with Domus at the wheel. Claribel and her kind hostess visited Franeker, Dokkum and the northern coast, taking narrow country roads so that she could see the villages and the prosperous farms, all built to the same pattern, the house in front, connected to a large barn by a narrow neck, the whole mostly thatched over red tiles. She had the dykes explained to her, too: the dead dykes, no longer needed because the land had been reclaimed from the sea; the sleepers, the dreamers and, nearest the sea, the watchers. In time, the baroness explained, as more and more land was reclaimed, a sleeper became dead, and they all moved back one. The villages, few and small near the coast, were mostly built along the dykes, small neat houses, too, with tiled roofs with strings of washing in their back gardens. So different from her own home but, in its way, just as peaceful and charming.

She explored the city, too, while her hostess rested after their lunch: strolling round the shops, gazing at the Weigh House, poking her pretty nose down narrow streets and going to the museums. The Frisian Museum was, to her mind, easily the best with its lovely old costumes and jewellery and the colossal sword of Grote Pier who had driven away the Saxons four hundred years earlier. Frisians, she had discovered, were large people, both men and women, but he must have been a giant among them.

It was on her fourth morning there that the baroness suggested that she might like to go off on her own. 'I have business to attend to,' she explained, 'and it is too nice weather for you to stay indoors.'

So Claribel wandered off into the centre of the city, not sure what she wanted to do. The days so far had been delightful, for there had been various friends and relations calling at the house, as well as their daily excursions, but right at the back of her mind was the thought that Marc had made no effort to see her. He had phoned, so his grandmother told her, but to all intents and purposes he had removed himself to the other side of the world. She told herself that she didn't mind in the least; he was a tiresome man, always wanting his own way and getting it, too. All the same, she missed him.

She went and leaned on the railings by the Weigh House, staring at nothing, wondering why she felt so dispirited. Perhaps she shouldn't have come, but then Irma might have made herself troublesome.

'Hello, Claribel,' said Marc from behind her, and she spun round to face him, suddenly alight with happiness—a lovely feeling, she thought bemusedly, like going out of doors very early on a summer morning or going home after a hard week's work and opening the kitchen door and seeing her mother—a lovely complete feeling in which content and delight and joy were nicely mixed.

He stared at her for a long moment. 'Pleased to see me?' he asked.

'Yes, oh, yes.' And then, aware of his intent gaze, 'I'm having a simply lovely time with your grandmother.'

'Good. I've given myself a day off. Would you like to see my home? We'll go back and have coffee if you will with Grandmother first, and then go on home for lunch.'

She nodded her head slowly, her hair golden in the sunshine. She wanted very much to go to his home for lunch; she knew with a suddenness she didn't try to understand that she wanted to go to his home and stay there. How could she not have known all these weeks that she loved him?

He stood quietly before her, smiling a little, his hands in his pockets, impeccably dressed as always only this time slacks and a tweed jacket replaced his more sober suits. His dark eyes were intent, watching her face. He must have found his scrutiny satisfactory for he observed softly, 'Well, well,' and then, 'Shall we go?'

They had their coffee on the veranda at the back of the house, and the regimented rows of flowers glowed in the sunlight.

'Charming, isn't it?' observed the baroness, 'but of course I'm old-fashioned enough to like a formal garden.' She glanced at Marc. 'Will you dine here, my dear?'

'Thank you, Grandmother, yes.' He looked across at Claribel. 'Ready? Shall we go?'

She had said very little while they had been sitting there, doing her best to breath normally so that her heart would stop its frantic thumping against her ribs, but she was finding it difficult. She had tried not to look at Marc, either, but once or twice his dark eyes had caught and held hers and she had had difficulty in looking away. She would have to do better than this, she told herself; the very idea of him discovering that she was in love with him made her feel quite ill. After all the fuss she had made about helping him in the first place…

They said goodbye and she got into the car beside him and, intent on being exactly as usual, embarked on a flow of small talk, something so unlike her usual manner that Marc, agreeing to her platitudes with every sign of interest, hid his amusement.

CHAPTER NINE

THEIR way lay through the city and then, once free of the suburbs, Marc left the main road south for a narrow country road running between water meadows, each with its quota of cows. Claribel admired the cows, the flat meadows and the occasional farm, keeping up a steady stream of small talk which really needed no answer, hardly pausing between one topic and the next for fear that there would be silence between them. Her tongue was in danger of cleaving to the roof of her mouth by the time Marc turned on to a narrow bricked road on top of a dead dyke. There were trees ahead and the glimpse of red roofs. Seeing them, she asked, 'Are we nearly there?' and heaved such a sigh of relief that Marc smothered a laugh.

'The village is behind those trees; I live just beyond. In a moment you will see the lake. There are a series of them; this particular one is at the end.'

He sounded just as usual and she decided that she had panicked for no reason; she would have to get a hold of herself. It wouldn't be for long now; soon she would be going back home and as soon as she could she would get another job. Somewhere where she would never see him again... She sighed again and Marc allowed himself a quick smile.

The village was small but compact, encircling a red brick church, very severe in appearance, but there were trees and pretty little gardens before the small houses and a shop or two. There were people about, too, housewives, and children playing in the street, and solid men going about their business. They saluted Marc as he drove by and he lifted a hand in reply.

'They all know you,' observed Claribel brightly.

'Well, we were all born here.' He had turned a corner by the church and slowed into a lane leading away from the village towards the lake. The trees were thicker here and presently there was a high iron railing with a vast lawn behind it and, in the centre, a castle. A small castle, but a castle nevertheless, complete with pepperpot towers, and a big double door, flanked by tall narrow windows.

'Oh, look,' cried Claribel, 'what a darling little castle. Does someone live there? I wonder…' She paused. 'It's yours, isn't it?'

'Yes.' He swept the car between high wrought-iron gates and up the drive, straight as a ruler, to his front door.

I don't know the first thing about him, thought Claribel miserably. He was just a consultant surgeon with a short temper and a liking for coffee in London, but here he's something quite different… She got out of the car reluctantly when he opened her door. 'You might have told me,' she said.

'Why? What difference would it have made? Don't be a silly girl and come inside.'

He took a bunch of keys from his pocket, unlocked the massive double doors and propelled her forward into a lobby which in turn opened on to a square hall, across the floor of which came a thin, elderly man with a solemn face. As he reached them he spoke to Marc in a reproachful way and shook his head. Marc laughed and clapped him on the shoulders. When he spoke it was in English.

'Warmolt, this is Miss Claribel Brown, from England.'

He bowed his elderly head and, when she put out a hand, shook it. 'Welcome, Miss Brown. We are pleased that you come.' He smiled widely and didn't look solemn at all. 'I'll fetch Sieke.'

'His wife and my housekeeper. Do come into the drawing-room meanwhile.'

She had a quick look round her as she went. The floor was paved with black and white marble and had a lovely old carpet down its centre. The walls were white plaster, hung with paintings, and the staircase was at the back of the hall, solid oak with a carved balustrade and dividing halfway up into two wings leading to a gallery above the hall.

Marc had opened an arched door and was waiting patiently

for her. She went past him into a very large room with french windows opening on to a veranda at the side of the house and a row of small windows at the front. Its high ceiling was plaster with pendant bosses and the chimneypiece was an elaborate two-tier dome, ornately carved. There were a number of handsome cabinets against its walls, displaying a vast quantity of silver, glass and porcelain, and there was a beautiful console table under the windows, which was curtained with old rose brocade, held back by great tasselled ropes. The chimney-piece was flanked by two William and Mary settees and on each side of the console table were a pair of eighteenth-century armchairs of gilded wood and covered with tapestry. But there were more modern pieces as well: wing-back armchairs, a ladies' work-table with its silk bag, lamp tables with a handsome commode with a serpentine front bearing a Delft bowl filled with flowers.

'Oh, how very beautiful,' exclaimed Claribel, rotating slowly so that she wouldn't miss anything. 'And lived in, too.'

'Hence the mixture of its furnishings—each generation adds something. And it's certainly lived in.'

As if to underline his words the door was pushed open and two bull terriers came darting in, going first to Marc and then to Claribel, to stand politely while she admired them and stroked their smooth heads.

She said shyly, 'I liked your flat in London, but this is your real home, isn't it?'

'I was born here, and I hope I shall die here. Here is Sieke; she will take you upstairs. When you come down we'll have a drink.'

Following the housekeeper, a stout woman with a nice friendly face, Claribel was led out of the room and up the staircase, to be shown into a charming room at the front of the house. Castle or no, it lacked none of the comforts and luxuries of the twentieth century; there was a bed of some pale wood, covered by a quilted spread, its rose-covered satin made to match the curtains at the two windows, between which was a sofa table with a triple mirror upon it. There were easy chairs, too, and a table or two and a roomy mirrored wall closet. And the bathroom adjoining it was just as luxurious. Claribel sat down before the mirror and tidied her hair and powdered her pretty nose and made a mental list of topics she could talk about with Marc; she must remember to be friendly but not too eager—a few well-chosen questions about the castle and its history, but she mustn't get too interested either. She went back downstairs, well primed, dreading and at the same time longing to be with Marc; the day stretched before her, probably full of pitfalls, but, after all, she had been alone with him on a number of occasions during the past few weeks... She would have to pretend that nothing had altered.

Only when she got to the bottom of the staircase did she become aware of voices in the drawing-room, and when she went in it was to find that she need not have got into such a fidget; the room was full of people. Well, not full, but there were seven people standing around Marc with drinks in their hands. He came to meet her.

'There you are, Claribel. I thought you would like to meet some of my friends at lunch. Come and be introduced.'

Four men about Marc's age and three younger women; they had strange-sounding Friese names like Sjamke, and Waltsjer, and they at once enveloped her in warm friendliness, laughingly pronouncing their names for her, explaining who was married to whom and who were merely engaged, asking her how she was enjoying herself. At lunch she sat between Marc and a slightly older man called Wobberen who it seemed, was a doctor with a practice in Dokkum and who knew London well, so that there was a great deal to talk about.

The table was large and round, gleaming with silver and glasses and everyone talked to everyone else while they ate cold salmon and a salad which looked too good to eat and then a Dutch apple tart with lashings of whipped cream. They had their coffee at the table, served by Warmolt, grave as a judge, going silently about the room; he suited his surroundings very well, Claribel decided, for the dining-room was as grand in its way as the drawing-room, with panelled walls and a great deal of strapwork on the ceiling.

It was well past three o'clock when Marc's guests went their various ways. He stood on his doorstep with Claribel beside him, seeing them off, and when the last car had gone to took her arm.

'Like to look round the grounds?' Not waiting for an answer, he walked her round the side of the castle along a narrow path with the castle walls on one side and a gentle grass slope on the other. 'There was a moat a very long time ago,' he explained.

There were sweeping lawns at the back of the castle and a knot garden, as well as a lily pond with goldfish, but there were no formal flower beds here. Instead there were flowering shrubs, great banks of roses and a lavender hedge bordering a grey flagged path which led them to a circular bed of colourful annuals. And, beyond that, trees and an expanse of parkland.

'Oh, it's beautiful,' cried Claribel. 'How can you bear to leave it?'

'Ah, but I come back to it, you see. It has been here for a very long time; it is ageless and timeless.'

He tucked her hand under his arm as they strolled along, and Claribel suffered a succession of what felt like electric shocks and tried not to notice them.

'I've a letter for you,' he went on, 'from Jerome's. Remind me to let you have it when we get back indoors.' Sooner than she had wished.

Warmolt, pacing in a stately fashion towards them, caused them to stop and wait for him. He bowed politely to Claribel, who felt that she should bow back, and addressed himself to Marc.

Whatever it was engendered a brief conversation before Marc observed, 'An aunt and uncle have called. We had better go back.' He said something to Warmolt who quickened his pace ahead of them. 'Tea,' said Marc, 'and light conversation.'

The two people waiting for them in the drawing-room were middle-aged, tall and inclined to stoutness; the man had the aggressive nose Claribel had rightly associated with the van Borseles. They greeted her kindly, made small talk over tea and biscuits and, in due course, went away. Claribel liked them both but although they were van Borseles she had been unable to pronounce their names. Not that it mattered; she wasn't likely to meet them again. The thought saddened her and at the same time reminded her that Marc had a letter from the hospital. He gave it to her when she asked.

'I'll go upstairs and change and you can read it while I'm gone,' he observed cheerfully.

They had got things sorted out at Jerome's. She could transfer to a hospital in the north of the city until such time as a new physiotherapy department could be built and equipped, or, if she wished, she could be released from her contract with Jerome's and find her own work.

It would have to be the latter, she decided immediately. For one thing the new hospital was too far away from her flat for her to be able to get to and fro within a reasonable time each day, and, far more importantly, she needed to be free to find a job wherever she wished. And that, she told herself decisively, was as far from Marc as possible.

She had pulled herself together by now and when he came back, elegant in one of his dark suits, she was able to tell him of the contents of the letter. 'It couldn't be better,' she told him. 'Just the chance I wanted to make a change.'

He nodded calmly. 'Then this is splendid news for you. I shall be going back in four days' time. There will be no need for you to answer the letter; you will be able to see them in person.'

'So I shall,' said Claribel. With the upheaval her feelings had undergone she hadn't given much thought to returning. The awful finality of it paled her cheeks, something which Marc noted with interest.

He said smoothly, 'I shall miss my visits to Meadow Road—that is, unless you plan to stay there?'

'I've no idea where I shall be,' Claribel said with a snap. She added recklessly, 'I'm told there are plenty of jobs in Australia and New Zealand.'

'Must you go quite so far?' asked Marc blandly. 'One doesn't need to run to the ends of the earth, you know.'

Oh, but one does, thought Claribel unhappily, and even that wouldn't be far enough away for her to forget him. She said rather too effusively, 'What a delightful day I have had; I liked your friends—and your aunt and uncle.'

'Splendid. We had better go now or we will arrive too late at Grandmother's. Have you any plans for your last few days here?'

She began at once on a recital, thought up on the spur of the moment, of the multitude of things she intended to do. 'Your grandmother is taking me to Dokkum again and she has kindly offered the car so that we can go to Groningen, only it may be too far for her to go. And then I have to buy presents to take home and—and go up the Oldehove Tower...'

They were in the car driving back to Leeuwarden, the dogs sitting side by side on the back seat. She had wished Sieke and Warmolt goodbye and taken a last look at the little castle, wishing with all her heart that she could have explored it; it was so perfect. She had felt the warmth of the generations of van Borseles who have lived there; no sinister corners or creepy passages, just an abiding contentment and happiness.

She said dreamily, 'It is a very beautiful castle; I'll never forget it.' She added quickly, in case he might think that she was too interested, 'Leeuwarden is a delightful place too...'

'You like heights?' asked Marc idly. 'The Oldehove Tower is quite high. It leans a bit, too, although there is a lift. The view from the top is quite something.'

She hated heights and she disliked lifts but she had just told him with enthusiasm that she was going to the top of the tower. She said airily, 'Oh, good, I'm looking forward to it.'

Back at Baroness van Borsele's house, she went to her room to change her dress and shower. She chose to wear the dark blue crêpe-de-Chine, aware that it highlighted her hair and added sparkle to her eyes. She took great pains with her face and hair and was rewarded by a cursory glance from Marc which did nothing for her ego. And anyway, why was she bothering? she reflected, sipping her sherry with pleasure and listening to his grandmother's very informed history of his castle; Marc had never once given her the impression that he had any interest in her other than as a useful dispenser of coffee and a means of getting rid of Irma.

'And what did you think of the castle?' enquired the baroness as they sat at dinner. 'Is not the circular room in the central pepperpot tower quite charming? Marc's mother used it as her own sitting-room.'

'I didn't see it,' said Claribel flatly.

'You didn't take Claribel on a tour of inspection?'

'No, Grandmother.' He sounded pleasant enough but he wasn't going to say more than that.

'Quite a good thing,' said Claribel chattily. 'My head is crammed with so many museums and churches and farms, not to mention whole streets of lovely old gabled houses, I don't suppose it will hold another thing.'

'Ah, but you must make room for the Oldehove Tower. Remember to take your camera with you,' Marc observed. 'You should have some impressive photos to show around when you get back.'

She stole a look at him. She was reminded forcibly of the first time they had met; his face bore a similar expression of impatience and somehow his aggressive nose registered hauteur. He looked at her before she could turn her eyes away and she flushed under the gaze from the black eyes boring into hers.

He left shortly after dinner. 'I've a list in the morning and a teaching round in the afternoon, but I dare say I'll see you before we go.' He kissed his grandmother and took Claribel's arm. 'Come and open the door for me,' he suggested. 'It will save Domus's feet.'

But when they reached the great door and she put out a hand to lift the massive latch he lifted it off. 'Have you any idea why I asked you to spend the day with me?' he asked her.

She thought about it for a moment. 'Well, I expect you thought that I might like to meet some people—and I did enjoy that, really I did. And it was nice to see your home…'

He nodded. 'I imagined that was what you might have thought. And you found my home, er, nice?'

She looked up at him. 'I found it enchanting. Quite perfect inside—as far as I could see—and out. Anyone who is fortunate enough to live in such a heavenly place…' She drew a long breath. 'You must be very happy there.'

'I am. And I intend to share my happiness with a wife and children.'

She went a little pale but she was composed enough. 'I'm glad. I'll think of you being happy there.'

He smiled a little. 'And where will you be, Claribel?'

How easy it was to tell lies when one was desperate. 'I've decided to go to New Zealand. Mother has cousins there.'

'You will leave broken hearts behind you.'

She gave him a questioning look.

'Enoch and Toots. You can hardly take them with you.'

She didn't know what she had expected him to say, certainly not that. A faint forlorn hope buried deep inside her finally died. 'They'll be happy with my mother.'

She bent to pat the two dogs standing patiently at their master's heels. 'These two are awfully good—you must miss them when you're away from home.'

He opened the door. 'It occurs to me that we are having a quite inane conversation about nothing at all, Claribel. Goodnight. I'll be in touch.'

A horrid end to a day which hadn't been as wonderful as she had hoped.

She was a sensible girl, even if her heart was in a thousand pieces. She spent the next two days being driven around the surrounding country with her hostess; Sneek and Bolsward, with its lovely old churches and town hall, the lakes where they stopped to drink coffee or tea, and Hindeloopen where Claribel bought some of the famous painted wooden bowls and spoons. She left the baroness in the car here at that lady's urging, and strolled along the sea wall to see the 'Gossip Bench' where the old men of the little town spent their leisure, looking out to sea and talking among themselves. On the third day they went to

Groningen, where they had lunch at the Crémaillère Restaurant and took a slow stroll past the university.

During the last day of all she packed her things, spent the morning with the baroness and then, at her suggestion, decided to go out for a walk. There had been no word from Marc other than a brief telephone conversation. They would leave on the following day, he told her, directly after breakfast, and get back to London some time during the late afternoon. 'And be sure and let your people know,' he warned her.

She sensed that he had no time to talk at length, so she agreed without quibbling and rang off. She had, she supposed, served her purpose, and then she chided herself for self-pity. She had had a lovely holiday and never for one single moment had he led her to suppose that he was even faintly interested in her.

It was a dull, warm afternoon, and she had bought her presents; there was still Oldehove Tower to visit. She told the baroness where she was going, promised to be back for four o'clock tea, and took herself off.

The tower was truly massive. She walked all round it and then, together with several other tourists, took the lift to the top. Now that she was actually doing it, she was sorry that she had been silly enough to show such enthusiasm about it. If it hadn't been for Marc she would have backed out, but some misguided pride had made her go ahead with it. The lift was small and full of people and she stood in the centre which kept the awful feeling of being shut in at bay. She got out at the top with a feeling of enormous relief which turned at once to dry-mouthed panic.

The view was indeed magnificent; everybody else was hanging over the railings pointing out landmarks and taking photos. There were a number of children, too, dashing to and fro, and several well-meaning sightseers who, with the kindliest intentions, urged her to go to the rails and look over too. To escape their puzzled glances when she shook her head, she walked cautiously to the other side, taking care not to look at the panorama below her. Thank heaven they would all go back presently and she with them. She wished there was some sort of seat but, since there wasn't, put a hand on the wall and stared at the stones. They were comfortingly solid under her hand—like Marc, impatient, wanting his own way, annoyingly monosyllabic at times, able to live in luxury and choosing to work all hours in hospital theatres, but, just like the wall, solid and dependable.

She made the mistake of looking around her and closed her eyes again. She would have to rejoin the other tourists; she could hear them laughing and talking. Someone put a head round the corner and called out to her in a cheerful voice. She waved and actually smiled and the head disappeared. At least she would be able to tell Marc that she had been to the top of Oldehove Tower. She started back, careful not to look towards the railings, but when she reached the lift door she found it closed. What was more, when she pressed the knob at the side nothing happened. They had all gone; she would have to wait until they were on the ground floor and get the lift back. She would hate going down alone but perhaps there would be other people coming up... Nothing happened when she pressed the knob a second time and then, after a few moments, a third time. It struck her that perhaps the head which appeared round the corner had said something to her, had even been telling her something vital about the lift...

She waited for a few minutes before trying to open the lift doors and then she went to the head of the staircase. it snaked away from her into a gloomy pit into which the narrow steps disappeared. There was no rail and it wound, as so many staircases did, in a spiral round a central pillar.

She made a tentative movement to descend and then withdrew her foot, in the grip of quite illogical panic. She had always hated heights but now she realised that she was acrophobic, a condition which had nothing to do with being cowardly, something she couldn't help. Clinging to the wall, she stepped back from the stairs, shaking with fright. Until somebody came back with the lift she was powerless to do anything. She edged herself up against the wall feeling sick.

* * *

The baroness looked up from her embroidery frame as Marc entered the drawing-room of her home. He greeted her with affection, refused tea and asked, 'Where is Claribel? I managed to get finished earlier than I expected. I thought she might like to explore the castle before we have dinner with you.'

The old lady snipped a silk thread. 'Well, dear, she went for a last walk through the city and intended to go to the top of Oldehove...'

'Has she been gone long?'

'Rather longer than I expected. She said that she would be sure and return for tea and it is now well past that hour.'

He stirred restlessly. 'I think I'll go and see if she is still there.'

'Yes, my dear. Such a dear girl, and so right for you.' She looked over her glasses at him. 'She is, isn't she? Or am I wrong?'

He smiled and bent to kiss her cheek. 'Grandmother, you are so right. I cannot imagine living a day longer than I must without her.'

'Run along then, dear. Don't bother to come back here until this evening—I'll put dinner back half an hour; that will give you plenty of time.' And, at his raised eyebrows, 'To propose, dear.'

Claribel had retreated as far as possible from the edge of the tower, with her back to the central wall, leaning so hard against it that she might have been trying to bore her way into its thickness. She was cold and still literally scared stiff, so that moving even a hand was an effort of will. She had given up wondering what to do; surely sooner or later the lift would return and until then she could only remain still. It was a good thing that she didn't know that the face which had addressed her had told her that the lift was out of order and that everyone was walking down...

She kept her eyes steadily on the wall and to keep up her very low spirits she began to recite all the poetry she could call to mind. Marc, climbing the stairs fast, was taken aback to hear her rather shaky voice: '''It is the little rift within the lute, That by and by will make the music mute.'''

'As I live and breath,' muttered Marc, taking the last few stairs at a gallop, 'she is reciting Tennyson.'

She had her eyes shut but she opened them at the sound of his feet. She stared at him wordlessly and he plucked her from the wall and held her fast.

It was too much. She burst into tears. 'I'm the most frightful coward,' she sobbed into his shoulder and tried very hard to stop weeping. Any moment now he would make one of his laconic remarks to deflate her, as though she wasn't already deflated enough...

'My poor darling girl.' His voice was tender with a hint of laughter in it. 'Never mind, I'm here now, you're quite safe. Didn't anyone tell you that the lift had broken down?'

She mumbled into his shirt front and he stroked her bright hair. 'I can't go down those awful stairs—I go all stiff. Oh, Marc...'

'My darling love, of course you will go down them, behind me, and you will be quite safe, and you need never go higher than the pepperpot towers in the castle for the rest of your life.' He put a gentle hand under her chin and kissed her very slowly. He said, 'We're going to be married, you know, and live happily ever after.'

'But you don't love me...'

'Oh, yes, I do, have done for a long time now; I've been waiting for you to discover that you love me, too—and you have only just done that, haven't you?'

She stared up at him. 'Well, yes—the other day you know, when you asked me to lunch and all those people came too.' She smiled shakily. 'I don't know what I would have done, trying to live without you.'

'Well, you're not going to live without me, my dearest, ever again. And now keep quiet while I kiss you.'

Presently Claribel drew away a little. 'I—I promised I'd be back for tea.'

'I called in and saw Grandmother; it was she who told me

you were here. We'll go there for dinner but now we're going to my home—our home—so that you can poke that charming nose into every nook and cranny.'

He took her arm and started for the stairs. 'Stand behind me and put your hands on my shoulders and keep your eyes on the back of my head. You're quite safe, sweetheart.'

Love can be a very powerful feeling; if he had told her to jump over the railings she would probably have done so; as it was, she did as she was told, listening to his calm voice planning their journey back to England and their future.

On the bottom step he turned and took her in his arms. 'My brave girl. Stop shaking, darling, I have you safe and I don't intend to let you go.'

Claribel took a grip on herself. 'Don't you? Don't you really? You didn't just say—the things you said—to coax me down?' She looked up at him and saw the look in his eyes and added hastily, 'No, you didn't. I shouldn't have said that.' She reached up and kissed him and was kissed breathless in her turn.

'Why were you reciting Tennyson?' he asked, and tucked a lock of hair behind her ear.

'To take my mind off things.'

'He wrote about you, too—did you know? ''Where Claribel low-lieth, the breezes pause and die.'' Only I'm not a breeze and I'm very much alive and in love with you.'

They smiled at one another and he kissed her once more, watched by a middle-aged couple who happened to be passing, a boy and the small dog with him. The couple sighed and linked arms, remembering their own youth, the dog barked, and the boy, in the manner of all boys, whistled rudely.

To Claribel, lost in bliss, he could have been a string orchestra playing 'Moonlight and Roses' under a perfect sky.

0702/73/MB45

Betty Neels Ultimate Collection Official Prize Draw Rules

NO PURCHASE NECESSARY

Each book in the Betty Neels Ultimate Collection will contain details for entry into the following prize draw: 4 prizes of a signed Betty Neels book and a weekend break to Amsterdam and 10 prizes of a signed Betty Neels book. No purchase necessary.

To enter the draw, hand print the words "Betty Neels Ultimate Collection Prize Draw", plus your name and address on a postcard. For UK residents please send your postcard entries to: Betty Neels Ultimate Collection Prize Draw, PO Box 236, Croydon, CR9 3RU. For ROI residents please send your postcard to Betty Neels Ultimate Collection Prize Draw, PO Box 4546, Kilcock, County Kildare.

To be eligible all entries must be received by **July 31st 2003**. No responsibility can be accepted for entries that are lost, delayed or damaged in the post. Proof of postage cannot be accepted as proof of delivery. No correspondence can be entered into and no entry returned. Winners will be determined in a random draw from all eligible entries received. Judges decision is final. One mailed entry per person, per household.

Amsterdam break includes return flights for two, 2 nights accommodation at a 4 star hotel, airport/hotel transfers, insurance and £150 spending money. Holiday must be taken between 1/8/03 and 1/08/04 excluding Bank holidays, Easter and Christmas periods. (Winner has the option of accepting £500 cash in lieu of holiday option.)

All travellers must sign and return a Release of Liability prior to travel and must have a valid 10 year passport. Accommodation and flights are subject to schedule and availability. The Prize Draw is open to residents of the UK and ROI, 18 years of age or older. Employees and immediate family members of Harlequin Mills & Boon Ltd., its affiliates, subsidiaries and all other agencies, entities and persons connected with the use, marketing or conduct of this Prize Draw are not eligible.

Prize winner notification will be made by letter no later than 14 days after the deadline for entry. Limit: one prize per an individual, family or organisation. All applicable laws and regulations apply. If any prize or prize notification is returned as undeliverable, an alternative winner will be drawn from eligible entries. By acceptance of a prize, winner consents to use of his/her name, photograph or other likeness for purpose of advertising, trade and promotion on behalf of Harlequin Mills & Boon Ltd., without further compensation, unless prohibited by law.

For the names of prize winners (available after 31/08/03), send a self-addressed stamped envelope to: For UK residents, Betty Neels Ultimate Collection Prize Draw Winners List, PO Box 236, Croydon, CR9 3RU. For ROI residents, Betty Neels Ultimate Collection Prize Draw Winners List, PO Box 4546, Kilcock, County Kildare.